P9-ELX-419

CITY OF SHADOWS

ARIANA FRANKLIN

CITY OF SHADOWS

wm | William Morrow
An Imprint of HarperCollins*Publishers*

This book is a work of fiction. References to real people, events, establishments, organizations, or locales are intended only to provide a sense of authenticity, and are used fictitiously. All other characters, and all incidents and dialogue, are drawn from the author's imagination and are not to be construed as real.

HarperCollins books may be purchased for educational, business, or sales promotional use. For information please write: Special Markets Department, HarperCollins Publishers, 10 East 53rd Street, New York, NY 10022.

FIRST EDITION

Designed by Judith Abbate / Abbate Design

Printed on acid-free paper

Library of Congress Cataloging-in-Publication Data

Franklin, Ariana.
City of shadows / Ariana Franklin.— 1st ed.
p. cm.
ISBN-13: 978-0-06-081726-8 (acid-free paper)
ISBN-10: 0-06-081726-7
1. Germany—History—1918–1933—Fiction. 2. Berlin (Germany)—Fiction. I. Title.

PR6064.O73H685 2005
823'.92—dc22
2005051114

06 07 08 09 10 WBC/RRD 10 9 8 7 6 5 4 3 2 1

To Frank McGuinness,
in return for the picture

CITY OF SHADOWS

PROLOGUE

Berlin, February 1920

If Ignaz Stapel hadn't been so afraid of his father, he would have reported the incident and perhaps saved the lives of all the people who were to die as a consequence of it.

But Ignaz's father thought that his son had been passing that particular February evening by singing healthy Teutonic songs at a meeting in Wilmersdorf of the Wandervogel youth club to which Ignaz belonged and of which Herr Stapel Sr. approved.

Ignaz hadn't. He'd spent it in another part of Berlin entirely, at the house of a slightly older male friend with whom he'd indulged in an activity for which, had he known about it, Herr Stapel would have beaten his son senseless.

Since Herr Stapel had seen no reason to give the boy tram fare, Ignaz was hurrying back across the city on foot, frantically rehearsing various explanations to excuse his late return. It was nearly midnight, and Wandervogel meetings ended promptly and healthily at 2230 hours.

It was quiet and very cold; Berlin had gone to bed to keep warm. Once it would still have been busy at this time of night: cafés and beer cellars full of loud, happy, confident drinkers. But the Great War had silenced too many of them forever, and the subsequent revolution—of which Ignaz privately approved, though his father did not—had left it divided.

A bitter, poor, strike-ridden city now, and getting poorer. Only the wealthy could afford to stay up late.

Ignaz was still rehearsing his excuse as he approached the Herkulesbrücke. A young woman was ahead of him, going in the same direction. She'd already gained the bridge.

Had Ignaz considered her, which at that point he did not—women weren't in his line—he would have put her down as one of Berlin's factory workers either returning from or going to a late shift. She was shawled and, from the back, seemed roughly but adequately dressed against the cold, neither her gait nor heavy clothes suggesting the prostitute.

The canal, puttering and noisy in daytime, ran silent beneath her. A gas lamp on the south side of the bridge's center sent light on turgid, icy water, intermingling with that of the blue lamp above the closed doors of the River Police station down on the towpath. The frosted, livid life preserver that hung on a stanchion nearby gaped like an astonished mouth out of the blackness.

A man, a big man, was coming over the bridge from the other direction, his boots clicking confidently on the iron of the bridgewalk. He and the woman would pass each other under the gas lamp.

There was no assignation. Ignaz, going over the event later, as he was to go over and over it for the rest of his life, could have sworn they did not intend to meet. When they neared each other, the woman swerved off the footpath so that the man could maintain his pace as he went by but, as she did so, she looked up and he looked down.

They stopped. Everything stopped. The man's arms, which had been swinging to his walk, froze so that one stayed ahead of his body, one just behind. The woman became a hunched statue. Their intensity halted Ignaz in the shadow of the bridge's far end. He stopped thinking about his father or excuses; there was only the couple on the bridge.

Long-lost lovers? No, there was something terrible here.

The city clocks striking midnight released them all. Ignaz thought he heard a squeak from the woman as she dodged to the other side of the bridge to run away. The man's big head turned to watch her, like a dog following the capers of a mouse. Two strides got him to her side. He took her by the neck and the knees and lifted her in his hands. For a moment he stood under the gaslight like a strongman at a circus, holding her above his head.

Then his hands were empty and the woman was flailing down into the water, shawl and skirts flapping as if from a badly tied bundle of washing.

Ignaz stood still, trying to believe he'd seen what he had seen. He thought later that he must have cried out, certainly the woman must have screamed, must have caused a splash, but if she did, he didn't hear her; he was looking at the man.

Who was looking at him.

Casually, his head to one side as if he were curious, the big man began walking toward him. Had he hastened toward Ignaz, shown anger, Ignaz might have run, but this interested stroll petrified the boy; he didn't move, couldn't.

The man padded closer. Ignaz heard his breath, smelled the feral stink.

There was a shout from below and splashing activity. The great head looked away, the heavy shoulders shrugged.

Ignaz was knocked aside, and then there was only empty space in front of him. He heard the click of running boots fading away toward Lützowplatz. Berlin reestablished itself around him, shabby and familiar.

He fell to his knees, partly from gratitude, mostly because they wouldn't hold him up. After a minute he crawled to the bridge parapet and looked over. A man was in the water, one of his arms around the woman's neck to keep her afloat, the other striking out toward the canal bank.

The doors of the police station opened, and men spilled out onto the towpath. One of them grabbed the life preserver from its hook.

Ignaz turned around so that his back was resting against the parapet, and retched. He'd seen one human being kill another, or certainly try to kill her. His nostrils had sniffed his own death so close he would never be the same again.

I must tell them. The thing's loose in the city. I must tell them.

But if he told them . . .

Guilt had been Ignaz's shadow since he'd first realized that he was not as other boys, abnormal, what his father referred to as "filth." He lived in terror that his secret would become obvious, that the word "sodomite" would pop out on his forehead in letters of raised flesh.

If he told them, they would ask questions. Why was he crossing Herkulesbrücke at this time of night? They would guess. His sin, so apparent to him, would be clear to them. They would tell his father.

He peeped over the parapet. The inert body of the woman was being slithered onto the towpath, men were bending over her, pumping her arms.

If she was alive, *she* would tell them what happened. Perhaps she knew the man and would explain to them who he was, and they'd catch him. All Ignaz could declare was that he was big. And that he wore an armband.

If she was alive . . .

Knowing he was adding another sin to the burden he already carried, Ignaz crawled across the bridge on his hands and knees so that he couldn't be seen by the men below and ran off into the darkness of his own particular hell, leaving yet another to be visited on a city that had already suffered its fair share and was to suffer much, much more.

PART ONE

1

Berlin, May 1, 1922

"ESTH-*ER*."

"What?" She tore off her Dictaphone headset, made a mark on a notepad, and went next door to his office.

He was sitting with his chair turned to the window that looked down onto the floor of his nightclub.

It was a fine nightclub, the Green Hat, one of the largest and most exclusive in Berlin. He'd hired Kandinsky to paint the walls—"Russian scenes," he'd told him. "I want Old Russia"—and been disappointed. "It's blobs," he'd said when he saw the result.

"It's wonderful," Esther had told him. And it was.

But his Russia hadn't consisted of blobs, so he'd insisted on lining the walls with huge stuffed brown bears and putting ribboned kokoshniks on the heads of the cigarette girls and hiring waiters who could squat-dance. "So they know this is a piece of Old Russia," he'd said.

"You're not supposed to say, 'What?'" he said now. "You're supposed to say, 'Yes, Your Highness.'" He was in a good mood.

"I'm busy. I'm translating your instructions to M. Alpert." She paused. "Are you sure you want to put them in a letter?"

"Why not?"

"Suppose the French police raid his office and find it?"

Prince Nick distrusted telephone switchboards, in case his competitors were bribing the operators to listen in, and since he spoke only Russian and German, she handled most of his foreign correspondence, which, she supposed, made her an accessory to corruption, tax evasion, not to mention fraud, all over Europe. But it was a job; she hadn't been able to get another.

"They won't. He's got the gendarmerie in his pocket." He blew out a redolent smoke ring. "And I've got the Polizei in mine."

His pockets were weighed down with them. His other cabaret clubs were popular with the high-rankers because he kept them discreet; politicians, judges, police chiefs, could cavort in privacy—and did. Lists of members and their sexual preferences were kept under lock and key. There was a price, of course: they had to keep Prince Nick from prosecution—they did that, too.

The police on the beat sold him information, usually about any vagrant good-looking young men and women who'd be likely recruits for his clubs. "I want them cheap, and I want them grateful," he used to say. He interviewed them himself. Nearly all came cheap, and most were grateful; working for Prince Nick was better than walking the streets.

In her case she'd had the choice of going on the streets or jumping into the Spree, and of the two she preferred the look of the Spree. It was the rabbi of the Moabit synagogue who'd suggested she apply to Prince Nick for work. The Jews knew of him because, for a price, he could get papers for those wanting to emigrate.

Papers—the Wandering Jew's eternal bugbear. But if you could afford Nick's, you could go to the U.S. embassy in the Tiergarten and get an immigration visa for America. "Go see this Prince Nick, Esther," Rabbi Smoleskin had said. "A crook, yes, but a fair crook. And a Russian like you, so maybe he'll give you a job."

"With a name like Solomonova? And with my face?"

"Brains you got. Languages. A brave heart. Who cares for pretty?"

Prince Nick did; his clubs ran on pretty. He'd taken one look at her and opened his mouth to say sorry, but . . .

She hadn't given him the chance. "I speak English, French, German, and Italian well," she told him in Russian. "I can get by in Polish and Yiddish and Greek. I can type, I do shorthand and bookkeeping. They say you're an international businessman—you need me."

Most of which was true. Not the shorthand, but she could learn.

"Oh, and Latin," she'd said, "I'm good at Latin."

"Always handy in cabaret clubs, Latin," he'd said, and she knew then that, if she could get him over the hurdle of her Jewishness, she'd have the job.

"How'd you get the scar?" he asked.

"Long time ago. In a pogrom."

"A Jew, then." In Old Russia pogroms happened to Jews.

"A Jew," she said.

"With an expensive education?" In Old Russia pogroms happened to *poor* Jews.

"My father was well-off. I had a mam'zelle and a tutor."

"What did your father do?"

"He was a banker."

"Yeah? So how'd you get mixed up in a pogrom?"

"Are you hiring me or not?"

He hired her, which confirmed that he was no more a Russian nobleman than Rabbi Smoleskin. Prerevolution Russia had been about the only country in the world where persecution of Jews was part of the constitution, and she'd never met one of its aristocrats who wasn't anti-Semitic.

Who he really was, where he came from, she didn't know even now. There was a slight slant to his eyes and a beautiful olive sheen to his skin that suggested Tartar, but he professed to be Russian Orthodox and made much of the estates he'd lost to the Bolsheviks. It didn't matter anyway; they were both frauds. And in a Germany that had lost the war, was losing the peace and its currency and, very nearly, its mind, it was only men like him who were making money.

His office had two windows, neither of them giving onto the outdoors. One looked down onto the floor of the club, two stories below, empty this morning. The other, which was small and had a sliding shutter, gave him a view of the large and illegal gaming room next door. Set into one wall was a safe like a miniature Fort Knox. Her own office, through a connecting door, was small and windowless, and she worked in it for a pittance.

He was in fine fettle today, smoking a cigar with his feet up on his desk, hair so sleek it might have been painted on, thirtyish, good-looking—and as ersatz as the sign on his door and the name on his monogrammed writing paper: PRINCE NICOLAI POTROVSKOV.

She'd told him once, "Nick, a prince of the blood doesn't have to say he's a prince. Just put 'Potrovskov.'"

He wouldn't. "It impresses the punters," he said.

SHE'D BEEN ABLE to tone him down a bit. She'd stopped him wearing scent—or not so much—sent him to a dentist to get rid of the gold in his mouth, and she'd redesigned his office. When she first came, he'd been trying for the German-country-gentleman look: an antique claw-footed table desk, a massive chesterfield leather sofa, and truly awful hunting prints set in an unlikely eighteenth century on the walls. It didn't suit him. She'd got him into chrome and hung up copies of Braque's stage designs for *Firebird*.

He wouldn't give up the chesterfield; that was for sex.

She shook her head at him—she did like him. "So what do you want?"

"Did you ever meet the grand duchesses when you were in Moscow?" He was regarding the tip of his cigar, which he did when he was plotting.

Dear God, she thought. "Who?"

"The grand duchesses. Olga, Tatiana, Marie, Anastasia. The czar's daughters."

"Romanovs didn't mix with Jews," she said.

"They did with rich Jews. Your father was rich, you told me."

She'd have told him anything to get the job. Now she said, "The Jews were expelled from Moscow."

"Rich Jews could live anywhere. And they were invited to St. Petersburg now and then, I know—I remember the priests yelling bloody murder about it. The czar wasn't that much of a fool he'd expel the moneymen. Your father went to official things, all the big *zhid* bankers did—Sack, Baron Günsburg, Don't tell me you don't know what the young princesses looked like."

Yes, she said, she knew what the princesses had looked like; their pictures had been everywhere. "They're dead. They're all dead."

"A*ha.*" He pointed his cigar at her.

"Oh, not that old tale, Nick, *please,*" she said. The Russian émigrés wouldn't let it drop; there'd been escapes from Ekaterinburg 1918; the czar had been seen walking down a street in London; little Czarevitch Alexei was alive and well in France; one or another of the grand duchesses had survived the slaughter; the whole Romanov family had been smuggled out of the cellar and put on a yacht to sail forever round the world like the Flying bloody Dutchman.

He sat up and stubbed out his cigar. "Let's go for a drive," he said.

"I'm busy."

"It's a nice day," he said. "Get your hat on, Scarface, we're off."

"Where to?"

"Loony bin. See a madwoman. Hurry up."

It was a beautiful late-July day. People strolled under the trees of the Tiergarten as if the sun had slowed down the inflation that was ruining everybody except those smart enough and unscrupulous enough, like Nick, to speculate in currency. Even those in a line waiting for food from a temporary Salvation Army shelter had raised their faces and closed their eyes like sunbathers.

Apart from the trams, Berlin was traveling on two legs or four—gasoline was scarce and expensive. His new Audi was almost the only car on the road, and he exulted over it. It had won the International Alpine Run, something about four-wheel hydraulic braking.

He slowed down and took his right hand off the wheel to wave it. "How'd you like to live around here?"

They were going along Bismarckstrasse, bastion of Berlin respectability.

She didn't bother to answer him.

"You could," he said. "I'm thinking of renting you an apartment."

Something was up; he was never generous without a reason. "Why?"

"You're my secretary. I can't have a secretary living in Moabit. It's not classy."

It had been classy enough so far. She suspected geese that laid golden eggs. "Good," she said.

For certain he wouldn't be setting her up in a nice apartment because he had designs on her virtue; he'd taken that, such as it was, on the day he'd hired her. She'd thought her face would preclude her but it hadn't.

It had been a form of apprenticeship initiation. The chesterfield in the office was there for that purpose. So were the packets of condoms in his stationery drawer.

She'd been so *hungry*. Ashamed of taking another meal from the canteen that rich Jews had set up for their suffering brethren in Moabit, she'd gone without anything but tea for two days. Even then, when she'd passed it in her search for work and seen its lines of desperate mothers and children, she'd felt guilty.

She'd thought, What does it matter? She was soiled goods anyway. Jews waited for better times. Dully, she let him.

He was a skilled practitioner; it was necessary to his self-esteem to leave all his women satisfied. What took her aback was that her body acted independently and responded with orgasm, as if it had become impatient with her mental numbness and was reminding itself that it was still young and needy. Memory was overwhelmed, blanked out in an eruption of voluptuousness.

There was no pretense on either side that the encounter was anything but physical gratification for them both, but all sensual enjoyment had been foreign to her for so long that she was grateful for it.

"We'll do it again sometime," he'd said. And indeed, when he felt it necessary to mark her as his territory and he was between mistresses, they had.

He increased speed through western suburbs that were still loosely connected villages, where cottages and, intermittently, the walls of mansions lined the route and goats grazed the roadside grass and the poverty was agricultural, which meant that the poor at least had milk from their cow and eggs from the hens now scattering from the Audi's wheels.

"What's the madwoman called?" she shouted.

"What?"

"The madwoman. What's her name?"

"She hasn't got one."

"Nick?" He was making her nervous.

"Oh, come on, Esther," he said. "One of those Romanovs escaped from Ekaterinburg. Everybody thinks so."

"People will believe anything," she said.

"And sure as hell it was one of the princesses. All right, the Bolshies shoot the czar and the czarina, maybe even little Alexei—he's heir to the throne, and he's sick anyway. But those girls? You've seen their pictures, all in their pretty white dresses? Like swans, every one of them. Maybe somebody's finger faltered on the trigger when it came to putting a bullet through those golden heads. Maybe one of them wasn't shot, or maybe she was just wounded and they let her go."

"That's firing squads all over," Esther said. "Tenderhearted."

"Russian firing squad, remember that. Bolshevik bastards, but *Russian* Bolshevik bastards; they'd grown up with the image of those sweet kids in their heart, and what harm did they ever do anybody?"

He'd actually slowed down so that she could attend to his argument better. They were into forest now, and she could smell the pines and hear birdsong.

"Nice, polite kids they were, opened a church bazaar here and there, rolled bandages at the hospital. Was that grinding the faces of the poor? I tell you, Esther, when it came to burying the bodies and they found one of those girls was still alive, they couldn't finish the job. They had to let her go."

"Sweet," said Esther. "What did she do then? Grow wings?"

"That's the trouble with you Jews," he said. "No soul. She's wandering alone in Siberia, she's found by true Russians, they smuggle her over the border, she's helped again, crosses Poland, arrives in Berlin. She's hurt, destroyed by grief, lost her mind and memory for a while maybe. . . ."

"Please don't tell me what I think you're going to tell me," Esther pleaded.

"Yep. She ends up in a German loony bin. It makes sense."

"Oh, it absolutely does," she said. "And which of the grand duchesses is she? Olga, Tatiana, Marie, or Anastasia?"

"Tatiana. One of the inmates recognized her from a magazine."

"That proves it, then," she said. "How did you hear about her?"

"Word gets around," he said vaguely. Nobody had his ear pressed more firmly to the ground than Prince Nick; he could hear a penny drop in Kazakhstan—and make a profit from it.

She laid her hand on his sleeve. "Don't do this, Nick. Whatever's in it for you, don't do it."

"This is sacred, Esther, in the name of God. You think I'm out to make money from it?"

"I bloody know you are."

"You hurt me." He put his foot on the accelerator. "All right, maybe she *is* Tatiana, maybe I help her to her inheritance, and maybe I take a percentage, but I tell you . . ."

He took his hands off the wheel to slam them on his chest. "If I do this, I completely do it for my dead czar, for the soul of Russia, for the Holy Church."

"Oh, shut up," she said.

It's another of his schemes, she thought. Like the time he tried to marry the kaiser's aunt. It'll come to nothing.

He was driving like a mad thing now, punishing her. People came out of their doorways at the sound of the car, only to find it had already gone by, leaving them in its dust.

It didn't worry her. She'd got used to being out of control and clinging on to life as it dragged her helter-skelter through its scrub, lucky when she didn't encounter anything too hard, not yelping when she did. At the moment it wasn't hurting too much, which was all she could expect of it. Numbness was her chosen state; after being in hell, limbo had much of heaven's attraction. Anyway, her body enjoyed being whipped by warm air. Physical sensation was the thing.

He was slowing now to look at some written instructions that he had, and crawled until he saw a sign above some gates, then turned into them, fast. She had just time to read the word "Dalldorf" before they were haring up the drive, scattering pigeons and rooks.

Dalldorf, then. A place with such echoes that its name had entered the Berliners' language as a euphemism for madness. *He belongs in Dalldorf. Let you out of Dalldorf, have they? Carry on like that, you'll end up in Dalldorf.*

The building was large and, on a day like this, didn't look oppressive, though one felt that it would if it could. A few people wandered the lawns at its front, watched by a man in a white coat.

The front door was opened by a large porter; their names and business were inquired into before they were allowed into a big hall smelling of antiseptic. The place was ordered and almost empty. Noise—a lot of it—was somewhere in the building, but not here. They were shown into the office of the matron, a large woman with starched white cuffs and cap, who asked them what they wanted. She had a bunch of keys hanging from her belt.

Nick kissed her hand. "Prince Nikolai Potrovskov, madam. This is my secretary."

He never gave her name at first meetings in case its Jewishness put people off. He catered to anti-Semitism in other people without having any himself; Jew, goy, black, white—they were all the same to him as long as they served his purpose. Esther often wondered whether his total amorality caused his total lack of prejudice, or the other way around.

Anyway, he'd discovered that people were flustered by her face and that this was useful, because they then obliged him in their embarrassment for having been caught staring at it. Their initial reaction always amused him. "Like introducing Medusa," he would say.

The matron didn't spend much time on it; in a hospital like this, there were other horrors. "What can I do for Your Highness?"

"Madam, here you have unidentified lady patient. With your permission, we see her, yes? Maybe she is compatriot of mine."

"Frau Unbekkant?" The woman's lips compressed. "I am sorry. This business is attracting too much attention for her own good. We're not permitting visitors."

Esther watched Nick slide a hand under the matron's arm and lead her to one side. It was merely a matter of waiting. The woman would do what he wanted; women always did.

Three minutes later they were on their way through bare, disinfected corridors tiled to waist height in pastel green. Some doors were open, showing people sitting at tables, weaving baskets, or doing jigsaw puzzles.

All very tidy, very decent, very German, she thought. In Old Russia a place like this would have been a snake pit.

They stopped at double doors with windows that were netted with wire as if against a bomb blast. In the anteroom beyond, a nurse sat at a desk, writing.

They went in. "These people want to see Frau Unbekkant, Klausnick," the matron said. "How is she today?"

"No different, Matron."

The matron nodded with satisfaction. "She won't talk to you," she told Nick. "She's not said a word to outsiders since she's been here."

"How long?"

"Two years. Very well, Nurse Klausnick will look after you. I have things to do." She bustled off.

Klausnick unlocked the door to the ward, and the noise came at them in a roar—the screechings, screamings, moanings of anxious animals in a zoo.

It was a long, clean room, hot from the sun coming in through barred windows. Antiseptic mixed with the smell of urine. It was full of women. Iron beds ran along each side, and two of the patients were jumping from one to the other, yelling like high-spirited children and being shouted at. Two more were rolling on the floor, pulling each other's hair.

Klausnick drew in a breath and roared, "QUIET!" from not inconsiderable lungs.

Everything stopped—the jumping, fighting, the moaning. Heads were turned to where they stood in the doorway and then, after a while, turned away.

Klausnick separated the two women on the floor and began pursuing the ones who had resumed jumping. She flicked a thumb toward the bottom of the ward. "Last bed," she said.

But they'd already seen Mrs. Unknown. She was the only still person in the room and the only one who hadn't looked up at their entrance. Her bed was a reservoir of quiet. She'd built a barricade of pillows around it, and they could just see the profile of her face upturned to the ceiling.

She was aware of them, though; as they approached, she pulled the gray hospital blanket over her mouth and hugged it there with tiny, nail-bitten hands. Huge and very blue eyes continued looking at the ceiling from a little skull like a marmoset's.

Nick spoke to her in Russian. "Madam, we have come to talk to you. I am Prince Nicolai Potrovskov, here is my secretary."

The woman's eyes didn't move.

He repeated what he'd said in German. There was a flicker, but no response.

"How old do you reckon, Esther?" Nick said. "Your age, maybe?"

"Maybe." The forehead skin was unlined, like her own, but youth had gone out of both of them.

"Recognize her?" Gently, he disengaged the blanket from the woman's grip and pulled it down. Immediately, her hand came up to cover her mouth again.

"Should I?"

He shrugged.

A woman had come up, adjusting the band that held back her long, gray hair—she'd been one of those fighting—and stood at the end of the bed. She was tall, bony, and aggressive. "You want to talk to her, you talk to me. She don't talk to just anybody. She's royal."

Nick turned to her. "I am also. Prince Potrovskov, at your service."

The woman stared at him for a moment, then ran up the ward, scrabbled under a mattress, and came back waving a dog-eared magazine.

"It was me," she said. "Clara Peuthert, you remember that, Your Highness. It was me recognized her."

Other patients were gathering around the bed, their eyes avid.

"Sure, Frau Peuthert. I'll remember." Nick took the magazine, an old edition of the *Berliner Illustrierte Zeitung* that had been turned back to a full-page family picture. The accompanying story on the opposite page had a headline: "The Truth About the Murder of the Czar."

Clara jabbed her finger on one of the pictured faces. "See? That's Tatiana." She transferred the finger to the quiet shape on the bed. "And *that's* Tatiana. Recognized her right off. You remember that. I been writing to every bit of family that's left. The czar's poor mother in Denmark and the czarina's sister, Princess Irene of Prussia. 'I found the Grand Duchess Tatiana,' I told 'em. Been waiting and waiting for one of 'em to come. Knew they would. Sent you, did they? Supreme Monarchy Council?"

"Sure." Nick was turning pages, his eyes going from the magazine to the woman on the bed. "You want to look at this, Esther?"

"No."

He shrugged. "She ain't the believing type," he told Clara.

The big woman transferred her attention to Esther, grabbing one of Frau Unbekkant's unresisting hands and waving it like an exhibit. "You can believe this. See this? How fine is this? That's a grand duchess's hand. See mine?" A thick, raw fist was brandished. Clara was getting angry. "Common, that's a common hand, and it can punch your snotty nose, miss. Who're you, you ugly thing, coming in here and telling me—"

The rising voice was an alarm bell, and Nurse Klausnick was at Frau Peuthert's side. "Calm, now, Clara. Calm yourself. You don't want solitary again." She led her off.

Nick jerked his head at Esther. Everybody to be kept away; this was private.

Esther approached the women gathered at the end of the bed. "Tell me, ladies, have you been here long?"

Gently, she shepherded them up the ward, listening to the answers. One tiny woman could make only inarticulate sounds but made them with such urgency that Esther had to turn to Nurse Klausnick.

"What's wrong with her?"

"Nothing much. She's just deaf. Never learned to talk."

"And she's in here how long?"

"Forty-two years."

Esther said, "There are ways to help the deaf now."

"Too late for her." Klausnick hurried away.

Clara Peuthert was crying into her pillow. At the end of the ward, Prince Nick had his head close to the unknown woman's. He'd given her a piece of paper and a pencil.

On the way home, he was subdued. "What do you think?"

"Sad. Horrible."

"Know why Unbekkant covers her mouth like that?"

"No."

"She had toothache. They pulled some of her teeth out. Cheaper. But we can fix that, good dentist, nice dentures, all dandy." He shot a look at her. "You think she's the grand duchess Tatiana?"

"No."

"You're right. Know who she thinks she is? Feel in my left pocket."

He smelled of pomade and the artificially scented carnation in his buttonhole. She pulled out a piece of paper.

He yelled, "I wrote down the names of the four grand duchesses. Told her to scratch out the ones that weren't her. Look at it."

She looked. Three names had been struck through. The one that remained was "Anastasia."

"Shook me," he said. "I was expecting Tatiana. Know when Unbekkant was born? Hospital register says 1901. Know when Anastasia was born?"

"In 1901?"

"That's right."

They stopped for lunch at a Spiesehäuser. He liked plain eating houses. The weeks of starvation that he'd endured trying to get out of Russia while dodging the Bolshevik army had instilled in him a passion for German food at its weightiest. With his wealthier clients and his fancy women, he ate French food at the Eden or the Adlon; with her he fell on pork and potatoes.

"You're not going to be difficult, are you?" he said.

"She's not Anastasia."

"Why isn't she?" he said. "Pass the salt. Right size, right eyes, hair, everything. I tell you, kid, she shook me. You notice her ears?"

No, Esther said, she hadn't noticed Unbekkant's ears.

"Exact same shape as Anastasia's in the photograph. You can't fool around with ears."

"She's not Anastasia," Esther said.

"By the time I'm finished with her, she will be. Empress Granny will fall on her neck: 'Vnushka, my long-lost little one. Here are the jewels of the Romanovs.' And I happen to know"—he tapped his nose—"there's a fortune the czar put for safekeeping in the Bank of England. You leaving that herring?"

She leaned forward and wiped food from his chin with her napkin. "She'll have relatives who know who she really is."

"Oh, yeah." He liked Americanisms. "Esther, she's been there two years, and nobody's so much as sent her a card—I asked. Two *years.* And in the hospital before that—the police fished her out of the Landwehr Canal in 1920. Nobody wants to know who she is." He chewed reflectively. "Except me."

"Was she? Fished out of a canal?"

"That's what it says on her record."

So she's been where I've been, Esther thought. She's stared down into the waters and wondered how long it took before they delivered oblivion. Only she decided to find out. Does that make her more cowardly than me? Or braver?

"All right, she's mad," Nick said. He shrugged. "But who ain't?" He held that the whole world was insane, a conviction Esther agreed with. "But suppose she is Anastasia. . . ." His eyes widened. He stopped shoveling food from her plate onto his. "Holy Martyr, *I think she is.* I completely think she is."

Alarmed, Esther saw him reassessing his evidence. "Holy Martyr," he said again. "I've found Anastasia."

"You are appalling," she said.

"What? See, all right, I got this tip-off. There was an unknown woman in Dalldorf, and one of the patients in there shouting around it was Grand Duchess Tatiana."

"And you thought Tatiana plus Romanov equals czarist treasure."

"Nothing wrong with that," he said, injured. "There's a fortune in Romanov jewels still floating around that didn't all disappear. Grandma Dowager Czarina took a king's ransom in precious stones with her when she escaped. She's an old woman. Who's going to get them when she curls up her toes? The Bolsheviks want them, say they're state property. The king of England says he'll distribute them around the family, but his old lady . . . what's her name?"

"Queen Mary."

"She's got a keen eye for a trinket, that one, so she won't let them go once they're in her claws." He poked the fork at her, like a stabbing trident. "And I'll tell you this, Esther, I'd see them go to the Reds before I let the fucking English get them."

"Very patriotic of you." King George V, the czar's first cousin, had ensured the death of the Romanovs by refusing them asylum in England. It had not endeared him to White Russians, high or low.

She said, "So the Bank of England and various Romanovs are going to say how nice, Prince Potrovskov, thank you for bringing the grand duchess Tatiana and/or Anastasia back from the dead, and here's our millions. I should have left you in Dalldorf."

"Yeah, but see, Esther, I'm beginning to think she truly is. Okay, maybe I was considering making my own grand duchess when I started out, but now . . . It fits. Think back to that kid we've just seen in that bed. . . ."

She thought back. There'd been intelligence, even craftiness, in those eyes. But mostly panic. The barricade around that bed had been a bunker. She'd lain like a leveret in the long grass hoping the fox wouldn't find it. Two years of it, two years of silence in a cacophony of the afflicted. Refusing an identity. Either very crazy or very frightened. Perhaps both.

"Nick, you saw her. She doesn't even speak Russian."

"Would you?" The fork summoned up a funeral drum. "If your own people took you down to a cellar, Russians, and shot your daddy, your mommy, your brother and sisters in front of your eyes, wounded you, maybe, would you want to speak the same as those bastards? Not if you didn't have to—and those girls were educated, remember. They had other languages. They were . . . what's the word?"

"Polyglot?"

"Yeah, polyglots. Why'd she want to talk Russian? With those memories? Too terrible. She sticks to German. That makes sense, the press'll understand that." He began eating again, swaying slightly to the symphony in his head.

"The press?"

"Obviously we'll call a press conference once she's ready."

"You're calling a press conference," she said flatly.

"Not yet. We've got a long way to go, but . . ." He faced her look. "Esther, we'll be doing people a favor. That was a terrible thing happened at Ekaterinburg. Made the whole world sad. Maybe as a Jew you don't feel it the same, but for us loyal subjects"—he thumped himself on the chest—"that pierced our hearts. We'll never get over it."

He was frightening her; he was sobbing. She wanted the cynic back. This was an alien being crying real tears. Her own eyes were stony dry.

"Beautiful things happen sometimes," he said. "Now and then the saints in their grace grant us a miracle. They just did. We got one of them back." He knuckled his eyes with his forefingers, wiping them. "I tell you, such a cheer will go around the earth. Stock market'll go up, maybe. I must get in touch with my broker."

That was better. Nick the opportunist she could cope with.

"It won't work," she said. "She's just a sick, scared young woman."

He became impatient. "Sure she's scared. Maybe she thinks the Bolshies are out to get her. 'You want to stay here forever?' I said to her—she understands German well enough. 'You've got me to protect you now.'"

"And suppose the Romanovs say she's not Anastasia?"

"They'll have to. New teeth, plenty of coaching . . ." He began tapping his own teeth with his fork and then waved it at her. "Listen, Esther, there's a hole in the market just waiting for her. People want a happy ending, I'm giving them one."

Another thought struck him. "What a movie it'd make. I could get rich out of the film rights alone."

"And Little Miss Unknown has agreed to all this, has she?"

"Anna Anderson," he said.

"What?"

"Anna Anderson. That's who she's going to be for now. I suggested the name, and she liked it. Nice and neutral. It's the name I'll get put on her identity papers."

Esther raised her eyes to heaven. "She's agreed to this arrangement, has she?"

"She will. Fifty-fifty, I told her." Absentmindedly, he took over Esther's plate and began clearing it. "Maybe I'll make it seventy-five–twenty-five, I'm going to have a lot of expenses." He beckoned to a white-aproned waiter. "Do you make palatschinken here?"

"Yes, sir."

"Two portions."

He was silent until the pancakes came, and then he said, "You could put her up in the new apartment I'm getting for you."

Ah.

"Suddenly Moabit's looking attractive," she said. "I think I'll stay there."

"Moabit's a shithole. I was going to take you out of it anyway."

"I'm not going to do it, Nick. It's fraud on a grand scale. It'll hurt people."

"Not if she's the real Anastasia. Who's it going to hurt? Her? I'm going to restore her to her rightful place, cherish her like she should be. At least she gets out of Dalldorf. The rest of the Romanovs? I spit on 'em. They can't even wipe their own asses without whining there's no servant to do it for 'em."

It was true. They had become shabby in their obsolescence. Since the revolution, princes, grand dukes, who'd once roamed Europe in their private trains, kept their mistresses in luxury, flung roubles to peasants lining the roadway, patronized great artists and gambled millions on a throw of cards at Monte Carlo, had become pathetic emperors without clothes, still clinging onto their titles and expecting to live on the generosity of others.

Grand Duke Cyril, Nicholas's cousin and now heir to the nonexistent throne, had declared himself "Czar of All the Russias" from a farmhouse in France where the occasional émigré turned up to bow to him. "Makes the farmhands walk backward," Nick had said.

Only Grand Duke Dmitry, Nick said, was showing a grasp on reality; he'd become a champagne salesman and was allegedly pursuing an American heiress.

None of the bluer-blooded émigrés would invite Nick, the arriviste, to the homes other people had given them. But they were glad enough to go to the parties he threw, Esther thought, quick enough to touch him for a loan that they had no means and no intention of repaying. She'd seen them at his clubs in lachrymose gatherings, remembering the good old days, still pretending to dignity, still unable to believe that the serfs they'd maltreated didn't want them back.

What right had they to look down on him? Bereft of their palaces and jewels, they'd been landed back in the primeval soup to begin the business of survival all over again. And they weren't good at it. The ruthlessness of their ancestors that had given them the palaces and jewels in the first place had been bred out of them. Instead the energy to crawl onto dry land belonged to men like Nick, hungry, unhampered by tradition or morals.

"I tell you, Esther, we've found her. We've made the discovery of the century. You want to leave her in that place?"

"No." Whatever happened, they were going to have to get her released if they could. Just seeing her had laid that responsibility upon them. Walk away from it and that silent little form in the bed would haunt her dreams forever. "Get her out by all means, but after that you're on your own. I'm not going to help you."

"Really?" He leaned back in his chair and slowly lit a cigar, watching the smoke as it curled up from his lips before he looked at her. "What are you going to do instead?"

"I see," she said quietly.

It was that important to him; she'd become his right hand, but for this he was prepared to cut it off. She met his gaze. "I'll manage. There'll be some other twister who needs his dirty work done in five different languages." And wondered where the hell she'd find him.

"Maybe," he said.

Then he changed gear. He's going to tell me I owe him, she thought.

"You owe me, Esther," he said.

And she did. A Russian émigré, a *Jewish* Russian émigré, a *disfigured* Jewish Russian émigré didn't rate high in the endless unemployment lines of a Germany with galloping inflation. She was only on dry land now because she'd clung to his back. Not just her, but the dozens of other poor White Russians he employed in his clubs—and what about the Jews who'd been able to get to the States and begin new lives because of him?

All right, it had been self-interest, not philanthropy. But that was capitalism for you: sharks allowing little fish to feed on the bits between their teeth.

She watched him shoveling in pancakes, persuading and cajoling. Automatically, she took the spoon out of his right hand and replaced it with a fork.

"I'll miss you," she said. And she would; in a fractured way they were each other's best friend.

"So don't," he said. "All you have to do is take in a poor female, be her companion. You got class, Esther, haven't I always said? You know things—art and books. Let some of it rub off on her. That's completely all you got to do, I swear. As for the Anastasia thing, you won't be involved. I'll find someone to coach her in the Romanov stuff."

"If she's a Romanov, why does she need coaching?"

"She's forgotten, for God's sake." He was amazed at her obtuseness. "It's been four years since Ekaterinburg. The saints know how she's had to live, what she's been through. Brain fever wiped out her memory, maybe. All you do is remind her how to be a lady again. Is that so much?"

His persuasion ebbed and flowed in and out of her mind as she considered—and weakened.

"Come on, Esther. It'll be fun."

Yes, she could see that. By God, to set a cat among the pigeons that still believed they had a right to the Fabergé eggs and the rubies and the pearls distilled out of a people's sweat and tears. She was amazed they could lay claim to them. They'd learned nothing.

"You want to leave her in that hellhole?" he continued.

Yes, I owe him, but he doesn't know what he's asking. It's not wickedness to him; he doesn't know what wickedness is. Neither do I anymore. I merely make a choice of sins.

". . . get her doctors. Who's the one that's good with loonies? Freud, I'll get her Freud. . . ."

Anyway, it's too impossible to come to anything.

Oh, God help me, I can't go back to being hungry, I can't. With my face I couldn't even earn a living as a whore.

"Be her friend, that's all I'm asking."

"Oh, shut up and finish your bloody pancakes," she said.

He grinned at her. "That's my girl."

"That's me," she said. "Sadly."

2

THE TROUBLE WAS that the woman who was now Anna Anderson refused to leave Dalldorf.

For three days she wouldn't even desert the dugout of her bed. During their afternoon visits, Esther kept the other women of the ward at bay while Nick, cajoling in a whisper across the pillowed barricade, extolled the marvels that awaited his protégée in the outside world—without result.

"Has she said anything yet?"

"Not a fucking word." He brightened. "But she's listening."

It wasn't that the asylum wished to keep her; the doctors were willing to sign her release. They'd made no progress with her in two years and feared she was institutionalized. The matron wanted her out; Frau Unbekkant, being indigent, was costing the place money.

"And she can cause considerable trouble," the matron told Esther.

"Really?"

"Indeed. She'll put the hospital in an uproar if she gets disturbed."

"I should think she gets enough disturbance in that ward." The place would send anyone mad within minutes.

"She refuses to leave it. It's secure, you see. She won't countenance transference to an open ward. It's men. A new window cleaner appearing at the window, an unfamiliar doctor entering the ward at night, especially if he's tall. Big men . . . I tell you, Fräulein, she can be almost uncontrollable."

"She was raped, then," said Esther gently.

The matron, as the one who had to impose order on chaos, lacked sympathy. "She should pull herself together; she could if she put her mind to it, of that I'm sure. She's not as defenseless as she likes to appear."

Clara Peuthert, too, maintained that her grand duchess was terrified, but she was more specific about the cause. "Bolshevik agents," she said. "Out to assassinate her."

"Really?" Esther was attempting—not very successfully—to keep Clara from intruding on Nick and Anna's tête-à-tête by sitting with her on her bed underneath one of the ward windows.

"You think I'm telling lies?" Clara's temper was quick to surface. "Seen him with my own eyes. Lurking in the shrubbery at nights, watching the building. Comes regular. Big bugger. All them Red agents is big."

"When was this?"

"I got out," Clara said. "Slipped past Klausnick when she opened the ward door. Got into the garden. Ran at him in the dark. 'You leave Her Imperial Highness Tatiana alone,' I told him. 'You kill her, you got to kill me.' That saw him off."

"She seems to believe she's Anastasia."

"She's Tatiana. I told her she was. Looks like Tatiana."

In Esther's view Anna Anderson looked vaguely like all four princesses—or what the princesses might have looked like if they'd lacked their front teeth and survived the trauma that Anderson obviously had. Perhaps people had commented on the likeness. Perhaps Clara's recognition of her as a grand duchess had acted as a catalyst, allowing Anna's hurt mind to accelerate and improve on a fantasy it had always harbored.

"Came back, though," Clara said gloomily.

"Who did?"

"The Bolshie. That agent. But this time they wouldn't let me get at him." She nodded toward the window. "He was out there. Watching."

It was said with a certainty that caused Esther to stand up and look out. A long back lawn gave onto copses and fields where Dalldorf cows grazed, flicking their tails—the asylum was virtually self-supporting, with its own dairy. The sun was high, shadows were short, an old man was mending a gate. Nursery-rhyme land. Oh, God, to be locked up here, unable to go out and lie under one of those trees. No wonder minds festered and created their own nightmares.

"We mustn't frighten her, Clara. There's nobody there."

"'Course there isn't," Clara said. "Ain't the sixth week, is it? That's when he comes, every six weeks. Oh, don't you smile at me, miss." Furiously, she delved underneath her mattress and brought out a large and creased calendar advertising Klingenberg Engineering. The dates on the page for July were below a large picture of nuts and bolts and had been filled in with pencil scrawls: "*Painters in,*" "*Solitary again,*" "*Shit on Klausnick,*" but dominating all of them was "*Here again!*" written across the squares for June 17 and June 18, through which Clara had drawn a dripping dagger in red ink.

"And see here." Clara's big hands flipped back the pages to a May represented by iron pipes of various sizes where, among the scrawls, another "*Here again!*" red and bloody dagger pierced the weekend of May 6 and 7, as another did on March 25 and 26 and yet another six weeks previously in February.

"That's when I spotted him first," Clara said. "February. I reckon that's when the Bolshies found out where she was."

"How?"

"Traced her from the hospital. Got somebody there who told 'em she'd been transferred here."

"The weekends," Esther said. "He comes here hoping to assassinate her every sixth weekend."

"Yep," Clara said. "Has to go back to Russia in between. Got to report to his masters in the Cheka."

"Of course."

"Just you wait, missy." Clara's fist was waved under Esther's nose. "Think I'm touched, do you? Just because I'm in here don't mean I lost my eyes. You come back"—she consulted her calendar—"July twenty-ninth. That's six weeks from last time he was here. You come back here late Saturday night, July twenty-ninth, and you'll see him standing in the shadows out there, waiting for his chance to kill the grand duchess."

"Peuthert's fueling that poor child's fear," Esther told Nick on their way home. Whatever horror had put Anna Anderson in here in the first place was being given an up-to-date shape to fit the grand-duchess legend. "She says there's a Cheka agent lurking in the grounds waiting to assassinate Anna."

"She does?" He put his foot on the brake. "Holy Martyr, wouldn't it be dandy if there were?"

"What?"

"It'd prove it, don't you see? Bolshevik Secret Service doesn't bump off just any old loony. The Cheka knows Anastasia got away. They've got to get rid of her. Afraid a counterrevolution'll put her back on the throne. Heir to All the Russias. I tell you, Esther, it fits."

"Really? Well, this assassin's part-time. He only turns up one weekend in six, according to Clara. Every sixth weekend she keeps a night vigil and watches for him—and there he is."

"Oh." He was disappointed.

"For God's sake," she said, "we're dealing with sick people, Nick, and you're sicker than any of them."

"Peuthert's a pain," he admitted. "Keeps interrupting. I got to find some way of getting Anna away so I can work on her in private."

They drove on. It was a glorious day.

"Picnic," he said, suddenly. "We'll take her into the grounds for a picnic. Sunshine, champagne, strawberries—she'll love it."

"With all those imaginary Cheka agents in the bushes? She won't go."

"Mmm." Another mile passed before he solved that one.

"We'll bring one of the bouncers along. Big Theo, maybe. Make her feel protected."

"She's scared of large men, and they don't come larger than Theo."

On the other hand, Esther thought, they didn't come milder either. The great Yakut, once a heavyweight wrestler and bodyguard to Prince Ivan, radiated a calm that usually reduced troublemakers at the Green Hat without the necessity of throwing them out. Or, if he had to throw them out, he managed it with the minimum breakage to their bones. "We could try, I suppose," she said. An afternoon in the fresh air could be a start to Anna's rehabilitation.

ANDERSON BEGAN TO scream the moment Big Theo appeared in the ward doorway. Esther ran to her bed, dragging the bouncer with her. "Look at him," she said. *"Look."*

She cupped the contorted face so that its eyes were aimed at Theo's, beaming down on Anna like a beneficent yellow moon. "It's not him," she said. Whoever *he* was, she thought.

The screaming stopped. The rest of the ward, which had become restless, settled down.

Theo had been rehearsed. He picked up Anna Anderson's hand, almost losing it in his, and kissed it. "Don't you scare now, Highness," he said in his bad German. "Ain't no damn anybody hurt you with me."

For the first time since they'd met, Esther saw something like youth return to the woman in the bed; not a smile, exactly, but a smoothing out of her features. She nodded.

Theo was chased from the ward, pursued by lustful catcalls from some of the beds, and Esther helped Anna into the dress she'd bought for her, the prettiest she'd been able to find in Kurfürstendamm's newest and most expensive store. Overlarge hospital slippers went oddly with it—Esther hadn't been able to guess Anna's shoe size—but since the woman's legs wobbled under the unaccustomed exercise of walking, they were just as well.

They picnicked in a summerhouse in the asylum's neat and scented rose garden. The huge figure of Big Theo on guard blocked light from the doorway, and the sun came through the slats in horizontal stripes to shine on the contents of a hamper that Nick's chef had filled with delicacies fit for a Russian princess—caviar, blinis, pelmeni—"so's your Imperial Highness can feel at home."

Anna looked at it with suspicion and, somewhat wisely in view of a stomach inured to hospital food, chose a chicken leg and nibbled at it cautiously with her canines.

Sniffing a choice of champagne and "good old Russian kvass," Anna—again wisely in the opinion of Esther, who'd always loathed kvass—agreed to sip a glass of champagne. Esther herself took the long-forgotten opportunity of wolfing down blinis stuffed with caviar and sour cream.

Nick was tremendous—talking, laughing, painting the future, recalling happy Romanov state occasions of the past, trying to draw some royal memory or acknowledgment from his guest.

Nothing. The great violet eyes studied him and Esther, and rested, perhaps with comfort, on Theo's back, but the sunken mouth didn't open.

It was only when Nick had admitted defeat and he and Esther were packing the food away that a soft voice said, "Want a dog."

Nick actually looked around in case somebody else had slipped in through the summerhouse slats. "Sure, sure, Your Imperial Highness, you have all the dogs you want. You ready to leave with us? I got the car outside."

Her Imperial Highness wasn't ready. "I go back in now," she said.

With Theo's bulk covering them, they helped her back to the hospital.

"You reckon we're making progress, Esther?" Nick asked on the way home.

"I don't know. At some time or another, that girl was terrified by some man—raped, probably. She can't get rid of the memory. It haunts her."

Enslavement to memory was something Esther knew about; freeing herself from her own was an everyday struggle. Sometimes she won, sometimes she didn't.

"Yeah, well I can't spend all my time in a loony bin. I got a business to run. What the grand duchess needs is sessions on her own with a nice lady companion like she was used to, discuss Old Russia, improve her German, girly talk, win her confidence—all that stuff."

"Me?"

"You."

Esther sighed, but he was probably right; with her distrust of men, Anna's rehabilitation was more likely to be achieved by a woman. "Am I going to be paid extra for this?"

"For spending afternoons chatting? You want extra?"

She was at least allowed the use of his car and, with Theo beside her, drove it every afternoon to Dalldorf, returning them both to the club in the evening, where she caught up on her typing and translation, not forgetting to point out that doing so kept her working into the early hours.

Anna was content to leave her bed as long as Theo was by her side and they didn't venture too far from the main building. Even then her eyes were never still, always aware and looking for movement. A rustle made by quarreling birds in the bushes could make her curl up like a hedgehog.

The sun continued to shine, it was nice for Esther to get out of an airless office to sit in the asylum's immaculate gardens—and the sessions with the unknown woman were compelling.

For one thing, she had no curiosity. Esther's attempts to fill in for her the years that had been spent in a hospital ward were useless. The revolution that had made Germany into a unified, if shaky, democracy, the reparations demanded by the victors of the Great War that were bleeding it dry—these things were met with complete lack of interest.

The latest fashions evinced a flicker of response, but it soon went out. She seemed to have taken Prince Nick at face value as someone who'd come into her life with the intention of helping her, but she was incurious as to why.

"What *do* you want to talk about?" Esther asked desperately.

"Russia."

"The revolution?"

"No. Was bad. Old Russia. Romanovs, tell me about Romanovs."

Even then she showed more interest in the magazine articles Esther brought her on the subject than in Esther's stilted attempts to describe royal state occasions.

Her German was ungrammatical and she spoke it with an accent Esther couldn't identify. Any inquiries about her past—how she'd come to jump into the canal and why—were met with silence, and the day Esther persisted with them ended in Anna's demand that she be taken back to her ward.

Esther watched her go.

Who the hell *are* you? What are you afraid of?

The questions remained unanswered. The only subject on which Anna would hold forth was her nurses and fellow inmates, all of whom, except Clara, displeased her. "They don' show me respect."

Respect. It was her only yardstick. She approved of Theo because he treated her like royalty; indeed, she spent a lot of the sessions ordering him around. "Go pick me flowers." "Fetch me a handkerchief." And smiled, always behind her hand, as he obeyed.

Esther failed the test by refusing to call her "Your Imperial Highness" when demanded. "No," Esther said, "I'm calling you Anna, or your real name if you tell me what it is, but I'm not using titles."

There was an immediate flash of temper. "Solomonova. Esther Solomonova. Clara says is Jewish name."

"It is."

Anna got up to go. "Don't like Jews."

"You're stuck with me, kid," Esther said calmly. "There isn't anybody else."

Anna looked toward the hospital for a long moment and then sat down again.

It was, Esther felt, a small triumph, an admission that Anna needed her. It didn't stop the gibes, though. As the young woman gained confidence in defining herself as one of the Romanovs, she was consistent in displaying their anti-Semitism.

It came up again and again as Esther tried to fit her for social life in the outside world: "It's better to use your fork. Like this." When they were alone over the picnic basket, Anna felt free to attack the beautiful food with ferocity.

She snarled at Esther, "What a Jew know? When you been hungry like me, you eat any way you can."

"Maybe, but ladies don't."

So she'd been hungry. Esther's impulse to slap her was invariably overtaken by compassion; whoever Anna Anderson was, she was vulnerable.

Even when it was with gritted teeth, Esther always reminded herself that the girl had tried to drown herself.

"She ready to come out yet?" Nick was growing impatient, afraid that some other entrepreneur might discover the golden goose at Dalldorf.

"Not yet."

And then, suddenly, she was.

It was a Saturday night when the Green Hat, though busy, was not expecting any celebrated guests, and Nick had gone across to the Adlon to dine, wine, and bed his latest paramour, a silent-film star, leaving Boris, his manager, in charge.

The call went through to Nick's office, where Esther was working late.

Over what sounded like a bad day on the Somme, Dalldorf's matron's voice was pitched at an unmatronly level. "Prince Nick said he would assume responsibility for Unbekkant. Come now. We can't put up with this."

"I'm on my way." Esther put through a call to the Adlon, where the desk clerk told her that Nick and his lady had just walked out of the hotel for a destination unknown. Damn it, damn it. She left a message for him, snatched his spare set of car keys from his drawer, and went downstairs.

"Boris, if Nick comes back, tell him I've gone to Dalldorf. I'm taking his car. And I'm going to have to borrow Theo for an hour or so."

"Okay, Esther, but bring him back quick—the von Schwerin boys just came in unexpected." German minor royalty spent freely but never felt it was having a good time unless it smashed furniture.

It was a warm night, and despite her concern for Anna, Esther enjoyed the drive—she loved the power of the Audi.

If Dalldorf had sounded like a battleground when the matron phoned, it now resembled a retreat before a vengeful army. Light spilled from its doors and windows, showing ghostly, night-clad inmates dodging around the grounds chased by doctors and nurses.

A naked woman—Esther thought it might be Clara Peuthert—was outlined against the moon as she sat on the roof ridge, diligently chucking tiles onto the terrace below.

Inside the hall two male nurses were fighting to put a straitjacket on a man twice their size, stepping as they did so in a pool of ink, which the splatters suggested had been thrown with force from the top of the stairs. The noise coming from all over the building was zoo-like: howls, screeches, whoops, combined with the crash of glass. Somewhere upstairs a battering ram was being employed.

The matron stood like a rock at her desk, telephone in one hand, the other clutching the pajama neck of a crying, wriggling, adolescent boy.

"Where is she?" Esther asked.

"Locked herself in a lavatory. They're trying to break down the door."

"What happened?"

"She thinks she saw a face at the window. . . . My man, if you'd give a hand over there." This was addressed to Theo with a nod toward the two nurses who were now hanging on to the straitjacket's ties and being dragged through the ink. "Nonsense, of course, but she went howling around the hospital, setting off one ward after another and— Thank you, my man. Take him back to his bed. The nurse will show you."

With the shouting, kicking patient slung over one shoulder, Theo went off.

As other captives were brought in, the matron saw that they were disposed of while simultaneously speaking to her superintendent over the phone, ordering the gardener to fetch a ladder and a maid to wipe up the ink, all in a calm but carrying voice and without letting go of the wriggling, whimpering boy.

A crash indicated that the battering ram had done its job. Some minutes later Anna Anderson, hanging limp between a nurse and a man with a doctor's coat over his pajamas, was brought downstairs. Her nightdress was stained, her feet trailed, and her eyes darted this way and that like a trapped animal's, then fixed on Esther's. "He find me," she said. Her voice was raw with screaming and sounded inhuman.

"I have tranquilized her," the doctor said.

The matron nodded. "Good-bye, Frau Unbekkant," she said flatly.

"But, but . . ." All at once Esther felt the weight of this new responsibility. "What do I do for her?"

"She'll fall asleep soon and will be out for some hours."

"Hasn't she any luggage?"

"Such as there is will be sent after her."

"But if she, well . . . Should she need more treatment, can I bring her back?"

The matron looked around her devastated hall. "No," she said.

As Theo tucked Anna into the space behind the car's two seats, there was a shout. "Remember it was me!" Clara Peuthert was gesticulating from the roof. "Remember me, Your Highness, I found you!"

One of the nurses helping the gardener with the ladder gestured for Esther to go; by staying she was making things worse.

She drove off.

"That matron," Theo said with admiration, "they make her a general and Germany win the war."

"Maybe, but don't tell me a little thing like Anna could cause all that." Esther was angry. "Two years, Theo, two years and no good-bye, not even a toothbrush."

"She tiny, maybe, but she damn trouble."

She still was. After a mile she began emitting hoarse, shuddering yelps. "He come after me, he's coming, he'll get me!"

"Where?"

"*There*. In the car. *He's coming!*"

"See anything, Theo?" They'd just rounded a curve.

"No." He was half turned in his seat beside her, holding on to Anna, who was trying to jump out.

"There's nothing, Anna. No car. Don't be frightened. You're safe now."

"No, no, he's coming!"

She kept it up for another mile, until the screams became shuddering little shrieks, then moans, and finally silence.

Esther put her foot down, mentally wrestling with the difficulty of where to lodge Anna. Nick had been handling the matter of Anna's apartment, but he hadn't told Esther where it was, nor, she knew, had he yet agreed to the lease; he was quibbling over the rent.

Where to take her? A hotel? Esther didn't have enough money on her. She thought of her own tiny room at Rabbi Smoleskin's house in Moabit, then rejected it. For one thing, she wasn't going to subject the Smoleskin family to Anna's anti-Semitism.

"Theo, does anybody else at the Hat know what Nick's up to with Anna?"

There was the inevitable pause that Theo accorded to every question. "Nick say keep my mouth shut, just say he being kind to another poor Russian."

Kind, she reflected, but it was a relief. There would be no questions if she took just another poverty-stricken émigré back to the club for the rest of the night. That's what she'd do, then. Nick could deal with the problem in the morning.

The moon was high now. The dry spring had turned the surface of the roads to dust, so that the Audi's speed churned up a cloud of it, leaving it hanging in the moonlit air like a trail of smoke.

At the Green Hat, she parked behind a line of limousines collecting the last of the guests, some of whom were unsteady and having to be helped into their cars by their chauffeurs.

Theo lifted Anna out of the backseat. They supported her into the foyer. Beyond, in the vast club room, the band was packing away its instruments and waiters were clearing the tables.

From the cloakroom came the voice of Olga Ratzel pestering weary hatcheck and cigarette girls out of their uniforms and into their civvies—the elaborate Russian costumes and kokoshniks had cost Nick good money; none of the girls were allowed to take them home.

Theo gathered Anna into his arms and followed Esther up the sweeping staircase with its heavily curlicued banister, relic of one of the kaiser's palaces and another item Nick had bought to impress the customers. The newel posts were turbaned Negro boys carrying torches.

Boris was in Nick's office, counting the night's takings. "What the hell you got there, Esther?"

"A package for Nick. Is he back yet?"

He wasn't.

Theo lowered the inert form of Anna onto the chesterfield; her eyes were slightly open; every now and then, she shuddered.

"We're going to have to spend the rest of the night here, Boris. I don't know what else to do with her."

"Okay." Boris was too tired to be curious—anyway, life with Prince Nick had taught him not to be. "You want I should leave Theo with you?"

"Oh, God, yes please." She'd need him if Anna became hysterical again.

She went downstairs and crossed the floor of the now empty club to the kitchens to gather provisions—water, milk, a bottle of brandy for medicinal purposes, some sandwiches, beer for Theo.

Boris had put the lights out before she got back so that the only illumination came from the chandeliers in the foyer, and she nearly tripped over a couple of broken gilt chairs lying witness to the von Schwerin brothers' good time.

Like all places built for a crowd, the club became eerie when it was empty. In the gloom Kandinsky's walls gained the depth of a tangled forest from which Nick's bears emerged, as if curious, to watch her pass by.

"Esther."

She jumped. "Don't do that."

Olga Ratzel, a thin, starched figure, was standing in the shadow of the doorway. They were old enemies.

Briskly, Olga asked, "Who is that woman upstairs, please?"

"She's a friend of Nick's, Olga. She's homeless at the moment. We're going to spend the night here."

"Spend the night? Does Nick know about this?"

"Not yet he doesn't. Excuse me."

Olga held her ground. "I need to know the circumstances, Esther. I am responsible for this club in Nick's absence. Should the Vice Squad do one of its inspections and find some street woman—"

"Just get out of my way, Olga." Esther sidestepped, concentrating on the tray she carried, and crossed the foyer. The last of the staff to go had left the glass front doors open so that warm night air came in to dissipate the accumulated smell of expensive cigars and perfume and alcohol.

Olga followed her upstairs, still lecturing. "Young woman, *I* arrange accommodation for the girls. If this female is homeless, I will find her a place right away, not here. . . . Camping out in Nick's office, it is not suitable. . . . Where we keep the receipts. . . . A stranger . . ."

Esther ignored her. Olga's responsibility for everything was self-imposed. The Russian-born widow of a Berliner, she'd inveigled herself into the Green Hat very early on under Nick's regime as a seamstress, laundress, and mender of uniforms. She'd made herself useful acting as dresser for such artistes as appeared on its stage, and gradually, without anyone's knowing how, she'd extended her empire to take in the cloakroom, waiters, cigarette girls, and cleaners. Nick, recognizing an efficiency, more Germanic than Russian, that kept everyday problems off his shoulders, had allowed her a certain autonomy in hiring and firing of nonmanagerial staff—a latitude that enabled her to rule by terror.

When Esther had arrived at the Green Hat, she'd put Olga's hostility down to anti-Semitism, only realizing later that the woman resented as a rival any female whose position took her closer to the management of the club than her own—which Esther's did.

Olga went with her into the office, tightening her lips at the sight of Anna slumped and unconscious on the sofa. "Is she drunk?"

"No."

"Well, who is she? What's she doing here?" She strode around Nick's desk and seated herself in his chair. "I shall stay. Somebody has to keep an eye on things."

"For God's sake, Olga . . ." Usually Esther was prepared to put up with a one-sided war in which she was the noncombatant—every organization had its Olga and even needed one—but she was tired, and the thought of spending the rest of the night catering to the woman's self-importance by feeding her curiosity was intolerable. "This is a nightclub, not a bloody convent. Go home."

Boris came in, and Olga appealed to him. "Somebody responsible must stay, Boris. Esther brings a strange woman into the office—how do we know what she may do?"

Boris's eyes met Esther's over Olga's head. "Nick's business, not ours," he said. He went to the safe and began cramming in the night's receipts—inflation was resulting in so much paper currency that they'd soon need an extra safe to contain it. He straightened up. "Get along home now, Olga." He put his hand under the woman's armpits, raised her gently, and steered her to the door.

"But, Boris, do you know about this?"

"We don't need to. Esther's in charge. Off you go."

Olga went, furious.

Boris said, "Thinks she owns the place. Doesn't own much else, I guess."

"I know. Thank you, Boris."

"You all right now? I'll lock up, then. Good night." He went downstairs.

Theo was making a pillow of his jacket on the baccarat table in the gaming room.

"I'm sorry about this, Theo."

"I slept on worse."

They all had. There probably wasn't one among the émigrés who hadn't bedded down on pine needles or the floor of a truck, a train compartment, or a barn during the flight from Russia—and they thought themselves lucky it wasn't a Bolshevik execution cell.

She left the gaming room doors open so that she could call him if necessary and went through her office into Nick's. Anna's eyes were still eerily half open, but her breathing was quieter. Esther took off her coat, tucked it around the girl, and switched off the light, relying on the dim glow from the window overlooking the club floor.

For a while she played Goldilocks, trying to emulate Theo and stretching out on Nick's desk—but that was too uncomfortable. So was sitting in his chair and putting her legs up on the desk. Eventually she dragged the chair to the window and rested her ankles on its low sill.

Better, though not much.

She was tired. Below, light from the entrance hall spilled over the dance floor, leaving the rest of the great room in shadow. Don't think about Russia. . . . But Kandinsky and Nick had done their work well, and the club became a silent, darkened forest through which the great, brown bear lumbered in its search for berries. Her father had made her a present of a cub—*"Ursus arctos,"* he'd said. "A little *Ursus arctos* for my little girl"—and taken it away when it got too big. Don't think, don't remember. . . . She could almost smell the scent of pine trees trapped in snow. . . . Clara Peuthert capered naked in the grove playing panpipes to a bear. . . .

Which had moved.

Her eyelids went up. One of Nick's bears, second from the left across the dance floor, was swelling to twice its size.

It became two. One of it stepped down from its plinth and began padding across the floor toward the foyer. It had something in one of its paws; everything else about the thing absorbed light, but this flashed back a gleam from the foyer chandeliers—a blade.

Slowly, very slowly, keeping the rest of her body still, Esther's hand searched for the telephone on Nick's desk, felt it, lifted the receiver, and found it dead. The receptionist had shut down all the lines except for the one to the switchboard behind the desk in the entrance hall.

Where the thing below was heading. It would gain the stairs, climb them. It would come in here, where the safe was, sniffing for money.

She was so frightened she almost had to lift her legs off the sill by hand; they'd frozen.

Moving fast, she crossed to the gaming room door and hissed: *"Theo."* She switched on the light. All the tables were empty. Oh, Christ, oh, God. He wasn't there.

She whipped back across the corridor into the office and shook Anna's shoulder. "Get up, get up, there's somebody coming." Her breath was a wisp of sound. Anna didn't move.

Lock the doors. She could lock herself and Anna in. But it was big, a big bear, and the doors were flimsy—it would break them down. She couldn't cower in here waiting for it to burst in on them, its arms wide, blade ready to strike.

Esther locked the door to Nick's office and went out of her own, locking that door behind her.

Movement was good, better. She stood at the top of the stairs and shouted: *"Theo!"* Then, desperately, added, "Boris, Vassily, Pietr, come here, boys. There's an intruder downstairs." Maybe that would frighten him off.

She heard her voice evaporate into silence.

Oh, shit, oh, God, there was just her and it.

It was at the bottom of the staircase. It was coming up. Again a sliver of metal caught the light.

In brain-melting, bladder-weakening terror, she could have begged it, *Don't worry about me, I'll hide. Break into the office, take what you want.*

But Anna was in the office.

As it was, she retreated back and back, out of sight, along the curving corridor, past the office, past the empty gaming room, to the door at the end, a broom closet, somewhere to crawl into, some small space where she couldn't see, couldn't hear, anywhere that would block out the ascending shadow and the soft touch of shoes on the stair carpet.

Back, back until her spine encountered the door of the closet. Still facing outward, she felt behind her and turned the handle. She moved out a little so that its door could open enough to let her in.

Galvanized iron buckets came clattering out, brooms, mops, jangling. The noise clanged through the silent building like lepers' bells announcing, *I am here.*

It released her. Suddenly she was furious. How dare he? She, Esther, had faced greater terror than this one burglar, whatever he was—terror administered by experts. And survived it.

She looked down at the tangle of buckets and implements at her feet, kicked one of the buckets out of the way, picked up a broom, held it like a spear and ran with it, shrieking, toward the stairs.

The man was lower down the staircase than she'd estimated—later she thought the clatter had made him pause—so that the broom caught him in the head rather than the body.

She saw the knife flash upward as the brush went into his face. He was knocked back, but the other hand clutched onto the rail so that he hung in a cruciform across the banister, the knife-hand arm crooked across one eye where the bristles had gone in.

She began going down the stairs, jabbing to keep him off as if at a giant spider. He was quick and hideously strong; he snatched at the broom and jerked her high off her feet in a parabola that sent her almost to the bottom of the staircase. As she landed, her left shoe was caught in an iron curlicue that sliced the skin off her ankle and left her sprawled with her feet four steps up and the back of her head on the hall floor. Breath went out of her in a *whoomph*. The pain was electric.

He was coming down the stairs, slowly, light flickering on the knife as his fist wiped his eyes.

She tried to hump her body backward, struggling to get away from him, but her foot was stuck in the ironwork of the banister and she couldn't dislodge it.

From somewhere to her right came the glorious sound of a lavatory flushing.

"Theo."

"Esther?" The bouncer came running to stand over her, unaware of the man staring down at him.

"Look *out.*"

Bodies clashed together. She was being trampled by feet, and then she wasn't. Twisting her head, she glimpsed a shadow flip away toward the doors with Theo limping after it, holding his arm.

There was a crash of breaking glass.

She lost interest.

3

As THE POLICE car entered Potsdamer Platz, its driver saw a figure dash across the road from one of the nightclubs into an alley, followed by another—this one staggering.

He nudged his passenger. "Trouble at the Green Hat, boss. Fella chasing another fella."

Inspector Schmidt opened his eyes. "Fuck it," he said.

"Fella doing the chasing, he's bleeding, boss."

"Fuck it."

"Fuck it we don't take no notice?" Sergeant Ritte asked hopefully. "Or fuck it we got to stop and deal with it?"

"Fuck it, fuck it." Schmidt was tired, they were both tired. A riot on the Western Docks between strikers and the Brownshirts brought in to deal with them had resulted in two deaths. He and Willi had been up all night trying to take statements from wounded and hostile men of both Left and Right.

He wanted to get home to his wife, Willi wanted to get home to his, and both happy returns must be delayed until they'd made their report at headquarters.

Bloody Saturday nights. You'd think there was enough blood

on the bloody streets without some drunk who hadn't paid his bill cutting his way out of a bloody nightclub. And now it was Sunday bloody morning.

But he and Willi were the bloody police, fuck it. This was their job.

By the time Willi had parked and switched off the engine, the absconder was out of sight with no chance of their catching him—the alley he'd disappeared into was too narrow for a car. The man who'd chased him was leaning against the wall, bleeding heavily, and the small crowd that popped up like bloody fungi on every crime scene was clustering on the pavement. Where did they come from? Café girls, mostly, from the look of them, on their way home, all except for a fancy-looking lounge lizard in white tie and tails who was rapping out questions to the injured man in a foreign language.

"Call an ambulance, Willi."

The frontage of the Green Hat glowed like a diamond from the setting of its glass doors, one of which had a man-size hole in it.

Willi stepped smartly through the hole, looking around for a telephone—an action that brought White Tie running. "What's that man doing in my club?"

"We're the police, sir. I'm Inspector Schmidt. My sergeant is phoning for help for that gentleman."

"Can't you use a street phone? He's my bouncer. I look after him. No need for police."

"It appears there is, sir." Schmidt walked to where the bouncer was sliding down the wall onto the pavement. He was in shirtsleeves, and blood was seeping heavily out of a stab wound in his left arm.

Schmidt knelt down, feeling in his top pocket for the crisp white handkerchief that Hannelore put into it every morning and applied it to the wound. "You'll be all right, my son. It didn't touch the artery. We're going to get you to the hospital. What happened?"

Flat brown eyes stared expressionlessly back at him.

"Theo don't . . . doesn't speak German," White Tie said, still displaying less anxiety about his employee than about the fact that a policeman was wandering loose inside his club.

Schmidt looked up at the women around and chose a couple. "Madam, if you'd hold this man's arm up in the air, that's right. And you, madam, press your hand here, against my handkerchief, and keep pressing. Bit harder. Keep pressing. The ambulance will be here soon. Excellent. Thank you."

He stood up. "And you, sir, are?"

"Prince Nikolai Potrovskov, owner of the Green Hat."

Russian lounge lizard. Schmidt said, "What happened?"

"I don't know. I just arrive. I have been out all night. Maybe the club is closing when this clumsy fellow step through the glass door. Accident."

"I don't think so, sir. He's been stabbed, and my sergeant saw a man running off. We'd better investigate. If you would lead the way . . ." He gestured courteously toward the club. When the man still hesitated, he stopped being polite. "Get in there." For all this bastard knew, his club was littered with dead.

A key was produced, and they crunched through broken glass.

Like bloody Versailles, Schmidt thought. Nightclubs weren't his line; the Vice boys usually dealt with them. With its chandeliers and mirrors and indefinable, expensive perfume, this one was a playground for the very rich—a fact that didn't endear it to him.

Willi was coming out of a cubbyhole behind the reception desk. "On its way," he said.

Schmidt walked through into the club proper. Potrovskov switched on lights and followed him. "What I tell you? Nothing here, no trouble." Watching Schmidt eyeing some splintered wood in the middle of the floor, he said, "So they break a chair or two. The von Schwerin boys, maybe, having fun. You know Count von Schwerin? Nice man, important. Lot of important people come here, all my friends. Minister of interior, good pal of mine . . . chief of police . . ."

Names buzzed past Schmidt's ears like warning shots as he peered into the kitchen and came out again. He ignored them. Something had happened in this club, and he was going to find out what it was even if Archangel bloody Gabriel was a regular.

He toured the dance floor. He didn't think much of the wall paintings—he wasn't one for modern art—but he liked the bears.

From the entrance hall, Willi shouted, "Over here, Inspector!"

He was pointing toward the stairs, where one of the newel posts had hidden the woman standing silently against it.

Schmidt's first sight of Esther Solomonova was almost immediately blocked by Potrovskov, who rushed over to her.

There was an exchange of Russian.

"What the hell happened? Can you hear me, Esther? What happened?"

"A man. He had a knife. He would have killed me—oh, Jesus, he was going to kill me. Theo . . . is Theo all right?"

"Where's Anna now? Quick, these bastards are police."

"In your office. Asleep. I locked her in."

"She's not here. You hear me, Esther? You never heard of her."

"I'd prefer it if you both spoke German, sir," Schmidt said. "*Does* she speak German?"

"My secretary, Esther Solomonova. It was a break-in. The man got away with completely nothing."

"Perhaps she could tell me herself, sir."

Reluctantly, Potrovskov allowed himself to be led away by Willi. The woman's eyes followed him.

God, she's lovely, Schmidt thought.

Then she turned toward him, and he saw the other side of her face. The worst thing about it was that she didn't mind if he flinched—which he didn't; he'd seen worse in the war.

The scar ran from the outside of her left eyebrow across the cheek almost to the corner of her mouth. No neat Heidelburg dueling scar this; somebody'd taken an ax or a bayonet to her, and somebody else had cobbled the wound together and done it badly. In between the gathers made by rough sutures, the flesh had been allowed to gape. Stretched pale patches showed where the skin had struggled to grow back.

She demonstrated none of the wary expectancy that most disfigured people did when meeting someone for the first time. But she was in shock; he recognized it. Time would be moving erratically for her, some things happening fast, others extending beyond normal. She'd be very cold without realizing it. Probably incoherent.

"Frau Solomonova?"

"Fräulein," she said—and he revised his opinion about her coherence.

He took off his jacket and put it around her shoulders. "Let's sit down before you fall down, shall we?"

She nodded, and he held his hand under her elbow to ease her onto a step. She winced.

He sat down beside her. "Are you hurt?"

"A bit. Not badly."

"What happened?"

"Theo," she said. "Is Theo all right?"

So somebody cares, Schmidt thought. "He'll need stitches, but he'll recover. Tell me what happened."

"There was a man. He must have got in when the club was closing and hidden behind one of the bears. When everybody'd gone, he came out. . . ."

Her account was lucid and cool—though her hands began shaking when she described seeing the bear spawn.

She'd called for the bouncer, she said, who turned out to have been in the lavatory. She'd shouted for nonexistent help, hoping to scare the man off by making him think the club was populated. After panicking she'd fetched a broom and gone for the man as he climbed the stairs. These stairs. He'd had a knife. The two of them had tussled, the man had thrown her down the staircase, the bouncer had come out of the lavatory. Another tussle, another glimpse of the knife, the man went off, followed by the bouncer, the crash of breaking glass . . . "And then I think I lost consciousness for a bit."

No self-pity, he thought. She'd been through the wars before, had Fräulein Solomonova.

"Can you describe the man?"

"Big," she said. "Tall. Not fat but . . . huge somehow. Fairish, I think. The light was bad."

"Did he say anything?"

"No." Her hands began to shake so badly she stuffed them between her knees. "He was silent."

"Would you recognize him again?"

She thought about it. "I don't know." She turned to look at him. "How did he get out? The doors were locked."

"Crashed through them. If it's any consolation, he's probably bleeding more than Theo."

"Good," she said, and tried to smile.

Schmidt got up and walked over to Potrovskov and Willi. "Sergeant, get back to headquarters—I'll walk. Alert hospitals and doctors for a big man coming in with cuts."

Potrovskov said, "Can I use my own phone now? We got to get that glass mended quick."

"What you can do is get that lady a glass of brandy, or hot milk, or some bloody thing."

"Sure, sure." He seemed surprised. "I take her to my own doctor when you finish with her."

"See you do."

Schmidt went back to the woman on the stairs, going through lists in his head. Big man, he thought. With a knife. Mopey Raab? No, Mopey always stuck to a cosh. Fritz Schaffer was a knife man, but he'd never come this far west. Schmidt reminded himself that growing poverty was leading to growing crime. Desperate amateurs were getting in on the act.

But there's something extra here, he thought. When they were talking in Russian, that bloody lounge lizard had been giving her instructions.

He sat himself down by Solomonova. "What do you think the man was after, Fräulein?"

She said, "Prince Potrovskov keeps the night's receipts in his safe." After a second she added, "They are considerable."

Schmidt was sure they were. "And you were alone in the club—apart from the bouncer?"

Pause. "Yes."

He looked at his watch. "That would be about four o'clock in the morning. Bit late to be working, isn't it?"

"I often work late," she said.

They heard the klaxon of an ambulance in the distance.

"You ought to be in the hospital yourself," he said, grumbling. There was blood on one of her shoes.

And suddenly she was looking full at him, smiling, astonishing him. "I've had worse," she said.

Walking back through the dawn to the Alexanderplatz, Schmidt knew he should have done more. Something had been going on in the Green Hat that wasn't a straightforward, thwarted attack in the course of burglary. The woman had wit enough to call out and pretend there were other men in the building to come to her aid, but that hadn't deterred the fucker on the staircase. He'd kept coming. Why?

I should have searched the whole bloody building.

But he couldn't have justified it to the big guns that slimy Russian would have brought in. *Lot of important people . . . all my friends.*

Christ, he loathed them: important men charged with running a country, *his* country, spending its taxes, *his* taxes, on chandeliered fucking opulence and, quite probably, sin. And their people scrabbling in poverty.

The chandeliers irked him. Yesterday Hannelore had anxiously mentioned the rising price of lightbulbs.

An even bigger mystery was what the scarred woman, the only honest thing in the place, was doing there. There'd been a quality to her that didn't belong in those ersatz surroundings.

And even she hadn't told him the truth. Not all of it. Whatever grubby secret her boss had been hiding, she'd kept it.

Fuck it, no point in puzzling about it. Or her. He had enough on his plate with another bloody report to type out when he got in.

4

Esther Solomonova and Anna Anderson left the Green Hat for their new home later that day.

The move involved climbing up a ladder to the club's skylight and a clamber over the rooftops of Potsdamer Platz, then down into an alley next to a cinema around the corner, in front of which a taxi was waiting for them.

Prince Nick had insisted on it, enjoying the drama. "I'm not having the Cheka follow her again."

"He wasn't the bloody Cheka."

But Nick had decided that he was; it was more exciting, more glamorous, and it gave a boost to his decision that Anna was Anastasia.

Esther sighed. Last night Nick had accepted that the intruder was a robber after the contents of the club's safe; by this morning the man had become a Bolshevik state assassin. Nick changed his theories as often as he changed the flower in his buttonhole—and this one suited him.

For herself the incident was beyond explanation. The man must have been in search of money, but there had been something . . .

something *personal* about the battle on the staircase, a meeting between hunter and hunted, as if the two of them had been removed from the time and space of Potsdamer Platz and faced each other far away in a lonely forest. And he'd hated her.

She didn't want to think about it—nor was she given much time to. Before she could accompany Anna over the rooftops, there were things to be done; she had to phone the hospital and make sure Theo was comfortable and see about hiring another bouncer to fill in for him when the club opened again on Monday. A messenger was sent to the Smoleskins in Moabit with an apologetic letter saying that she was leaving them and to collect her things. Olga, who'd turned up early to find out what was going on, was directed out into Sunday Berlin to try to obtain clothes for Anna from somewhere. Nick's luncheon appointment with last night's inamorata had to be postponed to dinner while he made sure the new flat was ready for Esther and Anna. He also rang every influential name he could think of to ensure that he was subject to no more investigation.

At last he was satisfied. He lit a cigar. "Could have been worse, kid. We've kept the police out of it. Our grand duchess is still our secret."

"Well, isn't that good."

None of this was passed on to Anna. She was not told that while she slept in Nick's office, battle and near murder had taken place a few yards away. She appeared to be drugged still and was quiescent at leaving the club by a ladder, as if it were a normal manner of egress.

Nick loved it, making both women bend low as they emerged in case a Cheka bullet hit them as they appeared on the skyline. But when he'd got them and their suitcases to the taxi, he hesitated. "You want I should come with you?"

"No. Get back to your film star." At that moment Esther wanted to be away from him, from everything to do with the Green Hat. The deep cut on her ankle had been treated, her bruises dabbed with arnica, but the sight of the staircase and her recollection of grappling on it with something she still thought of as inhuman was going to take a hell of a lot longer to fade.

They drove off.

. . .

Number 29c Bismarck Allee was a three-bedroom top-floor apartment in a block of houses served by a road lined with lime trees leading out of Bismarckstrasse, a good area of western Berlin, almost a suburb. There were a few dignified shops on the east side of the road—number 29 faced a bookseller's—but the west side was solidly residential, solidly lace-curtained, solidly respectable.

Frau Schinkel, the widowed landlady who lived on the ground floor of number 29 and acted as porteress, winced at Esther's face and last name. "Prince Potrovskov did not say you were Jewish." She was the sort of woman who believed in speaking her mind.

"Makes a difference to the rent, does it?" With her nerves still raw and her ankle painful, Esther believed in speaking hers.

"No, no." Frau Schinkel subsided; the prince was paying good money. "But I do not usually rent to foreigners. I expect good behavior in this house."

"So do I," Esther told her.

As they were shown upstairs, Esther noticed that the flat beneath theirs was empty. Times being what they were, Frau Schinkel had to take what tenants she could get.

It was a nice apartment, though Frau Schinkel's furniture, like Frau Schinkel, was on the heavy side. Nick, it appeared, had already required the landlady to make it ready for instant habitation; the bathroom was equipped, and so were the kitchen and larder—a bright new samovar stood on a surface near the sink. The sitting room was three times the size of Esther's bed-sit in Moabit, and as a joke—she hoped it was a joke—Nick had sent his hunting prints to decorate one of its walls.

The beds were made up in the three bedrooms. Her own—there was a card to say which was hers and which Anna's—had a plain cotton spread, whereas Anna had been accorded satin. The third bed, she was interested to see, was also made up, but it, too, was plain. It had no card.

At the far end of the sitting room, near the window overlooking a backyard, Nick had set up a small office area with a desk, a telephone, and a Dictaphone; Esther was to be no less his secretary because she was grooming his protégée with her other hand. She picked up the Dictaphone headset, pressed the button, and listened to his high, thin voice rapping out instructions. "Tonight, Esther, if you please. Needed first thing tomorrow."

It always was.

From this window she could see the gardens of the houses behind. Along the row a maid was hanging out washing and talking to two children on a seesaw. From farther on came the whir of blades where a man was mowing his lawn. It was all very comforting.

She unpacked for herself and Anna. The girl, still unnaturally tranquil from whatever drug it was she'd been given at Dalldorf, went straight to bed.

"You'll be safe here," Esther told her, tucking her in.

"Where the pretty lights? And the bears?"

"They were at Nick's club. We had to spend the night there."

"I like them." Anna closed her eyes.

Esther went back into the living room to go to the kitchen, welcoming its silence.

The kitchen was clean and sparse—in the days when Frau Schinkel and her family had been able to live in the whole house, it had been a bedroom. Now decorated with stiff oilcloth curtains, its window gave onto a view of the street below.

Esther opened the window, letting in a smell of sunny dust scented by the avenue's flowering lime trees. Below, a woman waited for her dog to finish sniffing a tree trunk while she chatted across the road to the bookseller washing down his shop door. A family of father, mother, and two children, prayer books in hand, was on its way to church.

So bourgeois, she thought, so safe. In Moabit you were never safe; people lived too close to the border between survival and starvation. Since the advent of the Brownshirts, there was no protection either from a jackbooted invasion that left broken heads and windows in its wake.

But here . . . she thanked God for the German middle class. No bears here. They'd never get past Frau Schinkel.

And there'd been at least one good thing from last night: she carried a healing memory of the concerned eyes of the policeman who'd sat beside her on the stairs. A stranger, a man whose name she didn't know, but kind. She wished she hadn't had to lie to him.

As she turned to go back into the living room, her head exploded.

By now she'd disciplined herself not to crawl on the floor when the noise and pictures started up, but her hands gripped at her knees to try to stop her shaking. She couldn't hear anything through the crack of gunfire. Time unraveled the pogroms into bits of chaos; one jigsaw piece illuminated dear dead faces, another showed Jews running the gauntlet of rifle butts.

She watched a rabbi's hat fly from his head, saw him stoop under the blows to pick it up and then continue the run. *It is forbidden to bare the head before the Lord.*

She held on to that picture as she groped her way to a chair; it always steadied her.

When it was over, she was left panting and resentful. Goddamn it, she'd been getting better; it had been weeks since the last one. The attack on the stairs last night had resurrected an older terror.

For Esther, memory was the devil horned and stinking; she fought it with the desperation of an old-time saint saving his soul in case remembering destroyed her own. She'd seen what it could do to émigrés who'd suffered, keeping raped women in a depression they couldn't escape, inflicting apathy on the old whose losses had been too great to bear, collapsing the nerve of others so that even a loudly ticking clock was reminiscent of a rifle being cocked—oh, God, she knew that fear. She saw it in Anna; memories could attach themselves to you like tentacles sucking away present sunlight, leaving you blundering forever in the grayness of the past.

The bastard, she thought. I'm not letting him resurrect all that. I'm going to forget him. He's gone. We're safe now.

In the evening Nick came by to see how they were settling in, still playing cloak-and-dagger games. "I parked around the corner, made sure I wasn't followed. Where's Her Imperial Highness?"

"Anna's asleep. She's still groggy."

"She like the flat? Good, huh?"

"Very nice."

"Definitely is," he said. "Cheka assassins won't find her here."

One thing about Nick, Esther thought, the tentacles of memory couldn't suck anything out of his hide. Automatically, tonelessly she said, "It was a bloody burglar."

"Wake up, kid, it was Bolshies wanting to get her. Who's out to bump off all the leading White émigrés? Who gunned down Petrovich in Paris the other day?"

"You said it was because Petrovich had been supplying weapons to the White Army."

"Sure. He was."

"I don't see Anna as an arms dealer."

"But who'll the White Army put on the imperial throne when it wins Russia back?" He sat down on the sofa and clasped his hands behind his head, luxuriating in the pleasure of it. "I tell you, our Anna's probably on the Reds' hit list. Top of it, maybe." He closed his eyes in joy. "If the Cheka is out to get her, she *is* Anastasia, pure and simple. I'm legal. I'm *completely* helping the rightful heir to the throne."

"Yes," a calm voice said, "the Cheka hate me." Anna, in the doorway of her bedroom, extended her hand. "I am Anastasia."

Nick got up to go and kiss it. "Your Imperial Highness."

"Oh, give me strength," Esther said. This was mutual masturbation. Not merely self-delusion, it was allowing Anna to explain away the real fear that had kept her moribund in Dalldorf for two years.

Anna walked across to the window and, keeping carefully to the edge, peered down into the road.

"They won't find you here, Highness," Nick said. "Nobody won't look for you here. This is good cover, better than a castle with a moat—"

"Cheaper, too," Esther said.

"And when you make your debut, I get a troop of Chevalier Gardes that nobody can't get past." He rubbed his hands. "But we got lot of work to do till then. Help bring back details, make you word-perfect. And I got just the person for it, someone you'll remember, maybe—Natalya Tchichagova."

If he expected a reaction, he didn't get it. Anna stayed looking out the window.

He turned to Esther, relapsing into Russian. "One of my own damn employees," he said, "I tell you, Esther, this was meant. The saints know about this. I was looking among the émigrés, someone who knew the royal family, and there she was all the time, working as a dancer at the Purple Parrot."

"A stripper?" Esther said. All Nick's clubs were next door to one another, though only the Green Hat had a lavish frontage. Entrances to the other two were more discreet and catered to differing clientele—the Parrot's customers appreciated the female form, while the Pink Parasol's preferred their entertainers to be male.

"Exotic dancer," Nick said.

Natalya, it appeared, had been a maid at Czar Nicholas's and Czarina Alexandra's favorite palace of Czarskoe Selo before the revolution.

"A personal maid?" Esther asked.

"No, no. Brass-cleaning floor sweeper—but she was born there. *Born* there. She can tell Her Highness everything, but completely *everything*. And me thinking I'd have to buy one of the fucking relatives to help coach her. It was meant, Esther, *meant*."

"She can't know much," Esther said. "They wouldn't have been short of floor-sweeping brass cleaners at Czarskoe Selo."

"Thousands, they had thousands." He flapped a hand. "But she knows the geography, she heard the gossip. Servants know everything. Little Anastasia falls over, wets her knickers, puts her tongue out at the king of Bulgaria, that's big news in the servants' hall. Stop being a doubting damn Thomas; you get on with your job, and Natalya'll do hers."

From the window Anna spoke. "Want a dog," she said.

"Sure, sure, Highness. Many as you like." He turned to Esther. "You finished those letters yet?"

"I haven't even started them."

"Holy Martyr, woman, I need they should go tomorrow. I've set you up in luxury so's you can sit on your fanny all day? Get on with it."

He went off, Anna retired to her bedroom, and Esther sat down at her new desk to get on with it.

She put a carbon between two pieces of paper, inserted the sheets behind the typewriter roller, realized she'd lost track of days and didn't know what date it was, looked it up in her diary, typed it—

It stared back at her. July 30, 1922.

July 30. Yesterday had been July 29.

You come back here late Saturday night, July twenty-ninth—Clara Peuthert's voice was as clear as clear—*you'll see him standing in the shadows out there, waiting for his chance to kill the grand duchess.*

Oh, dear God, had he been? And followed her?

He was taking shape again, coming up the stairs, no burglar now, but a hunting creature intent on the prey he'd been stalking for months . . . thwarted, *but with every intention of hunting again in six weeks' time.*

No. *No,* he wasn't. "Damn you," Esther said out loud, "you're not going to do this to me." She wasn't going to be in thrall to some phantasm conjured up by a deluded woman in an asylum.

"You're just a bloody coincidence," she told it, and began typing.

"WHO'S MADAM MIDNIGHT?" Natalya wanted to know on her arrival.

"She's the landlady, Frau Schinkel. She does the door opening."

"She sure don't help ladies with their luggage." Natalya was puffing.

Esther took the case from her and carried it to the third bedroom. "I'm Esther Solomonova. I'm pleased to meet you."

Natalya Tchichagova was guarded. "Yeah, I heard about you." She was pretty. Her bleached-blond hair was severely cut and plastered so that two ends curved around to her cheeks, where they stuck to her skin as if glued. Blue eyes peeped out from between heavily weighted black lashes, and lipstick rose in little twin peaks above her upper lip.

She approved of her bedroom and the fact that she didn't have to share it. "Classy." She turned her nose toward the kitchen: "Is that kotlety pozharskie I smell? Ain't tasted that since Czarskoe Selo."

Esther had to admit she'd bought it ready-made from the Russian delicatessen near the Inselbrücke. "I'm no cook, I'm afraid."

"You can afford to buy it cooked, you don't have to be. I ain't eaten chicken in a year."

Esther, honest to a fault, explained that the money came from Nick. His insistence that Anna must be well fed meant that Esther herself was eating better than she had done for a long time, though the sight of the lines at the food shops and of starving beggars on the streets flavored every mouthful with guilt. Without telling Nick, she was giving some of his money to the Salvation Army canteen around the corner in Cauerstrasse.

"Kotlety pozharskie," Natalya said fondly. "Maybe this job won't be so bad."

"Did you think it would be?"

It appeared that Natalya hadn't wanted the job of coaching Anna Anderson. Her removal from the stage of the Purple Parrot had caused disappointment to an appreciative audience and inspired her resentment. She'd enjoyed stripping. "I'm an artiste," she said. "One of my regulars says I'm a natural entertainer. He's going to put me in his next film."

However, like Esther, she owed her livelihood to Prince Nick and had been persuaded to do the work of tutor by a doubling of her salary.

"Gloomy old area, this," she said, though. "What am I going to do for nightlife?"

"You aren't," Esther told her.

"Yep, that's what Nick said."

"What else did he say?"

"He said"—Natalya squeezed her eyes shut—"I was to help Her Imperial Highness remember everything as happened at Czarskoe Seloe, who did what and where everything was, and if I was a good girl and the grand duchess got what was coming to her, he'd buy me my own film studio, but if I ever said a word about it, he'd cut my tongue out."

She opened her eyes. "*Is* she Anastasia? Nick says she is, but Nick'd say the moon was green cheese. Way I heard it, nobody escaped Ekaterinburg."

"I heard that, too," said Esther. Natalya was going to have to make up her own mind.

"Wouldn't it be peachy if she was?" For a moment, Natalya's face softened. "Near broke my heart, Ekaterinburg. Where is she?"

"In her room." Actually Anna was sulking; more and more she was spending her time in isolation.

"Ain't she going to eat with us?"

"It's me," Esther said. "She's decided she doesn't like taking her meals in the kitchen, especially with a Jew."

"I heard you was a Jewess," Natalya said cautiously.

"I'm a Jew," Esther told her. "I don't eat pork, but I'm partial to the occasional boiled baby, and I don't like the word 'Jewess.'"

"Why not?"

"It has derogatory connotations."

"What's that mean?"

"It means people spit when they say it."

Natalya nodded. "My pa and ma did."

"That was Russia. This is Germany." They might as well get the rules straight.

Natalya cut into her chicken. "Say this for you," she said. "You provide a nice boiled baby."

They toasted each other from a bottle of vodka—another of Nick's provisions. *"Za nas."*

"Za nas."

"To my career in Hollywood."

"To your career in Hollywood."

Anna was standing in the kitchen doorway watching them.

Esther said in German, "Nasha, this is Anna Anderson. Anna, this is Natalya Tchichagova. She used to work at Czarskoe Selo."

Natalya got up and bobbed a curtsy. "Your Imperial Highness. How are you?"

"She doesn't answer to Russian," Esther said.

Natalya repeated what she'd said in her accented German.

Anna looked her over. "I do not remember you."

"Well, you wouldn't, would you? But my pa was footman, Vassiliev, fourth in command to Trupp—you remember him. And Ma was maid to the czarina's personal maid."

Anna nodded. "Demidova."

"That's right, to Demidova. Ma's name was Lili."

Anna nodded again. "I eat now," she said. She got a tray, charged it with the plate of food that Esther had kept warm for her, procured a knife and fork, and disappeared with them back to her bedroom.

I'll let you get away with it tonight, Esther thought, but it's bad for you. After this you eat with us. There were times when she found Anna's self-imposed isolation heartbreaking, others when she wanted to shake her. Pandering to the grand-duchess fallacy was not helping the girl, was in many ways a criminal act. On the other hand, two years in Dalldorf hadn't cured her either, and to send her back to an asylum would be worse. Obviously she couldn't cope in the outside world alone; she was dependent on Nick for her survival—all three of them were. For each of them, this charade was now the only game in town.

"Why don't she use Russian?" Natalya asked.

"Nick says it's because she doesn't want to be reminded of the bad time," Esther said levelly. "Well? What do you think?"

"Could be," Natalya said slowly. "Looks like her, apart from she's missing her teeth. Same coloring, same blue eyes." She made up her mind. "Could be, but I got my doubts."

"Why?"

"The grand duchesses were polite." She lit a cigarette and put it in a holder. "I'm not staying in Berlin much longer neither," she said. "Think I'll do well in the films?"

"Very well, I should think," Esther said, and meant it.

"Yes, well, I got the looks," Natalya said. She regarded Esther. "And you should do something about that scar, if you'll pardon my saying so. They do miracles with plastic surgery nowadays. You got nice eyes and figure—you don't have to go around looking like the Phantom of the Opera."

Esther laughed.

Natalya blinked. "Well, you don't."

"I can't afford it. It doesn't matter anyway."

"Now, that's where you're wrong. People take you for what you look like; you mustn't let yourself go."

The evening ended with Natalya manicuring Esther's nails. Buffing away, she said, "I heard there was a to-do at the Hat Saturday night."

"Yes." Esther told her about it. She said, hoping it would amuse, "Nick thinks it was a Cheka assassin out to bump Anna off." She'd forgotten that the Cheka was every White Russian's nightmare.

"Cheka?" Natalya said immediately. "Does he know she's living here?"

"I hope not. We've been careful."

Natalya thought about it. "If the Bolshies are after her, she *must* be Anastasia, mustn't she?"

"If it *was* the Bolshies. I believe it was someone after Nick's cash."

Natalya said, "You don't think she is Anastasia, do you?"

"No." She wasn't going to begin this friendship with a lie.

"It's a con, ain't it?"

"In my opinion, yes."

"Might work, though, mightn't it?"

Esther was surprised by how unshocked Natalya was, thus realizing how shocked she had expected her to be and, therefore, how shocked she found herself at her own part in the exercise. Where had legality gone for her and Natalya and Nick? Swept away, perhaps, in the flood that had carried off everything the three of them had known, leaving them so stripped that trickery was the only tool left to them.

"Could be," Natalya said when Esther didn't answer. "It could work. Nick knows a thing or two." She considered. "She'd be famous. Heir to All the Russias." The phrase commanded the room for a moment, as it had commanded an empire.

"Well, actually . . ." Esther began.

Natalya wasn't listening. "I'd do it better," she said.

5

Anna and Natalya didn't get along from the first. Anna affected to look down on Natalya as a servant—an attitude that Natalya, sometimes prepared to believe that Anna was the grand duchess and sometimes assured that she wasn't, resented in both moods. "I ain't going through that again," she said. "I don't care if she's the Holy Ghost with knobs on. I had enough bowing and scraping as a girl."

The revolution had done Natalya one good turn in uprooting her from the sweeping and polishing and subservience at which she'd fretted. By leaving Russia she'd found space and opportunity that its claustrophobic class system would never have allowed her. She was ambitious; stripteasing, while enjoyable, was merely a rung on the ladder to an ill-defined future that contained fame in one form or another.

"Ma and Pa'd be horrified," she said. "What they wanted was for me to work my way up the household like they did. Serving the Romanovs was enough for them. Wasn't enough for me."

She hadn't been close to her parents, she said. "They always put the family first." But she worried about them. After the czar's abdication, the battalions of men and women who served his many palaces had been ejected into a world suddenly hostile to anyone who'd worn the imperial livery, seventeen-year-old Natalya among them. "It was like the world flipped over," she said. "Like everybody'd hated us and never shown it till then."

At that point the Romanovs were being treated not unkindly by the new Duma that had taken over government of the country led by Alexander Kerensky. They were confined in Czarskoe Selo, a reduced suite of servants with them. Natalya's father and mother had volunteered for it.

"I wanted them to leave, but they wouldn't. 'We're not deserters,' they said, as if I was. But I wasn't given no choice—us small fry were told to go. It all happened so sudden in the end, I didn't even get a chance to say good-bye." She hadn't seen her parents again.

She'd been lucky in having an aunt in Czarskoe Selo village with whom she could take refuge, and had hidden in her roof space when a detachment of revolutionary soldiers had arrived from Petrograd, where Kerensky was struggling to prevent a Bolshevik takeover of the country.

"They wanted to kidnap the Romanovs for their Soviet and take them to prison," she said.

Thwarted by Kerensky's guard on the palace, the soldiers had ravaged the surrounding area. "They found liquor and went wild. I'd have been raped for sure—some of our women were. They broke into the chapel where Rasputin was buried. They dug him up and set the corpse on fire."

She'd attached herself to the family of one of the palace cooks who had relatives in Poland, and together they'd made for the border through a Russia disintegrating into civil war. "Wasn't much better in Poland neither," she said, "so I thought, blow this, and headed for Berlin."

She made the terrible journey sound easy, a glossing-over Esther had noticed in other émigrés. As in crowd-trampling panics, situations had arisen, things had been done, viciousness shown, principles and virtue abandoned in the struggle to breathe free air—memories, like Esther's, not to be remembered.

Nick came around the next evening. "Making progress?"

"No," Esther told him. Anna was still refusing to leave her room. "She won't have anything to do with either of us. She thinks there's somebody watching the place, which there isn't, because I have to keep going out to look before she'll settle down."

"And you can ask her till you're blue in the face what she's afraid of. She won't tell you," Natalya said.

"Oh, and she wants a dog, which she can't have because you seem to have overlooked the fact that Frau Schinkel doesn't allow pets."

He stamped into Anna's room, slamming the door behind him. The words "Your Highness," "Dalldorf," and "bloody back to" were audible several times before he lowered his voice.

He came out saying, "And if you're a good girl, I'll buy you a whole damn kennel." To Esther and Natalya, he said, "She'll cooperate now. I told her it's either this or back to the loony bin."

"Let's hope she can tell the difference," Esther said.

"If she doesn't want to be the grand duchess, we can't make her," Natalya said. "Why don't you use somebody else? I could do it. I've always fancied wearing a diamond kokoshnik."

"What are you talking about, idiot?" His hands beat the air; he was at his most Russian when angry. "*Want* to be Grand Duchess Anastasia? She *is* Grand Duchess Anastasia, and no lèse-majesté from you two." He peered at Natalya. "You believe she is, don't you?"

"She looks a bit like her, from what I remember," Natalya said reluctantly. "That's if Anastasia had been a crackpot that was rude to her servants, which she wasn't, and bit her nails, which she didn't."

"She's changed," Nick said. "She's been through a lot. Just you think what she's suffered. But now her loyal subject Prince Nikolai Potrovskov is going to put her back on the throne."

"There isn't a throne anymore," Natalya pointed out.

"And women can't inherit it," Esther said.

"Can't they? What about Catherine the Great?" His knowledge of his country's history had been more concerned with its battles than its politics.

"They changed the system after her."

"Did they?" He barely listened; he was already invading Russia. "I wonder if I ought to marry her."

"Definitely," Esther said.

"I would," said Natalya.

He frowned at them. "I'm serious. I'm not paying out all this money so some other bastard can get her fortune. Well, we'll have to see how we go." He went to Anna's door and poked his head in. "As for you, Highness, one more tantrum and it's back to Dalldorf. Understood?"

There was a weak assent, and he turned again to Natalya and Esther. "In the meantime you two minxes can start earning your keep."

While unprepared to foster Anna as a grand duchess, Esther saw no reason the girl shouldn't at least be taught social graces. With this object she piled books on Anna's head to make her walk without slouching, made her sit upright with her knees together, and stopped her biting her nails by painting them with bitter alum.

If she'd ever had them, Anna had forgotten her table manners. "Will you *please* hold your fork like this, Anna?" Esther would say. And, "One dips one's spoon into the soup, then away from the front of the bowl, like this." And, "It's not done to chew with your mouth open." And, "You shouldn't yawn when someone's talking."

"Why not? I'm tired."

"Ladies are never tired in company."

"I am."

Esther found the stubbornness intriguing. If the woman really believed herself to be Anastasia, why did she not behave as Anastasia had been known to behave? If she knew herself to be a fraud, the same question applied. There was something almost admirable in her attitude of I-know-best, the only truly royal thing about her.

"Listen," Natalya told her, "it ain't enough to look like Anastasia, you got to act like her. People who knew her well are going to judge you."

"Aunt Olga?" asked Anna immediately. "Aunt Xenia? They will come?"

Natalya was taken aback. So was Esther. This was aiming high, but undoubtedly it would be the testimony of the grand-duchess aunts that mattered most.

"Maybe," Natalya said. "You got a lot of work to do till then." Moments like this shook her skepticism, if not Esther's. "She must be," she said in Russian. "Otherwise how'd she know about the royal aunts?"

"She could have read it."

The tragedy of Ekaterinburg had touched the world, and an international industry telling the story of the doomed family showed no sign of declining. Anna was avidly reading the books, magazines, and newspaper articles on the subject that Nick provided her with. "So I remember the happy time," she explained.

"Yes, but how'd she know about when she hit Tatiana with a snowball with a stone in it?" Natalya said. "I never read about that. You read about that?"

Esther admitted she hadn't. On the other hand, she didn't have time to read everything—she still had Nick's secretarial work to do.

Inevitably, she was drawn in; the line between teaching Anna to be graceful and teaching her to act like a grand duchess became increasingly blurred.

What weighed against Anna's authenticity most heavily with Natalya was the girl's slovenliness. She left the bathwater in the tub, she'd get up from the table leaving her dirty plate on it, she made crumbs, she wouldn't pick up her clothes.

Forced to remedy these sins, she would do so, but the effort of insisting on it was wearying, and the other two usually ended up doing it themselves.

Natalya, trained to neatness by her upbringing, was driven mad by Anna's negligence. "I don't care how Imperial your bloody Highness is," she said on one occasion. "I'm not cleaning the damned lavatory after you've been. I had enough of that with the maid-in-charge at Seloe. Here's the brush and there's the pan—next time I'll put your head down it." To Esther she complained, "Sure as hell, she ain't Anastasia. She's a slob."

Esther thought the slobbishness wasn't deliberate, more absent-mindedness or an incipient and unconscious protest against a regime that had once been forced on her. What happened to you? she'd wonder. It was no good asking—like hygiene, her past was another thing Anna had abandoned.

They had trouble getting her to the dentist because she showed real fear of going out into the street, even if a taxi waited. Eventually the mountain came to Mohammed when Nick bribed his dentist to bring equipment to Bismarck Allee and provide Anna with a set of dentures that declared falsity with their whiteness and regularity every time she smiled, but which, since she hardly ever smiled, nevertheless improved her appearance and would, it was felt by Natalya, account for any dissimilarity with Anastasia's looks.

Anna's refusal to speak Russian was another factor against her authenticity. "Nick says it doesn't matter," Esther said.

Natalya was unconvinced. "Seems to me she don't speak anything much. The Romanov girls talked all languages—German like their ma, French, English. Where do you reckon she's from if it ain't Russia?"

"I'm wondering if she's Polish. She called me a damn *Żydach* this morning, and that's Polish."

"Well, that'd account for why she's such a pain in the ass." Like most Russians, Natalya had no opinion of the country that her own had held in thrall for much of its history.

On Nick's instructions Esther had begun to give Anna English conversation lessons. His own researches had revealed that the Romanovs spoke English to one another in private. "She'll latch on quick when she remembers. It'll impress the customers. And open up the American market."

Anna was capable of surprising them both. She learned English quickly, and she could recount faultlessly the genealogy of both the czar and the czarina as well as practically every other crowned head in Europe. She knew the progress of the young czarevitch's hemophilia and the names of the two sailors who were set to guard him from the falls and knocks that brought on the agony of his condition. More than that, presented with photographs in the album that the czarina had published before her death, she could identify without prompting not only individual members of the immediate family but uncles, aunts, cousins, governesses, friends, personal maids, even pets, embellishing each picture with personal detail.

Natalya was once more spurred into reconsidering. "How's she know these things?"

Esther held up a book that Nick had just sent over that morning with Big Theo. "It's in here." It was Peter Gilliard's *Thirteen Years at the*

Russian Court. Gilliard, a Swiss, had been the Romanovs' tutor and had married Anastasia's nursemaid.

Natalya was still doubtful. "Looks kind of heavy for her to read. When did that come out?"

"In 1921. Last year."

That was the trouble: Anna had been in Dalldorf for the book's publication. Either she'd got hold of a copy, which argued considerable dedication for an asylum patient, or she knew someone who had. "Or," as Natalya said, doubtfully, "she was there."

Natalya's recollections of the imperial children were painful. "Lovely girls, the four of them, dressed in white mostly. Olga was the scholar. Tatiana—she was really elegant. Marie was the prettiest. Anastasia was the sassiest—she got into more trouble than the others. Never cried when she was slapped, never. And so polite—you didn't hear them saying, 'Do this, do that.' It was always, 'If you don't mind . . .' But it was the czarevitch who was everybody's favorite—we all loved little Alexei."

It was late. The summer was extending a blazing sun into September, and the heat of the day had soaked into the apartment, making its stuffy furniture seem stuffier. Esther switched on the light to dispel the memory of the darkness that had lain in wait for the royal children outside their bright, innocent arena of snowball fights, toboggan rides, toys, pets, and all-encompassing affection.

"He wasn't allowed to ride a bicycle," Natalya said of Czarevitch Alexei, "case he fell and set off his condition, but he was all boy, and I remember the day he sniped one of the gardener's bikes and wobbled across the parade ground—"

I can't listen to this. Natalya was resurrecting a child who was going to die, as thousands and thousands had died under the Romanov regime.

Esther got up and went into the kitchen, taking the day's newspaper with her. She sat down to try to read it, then pushed it away. Its headlines were of the rioting and strikes, crime and poverty, the spreading tuberculosis, the malnourished children, that lay outside the cocoon of this apartment where the three of them led what seemed to her as peculiar and unworthy a life as had the unheeding Romanovs in their enchanted palace.

The air was so still that she could hear the rushing rattle of trains on their way to and from the Anhalter, sounding to her like the shriek of a wind building up—the same red wind that had whirled her Russia into dust.

Oh, God, don't let it happen here. Not like that.

The telephone rang. She went into the living room to answer it.

"That you, Esther?"

"What's the matter, Boris?"

"It's Olga. Somebody beat her to death in her flat. Can you come?"

6

Olga's body had lain undiscovered for three days, possibly four. It wasn't until Monday and then Tuesday had gone by without her making an appearance at the Green Hat that Boris went around to inquire at her flat in Polenstrasse.

"Not until then?" Esther asked. She'd have checked earlier had she known about it; for Olga to take a day off, let alone two, was unheard of.

Boris was stung. "Look, Esther, I don't know what you're up to because Nick won't tell me, but *we're* busy. Nobody's going abroad for a holiday what with the mark at rock bottom—cheaper to stay in Berlin for your nightlife." He added, "Except His bloody Highness Prince Nick, mind you—*he's* sunning himself in the South of France, so I've got three clubs to run, and the new secretary's useless."

Boris could sound harassed even when he wasn't, but this time, Esther had to admit, he had cause.

He'd been waiting for her outside Olga's place with its key in his hand, a thin, gloomy, bowler-hatted figure, more like an accountant than deputy manager of one of Germany's most lavish and raciest clubs.

So far they hadn't gone in. Boris was bringing Esther up to date in the street rather than revisiting the scene that had met him on Wednesday.

It was quiet enough. They were within walking distance of the Green Hat—Boris had come on foot, Esther by tram as far as Potsdamer Platz—but here most of what was once an area of light industry had been torn down to make way for the advance of the new West End. Like everything else in Berlin, the project had run out of money, and Polenstrasse was now part of an empty, rubble-strewn plot of land with unexpected views. All that was left standing of the busy street Olga must have once known was a furniture repository and, next door, a square box of a building, its downstairs housing a printing works from which issued the clack of compositors at their keyboards.

"Where's the flat?" Esther asked.

Boris pointed to an open wooden flight of steps leading up the side of the printing works. "Up there."

"How did you get in?"

"The bastard left the door open when he'd finished with her. Seems he didn't break in—the police reckon either he was waiting for her or he followed her home."

"And nobody noticed?"

Boris inclined his head toward the printing works. "Police questioned the boys in there, but seems they come to work, go home, so it's deserted around here at nights. They rent the place off the owner—Olga did the same, never had much to do with them. Police gave me her key. They've finished up there, done the fingerprinting."

He looked down, twiddling the key—the police had given it to him, having found it in the flat. It was attached to a ring sporting a leather tab with a green top hat embossed into it—Nick had dozens displayed in a large brass pot on the reception desk for his customers to take.

Esther put a hand on his arm. "Bad, was it, Boris?"

"They've got to get this bastard, Esther." He was still looking at the key. "Really, they got to. She . . . he tied her to a chair. What he did . . . I didn't recognize her. . . . And her hair. You know how tidy she kept her hair. . . ."

Always. Plastered back into a tight bun.

"He'd torn bits of it out," Boris said. His protuberant Adam's apple jerked as he swallowed. "Why didn't she tell him right away where she kept her savings? That's what I can't understand. Why didn't she just let the fucker take it?"

"*Did* she have savings?"

"Don't know. Maybe she had jewelry. He must've thought so. Broke her neck to top it off. I tell you, Esther, I've seen some things but . . . I don't know what's happening to this bloody country, I don't."

She took the key out of his hand. "What do you want me to do?"

He was relieved. "Nick's telegram said for you to make the funeral arrangements. See when the police are releasing the body." He shrugged. "I don't know if she had relatives."

"Did she ever mention any?"

"Not as far as I know. There was a husband died in the war, but she never talked about him either. You'll find an address book up there, maybe."

"I'll go up, then," Esther said, not moving.

"That's my girl." Boris put up a thumb to her. "I've got to get back." He raised his hat and walked off. Then he turned. "Nick says to give her a good send-off but don't overdo it."

The sun was turning even this devastation into a vista; she could see the cathedral in the distance. Buddleia had colonized areas of rubble, and butterflies were hovering on its purple spikes. Sparrows made a kerfuffle taking baths in the dust. The clatter from the open windows of the printing works sounded like not unfriendly, automated gossip.

She dallied, wondered what was it like when the butterflies and the sparrows and the compositors had all gone home and darkness turned the piles of bricks into gravestones.

Just get up those stairs, Esther.

The wooden balustrade was warm under her hand as she climbed. A net curtain covered the glass in the upper half of Olga's front door. Esther fitted the key into the lock, turned it, and went in.

Heat slammed into her. Heat and the smell of corruption. She stood for a moment, then forced herself inside, leaving the door open behind her.

It was a bed-sitter and must have been a nice one—a large, wooden-floored space with metal-framed windows that now presented spacious views. And neat.

Or would have been neat, if it hadn't been for a wooden chair that lay on its side with ropes still attached to it. Dark brown splashes on the floorboards around it. There were scattered tufts of black hair. . . .

She walked briskly past it to get to the windows, trying to be furious. The police, Boris, *somebody* should have cleaned the place. There was something indecent in having left evidence of the woman's agony exposed.

It wasn't rope on the chair—stockings. He'd tied Olga up with her own black woolen stockings.

Esther pushed open the window with the cathedral view and leaned out, taking in summer air. This was more than the poor battening on the poor. He, they—perhaps there'd been more than one—had tortured at leisure. A woman had screamed for her life, and nobody'd heard her.

Esther jerked more windows open, then set about doing her job.

Olga had made it easy for her. A nonhoarder, Olga. The suitcase on top of the wardrobe was empty. The wardrobe itself contained few clothes, all smelling of the mothballs that lay scattered around them. On a rail with legs next to the wardrobe hung some of the Green Hat's costumes.

Here and there was gray dust with which, she supposed, the police had tried to find fingerprints; there seemed to be very few—a regular polisher, was Olga—and all of them small enough to be a woman's.

A stout pine table, also dusted, held a sewing machine with a swath of white linen still on the needle plate—Olga had been making herself a new nightdress. Esther pulled the material aside to reveal a drawer. Pins, needles, cotton, silk, some paper patterns, and, on one side, two stapled bundles, one of bills, the other of wage slips. *Jesus,* Olga, was that all Nick paid you?

In the kitchen area, a larder contained a small piece of cheese and half a rye loaf. Small wonder she'd spent every hour she could at the Green Hat; staff could eat free.

Everything tidy and neat, everything spotless. The bath in the tiny bathroom lacked patches of enamel but was scrubbed clean. A cupboard above the washbasin contained basic toiletries and a bottle of black hair dye. Esther shut the door on it quickly—Olga would have hated her knowing that. Olga would have hated her being here at all.

No photographs, no letters, no mementos of children—probably didn't have any—no war medals belonging to the dead husband, no address book.

She looked around. Come on, woman, there must have been more to your life than this.

She drew back the curtain separating the alcove containing Olga's bed from the rest of the room—and found Olga's life.

Prince Nick's face looked back at her. And looked back at her. And back at her. Dozens—perhaps a hundred—of photos and press clippings had been pinned up on the alcove ceiling and walls, all of Nick. Around and about the severely made bed was Nick bowing to the king of Albania, Nick saluting the Italian ambassador, Nick in fancy dress, Nick's portrait in profile, in full face, Nick with some comedian—both of them sporting a fez—with Gigli, with Nellie Melba. Nick in half a photograph that cut one of his arms off, presumably because it had lain around the shoulders of a pretty woman—Melba was the only female represented in the gallery; maybe her size disqualified her as a rival. Prince Nick winning a Grand Prix . . . Nick presenting a check to charity (a rare one, that, but Olga had noted and kept it).

The strips of newspaper had stirred as Esther opened the curtain—the untidy flapping of a prayer wheel. To a god who'd never noticed.

It was like being a Peeping Tom. Quickly, Esther closed the curtain. Then opened it again to begin tearing the pictures down.

I'm so sorry, Olga. Sorry I saw this. I'll never tell.

Keeping Olga's secret was the one thing Esther could do for her.

Before she left, she slipped one of the portraits in her handbag. It would go into the coffin.

She'd hoped that perhaps the policeman in charge of the case would be the one who'd attended the Green Hat. It wasn't. An Inspector Bolle assured her, "We'll catch him, Fräulein, don't you worry," but he sounded dispirited and echoed Boris's despair at what was happening to Germany, citing cases of old men and women being attacked for their pensions, housewives robbed on their way home from market, a milkman kicked to death by the man who stole his horse.

"Too many foreigners coming in," he said, oblivious of whom he was talking to. "It was never like this in the old days."

Were those the old days when there'd been a world war? Esther wondered. When you were fighting England? France?

Apparently Nick had been able to exert influence, even from the South of France, and both autopsy and inquest were to be expedited. The body would be released ready for burial the following Wednesday.

At the undertaker's, Esther ordered the most expensive casket available, to be drawn by black-plumed horses—the bill to be sent to Prince Nikolai Potrovskov personally. Still vengeful, she went on to the florist's and arranged for enough late roses to cover the entire coffin lid.

"That'll teach him to pay her peanuts," she told Natalya when she got home. "I'm going to see he walks behind that cortege with his bloody hat in his hand."

"Bit late to do Olga much good," Natalya pointed out.

"It'll do *him* good," Esther said. "And me." She went to her desk to put the date and time in her diary in order to make sure Nick kept to them.

Natalya heard her whimper. "What's up?"

"It was him." Esther was looking at the diary as into the face of the gorgon. "He killed her."

"Nick killed her?"

"It was him. It was the sixth weekend. Oh, God, oh, Jesus, it was *him*."

Natalya led her to the sofa. "Put your head between your knees. I'll get you a drink. We got any brandy?"

Esther didn't hear her. *That's when he comes, every six weeks.* Jostling for notice behind Clara's voice, other statements, other disregarded facts, were accumulating and joining up.

Boris: *The police reckon either he was waiting for her or he followed her home.*

Waiting for her. Followed her home. Déjà vu.

Natalya came back with a glass of schnapps. Esther clutched at her. "Where's Anna?"

"In bed. As usual."

"He was after her. That's who he wanted."

"Who did? Is this the Cheka we're talking about?"

"He waits and follows, that's what he does. It wasn't money he wanted from Olga. She didn't have any; he didn't even look for it. Her suitcase—it wasn't opened, not a drawer out, nothing disturbed. He didn't want money, he wanted Anna's address—that's why he tortured Olga." She took a breath. "I've got to tell the police."

Natalya was still holding the schnapps, concentrating politely. "Why would Olga have this address?"

"She didn't."

"Well, why would he think she did?"

"I don't know, I don't know." She rubbed her forehead. "Yes I do." She was back at the Green Hat. Anna was upstairs in Nick's office, asleep. The lights were out. Olga was in the doorway of the club room, scolding, coming up the stairs after her. *Young woman,* I *arrange accommodation for the girls.*

"He heard her say so. He thought she knew where we were taking Anna. But she didn't. He tortured her for information she didn't have." Esther stood up. "I've got to tell the police."

"Nick'll love that." Natalya pulled her back down and forced the schnapps into her hand. She went into the kitchen, returning with the bottle and another glass. "Let's go through it again, shall we? I ain't grasped exactly who you think done what."

Esther went through it again, this time from the beginning and with more clarity.

Natalya nodded carefully. "So this assassin, Cheka or whatever he is—"

"Not Cheka," Esther said irritably. "Anna was afraid of him before she got grand-duchess ideas."

"This guy with a grudge and a long memory wants to do Anna in—and after the day I've had alone with that cow, I don't blame him. Anyway, he's lurking around Dalldorf, sees you and Theo take her to the

Hat, follows, gets into the club with the idea of knifing Her Imperial Whatsit, but you shove him downstairs with a broom instead."

Esther sipped her schnapps; she knew where this was going. She could see her own logic—it was making her hands shake—but this was a matter where logic compounded the apparent absurdity.

Natalya went on, still carefully. "But he happens to have heard Olga doing her I-know-everything-that-goes-on-in-this-place, so he thinks, 'Okay, Olga'll give me Anna's address. Next time I get a couple of days off, I'll do some more lurking outside the Green Hat, follow Olga home, and beat the shit out of her until she gives it to me.' Which he does. Is that it?"

Esther said, "I know it sounds far-fetched. . . ."

"Phhh." Natalya's lips formed a perfect cupid's bow as she sucked breath through them. "I wouldn't say far-fetched, exactly. The police won't say it's far-fetched—they'll just treat you kindly and take you straight to Dalldorf to be with your pal Clara."

"I've got to tell them."

"Of course you have, of course you have."

"Stop that."

Natalya ceased her soothing. "All I'm saying is you've built this whole story out of a diary some loony kept in Dalldorf."

"You think the timing's just coincidence," Esther said.

"It *is*."

"But Anna's definitely afraid of something."

"She's another loony, for God's sake."

"Natalya, he tortured Olga. *Tortured* her. What for? She didn't have money. Her place wasn't turned over—he could see she didn't have money. Nick kept her on starvation wages. So what was he after if it wasn't to know where Anna was living?"

"Esther, my little rosebud, I don't like to tell you this, but there's men who *like* torturing women. Gives 'em a hard-on. All right, Olga was unlucky, but living in a place deserted at night, she was asking for trouble. Could've happened anytime. There's nothing to say it's the same man as the one at the Hat, is there? *Is* there?"

Esther sighed. "No."

"No." Natalya nodded. "Go to the police if you like, but your six-week murder theory'll just amuse 'em. I mean, what sort of killer only turns up when he gets around to it? What is he? A traveling salesman with a nasty disposition?"

"No." She almost smiled. Whatever he was, the killer was feral. The man on the stairs stank of the jungle; she couldn't see him selling vacuum cleaners door-to-door. She knew she was losing her case. If she couldn't convince sharp, streetwise Natalya, with how much less belief would that lumbering inspector at Alexanderplatz receive her?

She should go to him, nevertheless. He'd find her ridiculous, a crackpot foreigner, but she would have discharged a duty—that the whole matter be recorded in case, *in case,* in six weeks' time, the killer tried again and murdered somebody else.

The phone rang. "Esther? How's Anna? Get her ready, kid, we're going to put her through a little test. I've found a Romanov we can show her to. *Ne coupez pas,* for Christ's sake."

Nick was in Nice and having the usual trouble convincing a French telephone operator that he wanted to stay on the line.

"Nick, about Olga . . ."

"Yeah, terrible. You seeing to the arrangements? No, I've not finished, mam'zelle. *Ne coupez pas.*"

"Olga. Nick, did you tell her where Anna and I are living?"

"What's that? Of course not. Nobody knows, except me. Don't want the Cheka getting to her, do we? Now, listen, Esther, I've found this old lady, the grand-duchess girls used to call her Tante Swanny. She's willing— No, mam'zelle, I'm still talking. *Ne coupez pas.* Tell you what I'll do when I've finished the call, I'll put the phone down— You still there, Esther? I'm going to fly her up tomorrow. Anastasia was her favorite, she knew her well. We'll have a trial run with our filly, see how she goes over the jumps."

Esther tried to divert him: "Nick . . ."

"We'll be arriving Tempelhof eleven A.M. Okay?"

"Olga's murder, Nick . . . I think . . ."

But Nick had lost his battle with the French telephone system.

Esther put the receiver down. She went back to the sofa and poured herself more schnapps. "He's bringing some elderly Romanov to meet Anna tomorrow."

"She's not ready."

"It doesn't matter." Loomed over by Olga's death, the game they were playing was shabby and intolerable.

"It matters," Natalya said with energy. "There's a film to be made when she's recognized as Anastasia—and I'm going to star in it."

Esther stared at her.

Natalya was defiant. "Well, *she* can't play the part, can she? You imagine her on a movie set? She'd scream every time they clapped the clapper board."

"I see," Esther said. "That's why you don't want me go to the police. They might find out who she really is."

"Go," said Natalya icily. "They'll enjoy a good laugh. But I'll tell you this, if I believed the shit you believe, the last thing I'd do is tell the police—and get our Imperial Highness killed alongside of Olga."

"What do you mean?"

"I mean," said Natalya, leaning forward, "that half the Berlin police force is on the books of some newspaper or other. I got a friend on the *Morgenpost,* and he pays out for any good story. Anastasia back from the dead—that's a *very* good story. You tell the cops, and before Frau Schinkel knows it, she'll have flashlights and reporters ten deep outside her door." She sat back. "That killer you dreamed up, he won't have to torture anybody to find out Anna's address; he'll just have to buy a paper." Her eyes searched Esther's face for a moment, and then she nodded. "With that happy thought, I'm going to bed. We got a grand duchess to prepare in the morning."

Esther stayed where she was, clutching an empty schnapps glass to her chest. Self-interest, she thought. Every argument Natalya had propounded was in Natalya's own interest.

On the other hand, that didn't make them less viable.

Shit, *shit.* Go to the police and give them a chance to catch the killer. Don't go to the police, thereby ensuring that the killer didn't catch Anna.

If there *were* a killer after Anna. Which Natalya was sure there wasn't. And which, through the unaccustomed fumes of schnapps, she, Esther, was also beginning to doubt.

She'd sleep on it.

. . .

Marie Ivanova Narishkin had once been a ballet dancer. It was stretching a point to call her a Romanov; she'd merely slept with one, having at one time been mistress to a cousin of Alexander II. When her lover died, she'd occasionally been invited to St. Petersburg as a form of charity.

Now a fat, elderly woman, she'd been tempted out of retirement in France by Nick's offer of all expenses paid as well as the opportunity to pass judgment on a young woman claiming to be Anastasia.

On greeting her, Esther decided that Nick had chosen his subject well. Marie Ivanova's self-importance and delight at being taken out of obscurity would undoubtedly ensure that she proclaimed Anna to be the grand duchess, however slight her acquaintance with the imperial family had been.

Oh, God, Esther thought, I want nothing to do with this. Now that it came to it, they were crooks using an old woman in a confidence trick.

There'd been difficulty in getting Anna ready for the meeting. Anna had panicked. "I do not see this person. I am not meat to pick over. I see only Aunt Olga and Aunt Xenia. I do not see Swannies. I go to bed."

Natalya was infuriated. "Holy Martyr, even *you'd* be a better Anastasia, scar or no bloody scar." This was to Esther; they were tidying Anna's room, which was in its usual chaos. "Why doesn't Nick let me do it? I can play a lady. This one don't know the meaning of the word." She chucked a load of dirty underwear into a basket. "But oh, no, Natalya, you take the part of the maid because that's what you're good at."

"Marie Ivanova," Nick said, ushering his guest into the flat, "may I present Esther and Natalya, Her Imperial Highness's companions."

Marie Ivanova kept her eyes shut and wheezed from the climb up the stairs. Behind her, carrying wraps and handbags, was a thin, embittered-looking woman, her companion. Nick introduced her as Mademoiselle Mycielcka.

"Where is this creature I have come to see?" Marie Ivanova demanded when she'd got her breath back.

"Esther, inform Her Imperial Highness that Marie Ivanova is here."

Esther shook her head; she wasn't going to be party to this. Nick's eyes flicked at her and away. "Natalya, if you would be so good."

Natalya shrugged. "She won't come out of her room."

There was a gasp from Mademoiselle Mycielcka and a hissed *"Shit"* from Nick.

Marie Ivanova remained unconcerned. She nodded. "If she is whom you say, that is correct. *I* go to *her.*"

They followed her to the bedroom and stood in its doorway while Marie Ivanova went in and regarded a hump under the bedspread. "I am here, young woman."

The hump remained motionless and silent.

Marie Ivanova crooked a finger at her companion. "The feet."

Mycielcka darted forward, whipped up the bottom of the bedcovering, and laid it back, exposing Anna's legs.

"The shoes."

Mycielcka began untying laces.

"You should know," said Marie Ivanova, "that the grand duchess Anastasia had deformation of her feet. Hallux valgus. She was most conscious of it. We talked of it often, she and I, because, like most ballet dancers, I share the complaint."

The shoes were off.

"The stockings."

Anna's stockings were unhooked from her garter belt. Anna, her upper body and head still covered, did not move.

Peering over Mycielcka's shoulder, Nick, Esther, and Natalya stared at Anna's bare feet. They were small and rather ugly. If hallux valgus meant bunions, Anna had them.

Marie Ivanova studied them through her lorgnette, then passed her hand over them. She was crying. "I am here, my child," she said. "I am with you."

Anna's head appeared like a tortoise's from the carapace of bedclothes. "Tante Swanny?"

"Yes."

Anna disengaged her right arm and held it out. As the old woman bent to kiss her hand, she leaned forward and applied her lips to the wrinkled forehead. "Come back," she whispered in English.

"I shall."

Mycielcka began guiding her mistress from the room.

Esther heard Natalya's whisper: "She's backing out. *She's backing out.*"

Anna Anderson had been declared royal.

A grinning Prince Nick took Marie Ivanova and her companion off to lunch at the Adlon, turning around and jiggling his hips at the two women standing silently watching their departure.

"She did it," Natalya said.

"Yes."

"She did it *right.*"

"Yes."

"How?" Natalya was suspended between belief and disbelief, resentment and elation.

"I don't know." Esther felt very tired. She'd spent the night racked by indecision over what to do about Olga's murder. "I suppose Swanny was always going to believe it."

"But she really did—believe it, I mean."

"Yes."

Natalya allowed resentment to win. "It don't prove anything," she said. "Everybody's got bunions. *I* got bunions. *You* got bunions? How d'you get bunions?"

"High-heeled shoes," Esther said.

"Exactly."

Full of Anna's triumph, Nick came back from seeing the ladies off at the airport. "Got old Swanny eating out of her hand, didn't she?"

"And that's good, is it?" Esther asked.

He was surprised. "Sure, it is."

Natalya, anticipating the row to come, said good night and took herself off to bed.

Esther said, "I'll tell you what isn't good." She didn't spare him any details of Olga's death—if she was right about the murderer, there was a sense in which Olga had died for Nick. Then she gave him her opinion as to the reason for it.

He didn't argue. "You're probably right."

She was surprised. "You agree it was the same man?"

"Maybe. The Cheka doesn't give up that easy."

"It isn't the *Cheka.*" She was tired of saying it. "It isn't the Cheka because Anna's not Anastasia."

He lit a cigarette and puffed smoke at her. "Tante Swanny says she is."

"Tante Swanny's a credulous old woman. Nick, we must go to the police."

"We did, didn't we?"

"I mean, tell them that the man's been trailing Anna since Dalldorf, tell them to interview Clara Peuthert, get her to describe him."

"Sure," he said. "That's a great way to get Anna killed, but okay. Crazy Clara tells them Anna's the grand duchess—and she will. Next thing we know, Anna's picture's in the papers and she's a target. Bye-bye, Anna, but never mind, little Esther's been a responsible citizen." He stubbed out his cigarette in the saucer she always put on the table for him. "Look, kid. Maybe you're right and someone's hanging around outside the Hat trying to get a line on Anna. I say he's Cheka, you say he's . . . whatever you say he is. It doesn't matter. Why d'you think I'm keeping this address secret? Those ladies just now, they had no idea which street they were coming to because I didn't tell 'em. Why do I park two blocks away when I visit? Why do I dodge into doorways and look behind me? For fun? We're dealing in life and death here."

She considered. "You're certain that if we tell the police what we know, the newspapers will get hold of it?"

He displayed his hands. "Ring up the editor of the *Morgenpost,* why don't you? Cut out the middle man."

She went for the flaw in his argument. "So all Anna's schooling is for nothing. You'll never be able to present her in case the Cheka shoots her down."

"Esther, Esther." He shook his head at her obtuseness. "That'll be a big occasion, and I mean *big.* Guards, Secret Service men with shooters. Nobody gets in without being frisked. A proper press conference, international, radio, movie cameras—the whole borscht right down to the beets. How's Her Highness's English coming along, incidentally? The Yanks'll be there in force."

She was defeated. "Well, I won't be. It's still fraud—and Olga died for it."

He peered at her. "Ah, come on, baby. You're tired. Let's go to bed, uh?"

He picked her up and took her to her room, and for a while her body was able to separate itself from the film loop that went around and around in her head.

7

Marie Ivanova died four days after returning to France.

"The trip was too much for her," Mademoiselle Mycielcka informed Nick over the phone with a fury that was not assuaged when he asked if Tante Swanny, before her death, had contacted the Romanovs with the news that Anastasia had returned from the grave.

"She did not." The phone banged down.

Nick took the setback with equanimity. "Word'll get around," he said, and flew off to the funeral, partly to make sure word *did* get around and partly to woo the aristocratic young Frenchwoman he'd met on his previous visit and whom he had hopes of bedding.

Anna's reception of the news did not disturb the lofty confidence she'd acquired after Tante Swanny's authentication. "Like she's been crowned by the archi-bloody-mandrite," Natalya said.

It was Esther who experienced a sting of grief and guilt. Here was another death. They were collecting them.

Word *did* get around. It didn't reach the German newspapers, which had too much to occupy them with the by-now-runaway inflation and its inevitable consequence of strikes, unemployment, a rising death rate, and street battles between Left and Right.

But, whether it came from Clara Peuthert or Mycielcka or Nick, there was a sudden excited sprinkling of question marks in the Russian émigré press. IS ANASTASIA ALIVE? DID GRAND DUCHESS ANASTASIA ESCAPE EKATERINBURG? WHO IS THE MYSTERIOUS ANNA ANDERSON? To homesick, despairing White Russians, the idea that the czar's daughter had survived the slaughter and, like Persephone, returned to them from hell was almost unbearably beautiful.

At 29c Bismarck Allee, Anna searched for Anastasia's picture among the bundle of newspapers Nick had sent from France. "What they say? What they say about me?"

"They say there's a mystery woman in Berlin who claims to be Anastasia."

Anna became agitated. "They don't say where I live?"

"They don't bloody *know* where you live, do they?" Natalya said. Anna's celebrity was sticking in her throat.

"That woman with Tante Swanny, she knows."

"No," Esther told her, "she has no idea. She just knows she came to an apartment in Berlin. Lots of apartments in Berlin."

There'd been more street killings of White Russians, and one of the papers said, *"Her privacy must be guarded. If Her Imperial Highness Anastasia is alive, she may be a target for another assassin's bullet."*

Esther didn't translate that one. The decision not to pass her fears on to the police was validated; if there was this fuss over a mere rumor, the resultant jamboree—should the press track Anna down—didn't bear thinking about.

And she'd trapped herself in the confidence trick because, while there was the remotest chance that in six weekends' time the killer would be looking for Anna again, she, Esther, had to guard her—because she, Esther, was the only one who believed that he might.

And even she didn't really believe it.

On the clear, blue mornings of that St. Martin's summer, she'd castigate herself for thinking that Olga's murder was anything but a random killing. Yet when night fell, she'd see Anna go to the kitchen window—as the girl had begun to do now that the evenings were drawing in—to peer through a crack in the curtains, watching shadows form under the trees in the street below. Then Esther would remind herself that Olga's killer, random or not, was still at large.

"What the hell are you scared of?" Natalya demanded of Anna. "There's nobody bloody there."

"Cheka," Anna parroted. "They want to kill me."

"I know how they feel."

"Want a dog."

Natalya would appeal to Esther. "She's mad, she's bloody mad."

And Esther would think, Probably. But perhaps so is the man she's scared of. At nights, in an apartment darkened by constant electricity cuts, fear was infectious. The silence from the empty flat below was pronounced. A creak on the stairs made them all jump. More than once Esther went out on the landing to peep down the stairwell—and saw nothing. Every night, before going to bed, she made sure that windows were tightly closed and their front door bolted.

When Nick returned from Tante Swanny's funeral, Esther told him, "Think what you like, but on October twenty-first I want this place protected."

"That another sixth weekend?"

"Yes."

He humored her. "Sure, sure, you can have Theo spend the night, two nights. Want I should set up a machine-gun nest?"

"Theo will do."

His mind was on his new conquest in the South of France. "I tell you, Esther, this is the one, completely, you should see her."

They were always the one, completely. "Another thing, Nick, we think it's time Nasha went back to her old job."

"That's right," Natalya said. "I'll stay on to keep the girls company, but I'd like to start back at the Parrot at nights. I done what I can here, and I got my career to think of."

Nick turned on her in a temper. "Your job's finished when I say it is."

A shouting match ended in Natalya's stomping out of the room.

"For God's sake, Nick," Esther said.

"She's a blabbermouth. I'm not having her selling grand-duchess stories to the papers before I'm ready." He relapsed into sentiment.

"Eloise, now . . . Esther, you should meet her. She's got royal blood in her veins, this one. A real Bourbon. Descendant of Louis XIV." He sighed at his plethora of noblewomen. "I tell you, I'd marry her . . . but then I maybe have to marry Anna, so I think, wait a bit. That's my trouble, too many damn princesses."

"Must be a problem," she said. "Nick, you should let Natalya go."

"No. She'll give the game away before I'm ready. She's getting double pay—what more does she want? No, she's hired for the fucking duration."

"And how long is that going to be?"

"When I make my plans. You think you can raise a grand duchess from the grave just like that? You got to set the stage—international press, lights. Maybe I'll hire Tchaikovsky for the music. He writes a nice tune."

"He's dead."

"He is? Okay, somebody else. But first we got to get her authenticated."

Seeing it as a democratic duty to her student, Esther tried to interest Anna in *why* the Czar of All the Russias had fallen.

Anna believed that the situation was straightforward and temporary. The czar (good) had been toppled by the Bolsheviks (bad)—and the Jews had a hand in it somewhere. His people would soon see this. Soviet Russia would be returned to the good days of the monarchy.

"They weren't good days, and they won't come back," Esther told her. "Whatever happens, the world has changed forever." She wanted the girl to gain a different perspective of the Batiushka-Czar, father of the Russian people, and a revolution that had shifted the earth's political axis. Outside Czarskoe Selo, the czar's peasants had lived in a famine-stricken Middle Ages, his Jews in terror, and his Moslems consistently harassed by the Russian Orthodox Church. He'd employed, and listened to, ministers who regarded liberalization as a senseless dream—an immediate challenge to the revolutionaries.

"They warned him, Anna. Time and again he was told what would happen."

Anna wasn't interested. "Was a good man," she said. "You think Russia better now, under Bolsheviks?"

Forcing Natalya's memory of those precarious days was disturbing areas of it she'd suppressed for her own good. "Getting as bad as you," she said to Esther. "I'm having nightmares."

"*Do* I have nightmares?"

"I hear you shouting sometimes."

"I'm sorry," Esther said. In her dreams her head turned into a cinema in which she sat alone. The soundtrack screamed. On the screen was slaughter, frame by frame. "What are your nightmares about?"

"Ma and Pa. I know they're dead, but I want to know what happened to them. Nobody don't seem to know what the Reds did to the servants that went to Ekaterinburg with the family."

Only recently had anybody been able to find out what had happened to the family itself. The British government had promised Kerensky to send a warship to fetch them but had dithered; Prime Minister Lloyd George was reluctant to offer asylum, and King George, though fearful for his cousin, did not want to court unpopularity with his anticzarist public. With the collapse of the Kerensky government in 1917, it was too late anyway. Overnight a new man, Vladimir Ilyich Lenin, stood at the head of a new Soviet state. Czar, czarina, children, and servants were sent to Ekaterinburg, a town under the control of the most extreme Bolshevik soviet in the Ural Mountains.

After that . . . silence.

Rumor had intensified horror among the Russian émigré community, but now an official version, no less terrible, was emerging from investigators who had busied themselves taking depositions from those who could piece the story together.

You don't want to know, Esther thought. Humiliation first, that's how it works; degrade the thing you want to kill so that you can kill it. It's what was done to Jews.

"If they're dead, they're dead," she said. "Does it matter how?"

Natalya was vehement. "Yes it does, thank you for asking. I don't know what happened to your people, but what happened to mine bothers me."

"Was terrible for all of us," Anna said unexpectedly. "I don't want to hear. Too bad to remember."

"Then fuck off," Natalya told her. She appealed to Esther. "Don't any of the books say something about it?"

There was one. A new one that had just been published in France—also by the imperial children's tutor, Peter Gilliard: *Le Tragique Destin de Nicolas II et de Sa Famille.* Nick had brought it to Esther to translate. She had left it unopened. A pogrom was a pogrom, whether it slaughtered royalty or Jews; the same bullets smashed into flesh, the same bayonets caught the light as they slashed downward. And the aftermath was the same, bodies twitching on the ground, that sudden quiet into which a child whimpered and a dog barked before they were silenced.

I will not read it. I've been there.

But Natalya was becoming insistent. The once self-assured, perky stripper had become haunted by questions that, Esther knew, should not have been raised but which, now that they had, must be answered.

She opened the book and began reading aloud.

Of those who knew the whole story, not one had lived to tell it. Survivors who glimpsed the Romanovs in their last weeks gave vignettes scalded into their memories: soldiers lounging in the family's room, pocketing souvenirs, insulting Alexandra, spitting on the servants.

At Ekaterinburg railway station, Gilliard and some of the retinue were separated from their charges and got a last glimpse of the Romanov children as they were taken along the platform. Alexei, too ill to walk, was being carried in the arms of his attendant, Nagorny. Anastasia was carrying her little dog and struggling to pull along a suitcase too heavy for her. Alexei's spaniel followed them.

They were taken to a house that had belonged to a merchant named Ipatiev. It had been prepared for them.

"The House of Special Purpose," Anna said.

Esther looked up from the book. "How do you know that?"

"That's what the Bolsheviks called it."

"Yes, they did." She put the book aside. "I'm not reading any more."

But Natalya slammed the book back on her lap. "You got to. It's my ma and pa was there, not yours. What *happened*?"

So Esther took them back to July 1918 in a house in the Urals that had been prepared for a special purpose. . . .

On the night of the sixteenth, eleven people—all seven Romanovs, their doctor, and three servants—were woken up and taken down to a small basement room.

Esther said wearily, "This account came from one of the guards. The czar was told he and the others were going to be moved because the White Army was approaching to rescue them. There were rumors that loyalists were organizing an escape."

"Why didn't they, why the hell *didn't* they?"

"I don't know. It was all a mess."

By the time the White Army arrived, the House of Special Purpose was empty, the walls of its basement room were pitted with bullet holes. Alexei's spaniel, Joy, was whimpering outside.

"Even then they couldn't believe that the Reds had shot the children. Not the children."

Natalya urged time forward. "Who was with them when they were shot?"

"Dr. Botkin and Kharatinov—"

"He was the cook."

"Trupp, the footman, and Demidova."

"Demidova," Natalya said softly. "Funny little thing."

"And Jemmy." Anna's voice was harsh. "Don't forget Jemmy."

"Anastasia's spaniel?" Natalya said. She was weeping. "I remember him as a puppy. He piddled in the Grand Salon. I had to wipe it up. What they kill him for?" She wiped her eyes. "What happened to the others?"

Esther said, "Nagorny was taken away from Alexei. He was put in another prison, the same one as Countess Hendrikov and Mademoiselle Schneider and Prince Dolgoruky. Gilliard thinks they were all shot. Leonid Sednev—"

"They didn't shoot Leo, did they?" Natalya asked. "He was a kid, can't have been more than fourteen. Worked in the kitchens."

"No, they let him go, but I can't find out what happened to him."

The Whites put a trained legal investigator, Sokolov, on the search. Eventually, at the site of a mine several miles away from Ekaterinburg, he found evidence that bodies had been hacked to bits and then burned with acid. He'd reported back to Gilliard. The work had been hasty; hundreds of fragments belonging to the family—the czar's belt buckle, one of the czarina's earrings, Dr. Botkin's false teeth—identified them.

"But the children . . . the children?" Gilliard had begged.

"The children have suffered the same fate as their parents," Sokolov told him. He convinced Gilliard by showing him an odd collection of coins and nails and bits of string he'd found among the detritus.

Esther said steadily, "It was the stuff Alexei used to keep in his pockets."

For a while the sitting room was silent.

"No mention of my ma and pa?"

Esther shook her head. "I'm sorry."

Natalya shouted, "What about that, then, Your Imperial Highness? How did you escape being shot and cut up? Fairies took you away, did they? Angels flew you off?"

"I don't know!" Anna shouted back. "I don't know how. I faint. Everything is blue and noise. Everything . . . blood everywhere. I did not know days. I was mad, I think. The Tchaikovsky brothers rescue me."

"Who?"

"You don't believe, but is true. Peasants. They say they hide me. Took me to Romania, I remember Bucharest—was terrible, *terrible.* Then they disappear, first Alexander Tchaikovsky, then Serge—the Bolsheviki kill them, I think, because they would not tell where I was. The Cheka looked for me to shoot me. I am alone, so alone." She put her clenched hands up to her eyes and stood. "I don't tell more. You do not believe. Nobody believe."

They heard the slam of her bedroom door.

After a while Natalya said, "She'll have to do better than that." The stove sizzled as she spit on it. "Tchaikovsky brothers. Tchaikovsky, I ask you—I bet it's the only Russian name she knows." She began to cry. "Oh, Ma," she said. "Oh, poor Pa. What did they do to you?"

Since Nick brought most of their supplies and the milkman, baker, and coalman delivered the rest, there was no necessity for the three women to set foot outside the house. If Prince Nick had been given his way, they wouldn't have. "I'm not having Nasha slipping off to gossip with her pals at the Parrot. You see she stays in."

"Damned if I do. I'm not a prison guard." The autumn was glorious; Esther wasn't going to let it go by without Natalya or herself breathing some of its air.

"Okay, but she goes out, you go with her."

It suited them both: Natalya to get away from Anna, Esther to get away from the tension the other two women created when they were together. Anna didn't want to come—"Cheka will see me." She was equally scared to be left alone, and they had to ask Frau Schinkel if Anna could sit with her while they were out. It meant that the outings had to be restricted to the daytime, because Anna refused point-blank to be left, even in Frau Schinkel's company, when darkness fell.

Kurfürstendamm, the great street that had rivaled anything in the city center and had once been described as "the coffeehouse of Europe," wasn't the fun it had been. Due to inflation its shops, theaters, and cinemas were beginning to shut down. For a while the two women were able to order coffee in one or another of its cafés and eke it out for an hour or more while sitting at one of the pavement tables, but when the price of a cup became more than Esther earned in a week, that luxury was denied them and they took to walking instead.

Then the weather changed. Rain and wind became incessant, umbrellas were blown inside out. They were forced to stay indoors, a situation that fed the nerves, especially Natalya's; she would tense the moment Anna came into the room, eyes glinting sideways at her, waiting for a wrong move. And a wrong move was inevitable. Anna wouldn't, perhaps couldn't, judge the situation. She made the ill-considered remark, continually left the place in a mess.

Esther found herself yelling at them to shut up—and realized she was more on edge than either of them. Next Saturday would be October 21.

Stop it, she told herself. You are not going to live in fear, not again.

Nevertheless, she reverted to panic when the telephone shrilled on Friday evening and she walked into the living room to find that Natalya had answered it and was talking to somebody. "Yeah, just the same," Natalya was saying drearily. Seeing Esther, she said, "Got to go," and hung the receiver back on the wall.

"Who was that?" Esther demanded.

"Friend of mine."

"You gave him this number?"

"Why shouldn't I? I'm not allowed to talk to a pal now?"

"You gave him this number?"

"Yes I did," Natalya said, mouthing it. "Pal of mine at the Parrot. I was keeping in touch. I can do that, can't I? Stuck in this fucking tomb? And I gave him the number, not the bloody address."

"I told you," Esther said, "phone out by all means but nobody phones in."

"You think your guy can find us through a telephone number? What is he, psychic? You're paranoid, you are."

She pushed past Esther. "I'm going to bed. Fuck-all else to do."

Esther was left in an empty room. He's not my guy, she thought. He's Anna's, and Anna is my responsibility. I've got to be paranoid for her.

Was she paranoid? Was she scaring herself with an entity that didn't exist? *Could* you find out an address from a telephone number? Maybe not. But maybe.

Stop it, she told herself. Just stop it. It's being cooped up in this goddamned flat, it's making us all paranoid one way or another.

Nevertheless, she called Nick at the club to remind him to send Theo around on Saturday.

He was irritated that she was holding him to it. The Hat was going to be busy on Saturday. The von Schwerin boys were bringing a large party; Theo would be needed.

"Find another bouncer for the night," she told him.

"'Oh, Nick, it's the sixth weekend,'" he said, mimicking her. "'Our friend's been saving up his pfennigs for the train fare to come and knock Anna off.' Sweetheart, I don't like to tell you this, but the Cheka ain't that poor."

"Neither are you," she said. "Find another bouncer."

Natalya was as caustic as Nick, but by now Esther had the bit between her teeth. "Maybe I'm wrong," she said. "Maybe there's nobody after Anna. But if I'm not . . . well, believe me, you don't want to meet him on the stairs."

Big Theo, a hat pulled over his eyes, was unloaded in Bismarckstrasse on Saturday morning, and Esther, watching out for him, saw that Nick had given him instructions to make sure he wasn't followed. As he turned the corner and lumbered up the avenue, he paused to crouch behind every tree and peer around its trunk back to the way he'd come—about as conspicuous in Bismarck Allee as a hippopotamus.

She explained his duties to him. "I just want you here as a watchman. I don't want you hurt again. If somebody knocks on the street door, ask who it is before you open it. If he hears a man's voice, he'll probably run away."

"He the same fella stuck me at the Hat, he won't do no running. I'm tearing his legs off."

"Oh, God."

Explaining Theo to Frau Schinkel wasn't easy. "One of Fraulein Tchichagova's admirers from her theater days has been trying to find her new address. He may be . . . overenthusiastic, and we think it would be a good idea if only Herr Theo answers the front door for the next two days."

Esther's more fevered imaginings involved a knife cutting Frau Schinkel's capacious throat unless Anna was handed over.

Frau Schinkel's distrust of foreigners, modern young women, and theater people was confirmed. If renters hadn't been hard to come by—her second floor was still empty—the girls in 29c would have been out in an instant.

As it was, Theo charmed her. He carried coal, replaced a lightbulb too high for normal reach, and played choo-choo in the hall with Frau Schinkel's grandchildren when her daughter visited on Saturday afternoon. He was even given supper and only returned, replete, to 29c and his bed on the living room sofa in the evening.

Apart from the family visit, the one time the front doorbell rang all day was when a parcel arrived for Frau Schinkel by the second post. Esther, hearing it and going to the kitchen window to check, called down to Theo to answer it, more for the look of the thing than because she really believed that Anna's would-be assassin had dressed up as a postman.

The night passed peaceably to the tune of Theo's snoring.

Sunday came and went without incident.

"Told you," Natalya said.

When Nick turned up to fetch Theo on Monday morning, he said nothing so loudly that Esther told him to shut up.

She felt like a fool.

On the next sixth weekend, December 2 and 3, she didn't bother with precautions. Nothing happened then either.

8

ON AN EVENING toward the end of December, Nick arrived with a large suitcase as well as the usual supplies. "Here's a cache to keep you ladies in style while I'm away. Don't spend it all at once." He opened the suitcase, revealing an interior stuffed with high-denomination German banknotes.

"Where are you going?"

"I'm taking Eloise away for Christimas. Boris is taking care of the clubs. Eloise hates the cold—she's warm-blooded." He rolled his eyes. "Boy, is she warm-blooded."

Finding that his reception lacked enthusiasm, he said, "And great news, Esther. Come the New Year, we're going to launch the good ship Anastasia. I've heard from Aunt Grand Duchess Olga, got her interested. I reckon our girl's ready now. Where's Nasha?"

"Out."

"I told you she wasn't to go out nights. Where is she?"

"She's visiting a friend at the Parrot."

"Shit."

She let him rave. Natalya, too, had raved; her incarceration had begun to affect her to a point where Esther feared that if she were closeted with Anna much longer, there would be another murder.

"And while we're about it, Nick," she said, "I have to tell you that the day you launch the good ship Anastasia is the day I leave you. I don't approve. I never have."

He was quiet for a moment, walking around her. "You studied the secretarial job market lately, Esther?"

"I don't care."

He quoted a Russian proverb: "A dog is wiser than a woman. It doesn't bark at its master."

"I still don't care."

Now he was anxious. "You wouldn't give her away, though, would you?"

"She'll give herself away."

"Want to bet?" He recovered his good humor. "We'll see. You don't go to Tula with your own samovar." He was full of old Russian proverbs tonight—she'd never known what that one meant. He put his arm around her. "We're still friends, ain't we?"

"Yes."

"Of course we are. Of course we are. You and me, we've come a long way together. Just keep our Anna safe till I get back. A couple of weeks, that's all I'm asking. Can you do that?"

"I suppose I'll have to."

"That's my girl."

Soon after he'd left, Natalya came home, screaming with rage. "Well, that's done it! I can't go back. I burned my bridges for that bitch, and now I'm stuck with her. I'll kill Nick when I see him!"

"What on earth's the matter?"

"I mean there isn't a job for me anymore. The Parrot's closing down. Oh, yes." Esther had opened her mouth. "He's keeping the Parasol and the Hat, but he's closing the Parrot. Janni told me. Isn't paying its way what with inflation or some goddam thing." She tore off her hat and threw it across the room. "'Double pay, Nasha. Help the grand duchess to her rightful position, Nasha. Make a silk purse out of a sow's ear, Nasha.' He never said, 'If it don't work, you're on the street, Nasha.' Sneaky, slippery, swindling bastard!"

Esther agreed with her. Nick hadn't mentioned his intention to close the Purple Parrot to her either. Naturally Natalya was panicking; Nick was taking away her safety net.

She put her arm around the girl's shoulders. "There's always a place for talent. There are other clubs."

"And I've been in 'em," Natalya said. "Smoky little cellars where the customers put paper money in your spangles and stick their finger up your crotch while they're doing it. The Parrot was *respectable.*"

Probably why it's closing, Esther thought. As the mark's value went down, so did standards.

"Well, I ain't going back to that," Natalya said, "I'm an artiste, and I'm going to be a movie star." She shook herself free of Esther's arm. "That cow better turn out to be Anastasia, because if she don't, *I'm* applying for the job."

Esther was left alone, watching rain splatter against the windows. The year had been spent concocting a lie; it was as if time itself had become weary of it and broken down, exhausted, leaving them all trapped in a dimension that didn't move.

FOR SOMEONE WHOSE future was reliant on Anna—perhaps because it *was* reliant on Anna—Natalya was incapable of dealing patiently with her. Came the evening when Anna once more got up from the table without clearing it and, called back by Esther, refused. "Is not for me. Let her do it."

Natalya leaped with her hands out for Anna's throat.

Esther pulled both of them apart and did some raving of her own, ending with, ". . . and now get your coats on. We're going out."

"She's a shit madwoman," Anna screamed, holding a bitten ear.

"*I'm* a madwoman? Who ended up in Dalldorf?"

"We're going out," Esther said, "or we'll all end up in fucking Dalldorf."

"I do not go. Cheka will kill me."

"Let's hope they do."

"Shut up, both of you," Esther said. "It's Christmas Eve in case you two Christians had forgotten, and we're going *out.*"

They forced Anna into her teddy-bear coat and pulled one of Natalya's cloche hats down over her ears. Her protests were automatic; in fact, she was not too unwilling. This would be the first time she'd been out for something like three years.

With Anna walking arm in arm between them to guard her from Cheka bullets, they went forth into a Christmastide Berlin.

Which was gaunt. The cold air was even more bitter than the ill-feeling they'd left behind. Nativity candles that should have been in every window sent out light from only a few. In Kurfürstendamm well-dressed men and women were being handed from their cars into the better restaurants and hotels, but the cafés that should have been packed with ordinary, celebrating Berliners were gone.

It was the same in the Tiergarten. There was the usual municipal Christmas tree, but its decoration was subdued, and few people were listening to the carols played by an oompah band. Only the American embassy, which had guests arriving at its doors, showed signs of festivity.

"What's happening?" Anna asked.

"Inflation's happening," Esther said. Nick, with his supplies and his money, had insulated them from a crisis so deep that Germany, which had invented the modern Christmas, could no longer afford it.

The only color came from dozens of red posters surmounted by a huge black cross with horizontals on its end extending in the same counterclockwise direction. "What's that?" Anna asked.

"Tut, tut, Imperial Highness, you should know that," Natalya said. "Your ma put them up all over the place."

"It's a swastika," Esther said. "It's an Eastern symbol of light."

"Is nice," said Anna.

On their way back, they passed a flea-pit cinema advertising *Nosferatu* and the fact that its auditorium was heated. Anna and Natalya wanted to go in, Esther didn't. "It'll be depressing. It's about a vampire."

Natalya, her teeth still tasting Anna's ear, said, "Good, I'm thinking of taking it up."

They went in. At the box office, the manager pulled their tickets off a roll. "Four thousand marks, thank you," he said.

"What?" They stared at him. Frau Schinkel had complained with increasing panic at what was happening to prices, but this was ridiculous.

"I could've bought a stinking car for that," Natalya said incredulously.

"Or coal," the manager said hopefully. "I'll let you in for a nugget of coal each. Got to keep the boiler going."

"Oh, what a shame," said Esther. "We left the coal at home."

In the end he let them in, to increase his audience and on the understanding that next time they brought something negotiable. Esther offered him the thousand-mark note she had in her purse, which, she'd hoped, would buy them all a meal. He turned it down. "I already papered my living room," he said.

She'd been right; the film was scary. Anna and Natalya enjoyed it.

They went to the cinema a lot after that—Nick had seen to it that the coal bunker in the backyard was replete, though Esther noticed that each time she went to fill up their hod, the heap was smaller than when she'd left it. She didn't mention it to the others; even Frau Schinkel, she thought, didn't deserve to die of cold.

None of the films were new releases, and all were German, well made but very dark.

"For Chrissake, show something lively, Ernst," Natalya told the manager. "Give us a Hollywood movie."

"Sorry, girls, I can't afford the distributors' fee."

But the outings were a distraction—at least until the evening when they found the cinema closed.

Nick didn't return in two weeks, or three weeks, or four.

Inflation saw to it that the money he'd provided on December 21 to keep them for three weeks had run out in two, even with careful management.

"One thing," Natalya said. "Any bugger breaks into this flat looking for food's going to be disappointed."

Esther rang the Green Hat to ask for her wages, which hadn't been forthcoming.

Boris was harassed more than she'd ever known him to be. "Esther, it's fucking chaos here. Nick left me without enough to pay all the fucking bills, half the staff are on strike, and if it wasn't for American fucking playboys, I couldn't pay the other half."

"I can't pay the rent, Boris."

"Sorry, Esther."

It was an indication of how bad things were, he said, that the previous night a party of six Americans had feasted off oysters and champagne at the Green Hat on a single dollar. "*And* had change left over. *And* the fuckers tipped in marks."

"Where *is* he, Boris? I thought he was in Saint-Trop'."

"Wasn't warm enough for his latest, apparently. They've fucked off somewhere in North Africa."

Without Nick and his protection, the three women were exposed to the catastrophe that had overtaken the world outside their walls, naked as babies on a hillside.

Frau Schinkel refused to accept anything except currency for the rent. "What do I want with a coat?" They were offering Natalya's second-best, she being the only one of them who possessed two. "Can I eat it? Can I stew it with dumplings?"

"You can if you barter it," Esther said. "I'll do it for you. What do you need?"

"Cash." Frau Schinkel was too old and too respectable to barter; she refused to understand what was happening; she couldn't believe that her widow's pension had disappeared and that the war bonds she'd bought so patriotically in 1916 would never be paid back. Her suspicion that the apartment upstairs was Prince Nick's harem, a seraglio of foreign women no better than they should be and at least one of them Jewish, tainted their articles of clothing for her.

Esther, with great regret—she'd become interested in photography—went to the pawnbroker around the corner with a Leica camera Nick had given her for a birthday and hurried back with money to pay Frau Schinkel, who then hastened with it to the shops. In the time the procedure had taken, prices had gone up—a fact with which the landlady acquainted Esther on her return, ending her diatribe with, "That Herr Hitler has the right idea."

"Vindictive old bitch," Natalya said. "Who *is* Herr Hitler?"

"The man behind all the red posters," Esther said. "He's started a National Socialist Party down in Bavaria."

"What's he stand for?"

"It's more what he stands against, I think. Capitalists, homosexuals, liberals, socialists, and Communists. Oh, and foreigners, especially Jews."

"Good for him," Anna said.

She quailed—for once Esther had turned on her. "You will never say that in my presence again. *Never.* Do you understand?"

"Yes, Esther."

They tried pawning everything that wasn't vital, but most pawnshops had become overstocked and picky.

Esther set up a stall in the road and stood shivering by it for half a day, eventually selling the loathsome hunting prints to a visiting Dane who gave her enough money to enable her to stand in a line for the rest of the day and buy two eggs, which she turned into an omelette for three.

It was Natalya who suffered most. For one thing, it was her bits of costume jewelry that pawnbrokers accepted—the other two had none. For another, the price of cigarettes forced her to give up smoking.

She became increasingly restive and irritable. She blamed Nick "and whatever trollop he's gone off with." She blamed Esther for bad housekeeping. "You'd think a bloody Jew could manage better." And then was sorry. She blamed the czar for causing a revolution, she blamed the Bolsheviks for providing one, she blamed the German government for mishandling the economy, but most of all she blamed Anna Anderson, on whose altar, she'd come to believe, she had sacrificed her career. "I could've been in Hollywood by now if it wasn't for that crackpot."

Surprisingly, Anna bore all the privations with an uncomplaining stoicism that indicated she'd endured worse. She was concentrating on her English lessons, thus leaving Natalya at loose ends, which, illogically, Natalya also resented.

"When are we going to get our hands on all these jewels?" she demanded.

"What jewels?" Esther asked. She was tired and hungry. "There aren't any damn jewels."

"Yes there are." Natalya had been reading yet another magazine article on the Romanovs. Like the barbarian Golden Horde of Tartars from whom they were descended, the czars had encrusted themselves and their relatives with precious stones. There were jewels with names: La Pelegrina pearl, the Orlov diamond, the Polar Star ruby. There were Marie Antoinette's diamond earrings, Catherine the Great's black pearls, diamonds with blood on them, rubies, sapphires set by Cartier, by Fabergé. "Says here the imperial collection was estimated at eighty million dollars."

"The Bolsheviks got them," Esther said.

"The czar would have cached some outside Russia—he wasn't that much of a fool." Natalya, dazzled, her eyes reflecting facets of a thousand gems, saw chests of them waiting to be collected as if from an unclaimed-luggage office.

"And Anna's got the bloody ticket," she said. "We've given it to her. You and me. I want my share, and I want it soon. I can't go on like this."

They were huddled around the stove that had been filled with the last of the coal. There'd been more electricity cuts, and Anna was writing out her English exercises by the light of a candle, a notepad on her knees.

"I'm not going on with it either," Esther said. It was time to say it; she should have said it before.

Natalya looked up. "What's that?"

"I'm pulling out. All of us must pull out. We're hurting too many people."

"Who's it hurting? Her?" Natalya jerked a thumb at Anna. "She loves it."

"It's hurting all of us, her especially. She's sick, and we're colluding with her sickness. I'm not doing it anymore." She thought of the Romanov survivors and their wounds that the fraud would start rebleeding. If you lived with grief long enough, it became lodged so that you could go about your life somehow—she knew that, God, how she knew it—but to be reminded all over again . . .

So even if Anna Anderson had been the real Anastasia, could those who'd loved the grand duchess welcome a disruption to the accommodation they'd made with her death? Probably no more than a real Anastasia could fit herself to *their* lives—a woman in whom the intervening years inevitably wrought change of character and manners and experience of how the real world wagged and what wagged it.

"Anyway," she said, "Anna will never stand up to close inspection, not by those who really knew her. You know that."

"What are you talking?" Anna had heard her name.

Natalya turned on her, using German like a slap. "Esther says you're not going to be the grand duchess no more."

"Am the grand duchess."

"Then tell me that in Russian!" Natalya's arms went up, and she was suddenly screaming. "Fuck it, I'm wasting my life here! I've wasted half a year of my life! Fuck it! *Fuck* it!" They watched her go to her room and slam the door, heard her stomping.

Anna turned to Esther. "What she cry about?"

"Anna, it stops now."

"What?"

"I'm sorry, I apologize, I'm sorry I was ever part of it. I shouldn't have done it to you. It's time to stop, little one. We've all been using you. It's fraud, Anna. At least it isn't now, but it will be. You'll be claiming money under false pretenses, and that's a serious crime. Even if there is a fortune in the Bank of England, you're not going to get it."

"I don't want the money."

It was as calm a statement as Esther had heard her make, and the truest. For a moment, sane eyes looked into hers. Quietly, Esther said, "What *do* you want?"

The moment slipped away. "I am Grand Duchess Anastasia," Anna said.

"Listen to me. Think what your life will be like; the pretense will drive you insane. The Romanovs won't accept you; they won't want to. Be content with being ordinary. We'll stay together, if you want us to. We'll manage, I promise."

"I am not ordinary. Am not *ordinary.*"

Esther gripped her hands. "It won't be fame, it will be notoriety." She struggled for a way to pierce the incomprehension. "Newspapers may carry articles about you, but the Romanovs will refute them, they'll be unkind, they'll make you a laughingstock. Some people may take you up, but the Romanovs won't. They'll never recognize you as Anastasia. Anna, please try to see."

Astonishing violet eyes looked back at her, but what they saw, Esther couldn't tell. She felt a desperate tenderness for this abused creature—and guilt for her own part in abusing it.

"If I am well known, I have a dog," Anna said.

Esther released her hands and let her go.

In her room Natalya was sitting on her bed. Esther sat down next to her. It was very cold; the only light came through the door from the sitting room. "I'm sorry," she said.

"Six months of my life," Natalya said tonelessly. "There's not much left."

"Not much left of what?"

"My life. I'm going to die young, you know." She'd hooped her bedspread over her head and shoulders so that she was completely enwrapped except for nose and mouth. As she spoke, her breath made steam. Esther was reminded of the little charcoal burners' kilns in the Siberian forest.

"Nonsense."

"I am." Natalya's voice had taken on an elegiac quality. "There was an old woman in the village; she saw things. Poor peasants' Rasputin, she was. We were frightened of her, she looked like Baba Yaga, but she had the sight. She told me once, she said I'd be a shooting star, not long in the heavens but bright while I crossed them."

"For God's sake, Nasha."

"Could have been me, couldn't it? He should have chosen me, really. Nick should. Right height, right coloring. I know as much as she does, and I'm a hell of a lot saner."

"Doesn't sound like it." Esther reached out and touched the cold cheek under the quilt. "Come on, lovie. Get to bed. You're tired."

Natalya pointed to her pile of movie magazines. "Did you know Hollywood wants to make a film about Rasputin's killing?"

"Does it?"

"Make a great movie."

"I suppose it would."

"Anastasia coming back from the dead—that'd make a great movie, too."

"Not if she were a fake," Esther said.

"It's all fake. That's what movies are."

The telephone rang. Esther went into the living room to answer it and heard Nick's voice on the other end.

"He's back," she called, putting down the receiver. "And he's got cash, thank God. We can eat again. I'll go and collect it."

"Tonight?" Natalya appeared in the doorway like a pink bear in her bedspread.

"I've got to. We need to get food first thing tomorrow, before the prices go up. He says he can't come over—he's throwing a party for Yusupov at the Green Hat and can't leave."

"Yusupov?"

"Yes, he met him in Paris."

"Prince Felix? The one who killed Rasputin? He's in Berlin?"

"Yusupov?" Anna raised her head from her exercise. "He's a bad man. He put poor Rasputin under the ice."

"Oh, shut up about Rasputin. He was as mad as you are." Natalya was excited. "Esther, that film . . . the one I was telling you about, they want Yusupov to star in it. As himself, like."

"Really." Esther was putting on her coat. Get to the shops early, *very* early, before the lines grew too long. Maybe there'd be meat. . . .

Natalya was still in the doorway. "How well did he know Anastasia?"

"Who?"

"Yusupov."

"Only as a child. The czar banned him after he killed Rasputin."

"He's important, though, isn't he? Prince of the blood and all."

"I suppose. Where's my gloves?" Some vegetables before they sold out . . .

"I'm coming, too," Natalya said. "Wait for me."

"No, stay here."

There was an altercation through the door of the bedroom as Natalya retired into it to get ready. Anna had never been left alone in the flat at night and didn't want to start now. "The Cheka will get me."

"Who cares?" Natalya shouted.

Esther was dubious; she didn't like leaving Anna alone, and she distrusted Natalya's sudden excitement, but Natalya said, "You can't stop me," and Esther could think of no way, short of violence, to do so. She wondered whether she should send the girl to get the money on her own, then doubted whether, in her present mood, she'd come back.

In the end she persuaded a grumbling Frau Schinkel to let Anna sit with her until they returned.

Natalya joined her, carrying her handbag, in her best coat, and with what appeared to be a long skirt beneath it. She had on a pair of shoes.

"What's happened to your boots?"

"These are more comfortable."

It was too cold to talk; they adjusted their scarves over their mouths and walked fast through unlit streets, a wind straight from the steppes blowing on their backs. Herr Hitler's scarlet posters were black in the dark; they seemed to have proliferated.

They could hear the noise and see the lights from the Green Hat as they reached Potsdamer Platz. Flashbulbs were popping. A crowd had gathered outside its big glass doors in two lines to watch people going in. Autograph books were being proffered and signed.

"Oh, my God," Natalya said. "Look who's getting out of that car."

"Who?" The faces were vaguely familiar.

"Ruth Weyher and Fritz Kortner. You remember—*they've been in dozens of films.* And there's Fritz *Lang*. Oh, my God."

Film people. Esther became angry. Nick had found money enough to pull out the stops for Yusupov.

They pushed their way through the crowd, to be barred by a large man in an astrakhan hat and a uniform heavily frogged in gold braid. "Only invited guests," he said. "Oh, hello, Esther."

"Let us in, Gricha, we're on business."

The foyer was full of people handing in their coats and wraps. Esther tapped one of the cloakroom girls on the shoulder. "Where's Nick, Vera?"

"Just gone upstairs."

Esther turned to look for Natalya, found she'd disappeared, and went up.

The gaming room was getting ready for the suckers. Nick was handing out the banks to his croupiers and testing what Esther had always suspected were crooked roulette wheels. "Come for our money, Nick," she said.

"You girls, so mercenary."

"We girls, so hungry."

They went to his office. "How's Mademoiselle Eloise?"

He frowned. "Oh, shit, Esther, wait till I tell you. She is a complete disappointment. Not Bourbon at all. I think she's Mafia. I may *have* to marry her. What do you want? I don't have time, I got a party to throw."

"Money, Nick."

Grumbling, he opened his safe.

She went to the window that gave onto the club's great room, effacing the memory of the night it had been empty by seeing it crowded. A ragtime band was playing the Charleston and couples were dancing, legs kicking, arms swinging. The women were shimmering and angular in their straight, bosomless dresses, long necklaces bouncing, their neat bobs circled by jeweled headbands.

Watching money enjoy itself, wondering where it came from, comparing the glitter of wealth in this heated place to the bleakness of the streets, she recognized faces she'd seen in the newspapers, politicians, actors, actresses. How had Nick come to know these people? And they him?

Oh, hell, she thought with a sudden longing, it may be decadent but it looks fun. "Is Yusupov here?"

"Not yet. He will be; he never misses a party. Met him in Paris, down on his luck like the rest. I'm softening him up. He doesn't know it yet, but one of these days our Prince Felix is going to recognize the grand duchess Anastasia."

She took in a deep breath to tell him a thing or two . . . and let it out again: "Oh, *hell*."

"What?" He joined her at the window.

A figure had walked onto the flickering floor, matte and plain against the surrounding sparkle. The dancers were stopping to look at it, and it was inclining its head graciously toward them.

Natalya had dressed herself in a long skirt and an off-the-shoulder blouse. There was a single string of pearls around her neck; she'd borrowed a kokoshnik from one of the cigarette girls and had scraped her hair back under it, leaving only a fringe.

She looked very young; she looked like the picture that had adorned a hundred thousand postcards; she looked like Anastasia.

Nick picked up a speaking tube. "The girl on the dance floor. Get her up here. Now." Swearing, he began kicking his desk.

She's gone mad, Esther thought. We've sent her mad. She watched Theo and another muscled man in a tuxedo advance on Natalya and speak to her. Natalya smiled, laid her hand elegantly on Theo's proffered arm, and allowed herself to be led away. The band started up again, but the dancers remained in groups, talking.

The office door opened. "Here she is, boss," Theo said. "She was asking for Prince Yusupov, but he ain't here yet."

"Leave her to me."

There was silence. Unwillingly, Esther turned around from the window.

"Well?" Nick asked.

Natalya started to babble. "I can do it, Nick. Look at me. Somebody said 'Anastasia' down there—I heard them. We're wasting time with Anna. She'll never do it; she can't even speak the bloody language. Let me see Yusupov. Just let him look at me; he'll say. I know it all, I was *there,* for saints' sake—she wasn't. I'll do it for you, I can do it. *Look* at me."

"I'm looking," Nick said. He'd sat down on the edge of his desk. He was terrible when he was quiet.

Mascara was smudged below Natalya's eyes. Her short, too-blond hair had fallen out of her kokoshnik and assumed its flapper position on her rouged cheeks. Her eyes were wide and staring; she looked like a rag doll. She began shrieking. "It's bloody done now. They've seen me. I'm not going back. There's a film in it, Nick. Me as Anastasia, back from the dead. Oh, Nick, let me do it. I can *do* it."

"No."

They stared at each other.

"Why not?" asked Natalya, and she sounded reasonable.

"Because Anastasia isn't trash and you are."

Esther moved to Natalya's side, facing Nick. "Leave her alone. It's finished. You started this, and here's how it ends."

"Oh, no it isn't." Natalya's face had wizened with shock. "I'll tell, Nick. I'm Anastasia now, and you say I'm not, and I'll tell the newspapers what we've been doing with that Polish slut in Bismarck Allee these months."

"Oh, yes?" Nick got up. Gathering Natalya in one arm like a friend, he took her to the window. "Look down there, kid. See that fat man in the corner, the one with the floozy in the pink? Biggest publisher in Berlin. And him on the next table? That's the chief of police with the minister of the interior."

He turned Natalya around and put his face close to hers. "The powerful men of Germany are in the Hat tonight, kid, and most of 'em are taking my sweeteners one way or another. Who're they going to believe?"

Yes, Esther thought, I ignored this. Good old Nick, the corrupter. Good old vicious Nick. I didn't want to know. I should have.

"Now, you go home," Nick was saying. "You be a good girl, and maybe I'll forget this." He steered Natalya to the door and opened it. The bouncers were outside. "But one word, one *word,* and I swear on the fucking Bible you'll have no tongue to say another." To the bouncers he said, "Get her coat and one of you take her home."

When she'd gone, he turned back into the room, glaring at Esther. "And what the fuck were you doing bringing her here?"

"Nick, the game's over, whoever you use. It's dirty, and it's damaging those girls, and I'm not playing it anymore. There'll be no Anastasia. I'm stopping it."

"You are?"

"Yes. Try it and I'll do some telling of my own. And I know where the bodies are buried. Income tax, Nick." He stared at her, appalled; she'd used a dirty word: *Einkommensteuer.* "Income tax," she said again, enjoying it. "You can have half the government in your pocket, but you haven't got the Tax Department, and they don't like being bilked."

He picked up a paperweight from his desk, and for a moment she thought he'd throw it at her. Instead he smashed the glass of one of the Braque prints. "That's what I get for employing a fucking Jew."

"That's what you get," Esther said. "And while we're talking money"—she swept up the pile of thousand-mark notes he'd got out of the safe—"this is mine."

Theo was at the door, lumbering from foot to foot. "We lost her, boss. I was getting her coat, and she sort of slipped out—"

"Find her." His fists drummed on the desk. He began hitting it with his head.

Esther tapped him on the shoulder. "Give me your car keys."

He looked up. "What for?"

"She's out there somewhere without a coat. Give me the stinking keys."

"Oh, *fuck* it. Come on."

On the way out, he shouted for Boris to take over. "And if Yusupov comes, give him the real Veuve Clicquot. The bastard knows his champagne. Tell him I'll be back."

The number of people on the pavement had grown, as if the entertainment of seeing the rich and beautiful pass by kept them warm for a while. As had the peasants in Russia, Esther thought. Until they got too cold.

She slunk into the crowd and made her way around its back while Nick kept to the red carpet laid across the pavement, camera flashes flickering on his face.

A woman with a notebook stepped forward. "Prince Nikolai, I'm from *Film News*. Is it true you're backing a movie about the grand duchess Anastasia?"

Suddenly he was surrounded with notebooks. "Is she in there? Is it true she's alive?" "Do you know where she is?" "Where are you hiding her?"

"No comment."

So somebody inside the club had spread the news of Natalya's charade. Esther crossed the road to where Nick parked his car. He'd changed it for a Daimler. She stood for a moment, looking up and down the Platz for Natalya and not seeing her, then slid herself into the front passenger side. Come on. Come *on*.

Still shouting "No comment," he jumped into the driver's seat, started the engine, and slammed the car into gear. "See what the bitch has done now? Fucking press."

"Oh, shut up," she told him. "Bismarck Allee. And quick."

It was a straight run, and Natalya couldn't have covered it in the time. She hadn't gone home.

Opposite number 29, Nick did a violent three-point turn and began going back, facing a few cars that immediately started doing the same. "Shit," he said. "See what you've done? You've put the fucking press on my tail. Where now?"

"The river."

"She wouldn't."

"I don't know what she'll do."

Going slower now, watching the sidewalks, they went to bridges, to the canal, to more bridges. The cars behind them began to lose interest and drop away one by one. Nick was still swearing at them. Esther didn't care whether they followed or didn't. She was studying alleys as they passed, leaning out to look into black water.

Nick was agitating to get back to his party; it was nine o'clock, everybody would have arrived, and him not bloody there. "Shut up," she told him. But the streets were empty and dark; another electricity cut was affecting the whole city. Little flakes of snow showed white in their headlights.

"She'll be home by now," Nick said. "I got to go, Esther. This is hopeless."

It was. "All right, take me back."

As he stopped outside number 29 and she got out, the last remaining car to follow them slowed and then went on down the avenue toward Bismarckstrasse.

Frau Schinkel and Anna were sitting in the downstairs apartment, playing cards by the light of a candle.

"Has Natalya come in?"

She hadn't. Esther thanked the landlady, lit another candle from the supply kept in the hallway, and escorted Anna upstairs. "You away a long time," Anna accused her. "Where you been?"

"Looking for Natalya. We can't find her."

"Maybe the Cheka get her."

The apartment was cold. While Esther went to the cupboard for another candle, Anna took up her old position by the kitchen window. Her shriek shredded the silence and Esther's nerves.

"For God's sake, what is it?"

"He is there."

"Who is?" Esther joined her at the window. Snow came down in little rushes, allowing patches of moonlight. The trees' bare branches threw distorted shadows, none of them human-shaped. The doorway of the bookseller's opposite gaped empty, though Anna, backing away, still pointed at it. She was moaning, "Keep him off, keep him off."

"Keep who off? There's nobody there, lovie."

"Keep him off." Anna kept retreating in terror and moaning.

Esther bolted the door of the apartment. "See? Nobody can get in."

Anna began to chatter. "He's there. He find me again."

"Who has? For God's sake, Anna, you've got to tell me."

"At the asylum. He was there. I see his shadow, his face at the window, always I see it. Like the forest."

Esther sat her down, went and looked out, and then closed the oilcloth curtains. "It was somebody passing. There's no one there now." A reporter, blast him, she thought.

In the candlelight Anna's face was tight with terror. She was muttering. Esther caught the words "forest," "always," and "canal."

She poured a slug of the medicinal-purposes vodka she'd kept for emergencies into a glass for her. "Tell me," she said. Anna shook her head, trying to guide the glass to her mouth with hands that shook so fast they were vibrating.

She'd seen *something*. Esther got up to take another look out the window, waiting for the moon to appear. Still no one there. Had it been real or a phantasm?

Oh, Jesus *Christ*. She hurried into the living room and snatched up her diary. What's the date? With Nick away, she'd lost track. What's the goddamned *date*?

It was January 13.

She did a quick calculation. Six weeks ago would be . . . ?

He was here.

"What you doing?" Anna had followed her, clutching her drink.

"I'm phoning the police." Anna, Clara—the madwomen had been right all along.

"No." Anna snatched the receiver out of her hand, spilling the vodka. "No police."

"Of course the police. What else can we do?"

"Theo. Get Theo. Police . . . they check my papers. They ask questions."

"And about damn time you gave some answers." Esther was afraid and furious. She snatched the phone back and began dialing. "Inspector Bolle, please."

She heard the policeman on the other end of the line call across what sounded like a large and busy room, "Inspector Bolle, off sick, ain't he?" There was a reply. "Sorry, madam, he's not here. This is the desk sergeant. Can I help you?"

She wished she could remember the name of the inspector who'd been kind to her at the Green Hat, but she couldn't; the desk sergeant would have to do.

"Yes. There's a man outside our house." God, she thought, how often had some hysterical woman phoned in with that complaint? She tried to make her voice matter-of-fact. "He's dangerous. I have reason to believe that he's committed murder." Oh, *God,* Esther, can't you put it better than that? What way *was* there to put it?

She glanced toward Anna, but Anna had curled up on the sofa and was holding a cushion over her head and ears as if against bombardment.

"Your name, please. Address?"

She told him.

"Ye-es," said the voice at the other end of the line. She could hear a pen scratching, other voices. "And what's this man's name?"

"I don't know." She said desperately, "He's a big man."

"I see. A . . . big . . . man." More pen scratching. "Who did he murder, madam? And when?"

"A woman called Olga Ratzel. It was . . ." When was it? "It was in September. September ninth or tenth." Four months ago. She could hear her credibility thinning to wispiness, even to herself.

"Ye-es. And he's back again, is he? After you, this time, is he?"

"No, my flatmate. Look, I know it sounds ridiculous, but I'm not making this up. He's outside in the street. My flatmate's just seen him. You could catch him. I can make a statement."

"Is he trying to get in?"

"Not at the moment."

She thought, And he can't, thank God, not unless he's prepared to ax down two solid doors or clamber over garden walls around the back of the house and rise like a vampire to a third-floor window. Nevertheless, she looked down, out the rear window. Snow was beginning to settle, tipping the tops of walls and trash cans as if with an outline of white paint. The thin covering on the yard below was without footprints. "But I want him caught. He's dangerous. Can't you send a patrol?"

"We'll try, madam, but we got a riot at the Brandenburg Gate, half our men's down with the flu, and we're working by candlelight here." He went on, playing to his own gallery. Esther could hear somebody in the background laughing bitterly. "You just lock your door now, and maybe he'll go away."

"That's what I'm afraid of," Esther said. She slammed down the phone. "All right," she yelled at Anna. "We get Theo."

But the Green Hat's line was busy. She waited a moment and tried the number again. Still busy—a jumping night at the club, Saturday.

Dialing and redialing, Esther watched Anna, still crouched on the sofa with the cushion over her head. What the hell is worth all this? she asked herself. Terrified of the hunter who knew who she was, terrified of the police who might find out who she was, the girl was being kept in a suspension of fear by two opposing forces. And Esther with her.

The Green Hat was still busy.

Putting the phone back, Esther went downstairs to tell Frau Schinkel not to open the front door if the bell rang.

Frau Schinkel, who rarely had visitors, especially at this time of night, was aggrieved. "I can't open my own door now?"

"I want to see who it is first."

"We never had this trouble in Berlin until you foreigners came."

Suppressing a desire to point out that several capital cities could have said the same about the Germans during the Great War, Esther went back upstairs and persuaded Anna to go to bed.

"He can't get in. When Theo comes, I'll make sure it's him before I open the door."

The girl had recovered slightly; the cunning was back. "Is the Cheka, you know. They want to kill me."

"Yes, I know. Get to bed."

The compliance with which Anna obeyed was awful, as if Esther were her lone champion against the forces of darkness surrounding them.

Which, at this moment, she was.

She tried ringing the Green Hat again. Still busy. Wrapping herself in a blanket, she sat by the kitchen window, looking down on the deserted sidewalks, watching snow drift gently against the gape of the bookseller's doorway, waiting without hope for the police, waiting for Natalya to come home, responsible for two madwomen. What was I doing to let this happen? Three madwomen . . .

Something woke her, and she ran to the door to open it. "Nasha?" But her voice echoed down into an empty hallway.

She made another failed attempt to get through to the Hat.

In the kitchen Frau Schinkel's wall clock said it was half past ten. "Send her home, God, please."

She settled back by the window and tried concentrating on some plan whereby the three of them could earn their living now that their connection with Nick was severed. Natalya would have to go back to stripping. And little Esther could join a freak show. But that left Anna. Maybe the three of them could make a virtue out of these past months and become a singing group, wear kokoshniks: the Anastasia Sisters. Mileage in that.

This time when she jerked awake, there really was someone at the front door. She heard the key turn. "Nasha?" She leaned over the banister.

"Yes."

She still couldn't see her; Natalya had paused out of sight on the threshold; a draft of cold air came racing up the stairwell, flecks of snow blowing in on Frau Schinkel's brown linoleum. "Where've you been?"

"What?" Natalya sounded preoccupied. "Oh, the Parrot. Saying good-bye. It's closing tomorrow." The front door shut.

Of course. Of *course* she had. "Are you all right?" Maybe she was drunk. Esther started down the stairs. Natalya was still in the doorway, reading something, a letter. Her hair was covered in snow, and she had a man's coat on. Seeing Esther, she put the letter in its pocket. "Yes, I'm all right." She gave a defiant sniff. "Had a nice time, actually. Old friends."

"Where'd you get the coat?"

"Vlad at the Parrot lent it to me. One of the customers left it behind."

They went upstairs together. Natalya *was* drunk, not very much, but so preoccupied that every answer to every question came after a delay. Esther's account of how they'd looked for her, how they'd worried, how they'd been chased by the press, was met with lack of interest.

"And Anna said a man was watching the house."

"There is," Natalya said. "Saw him when I came in. Standing in Ullstein's doorway. Big man."

Oh, God. Esther lifted the curtain. The snow was thick now, obliterating everything. "It's the man who killed Olga. I've been trying to get hold of Theo all night, but there's something wrong with the line. I've rung the police."

"They coming?"

"I doubt it."

"Don't blame 'em. Did you tell 'em your six-week theory?"

"No."

"Of course you didn't," Natalya said. She jerked her head toward the window. "He's a reporter, bound to be. The press followed you, didn't they?" She picked up Anna's glass from the desk, went into the kitchen and filled it with the last of the vodka. She came back, grinning. "Got them interested, didn't I?"

"Oh, the hell with it." Esther was suddenly sick of other women and their troubles; she had enough of her own. Whoever was outside, the bastard could freeze. "I'm going to bed."

The snow fell steadily all night, smothering the city like a soft white hand over its mouth.

Hunger woke Esther up, and she dressed to go out; sometimes on Sundays farmers brought produce from the countryside to sell in the streets. From the window she saw other shoppers with the same idea silently struggling through the snow. A perfect curve of white piled up against the bookseller's doorway showed that no watcher had stood there for some time.

If there ever was one, she thought. Hysteria, that's what it had been. Anna's *and* hers. She was sorry now that she'd called the police; if they should turn up, she'd look like an even bigger fool than she'd sounded on the phone.

She was collared in the hallway by Frau Schinkel. "I won't put up with this, Fräulein. Such a night I've had. Don't answer the door. People going in and out, letters delivered, like it was daytime. I need my sleep. My doctor insists on it."

"What letters?"

"Letters, letters, pushed under the door. Late last night. It was on the mat. I'm not bringing it upstairs with my legs. And Fräulein Tchichagova banging the door as she goes out at midnight—it is unbearable."

"Natalya came in soon after half past ten, Frau Schinkel, quite a suitable hour."

"Am I a liar? She went out again at midnight. Well, nearly it was midnight. I looked at the time—half past eleven."

Esther turned and ran upstairs.

Natalya's room was empty. The man's coat she'd worn the night before was hanging from a hook by the flat's front door. Anna's coat was gone.

She woke Anna up. "Did Nasha tell you she was going out?" She had to pull the covers down and reassure the girl that nobody was outside before she got an answer.

"Maybe the Cheka get her."

"Oh, stop that."

Anna shrugged. "She has a man, maybe."

That could be the answer; it was the most obvious one.

There was no point in ringing the Purple Parrot if it had just closed. Instead she went out foraging, but even the purchase of four large potatoes from a farmer's stall in Cauerstrasse failed to lighten a worry that persisted all day.

She cleaned the flat, gave Anna her English lesson, and then was left with nothing to do but to start reading *War and Peace* for the fourth time.

Snow made a hypnotic, moving curtain outside, turning the room's daylight a dingy yellow. She had to sit by the window to see to read and eventually became so cold she was forced to move.

At five o'clock she tried phoning the Hat to see if anyone there knew any of Natalya's friends. No reply. At six o'clock she called again. She spoke to the hatcheck girl, Mariska, who gave her some telephone numbers. She phoned them all. Nobody had seen Natalya.

She tried Nick. He hadn't seen her, didn't want to. "I am completely finished with the blackmailing bitch," he said.

"I'm worried about her, Nick. She was very strange."

"You tell me?" He hung up.

She heard Frau Schinkel clearing snow in the backyard and went down to help her; together they set a little iron table in the center on which to put a wreath in remembrance of the young Schinkel who'd died of wounds on board the flagship *Seidlitz* during its sea battle with the British at Dogger Bank in 1915.

After that she shoveled snow off the pavement outside the front door. After that she did nothing. The tick of Frau Schinkel's large round clock on the kitchen wall was like a cleaver chopping up the seconds—until it became the click of rifles being cocked.

Dear Christ, she thought, fighting memory, my time has stopped. Other people's years are moving on without me. For the rest of my life, I will be trapped in a moment that has gone.

At ten o'clock she began putting on her coat.

"You don't leave me again." Anna began to breathe fast.

"I've got to find her. There's something wrong."

"You know where to look?"

"No." She took off her coat.

"Dirty girl," Anna said, grinning. "She has a man."

"Maybe." But there was something. . . . It persisted, a perpetual and growing fear.

At three o'clock in the morning, she dialed the police. This time it was a different desk sergeant. He took down Natalya's name and description but was manifestly of Anna's opinion.

Five hours later the phone rang. It was the police. They'd found Natalya.

9

"MAKES A DAMN change, straightforward murder," Sergeant Willi Ritte said as they drove toward Charlottenburg that morning.

Inspector Schmidt agreed that it was. Their last three cases had been political killings, always tricky.

He told Willi to use the klaxon, more to announce a police presence than to clear other cars out of the way. Theirs was virtually the only automobile on the road. No gasoline, no traffic. With tram fare into town costing anything up to ten thousand marks, people with jobs were choosing to walk to them. There was a guilty schadenfreude in being driven through those cold, laboring streets, even if heat from the engine enhanced the smell of Willi's feet, which hadn't recovered from the rot they'd acquired in the war.

Early-morning faces looked tired already from the effort of getting to work through the snow, from the sheer, teeth-gritting awfulness of surviving coalless, inflation-hit days that went on and on, scything the young and the old as they passed.

Everybody thought that the economy had hit bottom in 1922. "Can't get any worse," they'd said.

But 1923 was proving them wrong; this city was suddenly full of gaps—the deserted corner of the street where, until last week, Schmidt always bought his *Berlin Tageblatt* from the elderly newspaper seller, the depleted numbers of children on their way to school.

Willi's driving reflected his fury at it all. "Where's the bloody farmers? That's what I want to know. Where the hell are they?" At this time in the morning, the roads should have been filled with carts and trucks bringing food into the city.

Schmidt sighed at the forthcoming exchange. Willi knew where the farmers were; they were staying on their farms, refusing to sell their produce to shops for worthless paper money or waiting until prices went even higher.

"The wife stood in line for four hours yesterday and got two eggs. And us with five kids. Know how much those eggs cost?"

"Yes."

"Two thousand marks."

"I know."

"Each."

No point in explaining that prices weren't going up but the mark was plummeting down. Willi didn't understand hyperinflation. Schmidt didn't understand it himself. "We lost the war, Willi."

"We were fucking stabbed in the back, that's what we were." Willi subscribed to the view that if it hadn't been for "the enemy within"—that is, Communists and other revolutionaries—Germany would have won.

Schmidt had long decided Willi had been in another war altogether. "We lost the war, Sergeant," he said. "We just lost it." And the Ruhr, and all the German colonies, and the Rhine ports—everything that would make it possible to pay the reparations demanded by the victors. They were still demanding them, nevertheless. Who was it had said Germany was being squeezed until the pips squeaked? Damn right, whoever he was.

"Know who I blame, boss?"

"Yes."

"The fucking kikes."

He'd had to stop being angry with Willi at this or he'd have been angry with half the population, including his own wife. Willi was by no means the worst offender; the fact that the middleweight boxer Finkelstein was a Jew didn't stop Willi being his greatest fan and cheering him from the ringside. But in bewildering times people reverted to the simplicity of the Middle Ages. They needed someone to blame—and Jews, the old, old scapegoat, fitted the bill. They were different, they were here. Inflation? Fucking kikes. Bad harvest? Fucking kikes. It was easy.

He'd been lucky. He'd had Ikey Wolff in his regiment; a man like Ikey changed your perceptions. Wearily, he said, "It wasn't the fucking kikes. We were on the wrong fucking side, Willi—like we are now, so shut up and look where you're going."

There'd been birdseed for his breakfast.

"What the hell's this stuff?"

"It's porridge," Hannelore had said. "I made it out of birdseed. It was all the grocer had in his shop. It's not too awful, is it?"

"It tastes like the birds ate it first." Then he was sorry and ate it up; Hannelore had stood in line even for this, which wasn't good for either her or the baby she was expecting. Her first pregnancy had ended in miscarriage.

The gaps in the soles of his shoes were going to let in snow the moment he set foot in the Charlottenburg Gardens. He thanked God for his overcoat . . . well, not God. He thanked Thompson, J., for that—the poor bloody British lieutenant he'd stripped it off when he found the man's corpse lying in a shell hole at Passchendaele in 1917. A good coat, that. The maker's name, Burberry, was sewn into the lining along with the name Thompson, J.

There were times when he felt closer to Thompson, J., than anybody else. It had been like that on the Western Front; only those fighting—German, French, or British—had known the atrocity that war was. Everyone else was a bunch of *tricoteuses* knitting around the fucking guillotine.

It was a relief to draw up outside the Charlottenburg with this straightforward murder to investigate instead of trying to make sense of it all.

In the distance the schloss was a domed confectionary of spun sugar. The white covering on the expanse of its lawns rose here and there in perfect simulation of some statue beneath. Local flatfeet were gathered around something halfway up an avenue of trees where trampled snow suggested they'd been clog dancing.

"Willi, tell those morons to stand still."

Willi strode toward the uniforms, bellowing, "Freeze, you varmints." Willi marched like a soldier but got his vocabulary from cowboy films.

And the plaintive, "We *are* freezing, Sergeant." But the damage was done—footprints all over the damn place.

They'd dug the snow off most of her. One of the uniforms said, "Don't reckon she was buried, sir, not deliberate like. Killer cut her throat and left her, and she got covered natural. Arnie, that's the gardener here, he just saw a mound where there shouldn't have been. No sign she'd been dug in like."

"When was that?"

"This morning, early. She could have been here two days, judging from the snow over her. Weather was too bad for Arnie to do his rounds yesterday."

"Dinter, is it?"

"Yes, sir." Dinter's round face was happy at the recognition. "Worked with you on that business in Wedding, sir."

"I remember. That's intelligent guessing, Dinter." No need, in that case, to get exercised about the murderer's footprints; there wouldn't be any. They'd have been obliterated by the snow that had covered the body at the same time.

"Thank you, sir." Dinter was emboldened. "And reckon we know who she is. Foreigner." He consulted his notebook. "Terchichagova, something like that. Russian. Reported missing 0300 hours this morning. Answers the description. Fair-haired. Twenty-two years."

She lay in a sort of snow coffin in the avenue of beeches that led eventually to the schloss. Nothing else, just her and the snow and the trees.

"Whore killing, don't you reckon, sir?"

Very neat, apart from the stain that had leaked out of her throat. Very quiet. The silence the dead imposed was reinforced by the park's frozen stillness and the snow-muffled rattle of traffic in the distance.

Could be a prostitute. But her skirt was long—and it was a funny place to take a customer for hanky-panky in the depth of winter.

Summertime, now, there were copulating couples as thick as dandelions here, but in this temperature a man'd get icicles on it.

And she was tidy. Murdered prostitutes weren't usually tidy.

He bent down and lifted the ice-stiff skirt to peek up and under. He heard Dinter excusing the action to the others. "We have to do that, see. Find out if they've got their knickers on."

She had. Cami-knickers—unstained and untorn.

She lay on her front, arms straight by her sides, nose buried in the snow beneath, suggesting she'd been dead before she hit the ground. The toes of her shoes were squeezed forward, leaving the soles and heels sticking up at right angles, indicating the same thing. Schmidt thought how anonymous she looked. A tight-fitting black cloche covered her hair. The coat with its cheap fur collar gave no clue to the shape of her body apart from the fact that it was slim. She might have been a shop-window dummy that somebody had abandoned in the snow.

Not rape, then. He wondered if she'd met her attacker face-to-face or whether the bastard had waited in the trees to cut the throat of any woman who passed by. Unlikely. Only an optimistic killer expected a victim to visit the gardens in this weather.

"Has she been moved?"

"She's exact as we found her."

He knelt down and laid his cheek against the snow to peer at her neck. A wide blue eye stared appallingly back at him. A strand of dyed fair hair had escaped from the cloche hat and lay across her cheek. The incision began deep on the left-hand side and petered out toward the right.

So the killer had cut her with the knife in his right hand while holding her up with his left. His retaining arm would have been saturated with her blood, most of which now formed a congealed black mass down what Schmidt could see of her front. Stains in the snow they'd shoveled off her showed where blood had spurted farther.

Yes, he'd cut her throat and let her drop and gone away, both of them disappearing—he through the falling snow, she under it.

Twenty-two years old; she wasn't going to get any older.

Schmidt got up. "What makes you think she's a prostitute, Dinter?"

"It's the area for them. And look at them fingernails."

He'd seen them, little arcs of scarlet berries curled in the snow.

"And"—Dinter lowered his voice—"that underwear, sir. Not what respectable women wear."

Undoubtedly pink satin cami-knicks, silk stockings, and suspenders with silk roses on them wouldn't be what Frau Dinter wore. Old Germany didn't approve of them, or painted fingernails. Some archbishop had condemned them and short skirts as the devil's invitation to sin. Schmidt had once shocked Hannelore by buying her a pair of cami-knickers, though she'd subsequently loved them.

The woman could be a pro, except most of them saved time by not wearing knickers at all when they were working, but she could also be any one of the factory girls or secretaries now to be found in every capital in Europe.

"Where'd she live?"

Dinter went back to his notebook. "Bismarck Allee."

"Bismarck Allee?" Not a whore's address.

He'd have liked the knife and a handbag but decided not to dig around anymore until the police surgeon had seen her.

"On his way, boss," Willi said. They'd worked as a team too long not to know what the other was thinking.

A policeman came up from the gate. "Sir, there's a woman. Reported a friend missing. Says we phoned and told her to come. Wants to see the body."

"*Did* you tell her to come, Dinter?"

Aware he'd exceeded his authority, Dinter was flustered. "Seeing as we needed an identification quick as we could and—"

"And they're only foreigners." Strange, Schmidt thought. Dinter, not an unkind man, wouldn't consider letting a Berlin girl look at a murdered body until it had been tidied up in a mortuary, but he was prepared to inflict the sight on a non-German. "Go and tell her to wait, Willi."

Dr. Pieck arrived, stepping high over the snow like a thin black heron. As always he was in top hat, tailcoat, and striped trousers, no overcoat, the opinion of his staff being that he was too bloodless to notice cold. A good forensics man.

"Morning, Herr Doctor. Don't worry about footprints—nobody else has."

"Good morning, Inspector." Pieck put his bag down. "Now, then, young woman, what's up with you?"

He always addressed his bodies like living patients, a habit Schmidt found unnerving. Schmidt told him what he could and left him to it; he never liked watching the insertion of the thermometer, that ultimate indignity. He went down to the gate.

Willi met him, identity papers in hand, rolling his eyes. "You know this one, boss. Remember that Russian kike with the scar last year? At the Green Hat? The one that talked like she was the kaiser's missus? Still does."

He'd never forgotten her.

"Bit of a coincidence, ain't it, boss? And you like coincidences."

He did; in crime they were usually not coincidences at all.

Schmidt took the papers and walked over to where a figure dressed much like the one lying in the snow stood by the gate. She'd been lodged in his memory as extraordinary, but even as he wondered if she still would be, his policeman's eye marked the fact that she wore the same sort of hat, the same dark, long coat as the dead woman; another window dummy, only this time upright. Very upright.

She had her hands in her pockets, looking toward the schloss and away from the cluster of activity around the thing among the trees.

She was in profile as he approached her noiselessly across the snow, the late-dawn sun gilding the left side of her face like an Egyptian queen's, and once again he thought, She's beautiful, and then she heard him approach and turned.

"We've met before, Fräulein."

She could have arranged her hat or her hair to hide some of the mess that was the other side of her face, but she hadn't. She didn't even care if you pitied her; you could if you liked, but why bother? What other people thought about her didn't interest Fräulein Solomonova; what concerned her was the body in the avenue. Very blue, very intelligent, and very driven eyes stared into his. She didn't look Jewish, but what was Jewish? Ikey Wolff had been redheaded with freckles.

There were no preliminaries. "I must know," she said.

"Describe your friend, please."

"My age, about as tall as me, blond, pretty."

"Did she have a handbag with her?"

"I don't . . . yes, it's gone from her room."

Schmidt looked down at the papers in his hand. Solomonova would be twenty-two in June; she looked older. "It seems likely," he said. "I'm sorry."

He saw her hands grip in her pockets. "I heard somebody say it was murder."

"I'm afraid so."

He had to catch her arm as whatever had been holding her up went out of her. He said, "We'll do the rest of this in the car."

He guided her through the gates and into the passenger seat of the Audi. Before he got in with her, he told Willi, "When the doctor's finished, start looking for the weapon. And the handbag."

"Okay, boss."

"And see if somebody can produce a hot drink for the Fräulein." He turned on the engine so that she could be warm.

Reaching for his tin of Manoli, he wondered if he should offer her one. These were his last; his tobacconist had run out. After this he'd be puffing leaves. It had been the Yuletide joke: *Where's the Christmas tree, Father? Sorry, my dears, I smoked it.*

"Cigarette?"

She shook her head, good girl.

He lit up, giving her time, and wound down his window a crack to let the smoke out. "Now, then, Fräulein, who is she?" As he sat next to her, the Audi's right-hand drive presented him with the scarred side of her face.

"Natalya Tchichagova, Russian. We share an apartment—29c Bismarck Allee."

Name and number, Schmidt thought. As lucid as she'd been last time. This woman's been interrogated before; a Russian Jew would be used to it.

"Single?"

"Yes." Her voice was deep and her German excellent, but the slight Russian accent that was usually dramatic—in his experience most Russians could make "pass the salt" sound soulful—issued from Fräulein Solomonova's mouth with the bleakness of the steppes.

"When did she go missing?"

The scar tightened as she tried to concentrate. "Two nights ago. She went out on Saturday night. She went out . . . eleven-thirtyish, I think. Our landlady heard her. And she didn't come home."

"And that was unusual? Not to come home?"

"Yes." Still concentrating, she added, "She's never done it before."

"But you didn't report it until the early hours of this morning, Monday."

"No." She put the heel of her hand against her forehead and rubbed it. "One always hopes there's an explanation, a boyfriend or something."

"And was there one? A boyfriend?"

"Not to my knowledge."

"So why didn't you contact the police right away when she failed to return the first night?"

"I thought she'd come back. I called everybody I could think of—"

"You have a phone in the apartment?"

"Yes."

"Where did Fräulein Tchichagova work?"

"She used to be an exotic dancer."

Read "stripper," he thought. "Where?"

"At the Purple Parrot." The answers were coming mechanically now; she was staring into a void.

He loved inconsistencies—they always led somewhere. A stripper living in bourgeois-solid Bismarck Allee? And with a telephone? He'd bet there weren't many phones installed even in that area. And for the first time, Solomonova had referred to the dead woman in the past. She *used to be* an exotic dancer but wasn't when she died.

"And you, Fräulein? Do you still work for Potrovskov?"

"I am still Prince Nikolai's secretary."

"I thought you lived in Moabit." Hell, he thought, I remember everything about her.

"Prince Nikolai rents the flat for us."

So that's how she could afford Bismarck Allee. Schmidt had checked with the Vice boys after his last encounter with Prince bloody Nikolai. *A crook, with a bigger harem than a fucking sultan,* they'd said. So Solomonova was his moll after all; probably the dead woman, too.

"Anybody else live there?"

"Another friend, Anna Anderson."

"Scandinavian?"

Pause. "Russian."

It *was* a bloody harem. He was disappointed; he'd thought better of this one. She didn't stack up as a loose woman; the scar for one thing, too respectably dressed for another, too well spoken, and Willi was right: shocked, grieving, she still had the self-possession of the upper class. On the other hand, she was wary of him—which, if she were in a racket with that shyster, she would be.

Time to use the whip. "Who killed your friend, Fräulein?"

"I don't know," Esther said, and heard the lie resonate in her head.

In all the shock and the grief, terror had been her first reaction—terror for Anna. Hide her, he's found us. Before anything else, hide her. He's out there.

She'd phoned Nick at home, waking him up. He'd had trouble grasping it. *"Natalya?"*

"Yes."

"You been drinking, Esther?"

"I've got to go and identify her. I'm going to tell them everything, but first you've got to get Anna away. Take her abroad, anywhere. He was here, the man who's been watching her. He was here on Saturday night. He killed Natalya."

"Why? You sure it was him?"

"Yes."

"I completely don't know anything about this."

"I know you don't."

"Murder. Holy God, it could ruin me. I can grease palms against most everything, but *murder.*"

"Nick."

"Okay, okay, I'll see to it. Listen, Esther, don't say anything. Give me a couple of hours to get her away, and then we'll see."

"Just do it."

Then she'd gone downstairs to Frau Schinkel and virtually hauled the woman up to 29c. "Something terrible has happened. I've got to go out. Stay here and don't open the door to anybody unless it's me or Prince Nick, not a crack, do you hear me?"

She'd managed to frighten Frau Schinkel. "Do we call the police?"

"They know."

In the street, people were going to work. Shopkeepers were sweeping snow from their sidewalks. It's Monday, she'd thought, surprised at the banality of time's persistence. He doesn't kill on Mondays. Then she thought, I can't rely on it. Anna can't rely on it.

Housewives were setting up stalls to sell their possessions on the roadside; she'd done that, a million years ago. The everydayness of things shifted her mind into a no-man's-land between hope and awful certainty. Perhaps it isn't her. Natalya wouldn't go to Charlottenburg. Why would she? Natalya's preference was to go east, toward the city, where she felt at home; Charlottenburg's quiet gardens weren't Nasha's thing.

Yet at the same time, she knew it was Natalya they'd found, because it was the answer, the hideous logic of the fear that had attended her for two days, for months.

She knew when she saw the little crowd gathered at the gates to the park, had slowed because she knew. Almost strolled toward them, not wanting to know. And been slammed with confirmation, again and again, her head like a boxer's being rocked back and forth as a woman told her, "They say it's a foreign girl." Somebody else: "One of them blondes from the east." And a policeman not letting her go and see. And the terrible little group among the trees.

Ice. Not feeling anything really; metallic lips answering questions as if somebody else pulled the lever that moved them. Sure of only one thing: Anna must be got away. Once the story was out, the delay would be extensive, the questions, the disbelief attendant on her answers, the "don't leave town," the reporters, photographers. Anna'd be exposed to people going in and out—and one of them a man with a knife. A man who was ubiquitous and, it seemed to Esther, with a longer arm than the police.

So now she said again to the police inspector, "I don't know." And thought, Tomorrow. I'll tell you tomorrow. Then she said, "What did he do to her? She wasn't . . . tortured?"

He wondered if that was a euphemism for rape. "Her throat was cut. It was very quick. If it's any comfort, I don't think he interfered with her."

"I see," she said.

"Did she have any money in her purse?"

"No." He saw her lip twist. Even in Bismarck Allee, nobody had money anymore.

He said, "Why do you think she came to these gardens?" It was unlikely she'd been carried here to be killed. Either she'd walked here with her murderer or she'd come on her own.

"I don't know." That at least was true. Warmer now. The man beside her was thawing her with kindness. He'd put a hot drink in her hands. She turned in her seat to look at him; very ordinary, very German, hair the color of dishwater, mustache ditto, somehow familiar.

He said, "Fräulein, the last time we met was at the Green Hat when you were attacked. Do you remember?"

She nodded; she did now.

"I mistrust coincidence. You must tell me if there is a connection."

She temporized. "What?"

The stupidity of shock, Schmidt thought. They weren't going to get anything out of her until it had passed off.

Willi was tapping on the window. "Dr. Pieck's finishing up, boss," he said. "The ambulance is here. And there's this." He'd put gloves on and was holding up a handbag, shaking it free of snow.

"Is this your friend's?" Schmidt asked.

At once Natalya was dead. The moment that comes, delayed but unavoidable, arrived with an imitation-crocodile handbag, her second-best because the best was pawned, slightly scuffed around the clip, held in somebody else's official hand. Natalya joined the roll call of those who would never answer to their name again.

As he leaned over to reach for the evidence bag in the backseat, Schmidt's arm touched Fräulein Solomonova's shoulder. She was shaking. He took the cup out of her hand before she spilled it. "Are you up to identifying her?"

She nodded.

"We can do it later, if you'd rather."

"Now," she said.

They were bringing the sheeted body to the gates on an old army stretcher. He got out of the car to turn back the sheet, exposing the face but covering the throat. Dr. Pieck had closed the eyes.

She looked calm and very young, and, as always, Schmidt felt the surge of not just anger but astonishment at the effrontery and ease with which one person could erase the teeming complexity of life in another. He beckoned Solomonova, and she came over, hands in her pockets. He knew it was to stop them from trembling, but it looked casual. So did her glance down at the body.

"Yes," she said without tone. "That is Natalya Tchichagova."

Schmidt heard Willi shuffle; Willi liked tears at this point. Bloody kikes, Willi would be thinking.

"Take her home," Schmidt told him. "I'll see her later. And, Willi . . ."

"Yes, boss."

"Look after her."

10

HE HAD THE usual game with Dr. Pieck. "Just give me an idea, Albrecht. I won't take it down in evidence."

The doctor's thin nose whiffled with enjoyment. "If pressed, I should say that someone who is right-handed, and considerably taller than our victim, cut her throat."

"Oh-thank-you-Doctor. What with?"

"A knife."

"And I thought it was rhubarb." His shoes were letting the snow in. "What sort of knife?"

"On the record? I have no idea as yet. Off the record? No idea either. It might have been a trench knife. I'm not saying it *was,* but the cut indicates something of that curved shape. And I thought I got a whiff of cold bluing when I sniffed her neck. We'll see what the microscope shows."

"That's my boy. *Dinter.*"

"Yes, Inspector?" Dinter stopped shoveling snow and put his hand to his lumbar region.

"It's probably a trench knife." Pieck knew his war wounds; he'd been an army surgeon.

"Yes, sir." Dinter relayed the information to the other uniforms and went back to shoveling.

Schmidt returned to Dr. Pieck. "When?"

"Do you mean at what time did death occur?"

"Come on, Albrecht, I'm getting bloody cold."

"My dear Siegfried, it is *because* you are cold that I am unable to venture a viable opinion as yet. The external temperature, you see, has affected the usual postmortem processes."

"Yesterday? The day before yesterday?"

"Forty-eight hours. Possibly longer."

"Gratis tibi maximus, Pieckus."

The doctor bowed. *"Principus placuisse vivis non ultima laus est."* It was their little joke.

Schmidt took Willi with him to the schloss and in the kitchen interviewed the caretaker, learning nothing that he didn't know already; Arnie had seen nobody hanging about. He'd stayed indoors, out of the snow.

It was warm in the kitchen and Mrs. Arnie was offering coffee, so they took the opportunity to examine the contents of Natalya's handbag, spreading them out on a long pine table that had become grooved with Mrs. Arnie's scrubbing.

A cheap powder compact; a worn-down orange lipstick; a white, neatly ironed handkerchief; a knitted purse containing a thousand marks—of less value as monetary exchange than the handkerchief; a comb. Nothing of value, but all of it scrupulously clean.

And a note. There was a doubled piece of blue writing paper tucked into a pocket in the bag's faux-silk lining.

Schmidt teased it out with gloved fingers and flipped it open.

"I can authenticate you. Come to Charlottenburg Schloss at midnight, but come alone, no prompters." It was signed *"Prince Yusupov."* No date.

He handed it to Willi.

"What's it mean, boss?"

"I don't know, but it brought her here on Saturday night."

Willi said, "Yusupov, Yusupov? Only Yusupov I ever heard of was the Russki as shoved that Rasputin under the ice."

"Only one I ever heard of as well." *God,* he loved this. Some men stalked deer over the mountains; he stalked mysteries—and this was a ten-point-antlered beauty.

He took the note back from Willi. The paper was the sort sold in a million stationery shops. Writing: a careful sloping hand, light on upstrokes, heavy on downstrokes, as taught in a million schools.

"She was lured," he said. "He was waiting for her."

No envelope, a pity. She'd left it at home, maybe.

On the way back, he stopped beside a sweating Dinter. "Sergeant, I want you and your boys to knock on every door of every road in the vicinity and find out who was walking or driving around them on Saturday night, especially between the hours of ten and midnight."

Was he right? He became the man he was tracking. Dinter, watching him, saw the inspector's eyes dull and the sense go out of his face; he wondered if the man was having a mild fit.

I'm carrying my knife to the rendezvous. I'm going to kill her. I can't wait long in the grounds—too cold—therefore I shan't arrive too long before her. But I'm nervous that she'll be early. Do I have a car? Too noticeable, too traceable, too loud. I'm on foot, so I'll walk around, letting the snow camouflage me, turn me white. . . .

"Yep," he said, briskly. "Between ten and midnight, Saturday. Concentrate on the pedestrians. All right, Dinter?"

"Yes, sir. This digging for the weapon, sir . . . there's acres."

"I don't know why you're bothering. He took it home with him. If he dropped anything, we'll have to wait for the thaw. Good man, get on with it."

Typical bloody *Geheimpolizistkommissar,* Dinter thought, watching him go. *Took it home with him.* And us digging up half Charlottenburg for it. No thought for poor buggers in uniform and their backs. And knock on every door in the vicinity. In this weather. Typical Alexanderplatz, the creeps.

Before he did anything else, Schmidt went back to the Alexanderplatz to have lunch. He needed to do some research. And you didn't pass up a hot meal—not when you'd had birdseed for breakfast.

Since Willi'd taken the car, he had to walk, but he liked walking, and the feet of those going to work had cleared the pavements for him.

Thinking of his wife, he went into every food shop he saw on the way that didn't have a line outside it, asking for whatever they had and being told that the reason there wasn't a line outside was that they didn't have anything.

Usually he strode the streets of Berlin like a landlord; it was his city. He boasted that, even if he were blindfolded, his nose and ears would tell him where he was—heated, rich air issuing from the hotels in the Friedrichstrasse, automobiles passing the Brandenburg Gate puffing exhaust fumes, the stink of blood and the lowing from the abattoirs of the Thaerstrasse, the milky churning of Bolle's dairy in Moabit, green smells from the forests and the lakes, lime and coal dust from the barges chugging up the canals—but it wasn't really true. It was always changing. This was a town that kept you on your toes. Turn your back a minute and, wallop, they'd torn something down and something else was going up in its place. No dignified sense of history here like they said there was in Paris or London. In Berlin history kept happening: Napoleon came and went again. Kaisers flattened elegant eighteenth-century buildings to put up monstrosities to their own glory, but the last kaiser and his war hadn't been glorious, merely monstrous, and Berlin had revolted.

Schmidt had missed most of the revolution; on leaving the army, he'd gone down to Bavaria to get married. He'd brought his bride back to a different Berlin. The kaiser had gone, and a government that believed in liberation had come in. Buildings had disappeared, streets had altered.

He'd loved it all the more. The place where East met West, the heart of a railway and waterway system that went out to the world and brought it in. A great stew of a city. French Huguenots, Viennese Jews, Bohemian Protestants, Wends, Poles, Hungarians, Romanians, Russians—they'd all hopped into the pot to escape persecution at home, adding variety to the stock—and staying. When Napoleon occupied the city, the Huguenots had resisted his blandishments to join him. "We are Berliners," they said. "We want to remain Berliners."

Somebody'd once said Berlin wasn't a city, it was a situation. And Berliners were good at coping with situations. Terrible things happened to them, but after they were over, the Berliners settled back to doing what they were good at: eating, drinking, working, and making little Berliners. Basically, for all its variation, it was a mundane city—which, a mundane man himself, was what Schmidt liked about it.

But it's being tried too hard, he thought. Today its people were gray from fatigue under a grayer sky threatening more snow. A piano was being lowered from a third-floor window onto a cart below, watched by a little girl in tears. Middle-class housewives wrapped in shawls were setting up tables on the sidewalks to sell their possessions. Outside the Quakers' and Salvation Army's soup kitchens, well-dressed elderly men and women waited in line with tramps.

Tempers were as sharp as the cold. Exchanges between buyers and sellers were shouted; a couple of men tussled over a bag of coal. From the open door of a café came steam and the sound of an altercation over a cup of coffee that had been five thousand marks when it was ordered and eight thousand by the time it was drunk.

And probably, he thought as he passed, it wasn't even real coffee. Not even acorn ersatz. Nowadays ersatz was ersatz-ersatz.

A statue of Frederick William I lacked its nameplate, as did every other statue in the Tiergarten—brass could be exchanged for potatoes. The British embassy had complained to Alexanderplatz headquarters that not even its illustrious name had been spared.

Farther along the street, a group of wing-collared businessmen were despairingly pointing out to a policeman that the roof of their office building had been stripped of lead. Burglaries and theft had doubled, street crime trebled. Violence between the Communists and the extreme right wing was an everyday event. This, in what had once been one of the most law-abiding capitals in Europe.

It's not crime, he thought, it's desperation. It's what happened when the basket you carried your wages home in was worth more than the currency inside it. And what the hell was the government doing about it, apart from printing more and more paper money? The million-mark note was expected any day.

When he thought of Hannelore and the little Schmidt she carried inside her and the nourishment they should both be getting and weren't, he wanted to kill—he just didn't know whom.

God send us a leader who knows what he's doing.

The Communists thought they'd found one; the usual pictures of Lenin were pasted up on walls everywhere under signs saying it was verboten to stick bills. But the posters that really caught the eye were bloodred with a huge and hinged black cross. He regretted the adoption of the swastika, that symbol of light, by the National Socialist German Workers' Party; now it was the trademark for a bunch of gorillas whose only idea of spreading light was to make holes in the heads of those who didn't agree with them. He didn't like the vicious little shit who'd become their leader either. Eye-catching, though, he gave them that; the poster seemed to drag the only color in the city into itself.

Still, whatever happened, whatever government came into power, policemen like him had to be paid and fed—not much, not well, but enough. Children could become malnourished, old people die of cold, the middle class's pensions, insurance, and savings be wiped away, but if the police didn't survive, neither did the government.

The canteen was crowded and steamy with drying cloaks, thick with cigarette smoke. One of the liberal reforms introduced by the Weimar Republic had been to do away with the old headquarters' segregated dining rooms that had provided varying comfort according to rank, and replace them with a vast hall in which inspectors of the Kriminal-Abteilung, like himself, even higher commissioners, were expected to eat in fraternal companionship alongside beat-pounding, uniformed Schutzmannschaft.

Nobody liked it. The place had been tiled in the public-urinal school of design; it was noisy and uncomfortable. The lower orders were constrained by the presence of officers; officers, mostly ex–military men, hated having to eat like ordinary mortals in front of their subordinates. The food was bad and getting worse.

However, at a time when Germany was starving, when a third of the population was unemployed, a third on strike, and a third having to take their pay partly in potatoes, it didn't do to be picky.

He fought his way through the crush to the counter. "What we got today?"

An officer of the Fraud Squad nodded gloomily at a vast shape behind the counter. "She says it's hare stew, but I just heard it bark."

"Dumplings," Schmidt said winningly. "Nobody makes dumplings like you, Rosa. I'll have three."

"You'll have two." Rosa was one of only five women employed at headquarters, all of them, so it was said, chosen for their ability to tear men's arms off. "And you'll eat them here." She pointed her ladle at a sign saying it was verboten to carry food off the premises. Men had been taking it home to their families.

He carried his plate to a table occupied by a group of Meldewesen, the division in charge of immigrants and refugees, and insinuated his chair between two of them. "This taste as bad as it smells?"

"Worse."

After a period of communal, reflective chewing, he said, "Otto, any Yusupovs in Berlin just now?"

"Two." Otto Steiber knew his lists like a housewife knew her grocery cupboard. "Yusupov, Felix, and Yusupov, Irina. Prince and Princess respectively. Renting number 42 Pariser Platz. Three-week visas each."

"So he *is* in Berlin. What's he doing here?"

"Officially, he's visiting friends." Steiber spread out his napkin on the table and forked a piece of meat onto it. "That's not hare. That look like hare to you?"

"No." Schmidt did the same with his. "And unofficially?"

"Unofficially he's here to see his lawyers. Some Yusupov jewels from his czarist days have surfaced in town. He's claiming they're his; the Soviet government says they belong to the proletariat." Steiber folded up the meat in the napkin and put it in his pocket. "The courts will have to decide whether they belong to a fucking assassin or the fucking Bolsheviks—and good luck to 'em. What's your interest?"

"His name's come up in an inquiry. I need to see him."

"Keep me informed. And keep your back to the wall." Steiber crooked his left hand on his hip and flirted the fingers of his right in the air.

"One of them, is he?"

"Duckie, he invented it."

"Otto, while we're about it, what have you got on Prince Nick Potrovskov?"

Steiber laid down his fork. "Am I to be allowed to eat this meal in peace?"

"Do you want to?"

"Probably not. Well, then, Prince Nick . . . Arrived in Berlin five years ago without a rag to his ass. Now owns three nightclubs here and another in Hamburg. We've got him down as an illegal dealer in foreign currency, he's on the Vice Squad's books as a procurer, Customs' as a source of stolen passports, while the Fraud Squad's looking hard at his tax returns, and all any of us have pinned on him is a breach of fire regulations."

"A real prince?"

"Just some bloody jumped-up lieutenant out of the Cossack army with an eye to the main chance."

"How does he get away with it?"

"His clubs provide spare-time activities for the rich—and that includes Reich ministers. The bastard's got friends in high places with low tastes."

Schmidt folded up his napkin with the saved meat and one of the dumplings in it, put it in his pocket, and went upstairs to his office to start writing his report.

Willi joined him. "You ought to see the kike's flat in Bismarck Allee, boss. Massive. Real wages of sin, it is. And there's me and my missus and the kids with hardly a place to park our butts."

"Was she all right?"

"Didn't say much. Thanked me when I made her some tea."

Schmidt brought him up to date.

Willi rubbed his hands together. "Getting good, this. A regular Hans Christian Andersen, this is shaping up to be."

Complete with Snow Queen, Schmidt thought. "What do you think, Sergeant?" He liked Willi's opinions, often in order to compare his own, sometimes as entertainment. Usually the foreigner did it.

"Yusupov," Willi said immediately. "He's our man."

"So he murdered Natalya, did he?"

"Yep. He's in town. Our Natalya's trying to sell some jewels she smuggled out of Russia but doesn't know how. Contacts Yusupov. Little Felix says he'll authenticate them, meet me tonight at the schloss. He says they're mine, she says finders keepers, and—*schlipp*—bye-bye, Natalya."

"Hmm. The note said, 'I will authenticate you.' *You*. A person, not jewels."

"Slip of the pen. Bad grammar." Willi liked his script and was running with it. "We know he's a killer. Did he use a knife on Rasputin?"

"Can't remember. Poisoned him first, I think, shot him, then battered his skull in and shoved him under the ice. Took a bit of getting rid of, did Rasputin."

"What did he get for it? Yusupov?"

"Got off free, I believe."

"Fucking Russkis," Willi said. "Boss, let's go get him. Think of the publicity. I can see the headlines now: 'Murderer of Mad Monk Strikes Again.' Pictures of the arresting officers, Inspector Schmidt and Sergeant Ritte, looking stern but modest."

"Bismarck Allee first." If Yusupov was their man, the case against him would have to be watertight. The six years since the Russian Revolution had done nothing to abate interest in the Romanovs or the peasant monk believed to have been their evil genius—nor the man who'd assassinated him. Yusupov attracted publicity like a dog did fleas, and he was quick to bring actions when he considered himself libeled or slandered. A wrongful arrest didn't bear thinking about.

Willi was still speculating. "Or it could have been that Prince Nick forged Yusupov's name. If he was keeping three women in sin in one flat, he was asking for trouble; Natalya's jealous of the other two, gets the goods on his nefarious activities, threatens to tell—*schlipp*—bye-bye, Natalya."

"A happy thought." Schmidt liked it. However, the same applied; everything to be done by proper procedure.

On the way to Bismarck Allee, he made Willi stop at the dairy around the corner from Alexanderplatz but came out empty handed.

"Trying to find some milk for Hannelore," he said, getting back in.

"How far gone is she now?" Willi, father of five, was an expert on gynecology.

"Four months."

"Should be getting plenty of milk."

"I know."

"Listen, boss . . ."

"What?"

"Nothing." Willi drove on.

They stopped again at a taxi stand in Friedrichstrasse, where Schmidt got out and walked down the line to the fourth cab. The driver was smoking and reading the *Sovremennye Zapiski*.

"Good afternoon, Count."

Count Chodsko, formerly of the czar's Imperial Guard, leaped out and opened the passenger door with a loud "The Linden, sir? Yes, sir," and a hissed "Sacred God, get in."

Imprecations from drivers at the head of the line followed them as they drove off. Chodsko replied with finger gestures. He yelled at Schmidt over his shoulder, "Do I put up a sign? Paul Chodsko is a police informer? You want my balls before my compatriots cut them off?"

"Keep 'em. But I need what you know about Prince Yusupov." He'd found it useful to have his own contacts among the White Russians in Berlin, independent of the Meldewesen's, just as he did among all the other émigré communities; Chodsko owed him his cab license.

The count knew a great deal about Prince Yusupov, all of it scurrilous and most of it involving removing his hands from the steering wheel to clutch his hair.

"And a woman called Natalya Tchichagova. Know her?"

"No."

"Esther Solomonova?"

"A Zhid? I know nothing of Zhids. Zhids are all our misfortunes."

"Badly scarred on the right side of her face."

Chodsko said reluctantly, "Sometime I see freak at the Green Hat. She is Prince Nikolai's woman, I think. He has thousand. You pay me for ride?"

"No."

"Shit. Try look like American. Only American *touristi* afford cabs nowadays."

"What'd the Russki say?" Willi asked when he got back.

"He blames Yusupov for the revolution. He says if the bastard had killed Rasputin more quietly, or if the czar had punished him properly . . . and on and on. Anyway, it was all Felix's fault. He's a bum-licking, ass-fucking, skirt-wearing lizard, slippery enough to go down sewer pipes, only stopping to bugger the rats on the way—and that's the edited version."

"Them Russians," Willi said admiringly. "How'd they learn good German so quick?"

"And he says Yusupov was at a party at the Green Hat on Saturday night."

"How does he know?"

"He was there. The vodka was free. Prince Nick was there, too. Who, according to Chodsko, *did* leave at one point—just after he'd had a row with a girl. And that girl very much answers the description of Fräulein Tchichagova."

"Lovely," Willi said.

"He kill her? He kill Natalya?"

"Somebody did. They don't know who. Sit down, lovie."

But Anna was rushing around the flat, almost skipping in her panic, trying to push a cupboard against the door to the stairs, failing, and instead grabbing a chair and inserting its back under the handle. She turned on Esther. "I do not stay here tonight. You tell Nick get me somewhere safe."

"I have."

"And dog."

"Yes. I promise, I *promise*."

There was no time to dwell on why it was Natalya who'd been killed. He hadn't tortured her to get Anna's address as he had Olga—hadn't needed to; he'd known it, had waited outside it. Well, she could puzzle out the impenetrable once Anna was safe.

The girl's fear was horrible; the conviction that she'd be next drained the blood from the area around her mouth, leaving it so white as to be clownish.

Esther made her sit down. "You've got to tell me who he is. Now you've *got* to tell me."

"Cheka, it was Cheka."

Shit.

She phoned Nick. "Where the hell are you? Why aren't you here?"

"I'm seeing to it, I'm seeing to it. I'll be there in a minute. Listen, Esther. When did it happen?"

"Saturday night, I suppose. I don't know, I don't *know.*"

"But *after* the scene she made in the Hat?"

"For God's sake, *of course.* How could she make it if she were dead?"

She heard an exhalation of breath down the wire. "I completely got alibis for every minute from ten-thirty. Big names. Thank you, God."

There was something refreshingly stabilizing about his self-absorption; curiously, she felt better for it. "You're a rock of undependability, Nick," she said. "Just get around here. And bring a dog."

11

THE FRONT DOOR to 29 Bismarck Allee was opened to Schmidt and Willi by a lady who impressed them both by her marked resemblance to General Ludendorff. Despite the cold of the hall they stepped into, she was fanning herself.

"Is it true? About Fräulein Tchichagova?" she demanded.

"It seems so, madam."

"Foreign women. I'd never have taken foreign women in, but with times so hard . . . I should have known it would bring bad luck."

Schmidt went upstairs. It hadn't exactly been good luck for Fräulein Tchichagova either.

Solomonova had gained poise now and invited them into the apartment like guests. She lit the stove immediately and motioned them to chairs near it. A small plate of cubed bread with a dish of salt, the traditional Russian offering to a visitor, was placed on a side table for them; so were two glasses of tea. The bread was stale, the tea leaves so few that they barely colored the water, but obviously hospitality must be extended to all callers, even the police.

Her skinny frame was padded out with sweaters, the top one being a man's that hung down to her hips over a thick, embroidered felt skirt, its sleeves impeding her hands. Bouncy fairish hair was tied back with string. On her feet were overlarge, very worn fur boots. As she moved about, the dim light caught first one side of her face and then the other, like an old movie flickering back and forth between two different people.

Willi, Schmidt noticed, thanked her politely for each attention.

A typical nineteenth-century Berlin *Zimmer,* this, very like his own, the long, corridor-like salon running to the back of the house where a single window gave onto a courtyard, other rooms leading off it at right angles. At this end he and Willi occupied two easy chairs opposite a sofa. At the other end, to catch the light from the window, were an upright chair and a cheap desk with a telephone, a typewriter, and a Dictaphone.

As an abode of kept women, it was disappointing; close up, apart from the secretarial equipment, the contents showed disguised penury. Whiter patches on the whitewashed walls indicated that paintings had gone to the pawnbroker's. Bookshelves had swelled the fire, as had his own; books were in neat piles on the floor.

In fact, Willi's apartment was only a little smaller than this one, and the reason he and his family couldn't park their butts, his inspector always thought, was that they couldn't find the chairs. A nice and loving woman, Frau Ritte, but one with an un-German belief in clutter.

When they were settled, Solomonova sat on the sofa opposite them, back straight, hands in her lap. Willi got out his notebook, Schmidt opened his mouth, but it was Solomonova who took over, like an army officer presenting a report.

"There was a man watching this house on Saturday night," she said. "I didn't see him, but Anna did. Natalya saw him also. A big man, she said, though she gave no other description. Anna was frightened when she glimpsed him standing in the doorway across the road. I rang the police, but they were busy, they didn't come."

Esther didn't want to go into the matter of Olga's murder—that would be another thing for tomorrow—but, presumably, they would have been told about her call to the police, so she had to mention it.

Damn, *damn,* they hadn't. She saw Schmidt exchange an interrogative glance with his sergeant and the sergeant give a slight shake of his head.

Schmidt said, "Had either of them seen this man before?"

"Natalya hadn't. Anna is always frightened of strangers. She had a mental breakdown sometime ago. She's very frail."

She's hiding something, Schmidt thought.

The books piled by the wall indicated that someone in the apartment read several languages. He spied two ragged copies of *War and Peace,* one in Russian, one in German. *Das Kapital, Lettres de Mon Moulin,* a *History of England* by somebody-or-other, lots of Shakespeare in German and English, and the same edition of Virgil's *Eclogues* and *Georgics* that he kept by his bed.

Don't get charmed, he told himself, she's in this up to her neck. She's lying to you, Schmidt. Then he thought, Not actual lies, more *suppressio veri* than *suggestio falsi.*

"Let's start from the beginning, shall we?" he said. "Which is: Why did Potrovskov set the three of you up in this flat?"

She replied to every question lucidly, very kaiser's-missus, but she was just answering, not proffering information.

The prince, apparently, had rescued a fellow Russian he'd been told about, from an asylum where she did not belong.

"Very philanthropic of him," Schmidt said. "And Fräulein Tchichagova?"

Natalya had been brought in as a companion to Fräulein Anderson. Another act of philanthropy by Prince Nick, apparently. No, the other two girls in the flat had not been working. Natalya was between appointments as an exotic dancer, and Anna was still too frail to have a job. The only person employed in the household was Solomonova. "I work from here," she said.

"Doing what?"

"Secretarial stuff—translating, mainly. The prince has a lot of international dealings."

I bet he has, Schmidt thought. "Do you entertain men here?"

"No." She treated it like all the other questions: no indignation, no protestation.

Willi made a note on his pad: check with the landlady.

"Tell me what happened on Saturday, Fräulein."

She went through the events of Saturday. ". . . and then Natalya and I went to the Green Hat to collect our wages—"

"Where Natalya quarreled with Prince Nick," Schmidt said.

That surprised her; she lifted her head to stare at him.

"I have my sources," he said. "What was it about?"

"She was upset. Prince Nikolai was closing down the Purple Parrot. She wanted another job, which he couldn't give her."

"So there was a quarrel."

"Yes. She ran away. The prince and I went looking for her. We didn't find her. Prince Nikolai went back to his party. I came home to wait for her."

They went into timing—when Potrovskov had returned to the party, when Natalya had returned to 29c, when she'd gone out again. . . .

Prince Nick was qualifying nicely as the killer. He'd quarreled with the victim a few hours before she disappeared, he was a nasty piece of work. The fact that Chodsko had him back at the party well before Natalya had made her brief return to Bismarck Allee and that, again according to Chodsko, the bastard hadn't left it for the rest of the night, Schmidt was discounting. Who knew at parties? People came and went. . . . Anyway, they only had Solomonova's word for it that Natalya *did* return to 29c after the quarrel.

"Did Fräulein Tchichagova receive a letter on Saturday?"

"No. She never received letters."

He fished out his tin of Manoli and took his time lighting up. "I have reason to think that Fräulein Tchichagova got a letter on Saturday."

"No," she said. Then certainty left her. "Wait, yes, perhaps she did. When she came back that night, she was in the hall. . . . I looked over the banister. . . . She put a piece of paper in her pocket. A letter . . . Frau Schinkel complained about it being delivered so late. . . ." She was shaken now. "Oh, God, was it on her? Has it something to do . . . ?"

"Check the time, Sergeant."

Willi closed his notebook and went downstairs to Frau Schinkel.

At his going, the atmosphere changed.

"If you think it's Nick, you're wrong," she said, leaning forward. "I must make you believe it wasn't him. He's all sorts, but—and this is true—he wouldn't murder Natalya. Why would he send a letter? Can I see it?"

"Do you know Prince Felix Yusupov?"

She shrugged, puzzled. "Every Russian knows of Yusupov."

"Did Natalya know him?"

"No." There was almost a smile. "She didn't move in his circles."

"Why aren't you telling me everything?"

"I'm telling you what I can."

They were using shortcuts; it was like the resumption of a long and intimate acquaintance. Solomonova, surprised, drew back. Schmidt thought, Fuck it.

He said, "I'll see Fräulein Anderson now, if you please."

"She's very frail. You can't depend on what she says," Esther told him. She prayed: Please, Anna, don't play the grand duchess, not today.

Schmidt was waiting. She got up. "I'll go and fetch her."

Thank you, but he didn't want Fräulein Anderson prepared. The note to Natalya had said something similar: *"No prompters."* He followed her down the room.

A scuffle from behind the door as Solomonova tapped on it suggested that Fräulein Anderson had been listening at her side of the keyhole. He doubted if she'd been able to hear much; it was a long room and a small keyhole. Solomonova said, "Anna, the police want to talk to you."

A voice said, "I do not see them. I am ill. Send them away."

"You must, Anna. Unlock the door."

"No."

Schmidt said tonelessly, "Unlock the door, Fräulein."

The key turned. Putting out a hand to stop Solomonova from going in, he said, "While I'm questioning her, I want you to make a statement to my colleague when he comes back. Times, dates, biographical details."

"She is frail," Solomonova said again.

"I'll leave the door open."

The room was almost dark, its only light concentrated around a triptych with a single candle illuminating its autumnal reds and golds.

Stumbling over obstructions, Schmidt went to the window and pulled back the curtains, an action that revealed the untidiest room he'd ever seen. In contrast to the rest of the apartment, which was scrubbed and polished, this was heaped with discarded clothing, newspapers and magazines, dirty coffee cups and plates, hairbrushes, cosmetics, stuffed dolls, wadded-up bits of paper, books and photographs—all suggesting a substratum awaiting archaeological exploration. Frau Ritte's rooms were nothing compared to this. At least hers were clean; this smelled frowsty. He'd seen more ordered places after a burglary.

In the middle of it, perched on a crumpled bed clutching a teddy-bear pajama case, was—as Solomonova had promised—a frail young woman. Height five foot three or four, slim, blue eyes. About the same age as the other women, early twenties. But whereas Solomonova was grown up, Anderson displayed the vulnerability of a baby chimpanzee taken from its mother and seemed smaller. Big eyes, violet smudges, stared at him with an agonized hostility.

"Papers, Fräulein."

She looked around the chaos, helplessly. "I do not know—"

"Find them."

For a moment she didn't move, and then, happy thought, unzipped the pajama case, delved into it, and handed the documents over.

Yes, he thought, cracked, but not too cracked to use it.

She was Anna Anderson, Russian, born Peterhof June 5, 1901. Like Solomonova, she had been granted unlimited stay in Germany.

She watched him study the papers. "I do not like police," she said.

He looked around for a chair, found one, and tipped its contents onto the bed before sitting down opposite her at arm's length. "You want to help me find out who killed poor Natalya, don't you?"

"Silly Natalya. She should not go out in the dark."

"Very silly," he agreed. "Who do you think killed her?"

She looked down at the pajama case, stroking it. "I do not know."

"Was it the man who was watching the flat?"

That frightened her. "I do not see a man."

"Yes you did. Natalya saw him, too. Was it Prince Yusupov?"

Somehow that let her off the hook. She nodded. "Yes, Yusupov. Yusupov would like to kill me."

So she thought she was the intended victim. "Why?"

"Assassinate me, like he do Rasputin."

"Why?"

She shrugged.

He gave himself some time to think, and she let him. She sat still and very upright, and yet the wonderful eyes, always moving from one object to another, sometimes sulky, sometimes interested, gave an effect of extreme animation, as if she were jumping about the room.

He didn't know enough about Eastern accents to pinpoint hers but it had a different intonation from Solomonova's. During their exchange through the door, she and Solomonova had spoken to each other in German, not Russian.

Why did she think the man watching the flat was after her? And while that could be paranoia—and was almost certainly so in this little lady's case—it could also be the truth. But it was Natalya who'd died.

"We should have dog," she said. "I have told to Esther we must have dog. She say no, we cannot afford." She leaned closer to him, in confidence. "She is Jew. Is mean Jew. Dog would keep away Cheka."

"Cheka?"

"Cheka," she said, impatient, "secret police of Bolsheviki. They wish to assassinate me."

"Really?"

That was two politically opposed forces out to get her—Yusupov and the Cheka. Frail? It was like interviewing a veering bloody weathervane. But she could help if she wanted to; she was hiding something—both damn women were hiding something.

"Does Prince Nikolai treat you well?"

"Yes," she said grudgingly. "But he should give me dog."

"How long have you known him?"

"I have no memory," she said. "I was ill long time. In hospital—Esther will tell you."

"Before that?"

"I have no memory," she said. She was quite happy about it.

"Who is the man you saw watching this apartment?"

"I saw no man."

The hell with it. He said gently, "We've got to catch him, Fräulein. You must help me, because if it's you he's after, he'll try again."

The violet eyes of the woman opposite widened. So did her mouth; out of it came a squawk, then a monotonous scream: "Esther, Esther, Esther, Esther, Esther, Esther, Esther."

Solomonova came running, pushing past him to gather up the woman on the bed, rocking her like a baby and hiding her from him.

Somebody standing in the doorway said, "The interrogation is over, don't you think, Inspector?" The man came forward, smiling, right hand outstretched, voice raised over the screams. "Prince Nikolai Potrovskov, at your service."

When Schmidt didn't shake his hand, he laid it instead on Anderson's head. "Enough, Anna."

The screaming stopped. Anderson's face emerged, turned toward him. "They try to assassinate me, Nikolai."

"Anna, it is *enough.*" The rebuke was gentle but firm. The woman nodded, cast a glance at Schmidt, and returned her head to Solomonova's bosom. "I am a great friend of your chief of police, Inspector," Potrovskov said.

"Yes, sir, you were when we met before." He followed the man into the living room; Anderson had terminated the interview in her own individual way. Well, it hadn't been going anywhere.

"We've met before?"

You damn well know we have; Prince Nick was playing games.

Long black cashmere coat draped over one shoulder—a style affected in the moving pictures by John Barrymore, one of Hannelore's favorite film stars. Prince Nick was never going to be a favorite of Hannelore's husband.

Willi said apologetically, "I'm sorry, sir, he had a key."

"But of course," Potrovskov said. "I do not live here myself, but I have properties I avail to my compatriots in need. When I hear—*heard*—of poor Natalya, I drive at once to comfort these ladies, to share their grief. She was one of my employees, you know."

He looked as if he was bearing up. He sat himself on a chair near the stove, crossed one beautifully trousered leg over another, and produced a cigarette case. "Do sit down. Smoke, gentlemen?"

Black Russian cigarettes, fat and aromatic, lay in a row behind the gold elastic.

"No thank you." Schmidt stayed standing.

Willi, who'd been about to take one, desisted.

"It is true, then? Natalya was murdered?"

"When did you last see her, Herr Potrovskov?"

"Esther." Prince Nick raised his voice. "When did I last see Natalya? I have been away."

"Let's not piss about, sir. You saw her on Saturday evening, and you quarreled. What about?"

"Ah." Potrovskov blew a double stream of Sobranie smoke out of his nostrils. "Money, I think. . . . Always it is money with employees." His eyes went thin. "When was Natalya killed? After ten o'clock on Saturday?"

"Possibly." Damned if he gave this bugger information.

"Then I have alibis. Completely fifty alibis, and your chief is one of them. They will say I did not leave the Green Hat from around nine-thirty until next day. I give a party for Prince Felix Yusupov and his wife, Princess Irina. You know them?"

"No."

"Prince Yusupov left about midnight—he go on to another of my nightclubs with some friends, the Pink Parasol. Princess Irina stay—*stayed*—on at the Green Hat. Good party. Is on until dawn. I completely do not leave it, not once."

"We'll check, sir." But, screw it, he probably hadn't. The man was a type, a racketeer, a swerver under and around the law. The inflation was throwing them up: Germans, Russians, Poles, Jews—brilliant opportunists of misfortune. The armaments industry was full of men whose wealth had been made from their skill in turning the human body into shredded flesh without being murderers according to the law. Vicious, but not vicious enough to do their own killing.

"My sergeant will take a statement, Herr Potrovskov. When we've checked it, you can come down to Alexanderplatz headquarters and sign it."

He took Willi to the far end of the room. "Anything?"

"The old girl saw a letter on the mat; it'd been pushed through the slot. She's not sure of the time, but it was before Natalya got back, so the girl must have picked it up then."

"Was it in an envelope?"

"Yes. Addressed to Anderson, she thinks. Just her first name, Anna—only longer."

"Longer?"

"That's what the old girl said, boss. She doesn't remember very well. The letter wasn't for her, and that's all she was bothered about."

"Have a look for the envelope in the wastepaper baskets. And question Potrovskov till he sweats."

"Pleasure, boss. Oh, and they ain't had any men visitors—only His Highness and some tough from the Green Hat who was called in for protection once when they was nervous."

"Nervous, were they? All right."

Schmidt went back to Solomonova. "I'll see Fräulein Tchichagova's room now, if you please."

He switched on its overhead light, which had been covered with pink paper to give an impression of warmth but left the bulk of the room in shadow. The comparison with Anderson's bedroom was compelling; this one had the bone-dry neatness of a nun's cell, except that the hook from where rosary beads might have hung was decorated with a frilly garter. Corners of bedcovers were tucked in with right-angled precision, the braided mat on the floor was parallel to the washstand. A side table held a framed photograph that marched alongside an icon in cheap, well-polished brass.

From behind him, in the living room, he could hear Potrovskov painting a picture of the dead girl. ". . . nice, very gay, very willing, very pretty, well raised. . . . Yes, White Russian. She escape the revolution with nothing. I find her in rags, very poor. Gave her job."

Willi's voice: "Another of your aristocrats?"

"No, no. Serving class. But I am liberal man."

"Where did she work in Russia?"

Well done, Willi. Keep asking questions; look for a disparity in the answers.

Schmidt took up the photograph. An elderly-looking man and

woman stared stolidly back at him, both of them in embroidered tunics. "'Serving class,'" he said.

A voice behind him said, "Her parents." Solomonova was watching him from the shadows of the doorway.

"Where was it taken?"

"Czarskoe Selo. It was one of the czar's palaces, near St. Petersburg."

"They worked there?" He put the photograph back in its place.

"Yes."

"What did they think of their daughter becoming a stripper?"

"She left them behind to come to Berlin after the revolution. She hasn't heard from them since. They're probably dead."

"And your parents?"

"The same," she said.

He said, "I thought you were Jewish. The revolution was supposed to liberate the Jews."

"Jews, Gentiles, we all died in Russia." And after a minute, "Were you in the war?"

"Western Front," he said.

"Then you know chaos."

"Yes." What the hell was this connection between them? He wanted to be angry with her; she was yanking him about; they were all yanking him about.

He opened the table's drawer. Natalya had made partitions for it. One held makeup, nail polish, and a vicious-looking crimping iron. A second contained neatly ironed handkerchiefs, another a packet of letters secured with a rubber band. He riffled through the packet—no envelope—then put it in his pocket.

In the wardrobe were a pair of boots and a pair of scuffed high-heeled shoes. She'd worn her best pair to go and get killed in. A box held clean underwear, garter belt, and rolled stockings, a bit of nonsense with breast pieces consisting of spangles and tassels, and a matching bespangled, betasseled something to cover the pubic area.

"Did she like stripping?" In these times women were being compelled into professions, mostly the oldest, to feed their families.

"Yes, but what she wanted was to be a film star."

"Any other relatives?"

"No."

"Fiancé? Lover?"

"Not since I've known her."

He grunted. The letters in his pocket would tell him more.

The few clothes hanging on the wardrobe rail indicated a jaunty but careful owner: a woolen two-piece dress with a collar of faux fur, a blouse and skirt and a feather boa, all of them covered with tissue paper.

"Was she happy?"

There was a pause. "She was ambitious, which made her discontented, but yes, on the whole she was a happy person. A nice one."

He turned around. She was not weeping—perhaps she couldn't weep—but the eyes were desolate; she'd cared for Natalya Tchichagova.

He got down on his knees to peer under the bed.

"What are you looking for?"

"An envelope." It wasn't here; maybe she'd put it in the stove. Well, the fact that she'd got rid of it was significant.

"Can I see this letter?" Solomonova asked.

"No." It was with the fingerprint boys.

"Can't you tell me what it said?"

He turned on her. "I'll tell you what it *did,* Fräulein." He was angry enough now, in Natalya's room where she'd looked forward to a future, in a fucking flat where nobody was helping him find out why she wasn't going to have it. "I'll tell you what it did for your nice, happy friend. It lured her out into the snow so that she could be killed. 'Come to Charlottenburg,' it said, 'I can authenticate you. Come alone. *No prompters.*' It was signed 'Prince Yusupov.' And Yusupov, or whoever it was, waited for her. And got her. Held her up and sliced her neck and chucked her into the snow like a cabbage stalk."

She was very still. The good side of her face had whitened so that, in the bad light, she appeared to be wearing half a mask.

"'Authenticate you,'" he shouted at her. "Authenticate who? For what?"

She said something he didn't hear.

"Who wrote it? Yusupov? Potrovskov?" He was still shouting.

The mask flickered; she was shaking her head.

"Jesus," he said. "You're still going to tell me you don't know."

"I don't," she said.

He pushed past her, out into the living room, and took up a position by the window to listen to Willi's questions and Potrovskov's answers.

In the courtyard below, he could just see the shape of a wreath laid on the snow. Somebody in the tenement was marking the anniversary of a war death. In his own building, he and Hannelore and the rest of the tenants had contributed to a wreath like that in remembrance of their landlord's son who'd died on the Somme. At one time there'd been a wreath in nearly every courtyard in Berlin, but they were rarer now; people were forgetting. Or couldn't afford them.

Potrovskov was talking rapidly: what a shock, what a crime, so young, so pretty, so good a performer. "Everyone love her."

The man worked hard at his German, which was not as exact as Solomonova's but fluent, and with a twang of American. Everything about Potrovskov was nearly perfect—but not quite. The smooth hair was a little too brilliantined, his suiting cut too close to his slim body, the diamond cravat pin too big, the spats over his shoes too white—everything just the wrong side of the line separating sophistication from ostentation.

". . . the reason for the party, sir?"

"Noblesse oblige, Sergeant, noblesse oblige. What would you? Once the second-richest man in Russia, now poor Felix needs my charity."

"She have any enemies?"

"No, no, everybody love Natalya. Everybody." He called down the room to Solomonova. "That's right, Esther, uh? We all love Natalya. A popular girl."

Schmidt raised his voice. "I want a full account of her background. And Anna Anderson's."

"Anna's?" Potrovskov was unfazed. "But we don't know it. She has no memory. I rescue her from an asylum. Before that her past . . ." He spread his hands. "A blank."

Schmidt was sick of it; they were wasting his goddamn time. "That'll do for now, Willi. All three of you to report to Alexanderplatz tomorrow."

Potrovskov, it appeared, was staying. He bade them good-bye, smiling, with one arm around Solomonova's shoulders. He'd been declaring ownership of the apartment and everything in it since he came in.

Solomonova broke away to show them downstairs to the front door, and while Willi scraped ice off the car's windshield, Schmidt lingered in the hallway, watching her. He was reminded of a soldier. She had the detachment of an army veteran, the apartness he'd seen in men who'd survived the war. As if, at some time in her life, she'd looked on hell.

In which case we both have, he thought. For him the partition between ordinary life and what he'd seen at the front had taken years to melt; he'd watched people on the other side of it busying themselves with trivialities, worrying about what was proper, what was not, whether our Gretchen behaved herself, opening their mouths and making no sense. Some survivors adapted quickly, others had gone mad and were still finding better company in the lunatic asylums.

He said, "He's out there, still breathing and, for all I know, getting ready to do it again. Why don't you mind?"

"Give me until tomorrow," she said.

The Ludendorff woman with her hair in curling papers came out of the ground-floor flat, the smell of cabbage soup emerging with her. "Is that you, Fräulein Solomonova? This is terrible about Fräulein Natalya. This is a respectable house— Oh." She'd caught sight of Schmidt. "Well . . . please to shut that door. Are we to freeze to death?"

Schmidt shut the door and stayed inside it as staccato grumbling, in which the word "Jew" was audible, faded back into the apartment. He looked at Solomonova for a reaction; there wasn't one. She's used to it, he thought.

On impulse he said, "What happened to you?"

She pointed to her face. "This?"

"That," he said. "Everything."

"It was a pogrom," she said.

She opened the door for him. On the front steps, he paused again, angry. "Why the hell are you with a man like Potrovskov?"

Her head went up, and he expected her to make a defense, tell him how hard it was for women like her to make a living in today's Germany.

"Because every now and again he fucks me," she said, and shut the door.

Willi was warming up the engine. "Fucking foreigners," he said. "See the ring on that bloodsucker's finger? Bastard. Feed my family for the next three years, that could. Reckon he did it, boss?"

"Afraid not, Willi."

Somebody tapped on the window. Schmidt wound it down, and General Ludendorff's head inserted itself, curling papers, and the smell of cabbage soup into the car. "That letter," it said, "now I remember the name on the envelope. I thought it was for Fräulein Anderson because it was like her first name, but longer."

"Yes?"

"It was Anastasia."

"Thank you, madam," Schmidt said, and meant it. "Thank you very much."

"I always wish to help the police."

"Thank you." He wound the window up.

"Anastasia," Willi said. "Mean anything to you, boss?"

"It's beginning to."

Upstairs, Nick had dropped the assurance he'd assumed for the police and was panicking. He was on the phone.

"Baron von Kleist, please. Tell him it's Prince Nikolaevich Potrovskov." He covered the mouthpiece. "We're getting rid of her right away, if not sooner. . . . Baron? Potrovskov. We met at the— . . . That's right. I believe you hear from a Frau Clara Peuthert on a certain matter. . . . That's right. Yes, oh, yes, I am convinced. You will have no doubt. . . . Well, tonight, if you wish. Eight o'clock? I inform Her Imperial Highness." He put the receiver down, laid his head back, and closed his eyes. "Thank you, God."

"Who's Baron von Kleist?" Esther asked.

"One of Crazy Clara's correspondents. She's got him interested in our princess. I'm taking her to his place tonight—with luck I'll offload her." He passed both hands over his smooth hair. "Murder. If the papers get hold of it . . . Holy Mary, it could ruin me." He sat up. "Get me a drink."

"We haven't any. Can von Kleist protect her?"

"Sure." He patted his pockets, brought out a hip flask, and took a deep swig from it. "Who was it, Esther? Who killed her?"

"The man at the Hat. He's grown." She'd thought of him as elemental, some vicious, primary thing from nature that had pincered itself to them. But he'd enlarged, as if a single organism had multiplied, becoming complex, sophisticated. And patient.

God, the patience. Losing them, finding them again, finding *out.* He'd learned everything, written the note knowing it would tempt. Luring Anna. Always Anna. Come and be authenticated. Come into my parlor, come into the snow. But Natalya had read it first and had been lured in Anna's stead.

The scene returned to Esther, like a clip of film being replayed—herself on the landing, Natalya down in the hall having returned from the Purple Parrot, reading something. The delay before she came upstairs and, when she *did* come upstairs, the paper she'd put in her pocket.

Damn you, Nasha. Why didn't you show it to me? Why did you believe it? I could have told you it wasn't Yusupov—real princes don't sign themselves "Prince."

But Natalya, the state she was in, had believed it. Seen her chance to usurp Anna. Gone to answer it.

Why did he kill her? Why did he have to kill her?

She realized she'd spoken out loud because, Nick said, "I don't know, do I? And I'm not getting involved. If it's Anna he's after, he can get her at von Kleist's, not here."

"Goddamn you, Nick. I want her protected."

"She will be, she will be."

She took the flask out of his hand, went with it to the kitchen, and poured them both a drink. As she handed him his, she said, "Tomorrow I'm going to tell the inspector the truth about Anna. Every single thing I know."

"You can't do that."

"I have to. The killer knows. He's found it out bit by bit." Every six weeks, she thought. The patience. The persistence. The terrifying intelligence. She told Nick about the note. "It was meant for Anna. 'I will authenticate you.' Somebody talked. He worked it out. He knew where to come, what to write. Somebody told him about Anastasia. The police have got to be informed; they can trace him."

"Couldn't have been Yusupov, could it?"

"Of course it wasn't." She sipped the brandy, watching him figure the odds.

"After all," he said eventually, "what can you tell him? What have I done wrong? I hear Grand Duchess Anastasia Romanov is in a loony bin, and I rescue her. I've supported her cause—in which I most *completely* believe, by the way. Fed the woman, clothed her, provided her with companions."

She nodded. "You've done all that."

"I come well out of it, don't I?"

"You do."

"A fact you'll point out to the inspector?"

"Yes."

He began tapping his teeth. "Is she word-perfect yet?"

"As much as she'll ever be."

"I *do* believe in her, you know. And others will. The good baron's lapping it up already. By God, she'll owe me when she claims her fortune." The tooth tapping increased. "Trouble is, she might forget. . . . I need insurance. We don't want the lady overlooking my contribution when she comes into her own."

Esther thought, He's still going to go on with it. The brandy was making her head swim; she realized she hadn't eaten all day, and neither had Anna. "You promise she'll be safe with the von Kleists?"

"Sure, they got money, servants, bodyguards. Important people. Friends with the Grand Duke of Hesse. I'll tell them she's a Cheka target—they'll be thrilled." He wiped his hands on his handkerchief. "She couldn't be safer in Fort Knox."

As long as they believe she's Anastasia, Esther thought.

Nick said, "Maybe I should get her to sign a contract before I hand her over. What d'you think?"

Esther hauled herself to her feet. "I think she should have something to eat before she goes." She turned around. "Did you get her a dog?"

"Sure, I got her a dog. It's in the car." He went downstairs to fetch it.

Esther put potato soup on to warm, then went to Anna's room and told her about the von Kleists.

"Good family," Anna said calmly. "They are in the Almanack."

"Yes. Listen, Anna, they know the Grand Duke of Hesse."

"My uncle Ernest Ludwig," Anna said obediently.

"Yes. There's something you can say about Uncle Ernest. . . . Anna, if you feel safe with the Kleists, you must stay with them. Try not to be awkward."

It had come to this. Until the maniac was caught, it was imperative that Anna should prove her credentials as the grand duchess. She could retain the interest and therefore the protection of those dazzled by royalty only while they believed her to be Anastasia. If they didn't, difficult as she was, they'd drop her—and leave her vulnerable to the killer. Providing her with special information to help her imposture, what Nick called "a clincher," might be dubious morally, but it would keep her alive.

"During the war Uncle Ernest of Hesse— Are you listening to me, Anna?"

"Yes."

"In 1916 he made a secret visit to Russia, to try to get his sister and the czar to leave Russia or at least negotiate a separate peace with the kaiser."

"In 1916?" Anna frowned. "Russia and Germany at war with each other."

"Exactly. It's not something he would want known, but he did it—and the imperial family met him. It'll make him believe you are Anastasia."

"You know this?"

Esther patted her head. "Jews are international. They know a lot of things."

Nick was in the doorway. "Look what Uncle Nicky's brought his Anastasia." He had something in his arms.

"Good God," Esther said. "Is that the best you can do?" It was a Pekingese, one of the smallest she'd ever seen.

"The town's out of wolfhounds," he said. "It was short notice."

"It's a short dog."

"Costs like a wolfhound," Nick said. "Pisses like one. All over my upholstery."

Anna was transported. She opened her arms to take the dog, and for the first time Esther saw her happy.

When they'd packed for her, she was driven away into the night, too absorbed to lift her face from the dog's fur to wave.

"God bless you, Anna." Esther stood on the steps, watching until the car's taillight had disappeared.

Turning back into the hallway, she thought of the words with which she'd seen the police inspector off the premises. She knew why she'd said them; he was the man she'd dreaded meeting all her life, the intruder, the sweet last straw under which she'd sink. Get away from me. I can't afford to love you, and you most certainly can't afford to love me.

At the Green Hat, even in those terrible minutes at Charlottenburg, she'd been aware of being warmed, cared for, tucked in, as she hadn't for many cold years.

But . . . Schmidt the married man, she thought. It was all over him, in the neat darn on the back of his sock, the home-knitted pullover.

In the hallway the bridge between them could have been measured in inches and the chasm below it in miles; him with his bloody niceness, her with her scars and disrepute. And pride. So she'd kicked the bridge in there and then—better for both of them.

She went upstairs to grieve for Natalya. There was time now.

12

IT WAS DARK by the time they reached number 42 Pariser Platz, and they kept making mistakes.

"Felix Yusupov?"

A man wearing a top hat and standing on a pair of steps outside the house stopped trimming the ivy decorating its frontage by torchlight. "I am Count Rutkowski. Ring damn bell."

They rang it. "Felix Yusupov?"

"What you want?"

"Police."

The youth who'd opened the door staggered. "No, no. No, no." He pressed the back of one hand to his forehead and used the other to prop himself up against the doorpost. "You cannot have him. Take me, take me in his place." He began to cry.

He was pushed out of the way by an oak of a man wearing cavalry boots and an apron, balancing a tray of tea on one enormous hand.

"Felix Yusupov?"

The man snorted. "Do I look like? I am bastard cook."

Willi pointed at the weeping figure still clinging to the doorpost. "Who's that?"

"Bastard majordomo." He kicked open a door to the left of the entrance hall. "Get in."

They got in. The room was full of the elephantine furniture typical of rented nineteenth-century houses, but somebody had touched it with grace. A lighted candelabrum picked out the richness of Persian rugs and Indian shawls thrown with apparent carelessness over chairs. From an enormous birdcage of white wood fretted like lace, a gaudily colored parrot stared at them and said hello in English. The smell of good cigars mingled with incense.

For a man who, if Potrovskov were to be believed, was down on his luck, this prince lived in style. The mild, painted eyes of the late czar looked down from a massive carved and gilded frame that alone, Schmidt reckoned, would fetch enough on the international antique market to keep himself and Hannelore in comfort for months.

He touched the latch of a jeweled egg standing on the mantel shelf. Immediately its top flew up, there was a click, and a tiny train began running round the lines of a miniature golden track.

A voice from the doorway said, "Pretty, isn't it? Fabergé made it for me. One of the baubles one managed to save when one left. Alas, one fears it will have to go."

Schmidt shut the lid. "Felix Yusupov? We're the police. I'm Inspector Schmidt, this is Sergeant Ritte." He was tired of strange and beautiful Russians—one of whom at Bismarck Allee had just given him a metaphorical kick in the balls.

This man was the most beautiful of them all, if not the strangest. He was wearing lipstick and a skirt and blouse under a quilted dressing gown.

Willi, who'd heard the rumor, positioned himself with his back firmly against a painted cupboard.

"My dears," Yusupov said, "why does nobody tell me these things? I thought you were here for the meeting. Never mind, let's make ourselves comfy. And you must have a drink. What would you like? We've run out of champagne, I fear, but one always feels a Bloody Mary starts the day well, and I'm sure you do, too." His large eyes rested on Willi standing like a guardsman against the cupboard, his thumbs in regimental line with his trousers. "You, my darling, look like a beer man."

He went to the door and shouted, "Beer and bloody vodkas, Dmitri! He turned back to Willi, who was now pressing so hard against the cupboard it was tilting backward, and smiled at his discomfiture. "Big, isn't he?"

"Very big," Schmidt said, cheered; there'd be weeks of mileage to be got out of this. Himself, he found this declaration of effeminacy inoffensive because the man was so obviously at ease with it. Unlike Potrovskov, Yusupov was not straining after effect; outrageousness was his environment, and though the world that had pampered him in it was gone, he carried it with him, instilling it into this ordinary Berlin house and making Inspector Schmidt and Sergeant Ritte the oddities.

Lipstick apart, he was naturally and pleasantly good-looking, fine skin over fine bones, with a set to his jaw and mouth that suggested intelligence. His German was almost accentless, and he spoke it with the soft *g* of the Berliner. Only the eyes showed that he was mad.

Could he cut somebody's throat?

He'd cut Rasputin's. Stabbed him anyway. But that had been in the fantastically colored, highly charged, onion-roofed court of a fairy-tale empire where an insane and mystical Russian peasant had acquired too much power over the czar and czarina, alienating them from their people, and where this equally insane prince had, according to Schmidt's researches, assassinated him in the hope of nullifying said influence and bringing said czar and czarina to their senses.

Killing a little nightclub stripper with no political pretensions was hardly in that league. However, it couldn't be ruled out.

He began his questions.

Yusupov fielded them all, sitting on the arm of a sofa, swinging his feet in their turned-up Turkish slippers, alternately addressing his replies to the parrot and Willi, whom he teased by flickering his fingers at him every now and again in flirtatious hellos.

"My darling, but I was at a party. At the Green Hat. You must know the Hat, it's run by a perfectly piggy parvenu called Potrovskov—I say, that's rather good, isn't it? All those *p*'s. Oh, you've met him. Well, just ask him. I didn't move all night. Oh, yes, I did. Some pals and I went on to a truly awful dive called the Pink Parasol—another one of the parvenu's, I believe. Got a teeny bit tiddly, between you and me, and feel perfectly awful this morning."

"It's evening," Schmidt said.

"Is it? *How* time flies. Where's Dmitri with those drinks?"

Dmitri didn't appear; neither did the drinks. "He never does a *thing* I tell him." At one point a woman almost as beautiful as Yusupov, and similarly dressed, floated in, picked up the parrot cage, and carried it out. No introductions were made, and Schmidt was left to assume that she was Yusupov's wife, which, again if his researches were correct, made her the late czar's niece. He must tell Willi that they had a child.

Did he know a Natalya Tchichagova? Or an Anna Anderson? An Esther Solomonova?

One knew so many people, but no, one couldn't recollect those names.

Did he recognize this? Schmidt gave him the note that had been delivered to 29 Bismarck Allee to let him read it. He'd fetched it from Alexanderplatz; the paper had been examined for fingerprints and was now acquiring Yusupov's.

"Not my writing, dear," he said, handing it back. "Far too neat."

Schmidt tucked it away and produced a photograph of Natalya's face taken by the Forensics Department. "Do you recognize this young woman?"

"I don't . . . oh, *oh,* she's dead, isn't she?"

"She was murdered on Saturday night. We believe she responded to that note."

"Well, I didn't write it, dear. Didn't kill her either. Who is she?"

"Natalya Tchichagova. She's Russian."

Yusupov tutted. "Sometimes I think they're trying to wipe us all out." He looked at the photo more closely. "Poor little soul. No, I don't know her." He gave it back. "No, I can't help you."

"What do you think the note means by 'authenticate you'? Who or what would you be in a position to authenticate?"

"One authenticates things all the time, darling. I'm a positive *guru* among our poor scattered community. The big auction houses are constantly onto me to tell them whether this necklace or that was the same one I last saw on a bosom being whisked about the czar's ballroom. Some poor devil's having to sell it to stay alive, you see, and my word adds to its provenance, which in turn puts up the price. I *do* know my jewels."

"And people? Do you have to authenticate people?"

"Oh indeed. The nouveaux riches love employing impoverished aristocrats, and I'm always being asked is my chauffeur really the grand duke this or is my maid really the countess that. Hideously embarrassing, and *so* banal, so *offensive.* Only the other day in Paris, somebody actually turned up with a spotty youth they insisted was the czarevitch." He sighed at Schmidt's incomprehension. "The czar's son, Alexei? This acned wonder, my dear, was supposed to be the heir to all the Russias. Sacrilegious little bastard even had the impertinence to address me as 'Uncle Felix.' All the authentication he got from me was the toe of my boot up his carbuncled young ass, I can tell you."

"And he wasn't? The heir to all the Russias, I mean?"

"Of course he wasn't." The playfulness dropped away. "Nobody got out of that cellar."

"Cellar?" Keep asking questions.

"They were slaughtered in a cellar in Ekaterinburg." Yusupov got up and turned his back to them. "All of them—the czar, the czarina, the grand duchesses, little Alexei." He was silent for a minute, drumming his fingers on the mantel shelf. When he faced them again, he'd got himself under control. "Eleven souls—three servants were with them. Butchered like cattle by the fucking Bolsheviks, my dear. But for some reason the myth persists that one or the other of them got away—hence our adolescent impostor hoping to get his dirty little hands on the remains of the royal fortune. Really, the things people will sink to. Necrophilia gone mad."

"Is there one?"

"Fortune?" Yusupov shrugged. "There are rumors of money in England, but I doubt if dear King George will let it out of his clutches. He did fuck-all to rescue the Romanovs—and the poor czar his own first cousin. Can you believe it? His own *cousin,* and he wouldn't give him sanctuary. His Imperial Majesty Cunt George, I call him. I tell you, once we've got Russia back from the Bolshies, I've a good mind to invade England."

They all believe that, Schmidt thought. He hadn't yet met a Russian émigré who wasn't convinced that his or her exile was merely temporary, that Communism was a passing fad, and that within a year or two their subjects would be pleading, cap in hand, for them to come back. He stood up.

"You're not going? Won't you stay for the meeting? People are coming by to listen to me tell the tale of how I killed Rasputin. Everyone clamors to hear it—I really ought to sell tickets. You'd love it, big boy." This was to Willi. "So *gory.*"

He stood on his steps to wave them off.

"God save us." Willi was still sweating. "You should've arrested him."

"He didn't kill her, Willi."

"Doesn't matter. Thing like that ought to be behind bars."

"He'd probably enjoy it. Actually, I thought he was rather brave." Schmidt savored the moment. "And he liked you *very* much, big boy."

"You bastard."

"'Sir' to you, Sergeant."

"You bastard, *sir.*"

On the way back to Alexanderplatz, they stopped at the cabstand to ask Count Chodsko one more question and receive an answer.

The canteen, which was supposed to offer refreshment around the clock, had closed for lack of anything to refresh anyone with. A watercooler had been placed on an otherwise empty counter for those with a thirst.

"Go home," Schmidt told Willi. "Wait a minute—before you do, try to find me a dictionary. I'll be upstairs." He settled himself in his office. It was cold and smelled of the cigarette butts piled in his ashtray. Hannelore would be waiting supper for him, if she had any, but there were reports to read and another to make before the night ended.

He was hungry, and his brain ached with Russian voices clamoring for its attention, most of them saying significant things. Overriding all of them was the flattest: *"Because every now and again he fucks me."*

Uncalled for. An unprovoked attack. Like a bloody sniper bullet. He'd merely been showing concern for her—and why he'd felt it in the first place, he couldn't now remember. Potrovskov was welcome to her; they could fuck each other until their eyes popped, and good luck to 'em.

Willi came in with the dictionary. "Pinched it off the desk of some little bastard in Accounts trying to improve himself."

"Thanks, Willi. Good night."

"Boss . . ."

"What?"

"All these bloody foreigners today . . . We're getting overrun."

Schmidt regarded him cautiously. "We're not going to be discussing *Volkstodt* this time of night, are we?" An obsession of Willi's, and one so general they'd stuck a label on it: *Volkstodt,* the extinction of the German race. It wasn't just alarm that the death of so many men in the war had caused a drop in the birth rate—which it had—but that better living standards were fostering the survival of people who, in the good old bad old days, would have been weeded out by natural selection. There was an uprush of fear that the country would be overrun by a spawning of the weak, the ill, and the backward. And, of course, foreigners.

"No, boss, but what I'm saying is, this country needs more Germans. Good stock, before we're swamped by the other sort."

"I'm doing my bit for the Fatherland, Willi."

"That's what I mean. That's the sort of baby we need, and there's Frau Schmidt not getting the proper food."

"Nobody is." Newspapers were reporting that tuberculosis was once again becoming the scourge it had been in the last century. Malnutrition was giving children rickets. When he thought about Hannelore and the baby, he panicked. "What can I do? No point in talking about it."

"Tell Frau Schmidt to drop by my place. My missus'll see to it."

Bless him. "We're not taking your rations."

They were alone in the room, but Willi looked around like a conspirator. "We'll just ask for a bit extra. We got an arrangement with greengrocer." He paused. "And the wholesale butcher. Can't get you eggs, though."

"What arrangement?"

"Well, you know. . . ."

"*What* arrangement?"

Willi shifted. "It's nothing. I paid a call on 'em one day and looked at their books, that's all. They're all on the ramp."

"And you overlooked it. . . . *Shit,* Willi."

"How'd you think I'm feeding my five little brats? Six if you count their mother?" Willi was suddenly angry. "Don't you 'shit' me, Inspector. You see the cigarette case that ponce produced from his pocket today? Gold, that was, and don't tell me he got that by paying his fucking taxes. Him and his whores. Look at those greasy kikes who run the banks with their mansions and motorboats. You don't see any government minister's missus taking in washing like mine's doing, do you? And we're supposed to say yessir, nosir, and watch our kids starve. I tell you, they're all at it. Corrupt, *all* of 'em."

Yes, thought Schmidt, looking at him, they probably are. That kind always were. It's when decent men like you and me join the corruption that woodworm eats into the whole goddamn system.

Willi took his silence badly. "Suit yourself, sir," and went out.

Shit, shit, *fuck* it.

After a while Schmidt lifted his head from his hands. Thank God for the escape that was his job, *his* Hans Christian Andersen country. He picked up the dictionary. It didn't look like a particularly comprehensive volume, but it had the word he wanted in it. He'd known what it meant in general; he just wanted to see its particular definition.

"Pogrom: 1905. Russ:= destruction. An organized massacre in Russia for the annihilation of a body or class, esp the Jews."

Yes, that's what he'd thought it was.

He turned his attention to the papers lying on his desk.

Dr. Pieck had worked all day and turned in his usual punctilious and pedantic report. "A postmortem investigation on the corpse of the female alleged to be Natalya Tchichagova found it to be the body of a young woman between twenty-one and twenty-five who had died from a hemorrhage caused by severance of her carotid artery." (Sharp, these scientists.)

She hadn't been a virgin, but neither had she been pregnant, nor had she given birth at any time. Condition of the corpse showed she had been somewhat undernourished but was otherwise healthy.

The fingerprint department had discovered no prints on the note other than those of its recipient, suggesting that the sender had worn gloves while writing it. No prints on the handbag either, other than Natalya's own.

To judge from their preliminary report, the Charlottenburg boys had spent the day slogging round the streets, asking at doors. They'd concentrated on Spandauer Damm to the south of the schloss and Tegeler Weg to its east, both large thoroughfares, but what with the snow and the blackout on that Saturday night, they were having little result. Most people had been in bed, trying to keep warm.

In Tegeler Weg, however, near midnight, a dogged postman had been delivering mail that had been delayed by the snow. He'd been tracked down and interviewed and had provided a list of the few pedestrians he'd noticed on otherwise empty roads.

There'd been a Jew having trouble pushing a handcart of old clothes northward through the drifts; he'd turned left along Mierendorffstrasse. A large woman had been hurrying south from the direction of the Westhafen Canal. Three urchins had been throwing snowballs at people's windows—the postman had corrected them and sent them home. He'd also witnessed a short, sharp altercation between two men with Communist armbands and a man on the opposite side of the road wearing an SA armband, but all parties had passed on and it had come to nothing.

In Spandauer Damm the police had been fortunate enough to find an elderly female insomniac who passed the night looking out her second-floor window. Just before midnight she'd seen the Jew with his handcart making his way toward Tegeler Weg, a pair of lovers who'd lingered for a while in an opposite doorway, a night tram driver coming off duty early because of the electricity failure—but he was a regular, and she knew him slightly—and a tramp with a long beard that, as he'd passed, the moonlight had shown to be parted, like a sailor's.

Police suspicion had fallen on the Jew and the tramp, and efforts were being made to trace both.

Schmidt scribbled a note: *"The tramp is Rudi the Flasher, surname Mach. To be found lurking in Moabit Market most days. Well done, gentlemen, keep it up."* He put the note in his out-tray ready to be sent back to Charlottenburg next day.

He sat back, lit his last Manoli, and considered. The Jew. How had they known he was a Jew? By the handcart of old clothes—the two were synonymous; poor Jews had virtually cornered the secondhand-clothes market. But you didn't have to be a Jew or a secondhand-clothes dealer to push a barrow in order to seem like one.

The large woman coming from the Westhafen Canal? How large? What was a lone woman, however large, doing on a lonely, icy, unlit street at night? Again, you didn't have to be a woman because you were wearing women's clothes. And Natalya's killer didn't have to be a man either—he must rid himself of the conviction that it had been.

He leaned across and added to his note: *"Try to trace all the pedestrians mentioned except Mach."* On second thought he crossed out the "except Mach." Could just possibly be Rudi had graduated from flashing at girls to killing them.

As for the two Communists and the SA man they'd quarreled with across the street, they were less suspicious. Schmidt would have expected such men to be in that area. In the nineteenth century, Charlottenburg, once a small and elegant village gathered around the castle, had been invaded by industrialization, bringing with it a working class forced to live without electricity or sunlight in the back courtyards around Wallstrasse. Inevitably it had become a stronghold of the Communist Party, which, in turn, made it a target for raids by the growing Sturmabteilung—the SA, storm troopers, the upholders of the Right, capitalism, kaiser, and the damn traffic.

The two Communists would have been on their way to a late-night meeting and the solitary SA man on his to join a gang of fellow Fascists who would try to break it up. If there'd been more of each, the postman would have witnessed not just name-calling but another of the running street battles that were turning Berlin into a zoo.

Jesus, why didn't they *stop*? Hadn't they had enough with the war? Of the two organizations, the Fascists repulsed him most, Jew-hating, foreigner-baiting, muscle-bound, Mussolini-loving cretins that they were. But the Communists were little better. Couldn't the bastards see that Soviet totalitarianism was just Fascism in another hat?

After the war, ex–Lance Corporal Siegfried Schmidt had joined the police force in order to protect an ideal formulated in the small town of Weimar, a *democratic* ideal, the third wonderful thing to come out of Weimar—Goethe and Schiller being the other two.

The Republic hadn't proved itself to be perfect, God knows. At the moment it was proving itself bloody incompetent, but it was the first democracy a unified Germany had ever known, a chance to snatch the frail maiden of civilization from the jaws of dragons. Between them, Communist and Fascist were ripping the poor bitch apart before she could draw breath. Bastards. If he had his way, he'd arrest the lot.

Suddenly he realized what it was about Natalya's murder that made him angry. He was used to death; he'd seen bodies of small children raped and mutilated, and that had sent him mad with despair, but the monsters who'd done it were *driven* monsters, sating some urge that they themselves didn't understand. It was as if those boys and girls had been victims of a blind primeval force, ripped apart by a hurricane.

In Natalya's case there'd been planning. Somebody had deliberated over it quite sanely, like the staff officers in war headquarters considering whether the next push would be convenient—*"We can expect forty percent casualties, old boy." "That's all right, old boy, we should inflict sixty percent on the enemy"*—wiping out in a couple of sentences the lives of men who'd wanted to study, marry, start a business, return to their children and wives, to their quiet farms. He hated the bastards.

Taking from his pocket the packet of Natalya's letters, he saw her murderer as another staff officer. The man had thought it out, weighed the percentages, sent the note, waited, killed. A trivial death, just another to add to the trivial millions murdered by the generals.

And you got it wrong, you fucker. Like they did. You got the wrong woman.

This was no good; he was tired and not making sense. Keep your mind on the job, or you'll miss something.

He took the rubber band off the packet. If Natalya'd had a boyfriend, he hadn't been a letter writer. Most of these were notes, some of them scrawled on Purple Parrot napkins from men in her audience: *"Greetings, beautiful. Come and have a drink. Table Three." "Hello, pretty one, let me take you to dinner after the show. Table Eight."* All different handwritings. None of them showing the persistence of obsession. Had she gone with any of them, he wondered, or merely kept the notes as tributes?

None of them either in the same hand as the one that had lured her to Charlottenburg.

There were two magazine clippings, both identical, which stated that *"the sauciest show in Berlin is presently at the Purple Parrot where customers can be delighted by seeing a great deal of Mesdames La Bon-Bon and Frou-Frou."*

"Frou-Frou" had been underlined in pen, presumably Natalya's stage name.

He yawned and got up. Time to report to Ringer. The captain was a stickler for hearing from his inspectors about their cases before the day ended. Which, thought Schmidt wearily, was bully for him; *he* hadn't been up since the crack of bloody dawn.

They were never happy interviews, his and Ringer's. Schmidt's fast rise through the ranks had occurred because, as a young policeman on the beat in 1919, he'd come to the notice of a Social Democrat member of the Reichstadt—he'd saved the man from injury during a riot—and thereby to the attention of the government's chief of police.

In any case, with 13 million men lost to the war, there had been room for swift promotion. This had not, however, endeared Schmidt to the Old Guard, mastodons like Ringer, who'd had to wait out the years stipulated by a creaking prewar bureaucracy before they'd achieved their present positions.

Some minutes passed before his knock on Ringer's office door gained him admittance. More minutes while Ringer ignored him in favor of some papers he was pretending to read.

Schmidt spent them speculating on how the man remained so fat when everybody else was losing weight. Ringer disapproved of the canteen's democracy and was never seen in it. The rumor was that he fed on orphans fried and served in his office with parsley.

As usual, his rigid collar cut into his neck so that his head looked like an overlapping piece of roast beef cooked rare. His mustache was waxed into points sharp enough to pick snails out of their shells.

"Well, Inspector?" Ringer initialed a piece of paper. He sat back and looked at Schmidt with disfavor, allowing his gaze to travel from the rimed shoes up to Schmidt's hair, which, for lack of time to go to the barber, was beginning to rest on his ears. "This prostitute—Natalya Something-or-Other—we needn't spend manpower on her, need we?"

"She wasn't a prostitute, sir." And what if she had been? Did that make her expendable?

"Nevertheless . . ." Ringer consulted his paper. "I see you've asked for house-to-house inquiries. I've told you before, in these hard times—"

Schmidt interrupted. "She wasn't the intended victim, sir. And there's Russian royalty involved." He hadn't made the rank of inspector by neglecting the art of manipulating his superior's prejudices.

"Really?"

"Yes, sir." He got Yusupov's name and title into the story quickly, moved on to Count Chodsko and Prince Nick, weaving in the two mysterious Russian women of 29c Bismarck Allee on the way. He needed men for those house-to-house inquiries—all the alibis required checking.

After a while he wondered if he could sit down. He dragged up a chair, still talking, and experienced a moment of triumph when Ringer didn't object. I'm Scheherazade enchanting the fucking sultan, he thought.

"Fascinating, fascinating," the sultan said when Scheherazade paused.

"Yes, sir. You see, I know what they're up to, Prince Nick and Fräulein Anderson."

"You do?"

"Yes, sir. It's fraud. Any moment now she'll be presented to the world as the long-lost daughter of the czar."

Ringer surprised him. "Which one, Inspector? There were four grand duchesses: Olga, Tatiana, Marie, and Anastasia."

So Ringer's bedside reading wasn't only police statistics; it included popular magazines; there was hardly one that hadn't displayed the picture of the four young girls in white dresses.

"Anastasia, sir. There's money to be made. Yusupov thinks there's a cache in England, and presumably she'd be entitled to it—if she can convince everybody she's the czar's surviving child."

"You're sure of this, Inspector?"

"Pretty sure, sir." He started building the bricks of his argument: (a) Prince Nick's shady reputation.

(b) Solomonova's reluctance to cooperate—"She's in on it, I'm afraid, one of Prince Nick's women. He pays her rent."

(c) The note itself: *"I can authenticate you."* "It was for Anderson—the killer knew enough to think that would tempt Anderson into meeting him, but Tchichagova picked it up and acted on it. She was an ambitious young woman, and I think she saw her way to film stardom."

(d) Anderson's fear that she would be assassinated. "She talks about the Cheka wanting to get rid of her."

"The Cheka, eh? Nasty."

"Yes, sir."

(e) Czarskoe Selo. "It was the czar's favorite palace, sir." He'd asked Chodsko about it. "Natalya's parents were servants there, familiar with royal procedure. Ideal for grooming somebody for the role of a grand duchess."

(f) Yusupov's account of the boy claiming to be the czarevitch.

"You see, sir, the White Russians were advancing on Ekaterinburg at the time the Romanovs were killed. Ekaterinburg was the place—"

"Where the Reds shot the czar and his family. I know that, Inspector. Frau Ringer was very upset by it."

Good God, there was a Frau Ringer? He'd never thought of Ringer as having a wife, especially one with susceptibilities. "Yes, well. A White Russian force was advancing on the place. Which was why the family was killed, to stop them from being rescued. And there's a strong rumor that one of the Romanovs got away."

He looked up from his notebook. "In my view, because of that belief, we're going to see a spate of impostors saying they escaped the slaughter and claiming to be the czarevitch or a grand duchess or some damn thing. There's already been one. Anna Anderson will be another. Prince Nick's got her under his thumb. She's not very stable."

"She wouldn't be, would she?"

Schmidt sat up. "Beg your pardon, sir?"

"After all she's been through, if she *is* the grand duchess," Ringer said. He waggled a reproving finger. "We can't rule it out, Inspector."

Schmidt said, "I don't think she can be, sir." *Nobody got out of that cellar.*

The finger wagged on. "They haven't found the bodies. One at least might have survived—with the aid of a servant, perhaps, and . . . and helpful people sympathetic to the czar who were living nearby."

Jesus, he wanted it to be true.

Then and only then did Schmidt fully believe in the structure he'd made from his bricks. Its cement had consisted of a good deal of intuition; he'd believed it but had reckoned on having trouble persuading Ringer. Now he knew his case was solid, not because Ringer had followed his reasoning but because Ringer was prepared to buy what Potrovskov would be selling.

His respect for the crook went up. Potrovskov had seen what he hadn't—that it would be easy. It was the perfect confidence trick: people *wanted* to believe it. The age of fairy tales still spun its magic in the hearts of men, even bureaucratic old farts like the one opposite him. This fairy tale had ogres. *Red* ogres. A princess escaping from them through Siberian wastes, disappearing into the wild woods, popping up again to claim her inheritance. Hans Christian Andersen was nowhere. Schmidt wondered if, as in all good fairy tales, any of the grand duchesses had possessed a birthmark to identify her.

Potrovskov'll tattoo one on, he thought.

He heard Ringer say, "It seems we must look deeper into Romanov history for our killer. Do you want any assistance from the Counterespionage Section?"

"What for?"

"Well, if it *is* the Bolsheviks who are on her trail . . ."

He does, Schmidt thought, he loves it. Communist assassins are the icing on his bloody cake. He said, "We'll see how it goes, sir, shall we?"

"Very well, Inspector." Ringer went on, "You may have what men I can spare. And keep me informed—this promises to be interesting."

Dazed, Schmidt had reached the door before he remembered to turn around and salute. He'd been expecting a battle; he hadn't even had to argue.

But if Ringer thought he was going to waste time buggering about with cloak-and-dagger crap and inquiries into Russian royalty, Ringer had another think coming. *"Nobody got out of that cellar."* Yusupov had said it, and Schmidt believed him; butchers weren't in the business of allowing lambs to escape the shambles.

Anna Anderson was an impostor. Maybe—*maybe*—she was being targeted because she was an impostor, but it was much more likely that the killer had emerged out of the apparent no-man's-land that was her past.

But we don't know it, Potrovskov had said.

About time they did.

Nick popped into Bismarck Allee after he'd settled Anna with the von Kleists to tell Esther that it had gone well and to see if she wanted to go to bed with him.

"Not tonight, Nick." She was too tired to tell him that she would be neither working for him nor sleeping with him again. *Sufficient unto the day is the evil thereof*. And this, if any, had been an evil day.

"Okay." He never pressed her; his sea was full of amenable ladyfish.

She warned him again: "I'm telling the police everything, Nick."

"Sure, sure. I've got nothing to hide." He was restive. "You think it was Cheka did in Natalya?"

"There is no Cheka," she said wearily. "You know that."

"I don't," he said. "I completely believe in Her Imperial Highness. Completely."

"But what?" There was something bothering him; she knew him well.

"I need insurance. Maybe we ought to find out a bit more about her."

Schmidt went up the stairs leading to his apartment with much use of the handrail, not because he was weary, though he was, but because Hannelore insisted on polishing the wood of each step until it shone like ice—and was as slippery. He'd tried pointing out the hazard to his and her neck and that of every visitor, but she held to the view that unpolished stairs were un-German and disgraced her.

"Sorry I'm late." He always said it, though she never complained.

"Hard day?"

"Fairly."

As always, the table was prepared for dinner. His slippers awaited him at the door. Artistically crumpled red paper in the fireplace did its best to simulate the flames they could no longer afford. She'd found ivy from somewhere, and it trailed with brave artistry along the mantel shelf that used to hold her pieces of Dresden.

He kissed her; invariably a pleasure, but her freshness made him realize that he smelled of sweat and cigarettes—and something meaty. Reminded, he brought a nasty-looking napkin out of his pocket. "Some hare stew, *madame,* and a dumpling. For *madame's* dinner."

She took it but stood still, smiling expectantly at him.

He sniffed. "Pork?" he said. *"Pork?"*

"And potatoes," she said.

"Good God, woman, have you been sleeping with the butcher?"

She'd stopped being appalled at jokes like that. "I didn't have to. A consignment came in just as I reached the head of the line."

"How long did you have to wait?"

"It doesn't matter," she told him. "Go and wash, and I'll serve up."

She was an excellent cook and had stretched the small piece of pork as far as it could go; it was also one of her tenets that the man should have the lion's share, so he had to make sure she gave herself a decent portion. "You're eating for two, woman."

"I know. Siegfried, isn't it wonderful?" To be childless was another state she regarded as un-German, a conviction she shared with, and was supported in, by almost the whole nation. Even left-wing public-health reformers were urging good German couples to start families. Magazines and newspapers were full of advice on eugenics counseling, how to raise children, on breast-feeding, potty training, preventive medicine, and the general production of improved human beings.

To Schmidt, in the first two years of their marriage during which Hannelore had not conceived, this propaganda had been a vague irritant; to Hannelore it was a dagger in the heart. It had been gall and wormwood for her to watch the shiftless Lammers family across the road produce more and more babies on welfare.

When she'd become pregnant, she'd said, "Now I am a proper woman."

"You were always proper woman enough for me," he'd said, but she wouldn't have it. The consequent miscarriage had nearly sunk her. This time she hadn't told anyone she was pregnant again until the three-month point had well gone by.

It had caused Schmidt to wonder at the burden this imposed on all the leftover women whose prospects of marriage and children had died on the battlefields. If you weren't a virtuous hausfrau with a Teutonic pedigree having babies on a production-line basis, you weren't doing your bit for the nation.

Tonight he found himself speculating on how it also isolated already-isolated women like the Jewish Solomonova who didn't qualify under any of those categories.

Hannelore was full of news. Frau Busse in the ground-floor apartment had offered the youngest Busse's baby clothes and might barter its carriage for something—they could keep it in the entrance hall. She had already unraveled a primrose-colored jersey of her own and was knitting a baby jacket from it.

"Siegfried, I am considering selling my hair. What do you think?" She had wonderful hair, ash blond and wavy; she kept it long, plaited around her head.

"How do you feel about it?"

But it was no good trying to get her to make her own decisions; she had to have his approval—he liked her hair spread about them both when they were naked in bed—so they spent time analyzing her motive. Fashion? Or what a wigmaker would pay for it? She wouldn't say, so eventually he took the initiative and told her to keep it, which pleased her.

He'd known he wanted to marry her the moment he saw her in 1916, a nervous, adolescent, honey-colored confection in Bavarian national dress sitting with her mother at a dance put on for soldiers, like him and Ikey Wolff, who were recovering in a Munich convalescent home after the Somme. He and Ikey were still trying to get used to their survival from the 142 days that had claimed 650,000 German soldiers. Hannelore had appeared as a seraphim to one rising from a muddy grave. He'd said to Ikey, "That, my son, is going to be my bit of home comfort."

He'd pursued her with ferocity for three years, against her parents' hopes for her—they were small-time winegrowers and wanted her to marry the local vintner's son, not a damn Prussian without a penny to his name—holding her image in his head while up to his thighs in filth, writing her letters under bombardment, thinking of her even when he was with other women, using everything he knew to outbid his rival.

After the war he'd brought her back to a Berlin so changed even he'd barely recognized it, to find that the greatest change of all had taken place in its women—a new breed accustomed to working, managing, making decisions, who'd cast off corsets and hampering skirts along with deference, who had opinions and the vote, who smoked and swore and generally kicked over the traces of an older generation that had expected its daughters to remain untouched by the war it had inflicted on them.

Hannelore, having been insulated from all conflict on her mountain farm, rosy with homegrown food and brought up to respect her elders, was a Sleeping Beauty in comparison; waking up to Berlin had shocked her.

It had been unfair on her, Schmidt realized—not that it occurred to her to complain that she'd been landed in a bankrupt city with a poorly paid, often absent husband.

She'd adapted to his vagaries, learned not to be repulsed by his Jewish friends, *probably* voted SPD in elections, as he did, put up with his swearing, his bad jokes, his sympathy for the detritus of society with whom he dealt, but she'd done so on his account, because it was a wifely thing to do; husbands were to be catered to. He was, he sometimes felt, her standard issue and that she'd have adapted equally sweetly to the lifestyle of a red-kneed, red-necked Bavarian.

For his sake she tried to read translations of his loved Latin poets and had tackled Shakespeare, but literature was their dividing ground, as was music—she liked waltzes and oompah bands, he preferred Beethoven.

"Where did you get all this from?" she'd once asked, as if he'd caught some disease while in foreign parts.

"A godless radical," he told her. Which is what Herr Müller, his elementary-school teacher, had been and why, after their first five years together, Herr Müller had been dismissed by the school board. By that time, however, the two of them had caught each other's attention, and for a few of his mother's hard-earned pfennigs a week, the young Schmidt had continued his education during the evenings in the garret in which Herr Müller had paced and talked and read aloud and played his gramophone and opened the gates to anarchic, terrifying, entrancing, jaw-dropping wonders of the mind and, eventually, smoked himself to death.

To get a job hadn't occurred to Hannelore—not that he'd suggested it; she'd been brought up to be a wife and mother, job enough for anybody. In the last year, her friend and neighbor Frau Busse had tempted her into the *volkisch* movement, and she'd joined one of its women's groups—Daughters of the Teutonic Dawn, he thought it was; the name kept changing—where like-minded females alternated jam making and sewing pot holders with pagan-looking dances around a campfire and discussions about the future of the Aryan race.

All very harmless, and if that's what she wanted, fine—though Schmidt was uneasy with the Daughters' stenciled newsletter in which editorials about the Aryan race seemed to take it for granted that other races, especially the Semitic, didn't actually have a future.

What concerned him more was that she seemed to block out the reality that faced him every day or, rather, to think there were simple solutions to it. "But how are they allowed?" she would ask of the prostitutes, homosexuals, rapists, murderers, burglars, fraudsters, and general evildoers with whom he had to deal—as if a good spring cleaning would get rid of them.

Eventually, to close the gap, he stopped talking over his cases with her and kept the discussion at dinner to matters of mutual concern.

Tonight, though, knowing she was fascinated by royalty and without mentioning names, he said, "Strange case today. I met a woman who thinks she's the grand duchess Anastasia."

She was gripped immediately, asked questions, fetched her scrapbook in which the familiar picture of the four girls in white dresses had been pasted. "Does she look like her?"

"She does a bit."

"Oh, Siegfried, perhaps she is."

He had another Ringer on his hands; the whole world was prepared to be conned. "And I'm the bloody pope," he said.

"Siegfried."

"What? All right, I won't say 'bloody pope' to little Bocksbeutel." They'd agreed the child was to be brought up in her religion, as a Roman Catholic.

"Bocksbeutel," she said with pleasure—it was the rounded bottle into which her home region put its wine. "We'll have to think of a proper name soon."

"I don't know. Bocksbeutel Schmidt—got a ring to it."

She laughed, and he thought, What the hell have I got to complain about? She was the wife he'd dreamed about in the trenches. He was the envy of Alexanderplatz; at police get-togethers everybody loved her. *He* loved her. She loved him, and if their marriage was not the meeting of true minds that somebody—possibly Shakespeare—had talked about, it was still a happy one.

He offered to wash the dishes, but she wouldn't have it—this was the time when husbands sat by the fire and read the paper.

When she came in, he made her put her feet across his knees so that he could massage them. "Your poor ankles are swollen."

"It's only from standing in the lines."

"Only?"

Bless her, she looked exhausted; the once-rounded cheeks were showing their bones. He was swept by a caveman savagery. Christ, why should she suffer because *he* had scruples? What sort of man allowed his pregnant wife to go without when others were not? She wasn't going to lose this baby, too. The particular little Isaac in her womb wouldn't be laid on the sacrificial altar its father had built to the demanding deity of virtue. He was no Abraham—never liked the nasty old bugger.

He said, "Tomorrow I want you to go to Frau Ritte's and tell her we'll go in on Willi's arrangement."

He wasn't even stricken by conscience. What else could he do? But he was sorry, very sorry. Weimar Germany had come to this—its police forced to join the ranks of its crooks. Fuck it, *fuck* it.

He was haunted by Latin. *Quis custodiet ipsos custodes?*

13

When Schmidt arrived at his office in the Alexanderplatz the next morning, his wife was much on his mind.

He couldn't look his sergeant in the eye. He said, "If it's all right by you, Willi, Hannelore will be calling on your wife today. We'd like to come in on the arrangement."

Willi held out his hand, Schmidt shook it, and that was that.

Willi said, "The piece from Bismarck Allee, the kike with the scar—she's downstairs, boss, waiting to see you."

"Let her wait."

He gave orders for the house-to-house around Charlottenburg to be continued and a new one to be instituted in Bismarck Allee. He sent two men off to roust out of their beds those who'd been at the Green Hat on Saturday night in order to account for every minute of Prince Nick's and Yusupov's presences at the party. Another uniform was dispatched to find employees of the Purple Parrot and get information about Natalya. "And while you're about it, I want the names and addresses of the men who were with Yusupov at the Green Hat and who went on with him to the Pink Parasol. They won't want to give them—they're probably homosexuals—but every one of the bastards is going to be interviewed." Schmidt had more or less eliminated Yusupov—and Potrovskov—but he was a thorough man.

He thought about Solomonova, Anderson, and Tchichagova, those three Russian witches stirring their cauldron in 29c Bismarck Allee. For all he knew of their past, they'd arrived in Berlin on broomsticks—he sent to Immigration for details of their entry papers.

Was he missing something by automatically assuming that Anderson was a fake? Perhaps he was; every other bugger was showing an open mind on the subject; maybe he should. *"There are more things in heaven and earth . . . than are dreamt of in your philosophy."* Shakespeare said every frigging thing.

Finally he acknowledged that by keeping Solomonova waiting downstairs he was cutting off his nose to spite his face; of all the people in this inquiry, she was the most likely to give him the information he needed.

You've gone beyond punishing people for their way of life, he told himself. What do you care who she sleeps with?

"Show her up."

Regulations stated that witnesses and suspects be seen in the interview rooms, but interview rooms were on the ground level and cold, whereas his office was two floors up from the canteen and absorbed some of its rising heat.

He cleared papers off his desk so that Hannelore's picture could stand more prominently on it, emptied his ashtray, put a chair on the opposite side to face the window, and set another one farther back for Willi.

He reached for a cigarette and remembered he didn't have any. He'd stopped to buy some this morning, to find that a packet of Manoli cost 3,800 marks. He'd sworn at the shopkeeper and left, vowing to give up tobacco. He fought down the impulse to grub among the butts in the wastepaper basket and see if any were smokable.

"Good morning, Fräulein." He didn't get up.

She wore two scarves Russian peasant style, one straight across the forehead and the other around so that it framed the face. The snow-reflecting light coming through the window from the parking lot outside was hard on her, showing every detail of the scar and emphasizing her pallor, but her eyes were more alive than they'd been yesterday, as if she'd joined the rest of the human race sufficiently to take part in it. She wasn't nervous either, and whatever it was about her presence that activated politeness in Willi was still working; he held the door and then the chair for her.

Yes, Esther thought, here he is. And emanating less kindness than he had yesterday; he'd categorized her as a loose woman, of course. She supposed she was, but damned if she'd apologize for it to some bourgeois male in a safe job. You've no idea of fighting to survive, she thought. And then remembered he'd been on the Western Front. He did.

Well, she'd deliberately repelled him so that he didn't get too close, and here he was—repelled.

From the first she skewed the story to exonerate Nick: "Prince Nikolai heard that an unknown woman was in Dalldorf Asylum and there was a possibility that she was the grand duchess Anastasia. Naturally, being a loyal White Russian, he was concerned."

"Naturally."

She ignored his tone. She told him about Dalldorf. She told him about Clara Peuthert and the daggers Clara had drawn on her calendar every sixth weekend. "She told me she scared the man off once, so she may be able to give you a description."

She told him about the drive from Dalldorf to the Green Hat. "Anna said the man was following us. I thought her paranoid, but after the incident on the stairs at the Hat, Prince Nick thought it safer for us to smuggle her out to our new flat."

Her scar tightened as she told him about Olga Ratzel's death, but her account was toneless. "An Inspector Bolle was in charge of that case," she said. "The fact that Olga's death fitted in with Clara's theory made me think, but I convinced myself that it was coincidence. Now I know it wasn't—he thought Olga knew where we'd taken Anna." She told him how she'd asked for Theo to protect them the following sixth weekend, but, when nothing happened, she'd decided she'd been overfanciful.

"But on Saturday he found you again," Schmidt said.

"Yes." She spoke almost to herself. "Yes, he's become clever. When you think of it, he's been hanging around Nick's clubs. . . . Somebody's been talking to him. Somebody . . ." Her eyes were sapphire hard now. "I'd like to know who."

"That's our job, Fräulein."

She gave a brief nod. Then do it, it said.

He said, "Fräulein Anderson insists that it's the Cheka who're after her. Or Prince Yusupov, of course."

"Yes, but when she was *truly* frightened, she told me the man had followed her always—she used that phrase. She mentioned past encounters at a Canal and in a forest."

"Canal?"

"Yes." Solomonova put up the heel of her hand to rub her forehead in a gesture with which Schmidt was becoming familiar. "I'm sorry. . . . Prince Nikolai once mentioned it, that she'd been fished out of the Landwehr Canal—1920, I think it was. You'd have to ask him about that."

Schmidt looked over to Willi, who made a note. "Did she give a description?"

"No."

"You can, though, if it's the same man who attacked you at the Hat."

"Yes, but whether I'd know him again . . . a big man."

"Narrows it down nicely," intoned Willi from his notebook.

Esther told them about Natalya's ambition, her growing irritation with Anna, and the culmination of both—the scene at the Green Hat.

"She wanted Prince Nikolai to present her to the world as the grand duchess. That was what the quarrel was about. Naturally he refused."

"Naturally."

She ignored his tone. "Natalya was in an overwrought state after that. I suppose it made her judgment unsound when she found the note. She must have believed that Yusupov wrote it and would present her as Anastasia."

Schmidt got up and turned his back on her to think. In the parking lot below, a couple of uniforms were trying to push a van out of a snowdrift.

He'd got it right. God, I'm good, he thought.

And she was an examining magistrate's dream: concise, clear—and honest, as far as it went. He wondered how far it did go.

"Do you think the canteen could supply three cups of real ersatz coffee for us, Sergeant?" he said.

"I'll inquire, sir."

"And . . . cake or something." She looked famished.

Behind Solomonova's back, Willi rolled his eyes. Cake yet.

When he'd gone, Esther said, "Why did he kill Natalya?"

"By mistake," he told her.

He'd worked it out. The killer's standing under the trees of Charlottenburg at midnight. It's dark; all streetlights are out, owing to the latest electricity cut. (Schmidt had checked.) Everybody in the area has gone to bed to save fuel. He's waiting for the woman to whom he'd sent the message. And here she comes, on time, through the snow, an intermittent moon washing out features so that her face is a pale, indistinguishable disk under the cloche hat. In her dark coat, Natalya is the expected woman in the expected place.

She doesn't see him. He lets her get ahead of him, then pads after her, no sound but the creak of branches under their weight of snow. She doesn't even cry out. The knife slashing into her neck is the only warning she has that she's about to die. Shock probably precludes even that knowledge. It doesn't take long in any case. Seconds.

"He thought she was Anna," he said.

"Let's hope he still does," she said. "I'm afraid for her."

Schmidt sat down. "It was fraud, wasn't it? You were going to pass off Fräulein Anderson as Anastasia and claim the Romanov fortune."

Her mouth opened slightly in surprise. Yep, I'm good, he thought. Then her eyes met his; she almost smiled. He thought she was going to admit it. What she said was, "Fraud implies gaining money under false pretenses. There has been no money gained."

She was right, of course. "But it was the intention."

She said, "Does it matter now? I want you to catch the man who killed Natalya. I am here for that."

"Does Prince Nick believe that Anna is the grand duchess?"

"You must ask him," she said.

"Do *you*?"

"No."

He sat back, relieved. "Who is she?"

"I don't know. None of us does. She was Mrs. Unknown in Dalldorf, and according to Nick she was Mrs. Unknown in the hospital before that. Sometimes I don't think *she* knows. What's worrying is that most of the time she really believes she is Anastasia."

"Which you helped her to do," he said—he couldn't leave it. "You were coaching her, you and Natalya."

She leaned forward, her hand on the desk. "Are we going to spend time on my sins? Because if we are, we'll be here all day. Look"—she moved farther forward—"I don't think this has to do with grand duchesses or fraud or anything. Anna is frightened of something in her past; it's why she's tried to forget it. Whoever this man is, he's come out of it to kill her."

"It's a possibility," he said.

"It's a probability. *That's* why I'm here. *That's* why I'm telling you all this. I'm afraid for her."

The scar, and her indifference to it, did something extraordinary for her, just as damage to some art object threw into relief how beautiful it had once been, tarnishing and tempering her face with the reminder of what humanity did to lovely things and how they bore it.

He kept on punishing her. "So you've left her on her own at Bismarck Allee."

"For God's sake," she said irritably, sitting back. "Of course I haven't. Nick's taken her to some family called von Kleist. Wealthy people, romantics, thrilled to bits to be guarding a grand duchess from the Bolsheviks."

He saw that "romantics" was a dirty word to her. "Address?"

She gave it to him. "You see, you've got the means to find out who she is and catch the man, or I wouldn't be here—"

"Bothering with me?"

She almost smiled. "Jews don't usually have much faith in the police, but . . . I trust you."

Again they were both taken aback.

But I do, Esther thought. Integrity was this man's milieu; he swam in it like a lone fish. She knew him. He didn't approve of her. She didn't approve of herself much either.

"Thank you." Schmidt, newly enrolled buyer in the black market, felt flattered and guilty.

They began chatting. "She couldn't actually be the grand duchess by any chance?"

"You met her," Esther said. "What do you think?"

"I'm not conversant with royalty. As far as I'm concerned, they all come out of lunatic asylums."

She smiled. No, she grinned. Devastatingly. Youth and amusement had been there in the past, and for a moment they broke through. Like a miracle, he thought. Like bloody snowdrops in winter.

"Until you've caught this man, I'd like the von Kleists to go on believing in her," she said. "Is that possible?"

"Why?"

She shrugged. "I may be wrong. I don't know them, but they'd probably drop her otherwise, and she'd be at risk again. She's not an easy person to live with." She said wistfully, "A pain in the ass, Natalya used to call her. We think she may be Polish."

He nodded. "That'd do it."

And she laughed.

"No cake," Willi said, elbowing through the door with a tray.

Schmidt asked standard questions, more to give her time to drink the coffee than because she had anything else to contribute—except who she was. When he asked her where she came from, she said, "You have my details."

"We could do with a bit more background."

"Is it relevant?"

He supposed it wasn't. Nor could he detain her because she wouldn't elaborate; she didn't have a record—in Germany at least.

"Don't leave town," he told her when she was going.

"I don't intend to," she said, and then, graciously, "I'm a Berliner now."

Esther left Alexanderplatz police headquarters feeling cleaner than she had for some months. Like a Roman Catholic after confession. Schmidt hadn't exactly given her absolution, but it had been noticeable that his more penetrating questions had been kept until his sergeant had left the room.

No point in trying to save my face, Inspector; that was lost years ago. Just find Olga and Natalya's killer. Save Anna.

Last night the apartment had seemed extra dark without Natalya's bright, dyed-blond presence. She'd stood at the window for a long time, menaced by hopelessness, watching the street's gathering shadows. How could one be pinpointed among so many? Especially one that knew so much about them—*"I can authenticate you"*—when all they knew about *it* was its bigness.

But on this clear blue morning, things were better. An intuitive man was on the job with fingerprint experts, all science to help him. A clever man, a nice man, a very nice man. With a picture of a pretty wife on his desk. Leave it to him.

Leave him.

Esther walked briskly; there was more cleansing to do yet—like finding a new and better way to earn a living. Natalya's death had been a watershed. If she—if all of them—hadn't been involved in a sleazy conspiracy, it wouldn't have happened.

In the Tiergarten, tourists were taking pictures of one another and of Berliners passing by with currency piled in baskets and trolleys. One or two Americans were buying bags of hot chestnuts from a man with a glowing fire bucket, handing over a dollar and photographing the resultant mountain of change, laughing.

Esther dawdled to watch them. She envied them cameras that had probably cost them, in their currency, little more than they were paying for the chestnuts. Cameras were magical to her. She must get her Leica back from the pawnbroker—she'd suffered a greater pang pawning that than anything else. If she could wish any artifact back from the past, it was the beloved box Brownie her father had given her on her tenth birthday.

Don't think about it, don't think about it.

She lingered a while longer. One of the vacationers handed his camera to the chestnut seller, asking the man to take a picture of him and his wife.

Now, that was an idea. Maybe there was a living to be made in taking photographs of tourists.

Well, perhaps. She wasn't ever going to be anybody's wife—and damned if she'd be somebody's kept woman much longer.

She stopped dawdling and set off for Nick's house to tell him so—and ask him to get her camera back.

Willi came back into the office after seeing Solomonova off the premises. Schmidt said, "What do you think, Sergeant?"

"Funny woman," Willi said. "Most kikes say 'sir.' I reckon there was money there one time. Two-faced, I mean *really.* One side she's the Queen of bloody Sheba, other side she could be Scarface Sara from Steinplatz. I reckon that kike quack of yours could have a field day with her."

"We're referring to that distinguished Viennese psychoanalyst Dr. Sigmund Freud, are we, Willi?"

"Yeah, him." Willi had been introduced to the theories of Freud when Schmidt had once tried to explain something of them in connection with a case of patricide; ever since, Willi had added deviousness to the sins he attributed to the Jewish race.

"Funny woman," Schmidt agreed.

But she's right, he thought. That Natalya had been murdered by a random killer wandering Charlottenburg was to lean too heavily on coincidence. *"I can authenticate you."* And now the death of the Olga woman would have to be investigated. There was no doubt Anna Anderson was at the center of this particular maze. Trace the trail she'd made and they'd find the man who wanted to kill her. The trick would be to find which path led to her: the grand-duchess way or via her true identity. What *was* her true identity?

Eisenmenger was in the canteen, examining a sausage through his monocle as if he'd found it stuck to his shoe. "Cheka, old boy? Are we talking about the All-Russian Extraordinary Commission for Combating Counterrevolution and Sabotage?"

"Is that what it stands for?" Usually he couldn't be bothered to humor Eisenmenger; like most officers in the Political Section, the man had been recruited from upper-class Junker military intelligence—a type Schmidt had loathed in the army.

"You might say so. You might also say that it stands for cutting the guts out of anybody who doesn't agree with it."

"Would it have agents operating in Berlin?"

"Has agents operating everywhere, old boy." He cut into the sausage and peered at its interior. "I hope this dog had a pedigree."

Schmidt sat down next to him. "Suppose a Romanov was running around loose in Berlin. Would the Cheka be interested in assassinating it?"

"Depends which Romanov."

"Somebody pretending to be one of the royal children, maybe. Escaped the massacre."

"Grand Duchess Anastasia, for instance?" Eisenmenger inclined his chin at Schmidt in satisfaction at preempting him. "One's heard the rumors. The Russki community is becoming exercised on the subject. Have you met her?"

"What I want to know is, *if* the Reds thought it was her, would they consider her a danger? Say"—he waggled his hand—"maybe that our government wanted to use her as a bargaining chip or a rallying point or some damn thing."

"A valuable pawn in the great game of chess against Bolshevism, you mean." Eisenmenger always sounded sarcastic, whether he meant to or not.

"Yes, that's what I mean."

"No."

"You're sure?"

"Old boy, we wouldn't waste our time, and the Bolshies know it. They know that we know that Czarism is dead. The great people of Russia may be dying in the thousands under Communism, but they did that anyway under the czars. Dying is what they're good at. National pastime."

"So the Bolshies wouldn't assassinate somebody they believed to be the grand duchess."

"That, old boy, is what I am trying to convey. Not planning a coup, is she? Not intending to storm Moscow at the head of a Tartar army or anything?"

Schmidt grinned. "Not as far as I know."

"There you are, then."

As Schmidt got up, Eisenmenger said, "*Is* she the grand duchess?"

"You're Intelligence. You tell me." God Almighty, he thought, if even Eisenmenger was prepared to be hoodwinked, Anna Anderson has a good career ahead of her. Automatically he wrapped one of his sausages in a napkin, just in case Hannelore hadn't had time to begin her black-market activities.

Eisenmenger watched him. "I thought that lovely wife of yours was pregnant."

"She is."

"Then see that the baby doesn't come out snarling. This dog didn't die happy."

Back in his office, Schmidt said, "Sergeant, I want you to fetch the file on this Olga Ratzel from Inspector Bolle. Ask politely. And after that I've got a nice job for you, right up your alley. Go to Dalldorf and interview Clara Peuthert. Ask around, see who she's been talking to, get a description, find out who's been hanging around there. If they want to keep you in, don't you let 'em."

"Thank you kindly, boss. And where are you going?"

"Me? I'm taking a stroll down to the Landwehr Canal."

For a city threaded with canals, Berlin had never quite come to terms with them. Rivers, yes. The rich had built beautiful houses on the river islands, lakes provided weekends of pleasure for bathers and picnickers, but architecturally the canals led a stern, almost secret life of their own along waterfronts that, with their angular and dirty warehouses, had not been integrated into the townscape.

On the Herkulesbrücke, men with time on their hands—plenty of those nowadays—leaned on its parapet watching a dredger do its stuff, water pouring off its pail as the crane lifted it. At their backs, pedestrians crossed to and from the Lützowplatz intent on other business, while below them, quietly chugging, disregarded barges supplied their city with its necessary coal, stone, lime, gravel, and clay.

He didn't quite know why he'd come; it would have been more sensible to go with Willi and get a sniff of the man who'd been hanging around the asylum. Or examine the Olga Ratzel file. Or put Potrovskov to the inquisition. Instead he was leaning on a bridge inhaling the smell of canal silt. But he loathed the pain in mental asylums. And, according to Solomonova, the inquiry into the Ratzel death hadn't got anywhere. And it probably wasn't a good idea to interview Prince Nick while he wanted to thumbscrew the bastard for maneuvering women like chess pieces and getting one of them killed.

Anyway, the thing about canals, he decided, was that bad men could push people into them. And this one was where the woman at the center of his case had suffered a reverse baptism—her identity, if not her sins, washed out of her.

He roused himself and went down the steps to the concrete canal path along which, among flaking buildings and shops, stood a small police station. A smart little launch with POLIZEI painted on its cabin was moored to a landing stage, its fenders gently bumping against the canal wall from the wash of more barges going by. The station itself, however, was reminiscent of a stable and probably had been one in the days of horse-drawn shipping.

Behind the table that served as a reception desk was a long, rectangular room, at the end of which uniformed men were sitting around a stove, their collars undone, smoking their pipes, lucky bastards. Probably tobacco they'd confiscated off some unfortunate, smuggling bargeman.

He raised his hat to the desk sergeant, showed his warrant card, and explained his mission, without much hope. The written record of Anna Anderson's salvation would be extant somewhere, but what he wanted was living memory. Cooperation wasn't too likely either; canal and river police led a life apart and frequently resented having their more interesting cases transferred to a stuck-up *Geheimpolizistkommissar*. This case, he presumed, hadn't been overly interesting, since they'd been left to deal with it.

The sergeant was not encouraging. "Jumper," he said without tone. "Get a lot of jumpers here, especial nowadays. Drop in like raindrops."

"This was a woman," Schmidt said helpfully.

"Nearly always is."

"Didn't have a name, refused to say who she was."

"Often don't."

"Frau Unbekkant, they called her at the hospital she was taken to. Sometime in 1920."

"February," said the sergeant gloomily.

"Youngish, blue eyes— *What?*"

"It was February. Not sure of the date. Let's have a look."

Marveling, Schmidt watched him lumber over to a cupboard, choose a key from a ring attached to his belt, open the cupboard, and select one of the black ledgers lining its shelves. He brought it back to the table, blowing the dust off it, sat down, and, licking his thumb, began turning pages. He swiveled the incident book around so that Schmidt could see it.

A date, 18 February 1920, had been carefully inscribed at the top of the right-hand page. A busy day on the canal, that. Two drunks had been arrested in the morning for fighting on the towpath, a dredger propeller had got fouled on a tree branch, a bargeman's child had fallen in and been fished out, two of the station's policemen had been required to help riot police during a workers' demonstration in the Tiergarten and a counterdemonstration by Right-wing militia that had got out of hand, an old-clothes man had been charged with peddling along the bank without a license, someone had been fishing for eels—also without a license—more drunks had been restrained as the night went on.

And at 2345 hours . . .

"Unknown young woman, about 20 years, jumped off Herculesbrücke, saved by Sergeant Hallman patrolling the canal bank at the time. Sgt Hallman successfully administered artificial resuscitation. She was admitted to the Elizabeth Hospital in Lützowstrasse. No papers or money found on her person. She refused to give her name or make a statement."

The sergeant said, "Be written up proper in the official report to headquarters, but that's the gist."

"Is Sergeant Hallman still around?" Schmidt asked.

"Retired."

"Does anyone remember the incident. Do you?"

"Off duty that night, I reckon."

Schmidt nodded; it had been too much to expect.

"But Gustl probably remembers," continued the amazing sergeant. "You could ask him. Hey, Gustl." He escorted Schmidt to the group around the stove. The seating was varied—an old chintz settee, lopsided armchairs—but comfortable. Schmidt took the arm of the settee, and introductions were made.

River Policeman August Schulz *did* remember the incident—a feat Schmidt found curious; after all, it had been nearly three years ago, and, if the desk sergeant could be believed, female suicide was a local industry.

He was a huge man, Schulz, and, considering the time he spent puffing his pipe before he uttered them, one of few words. He remembered that night, he said eventually, because if he hadn't heard Sergeant Hallman's bellows for help, the good sergeant would have drowned alongside the girl he was trying to save.

"February," he said. "Weren't warm."

Schmidt could imagine it. The water would have been as cold as it was now; death for the two people in it would have been quick. Only a man of Gustl Schultz's strength could have hauled a policeman in a heavy uniform and a girl in woolen petticoats—Anna had been well wrapped, apparently—up the sheer sides of the canal.

"Is there any other reason you remember the incident?" Schmidt asked, accepting a cup of coffee. After a while he was forced to wonder out loud whether Gustl had heard him, but his neighbor, grinning, said, "He's thinking about it."

Eventually Gustl took his pipe from his mouth. "Something about her," he said.

"What? Was it because she wouldn't give her name?"

There was an enormous shrug. "She were scared."

"Of what?"

Another shrug. "Scared." Whatever the "something" that had made the girl and her fright unusual, Gustl didn't have the vocabulary to express it.

Schmidt said carefully, "Was there anything, anything at all, suggesting she *hadn't* been trying to commit suicide?"

This would be a long wait, he could tell by the puffing. One of the other policemen, somewhat tentatively, held a small tin out to him. It contained cigarettes, lots of them, Wimpels. He took one and realized at the same time that the coffee he was drinking had been made from coffee beans. He lit up, luxuriously. "Should've joined the canal police," he said, and felt the atmosphere relax.

"Funny, that," Gustl said.

"What? What was funny?"

"As Sergeant Hallman wondered the same thing. Kept asking her was she pushed, did someone push her in."

"And?" God, he would grow old in this place.

"They didn't."

"How do you know, if she didn't say anything?"

"Kept shaking her head."

"Well, did Sergeant Hallman see something, or hear something, that made him think she was pushed?"

But that was it. Sergeant Hallman had been shivering, the girl had been shivering, it had been necessary to deal with them both before they got pneumonia. Unbekkant had been taken to the hospital, Hallman to his home. The incident had been filed as an attempted suicide.

A request for Sergeant Hallman's home address elicited the fact that the man had fulfilled a dream and retired with his wife to the Black Forest.

Shit.

As he got up to go, the policeman with the cigarettes took a small handful of them from his tin and dropped them neatly into Schmidt's Burberry pocket. "There y'are, son, compliments of the canal." He'd made a good impression. Accepting illicit goods, this was; he was becoming an old hand. Conspiratorially, he patted his pocket. What the hell.

Before he left, he copied down the incident page for February 18, and, on the off chance, made a note of Sergeant Hallman's address; perhaps he could write to him. The man had suspected that Anna's fall into the canal wasn't suicide. Which, Schmidt was nearly becoming sure, it wasn't. Were you that scared if you'd attempted suicide and been rescued? Bewildered and shocked, perhaps. Unhappy, certainly. But frightened?

He buttoned up his coat against the cold and wandered back to the bridge. *Why* hadn't she given them her name? Had she even then been planning on resurrecting herself as the grand duchess? Doubtful. According to Solomonova, that bright idea hadn't occurred to her until two years later, when she was in Dalldorf. So why hadn't she given her name?

They'd sat her in the warmth, Schmidt thought, seeing it. Probably on the settee he himself had just vacated. Concerned, homely faces around her asking questions, telling her she was safe now. But she hadn't felt safe. Why?

Because whatever was out there was still there. And whatever it was out there was so dreadful that it terrified her to this day.

Who is he, Anna?

14

WHEN ESTHER FINALLY caught up with him in his office at the Green Hat, Nick was throwing things. He'd been to see Anna at the von Kleists.

"Know what that bitch did to me? Cut me dead! Do you believe it? *Me,* who took her out of the loony bin. Had to report to some sort of guard. Then I'm kept waiting in the fucking hall, and a flunky comes up and says, 'Her Imperial Highness is not at home.' *Not at fucking home*—and I heard her voice coming from the *next room*!"

"Oh, dear."

"Yes, oh, dear." He turned on Esther. "So now I'm not good enough for her. Christ, if they'd have let me at her, I'd have done the Cheka's job for them. You smiling, Esther?"

"No." Her lip was being firmly bitten. "I gather you didn't go quietly."

"You're fucking right I didn't. Von Kleist comes out and says Her Imperial Highness is not well and can't receive visitors. Her Imperial Highness is as tough as old boots, I tell him. Don't be fooled by I'm-so-scared-and-on-the-edge-of-fucking-breakdown,

I tell him. She'll outlast you and me. Pity the poor Cheka agents try to do *her* in. They're welcome, I tell him."

Esther swiped up the only object remaining on the desk, a nice little Degas bronze it would be a pity to see broken.

Nick flung himself into his chair. "I spoiled the cow, that's what I did. Put her with some fucking baron and she thinks she's in shit-shovel city."

Which, Esther thought, was probably true. Anna was discovering Anastasia's milieu; she wouldn't want to be reminded of the crook who'd put her there. Or, for that matter, the stripper and the Jew who'd helped him. "They believe in her, then?"

"Believe in her?" Nick's head went up like a wolf's. "She's got them eating out her fucking hand. Told them some tale about Grand Uncle Ernest Ludwig going to Russia during the war that had 'em gasping. Kleist's checked up on it with some of his diplomat pals, and turns out it could be true, only no fucker knew."

"It's put her in good odor with the von Kleists?"

"Like the smell of sainthood. Christ, they got more guards around her than Fort fucking Knox."

"Good. She's safe."

"Good. Lovely. Perfect. They're starting to look for lawyers to get at the Romanov fortune for her. And where's that leave me? *Me,* who's paid out good money for the hag, taught her everything she knows." He was on his feet again. "I should have married her, Esther. I should have had a fucking contract. Who said, 'Put not thy trust in princes'?"

"A psalmist."

"Well, he knew what he was fucking talking about. She's not going to get away with it. What was Her Imperial Highness doing in the time between Ekaterinburg and jumping into the canal? We need to find out—*you* need to find out. I want a lever for some of that inheritance money."

"That's blackmail," Esther said, shocked.

"It's insurance. What you sitting there for?" he shouted at her. "Start, start." He flapped his hands.

After all, she thought, continuing to sit, the inspector wasn't the only one with investigative resources in this city—Nick had contacts among the men who ran it that Schmidt could only dream of.

"Start where?" she asked.

"I don't know. Just start."

"If I do, it's only to protect Anna, Nick, not so you can get your hands on the czar's jewels and *not* so you can threaten her with exposure."

"Sure, sure." He was calming down now that he had a plan.

"Do you know anybody in Immigration? Perhaps they have more information than they put on her papers."

Nick peered at her. "You going gaga on me, Esther?"

Esther sighed. "She didn't have any papers."

"Of course she didn't. Frau Unbekkant, wasn't she? That's another thing she owes me for—I had to pay Solly Hirsch for a rush job." Solly was Nick's forger.

"So all we know is, she was dragged out of a canal in 1920."

"The Landwehr, so Clara said."

"Which hospital did they take her to? Before she went to Dalldorf?"

"How the hell should I know? The Elizabeth, I think. Have I got time to sniff around? Use your bloody initiative. Find out."

She felt this wasn't the time to tell Nick she was leaving him; in this state he wouldn't even hear her.

He was on the trail now. Schmidt's nose led him along the route that had been taken by the ambulance carrying an unnamed, half-drowned young woman from the canal to the Elizabeth Hospital in Lützowstrasse three years before. He hated hospitals; their universal smell of disinfectant and suffering took him back to the bedside of Ikey Wolff dying from a British bullet in the stomach as the crowds in the streets outside celebrated the signing of the Armistice.

A nurse at a desk sent him to the matron's office down a corridor lined with mothers and children.

The matron refused his request. "Patients' records are the responsibility of the superintendent. I'm sorry, I have no authority to open them for the police or anyone else."

"Can I talk to the superintendent?"

"He'll be here tomorrow."

As she showed him to the door, he nodded at the crowded corridor. "Epidemic broken out?"

"Malnutrition," she said.

AT ALEXANDERPLATZ, Willi had returned from interviewing Clara Peuthert. He was sitting in Schmidt's chair, ostentatiously fanning himself with his notebook. "I want danger money."

"Bad time?" Schmidt asked.

"I had to track her down, boss. She's been let out, Christ knows why—she bloody near raped me. I don't know how long she was in the bin, but . . . You know how men come out of prison desperate for a bit of the other? Seems it's the same with women. I had to fight her off."

"It's your sexual magnetism, Willi." Schmidt took off his coat. "I hope she's as pretty as Yusupov."

"She ain't Clara Bow, I can tell you that." He surrendered his chair to Schmidt and found another.

Clara Peuthert, discharged from the hospital, had found a room in a cousin's house, from which she was continuing her campaign to gain recognition for her protégée, the grand duchess.

"Does she know where Anderson has been living?"

Willi shook his head. "No, but she knew she was with Prince Nick."

"And told somebody."

"Didn't keep it secret," Willi said. "If there's a crowned head in Europe she hasn't written to, I'd like to know who it is."

"It wasn't a crowned head cut Natalya's throat," Schmidt said. "Not that I'd put anything past them. Who else has she talked to?"

"Reporters, mainly. This Anastasia business is starting to get attention. She had a copy of the *Double Eagle* with a story in it that she'd given them."

"*Double Eagle, Double Eagle,*" Schmidt muttered. "I'll remember it in a minute."

"Magazine of sorts," Willi told him. "Published by the Supreme Monarchist Council, whatever that is."

"Ah, yes. Exiled Russians politically to the right of Attila the Hun."

Willi nodded. "Thought it went a bit strong on the Jews, the copy I saw. And another reporter turned up at the house while I was there."

"*Did* he now?"

"A she, it was. Lady representing an American paper, she said, wanting to write a piece on 'Anastasia, Europe's Deepest Mystery.' I told her to shove off. Ought we to say Anderson's a fake, boss? I did wonder."

"It's not our business unless she tries to get money out of it."

"And we don't *really* know she is, do we?"

Et tu, Brute?

Schmidt said, "Did you stop flirting long enough to get a description of the man in the grounds? Peuthert must have seen him. She's supposed to have frightened him off at some point."

"Yeah, well, descriptions ain't Clara's strong point. She gave me all that stuff about him turning up every sixth weekend, but she couldn't tell me his coloring, what he wore, how old—not anything. She may say she scared him off, but I reckon he scared her a good deal more. Seems nervous now she hasn't got the protection of the asylum. All she'd say was . . ." Willi paused from reluctance.

"What?"

"She just said he reminded her of me. Or I reminded her of him."

"You?"

Willi turned pages. "Her exact words: 'He was something like you, Sergeant.'"

"And what's that like when it's at home?"

Willi shrugged. "Good looks, charm."

Schmidt thought, I should have gone myself. "And she couldn't remember anything else?"

Willi shook his head. "Like I say, she's difficult to pin down. And half the time I was having to fend her off. They shouldn't've let her out."

Schmidt pondered on a man who so frightened women that they couldn't describe him. Even the self-possessed Solomonova had been unable to say much more than that the man was big. Olga Ratzel's file had got him no further; apparently nobody had seen anything.

He felt in his pocket, tossed one of the river policeman's Wimpels to Willi and lit another for himself. Big and frightens women. That's if it *is* the same man and our Anna isn't being pursued by a posse of different murderers and I'm not on the wrong fucking track altogether.

Why the gaps between his appearances? And what the hell connects him in Clara Peuthert's poor mind with our good-natured Willi? Size? Bad feet? Schmidt allowed his gaze to linger on his sergeant, upright in his chair, his cigarette's lit end turned in toward his palm in the way men had learned in the trenches when to show a speck of light attracted a bullet.

Hell. I don't know.

"I don't know, Willi," he said. "Tomorrow we'll have to start on Potrovskov's nightclubs, see if any of them have been providing a big scary monster with information they shouldn't have. Now I'm going home to my pregnant missus. You can present the report to Ringer tonight—serve you right for carrying on with Clara. Ought to be ashamed of yourself."

THERE WAS HOMEMADE bratwurst with onion gravy and sauerkraut for dinner. Hannelore had been shopping with Willi's wife.

"There was pork and veal, Siegfried," Hannelore said in the tones of one who had not only seen the Holy Grail but been allowed to bring it home. "And onions and cabbage. And so *cheap*."

Guilt flavored his every mouthful. The eyes of the starving children at the hospital were only slightly averted when Hannelore said, "I took some downstairs to Frau Busse for the little ones. Is that all right?"

"It certainly is." The Busses had three children and, since Herr Busse had lost his job as an accountant, were having a hard time of it. He suspected that Frau Busse had a hard time of it anyway; Franz Busse was frequently to be heard barking orders at his family and to be seen herding them off in all weathers to march through the Grünewald and enjoy themselves. Schmidt didn't like him, although, having to explain why to Hannelore, he'd only been able to come up with "He wears shorts."

"Siegfried."

"All right, he makes Frau Busse wear shorts."

Tonight was not improved by a visit from the very man. Hannelore ushered him into the living room, where he bowed. "I have come to thank you both. It was a fine meal." He was long and thin, with steel-rimmed glasses and a way of sounding, even when grateful, as if he were making an accusation.

Shamefaced, Schmidt mumbled, "Hannelore . . . They happened to have . . . Think nothing of it. . . . Lucky . . . Procured through a friend."

Herr Busse lifted a finger to stop him. "I do think much of it. Nor is there need for explanation, Herr Inspector. It is right in these times that the police should keep themselves fed and strong."

He wasn't being ironic, Schmidt thought. He meant it.

"Also," Busse continued, "I have to tell you that Frau Busse and the children and I are moving." Another finger stopped their expressions of concern. "We can no longer afford the apartment and are going to live with Frau Busse's mother in Wedding."

It was awful; *Wedding* was awful—one of the poorest districts in Berlin. "We're sorry to lose you," Schmidt said, and under these circumstances he was. Busse had struggled out of poverty to become a hardworking member of the middle class; inflation was sending him back to a district of poor housing where, the last time Schmidt saw the statistics, the infant mortality rate was 30 percent.

And, from the look behind his spectacles, somebody was going to pay for it. Busse's eyes were narrow with rage.

Schmidt walked him to the door, commenting on the band newly adorning Busse's left arm. "Haven't seen that one before. Wandervogel?" The *volkisch* movement had spawned dozens of youth groups, all dedicated to ensuring that German boys and, to a lesser extent, girls breathed good German air and sang good German songs around good German campfires. He'd belonged to such a one as a boy, but now there were so many he'd lost track.

"An offshoot. It is the Jugenbund—you know I am interested in the youth movement—we are the first, I think, to affiliate ourselves to the National Socialist Party. We have placed ourselves under the order of the Sturmabteilung. You know the NSDAP?"

"Seen the posters," Schmidt said.

"You should join, you know. Adolf Hitler is the only man who can get us out of the mess all these traitors and Jews have got us into."

"Yes, well, as a policeman I've got to stay neutral."

"There can be no neutrality," Franz Busse said.

"I am so sorry for them," Hannelore said, nearly weeping, when Schmidt rejoined her.

"So am I. I'd be more sorry if the bugger hadn't joined the Nazis."

They sat together in front of the ersatz fire, Hanne's legs on Schmidt's lap while he massaged them. Her ankles were still swollen. "I carried too much shopping back," she said. "I was greedy. They'll be better tomorrow."

She went to sleep, her legs still in his lap, and he laid his head back against the crocheted antimacassar to think.

For the tenth time, he put himself by the entrance to Charlottenburg Park, keeping in its shadows, watching for the figure that would come stealing in to wait for the girl he'd lured to it. It was male and it was big. It had come on foot via Spandauer Damm or Tegeler Weg—there'd been no sightings of a car. Here it came, a huge shadow, a woman frightener with something about it, if a troubled lady were to be believed, that resembled Willi.

He woke Hannelore by sliding his hand up her thigh and tickling her.

She smiled at him. "You are a naughty man, Siegfried Schmidt."

He said, "Imagine you're meeting Willi Ritte for the first time. What's your impression?"

"A big, kindly man."

"No, that's because you know him. Your *first* impression."

"Well." She squeezed her eyes shut to concentrate. "He's very much a sergeant, isn't he?"

"Military, do you mean?"

"Yes. Yes, I suppose I do."

They went to bed.

Schmidt dreamed. What the dream was, he never remembered, though Franz Busse was in it somewhere, but in the middle of it he woke and sat up.

"Jesus Christ," he said. "I know who he is."

15

"ALL RIGHT, who is he?" Willi asked, regarding Schmidt's desk, on which papers were being pushed this way and that.

"I don't know his fucking name, do I? I just know who he is." Schmidt snatched up some of the papers and came around the desk, jabbing his finger at them. "See this?" It was the report from the house-to-house inquiries made near Charlottenburg Park. "See who was on the streets the night of the murder?"

Willi ran his eye down the list. "Jew with handcart, courting couple, large woman, two Communists, SA man, Rudi Mach—it's not Rudi the Flasher, is it?"

"No, it isn't," Schmidt said irritably. "Now, look here—this is the incident report about what was going on at the Landwehr Canal the day our Anna went into it."

"Couple of drunks, kid fell in, secondhand-clothes man, Tiergarten demonstration and the usual trouble, illegal fishing."

"Now then." Schmidt shook the papers at him. "What's the common denominator?"

Willi went over the lists again, and his face was touched by a dawn. "Jew with a handcart at Charlottenburg, secondhand-clothes man at the Landwehr. It's a Jew."

"For Christ's sake, Willi. Our man's big. Solomonova said so, Clara said so, Natalya said so. How many big Jews do you know?"

"Well, there's Manny Finkelstein. He weighs in about—"

"It's not fucking Finkelstein." Schmidt gave up and went back to his desk. "I'll give you a clue. Pieck thinks a trench knife was used to cut Natalya's throat."

"Yes?"

Schmidt expired. "Look, our man's big and he's military—that's why he resembles you. You look like a soldier, so does he. On the night Natalya was murdered, an SA man, a storm trooper, quarreled with a couple of Communists. He was alone, so he was careful not to get into a fight. Now, that's unusual—the Brownshirts usually travel in packs, the bastards. Am I right?"

"Ye-e-es," Willi said.

"Good. At Dalldorf a big man turns up and frightens Peuthert. He's big, he resembles you, which means he's military. All right? Turns up again at the Green Hat, still big, uses a knife."

"Ye-e-es."

"Very well. Go back three years, to Landwehr Canal and Anderson plopping into it. What was happening that day? And not far away either?" His eyes rolled with exasperation at Willi's frown. "There was a demonstration by the Communists, wasn't there? At the Tiergarten? And who turns up at Communist demonstrations in order to start a riot?"

Willi hit the side of his head. *"Storm troopers."*

"The Sturmabteilung. Exactly." Schmidt leaned back in his chair. "And that's who our killer is. He's SA, sport trooper, storm trooper—whatever they call themselves nowadays."

Willi bared his teeth, clicking them as if tasting the argument. "Sure we're not being carried away by politics, boss?" Schmidt's loathing of the far Right was something that his sergeant regarded as an obsession—he himself was conservative with a small *c* and merely disliked troublemakers of all political persuasions.

Schmidt thought about it. Was he? No, damned if he was.

"I'll tell you another thing," he said. "He's not a Berlin man. He does his soldiering elsewhere. That'd account for the periods when he left Anna to her own devices."

"Only does his murdering on leave, you mean?"

Schmidt grunted. Put like that, it sounded silly.

"It wouldn't stand up to an examining magistrate, boss," Willi said.

"Maybe not. But that's who he is. And I'm going to prove it. I'm off to see Eisenmenger."

The Political and Intelligence Section had a corridor to itself. Which was carpeted—something that had not gone unnoticed by the lesser mortals in Crime who had to make do with linoleum. Eisenmenger's office was also carpeted. He had some small, exquisite landscapes on his walls, while his large posterior was fitted into a padded leather chair beside not a desk but an escritoire.

Schmidt was offered real coffee made in a French *cafetière*. He stated his request.

"Well, you won't find them in the phone book," Eisenmenger said, "their activities being frowned on by authority. Recruitment's through personal contact at rallies or the less salubrious beer halls. And they get their publicity by doing what they do, fighting the Reds and beating up the occasional Jew. Cheaper than giving out handbills."

"They must have an HQ," Schmidt said.

"Munich," Eisenmenger said. "They're all run from Munich. Very big there, as you know, very organized. Down there they've progressed from acting as Herr Hitler's personal chuckers-out to being his National Socialist private army, equipped and trained. My opposite number in Bavaria is expecting a putsch any day now."

"A putsch? They'll try to take over down there?"

"Looks like it." Eisenmenger might have been forecasting rain. "Röhm seems keen on it." He raised his eyebrows. "Ernst Röhm? My dear Schmidt, if you're investigating the Sturmabteilung, you should know their leader. A rather common fellow of questionable sexuality, but an excellent soldier, wounded at Verdun. You can't miss him; a shell fragment took away part of his nose. Rabid right-winger, of course, but as a military organizer he is nonpareil. He can make soldiers out of sewer rats, they tell me. And does. He's also the deviser of their uniform." Eisenmenger's own fastidious nose wrinkled. "He threatens to submerge the republic under a sea of brown."

"Like shit, you mean," Schmidt said.

"Don't underestimate him. My information is that he's in Berlin at the moment in order to invigorate the local thugs, who, since they lack the sympathy from our police that Munich boys are used to receiving from the Munich force, have not been killing enough Communists for his taste."

"The ones I've seen brawling in the streets are invigorated enough for me," Schmidt said.

"Oh, I agree, I agree. However, in Bavaria they'd be drummed out of the SA for sensitivity. Here's the address. . . ." Eisenmenger screwed his monocle into his right eye socket and plied a gold fountain pen on an embossed notepad. "As far as we can tell, such administration as the SA has in Berlin seems to be centered here in Kreuzberg. I'm told it's an unlikely-looking venue—that's deliberate, of course—midway between the railway and the water tower." He paused before handing over the note. "Should you be thinking of paying them a visit, and *should* you want to see Mother again, may I urge on you the necessity to be polite."

IT WAS AN old fire station, long abandoned by what had been a horse-drawn fire brigade. Both of its two huge and dirty doors were shut. Nailed to the central pillar was an equally dirty piece of cardboard, which said KREUZBERG SPORTS GUILD.

Like Eisenmenger, Willi was stressing the need for restraint as he and Schmidt awaited an answer to their knock on the great doors. "We don't want to rile them, boss, not till we find out what we want to know. What *do* we want to know?"

"I'm not sure yet."

There were sounds of activity beyond the doors, and somebody yelled, "Password?"

"Police," Schmidt shouted back.

There was no answer, not even to the kick Schmidt applied to the bottom of the door.

They were returning to the street after a fruitless attempt to find a back entrance when they saw a contingent of small boys, led by a tall, skinny youth, marching up to the doors. They reminded Schmidt of the Wandervogel of his youth, though these kids looked even poorer than he'd been; one or two had knapsacks and proper boots, but the rest had homemade sacks strung on their backs and worn-out shoes. Each of them, though, was equipped with a smart khaki peaked cap.

"Wayfarers," said Willi sentimentally.

"Never liked it," Schmidt said. "My group didn't take girls."

"Mine did. Unofficially."

On an order from the youth, the urchins lined up in professional military formation, shuffling into arm-measured distance from one another.

"Atten-*shun*." They snapped to it. "Hats off."

The caps were whipped off, collected by a small child with a corporal's stripe on his ragged sleeve, and handed to the youth.

"Heil Hitler!"

Twenty sets of breath puffed into the cold air, and twenty arms went up in the salute given to Roman emperors. "Return for inspection at five o'clock," they were told. "Dismiss."

The children scattered. The youth knocked on the door. They heard his shout: "Robber Baron. Lieutenant Alvens to report."

As one of the doors grated back, Schmidt and Willi moved up to push in behind the young man. The door swung back on them but was hindered by Willi's boot, and they went inside.

It was a gymnasium, startling in its size and cleanliness and—considering the poverty of the Kreuzberg district—lavish sports equipment.

Against the white walls were climbing bars, ringed ropes hung from the ceiling, and a vaulting horse stood in the center of the room, surrounded by exercise mats. One corner was a boxing area, complete with punching bags and a raised ring in which two boxers, both of them bleeding from the nose, had suspended activity to stare at the two policemen. As had the rest of the occupants—forty or fifty of them, all of them male, most of them young, and none of them showing a welcome.

It was not a comfortable moment. Ill will emitted by half a hundred youths, all in splendid physical condition, tends to daunt.

Schmidt knew he and Willi had only two advantages. One: they were fully clothed, which gave them the superiority of normality over opponents who wore only breechcloths—a group of boys just emerging from a side door, toweling themselves, were totally naked. Two: they belonged to a police force that had inculcated respect, not to mention fear, into its law-abiding and criminal citizens alike over many years. A new god was being worshipped in this place, but Schmidt had to count on the fact that the old one still spoke to blood ancestry.

"I am Inspector Schmidt, Berlin City Police. This is Sergeant Ritte. Who is in charge here?" He snapped it out—he wasn't going to get anywhere with this bunch by saying please.

The scales trembled. Glances were exchanged, fists tightened, but in the end nobody moved.

They were fine looking, thought Schmidt. Some, if not all, must have come from the slums, but, if so, the SA had been feeding them well. Where the hell did this organization get its money?

The smell of liniment from their shining white muscles mingled in the air with that of sweat and fresh paint. They looked like a beautiful frieze on a Greek vase; he could have been proud of them if it hadn't been for the massive swastika that hung from the ceiling.

Menaced though he was, he felt pity—and shame. We let them down, he thought. We lost the war for them, and nobody has pointed out to them that it shouldn't have been fought in the first place. Instead of the sword-waving, Wagnerian, "Deutschland über Alles" romances their heads have been filled with, we've handed them a feeble, poverty-stricken republic that promises nothing. Hitler offers them glory and power.

Eventually the youth that had been leading the wayfarers said sulkily, "Captain Schwerte is out."

"When will he be back?"

"Soon." It was spit out, suggesting *And then we'll see.*

"And you are?"

"Lieutenant Alvens."

Schmidt looked him in the eye, stuck his chin up, put a deliberate sneer to his mouth, like an officer, he thought, like a bloody lion tamer. Without moving his eyes, he pointed to a half-glazed door marked OFFICE. "I'll wait for him in here."

"You can't do that."

Schmidt strode into the office. "Hold the door, Willi."

He heard the youth's voice go high. "He can't do that."

And Willi's: "Oh, yes he can, sonny."

Schmidt partly closed the door so that it and Willi's bulk concealed him from outside but enabled him to go quickly to his sergeant's help if necessary. The office was military in its neatness. An iron table served as a desk. A chair. Army-surplus filing cabinets—all locked. The only books on display were large diaries on a shelf.

A framed picture of Adolf Hitler hung on the wall, looking so like the fishmonger whose stall Hannelore had patronized in the good old days that Schmidt mentally added a large cod to it. Below it were other photographs showing tiered rows of youths and bearing inscriptions: "SA Boxing team. Berlin. May 1921." "SA Jujitsu team. Berlin. August 1922." "SA Rifle team. Berlin. December 1922." In one, the largest, a line of uniformed men stood behind some squatting boys, all sternly facing the camera—nobody smiled in these photos—taken recently, apparently, at "Sports Conference. Berlin. 1923." A collection of silver cups and trophies on a shelf declared the teams' successes in various championships.

The only female contribution to all this male achievement was contained in an untidy, much less structured photograph, but when Schmidt looked at it closely, he saw that its subjects, who'd been caught in midcaper, were not women but boys with straw wigs for hair and balloons stuck down the bodices of their dresses. A high old time was being had by all, and none more than the figure of an older man dressed in hunting clothes, flourishing a horse whip over two grinning "girls" kneeling before him, their hands held out in a mock plea for mercy.

Even less healthy was a large cardboard box in one corner with "Erasers!" written on its label. Smith pulled back its flaps; it was full of brass knuckles and rubber truncheons. Storm-trooper humor, he thought.

On the desk, usually the place for a family picture, was a framed black-and-white photo showing two men, both in a uniform Schmidt didn't recognize but presumed to be brown. One, smaller and fatter than the other, had had to raise his arm to put it around his comrade's shoulders. Both had adopted a pose for the camera that suggested either arrogance or defiance. Across the bottom of the photo was a large scrawl: *"Revolverschnauze, herzlichst, Mollenkönig."*

He wondered at the affection existing between two men who knew each other as Revolver Muzzle and King of the Beer Barrels, but switched his attention to the more interesting diaries and took down the one most up to date.

The entries were neat and restrained. Today's read *"Meet E.R. at Anhalter Station 3:00 P.M. Sports display 4:30 P.M. Rally Viktoria P. Dinner with K."*

E.R.? Ernst Röhm? Big day for the SA. He and Willi seemed to have intruded on preparations for a celebration of the Bavarian leader. God, he hoped so.

Activity had resumed in the gym hall. He heard the run and thump of takeoffs and landings over the vaulting horse and Willi calling advice to one of the boxers: "Keep your guard up, son. Watch his left."

Good old Willi, always made friends.

A young voice sneered, "What do you know about boxing, old man?"

"Me? I taught Manny Finkelstein everything he knows."

"He is not a boxer."

"Not a boxer? He's middleweight champion!"

"He is not a boxer. He is a Jew."

Schmidt turned back the pages of the diary. What had these likely fellows been doing this last weekend when Natalya was murdered?

Nothing on the Sunday, apparently. The page was empty. But the previous one was headed "January Instruction Conference" and suggested that the Berlin SA had been paid a visit by representatives of its counterpart from other cities. Herr Revolver Muzzle (if it was he) had reminded himself of the arrangements he'd have to make for them. *"Book the Tabagie,"* he'd written. *"Accommodation and transport for T.S. (Hamburg), W.H. (Stuttgart), B.L. (Leipzig), R.G. (Munich), A.V. (Frankfurt), J.M. (Kiel), R.F. (Vienna), P.J. (Potsdam)"*—the list was long.

God Almighty, how far did this bloody organization spread? And screw you, Revolver Muzzle, for using initials. Out of caution, perhaps—some of these men probably had police records.

Schmidt looked around at the other diaries. He took down the one for 1922. When was it Prince Nick had fetched Anna Anderson from Dalldorf Asylum? July. The bastard he was after had been in Berlin in July 1922.

He flipped over pages. And there it was: "July Instruction Conference."

This time fewer men had come—the right-wing paramilitaries were only just getting themselves organized in '22; these would be representatives of various Freikorps—but A.V. had turned up from Frankfurt, accompanied by a G.N. Munich had sent R.G. again, this time with E.R. himself. Men with initials differing from those in '23 had come from Leipzig and Hamburg. Vienna had sent R.F. once more, Stuttgart had sent W.H. Kiel hadn't sent anybody. P.J. had come again from Potsdam.

Schmidt licked his thumb and forefinger to turn more pages. I'm pinning you down, you fucker. "September Instruction Conference," "October Instruction Conference."

Regular meetings. There was a lot to arrange when you were undermining a government, and, despite the fact that the headquarters were in Munich, it was more convenient for the bastards to meet each other in Berlin, the transport center of Germany.

Regularly.

His hands shaking, Schmidt turned back to the diary's beginning and then forward, counting. Every sixth weekend. *They met every sixth weekend.*

Schmidt straightened his back and expelled a long breath. The Wisdom of Solomonova. She'd been right: the killer lived somewhere else and traveled to Berlin every sixth weekend.

And *he* was right: the bastard was an SA man.

Names, that's what he needed, not initials. Maybe Revolver Muzzle had put them somewhere else. He reached for the 1921 book but was disappointed; there'd been no conferences until November 1921, and none of the entries had any relevance he could see, except to indicate that Revolver Muzzle had split his time between Berlin and whatever

Freikorps he then belonged to in order to beat up people, with trips to fellow Freikorps in Munich to help beat up people there.

There was no diary for 1920, when, if his assumption was correct, the first attempt on Anna Anderson's life had been made at the Landwehr Canal. Which, now he came to think of it, ran not far away from this very gymnasium.

You're here. You're in these pages. You've been in this room.

With the two relevant diaries open in front of him on the table, he got out his pencil and notebook and copied down the initials mentioned under all the conference headings, writing fast—Revolver Muzzle could return with E.R. at any moment.

When he'd finished, he crossed out the initials that hadn't turned up on up the pertinent dates. What was he left with?

W.H. of Stuttgart, R.G. of Munich, A.V. of Frankfurt, R.F. of Vienna. P.J. of Potsdam.

Shit. He imagined himself contacting the police forces of five cities and asking them if a particular storm trooper was on their books. *Sorry, old boy, I only know his initials.* They'd love him.

Well, what did he know about Natalya's murderer? A big man. Aryan. Probably ex-army. And, since he was being sent to Berlin to represent his city's storm troopers, someone high up in the SA hierarchy.

Like smoke issuing forth from the uncorked top of a genie's bottle, a figure was forming, shadowy, still insubstantial, but gaining the form of as weird a killer as he'd ever come across, a man who was too busy to come to Berlin and commit murder other than when, conveniently, he was sent—presumably with all expenses paid.

No other time off? Unable to plead the excuse of a grandmother's funeral in order to come and arrange Anna's?

Unless . . . unless, he *had* to come to Berlin on these conferences but the capital was dangerous for him because Anna was in it, would see him and give him away. Was that it? When you come to Berlin, you're vulnerable? Why, in a city that now encompassed—what? four million people?—are you likely to bump into *her*?

Schmidt held his pencil like a drumstick and beat it on the table in a tattoo that Hannelore would have recognized as echoing her husband's thinking at its most agitated.

Was there any reason Anna and the killer *should* come face-to-face in Berlin? Likely to make coinciding visits at his mother-in-law's? Belonged to the same club?

That's not it. Wrong track, Schmidt. No-no-no-no-nononono. The tattoo increased speed.

The two men in the photograph taunted him, as if they knew. *Did* they know? Would they stand for murder? Yes, in a way they did; the very existence of their organization was based on violence. Hitler's most recent speech, as reported in the papers, had said that the only revolution he wanted was racial, that Marxism could be counteracted only by the brutality of execution. Didn't his followers swagger through the streets on marches designed to spread fear? Weren't their rallies a celebration of malevolence?

And then Schmidt knew why Natalya's killer was afraid when he was in Berlin.

You're on display, you bastard. You have to strut in front of the public, march, speak from a rostrum, have your photograph taken with the other fascist luminaries, appear on newsreels at rallies. The man was in the open, his face bared—it had to be. He couldn't act like a shrinking violet; publicity was the SA's oxygen.

And it was terrible for him. All the time he was aware that Anna might see him—in a newspaper, at the cinema in a newsreel. She could be standing in the crowd watching as he marched by.

And she could say, *Ecce homo.* "Here is the man."

She hadn't. Probably hadn't even seen him. But perhaps the man couldn't depend on her silence. *Here is the man* . . . who did what? What did Anna know that was so awful she mustn't be allowed to reveal it? What crime so ugly that even Hitler and his storm troopers would cast out the perpetrator—that, presumably, being the killer's fear, because if he belonged to the SA, he wouldn't go in terror of the police. Rape? Murder? In the SA those were practically conditions of membership. What accusation could Anna bring against the man who wanted to kill her?

The drumming of Schmidt's pencil stopped at the sound of an engine outside in the alley that ran alongside the gymnasium. A motorcar was a rarity in this area of Kreuzberg—when he and Willi had parked, theirs had been the only one on the street.

Schmidt looked at his watch. It was 3:15 P.M. This would be Revolver Muzzle, back from Anhalter station, having collected E.R.

He put his notebook and pencil in his pocket and replaced the diaries on their shelf, took a quick look around, knowing he'd left something undone. There it was—the photograph on the wall of the 1923 Sports conference, a big gathering. With luck, he might have a picture of Natalya's killer. He took it off its hook, frame and all. The gap it left on the wall glared at him, and he stuffed the picture under his arm inside his coat. It wasn't that he had no right to take it—he was the bloody police investigating a murder, wasn't he?—but he wanted to leave this place alive.

He walked out of the office and joined Willi, shutting the door behind him, as two men entered the gymnasium.

They were the couple in the photograph on the desk. The tall one was handsomer and more elegant than he'd appeared in the picture, but it was the shorter of the two who held the eye. Plump, bordering on fat, his brown uniform stretched tight over bosoms and belly, his gait a travesty of a march that waggled his shoulders from side to side, he had a pit where the lower half of one side of his nose should have been—and he was smiling.

"HEIL RÖHM!" The gym shook with the greeting as half a hundred right arms went up.

"Heil Berlin Sports Club." It was a grin now, roguish, and some of the boys laughed.

Then, as one man, they turned to look at the two policemen, and Schmidt knew he and Willi were as close to danger as they'd been on the Western Front. The boys had lacked a leader until this moment; now they had one. This little man carried a charge that crackled around the hall. The place was as electrified as if he'd turned on a switch. Schmidt could hear a boy next to him panting. Maenads, he thought. Bacchus here has only to give the word, and they'll tear Willi and me apart.

Young Lieutenant Alvens was gabbling to the taller man, but it was Röhm who held up his hand to calm him and came forward. He clicked his heels. "And what do the Berlin police want with our little sports club? Have any of our boys been naughty, eh?" He was playing to the gallery.

"And you are?"

"Captain Eric Röhm of the Sportsabteilung. Who are you?"

"Inspector Schmidt. This is Sergeant Ritte." To Schmidt's annoyance he heard Willi click his heels. "We are investigating the murder of a woman, Natalya Tchichagova, killed in Charlottenburg Park on Saturday last. In connection with that murder, I wish to interview a member of"—hell, why should he pander to the pretense that this was a sports organization? it was a training ground for killers—"your *storm troopers* who was in Berlin at that time. Possibly he came from out of town." He fetched out his notebook. "You will please give me the names relating to these initials and locations." He read them out.

"The bastard's been at my diary." It was the taller man, pushing forward.

Röhm held him back. He took his cap off, revealing wavy black hair parted in the middle like a grocer's. "We must help the police, Dietrich. We are a law-abiding organization."

"Then you will supply me with the information I want," Schmidt said.

"Certainly," Röhm said. His pudgy hand took the notebook and he half turned so that his audience could hear him. "W.H. of Stuttgart—that would be Wilhelm Hagen, wouldn't it, Dietrich? You know him better than I do. Reinhardt Gunther is the R.G. of Munich. A.V. of Frankfurt? That's Albert Vali. And R.F. of Vienna is Rolf Freischütz."

Willi was writing it down.

"There." Röhm handed back the notebook. The youths were laughing openly. "Most respectable men, Inspector. Examples to us all."

"I see."

"Do you?" Röhm moved closer.

Schmidt looked back at the bright brown eyes that were gazing into his, perkily, like a robin's. "The man I want is big," he said. "A military man, and he was in Berlin for your organization's conferences—certainly one of them this weekend, again in July 1922, and, most probably with a Freikorps, in February 1920."

He watched the intensity of Röhm's stare dissolve for a second. *You know him now,* he thought. He said, "He slit the throat of a young woman three nights ago and tortured another woman to death before that, and I'm going to get him. I want you to believe it."

"What were they?" Röhm said. "Whores?"

"No, they weren't."

Suddenly Röhm was so close to him that Schmidt could smell his breath, which had whisky on it, and the lavender-scented pomade on his hair. "You were a soldier in the war, of course?" As if to have been anything else was unsound.

"Yes." He wished he weren't standing so militarily stiff, but he had to keep the photo pinned tightly under his arm.

"And you?" Röhm asked of Willi.

Willi clicked his heels again. "Yes, sir. Machine Gun Company, Infantry Regiment Number 156. *Sir.*"

Röhm nodded and turned back to Schmidt, speaking as one veteran to another. "They betrayed us, didn't they?"

"We lost."

"We didn't lose. *They stabbed us in the back.*" It was a shriek that sent a spray of spit onto Schmidt's chin. "The Reds and the Jews and the pencil pushers at our rear—they crumbled, they gave in because they were women. *Women!*"

He stepped back. Schmidt wiped his chin.

Röhm went on more quietly, "You should not be investigating us, Inspector. You should be joining us." His arm jerked out toward the watching youths. "See here the new warrior elite. Here are the ones who will give Germany back her pride, and if it takes brutality to do it, then they are ready. The masses need wholesome fear. They want it. They thirst for a leader that will frighten them into following him to glory. What are a couple of tarts to that?" He raised his arm, his voice crescendoing. "We are the real German revolution, and this time we will not be betrayed by noncombatants. We will march over them to the triumph of the Fatherland. Who are you to question the action of heroes?"

The gym erupted in ecstasy. A couple of boys hand-flipped joyfully over the vaulting horse. Fists punched into the air. Some voices screamed "Hitler!" others "Heil Röhm!" and a few "Get them!"

Willi nudged Schmidt. "Move." They edged toward the door as the yelling began to synchronize: "Heil! Get them! Heil! Get them! Get them! *Get them!*"

One of the doors to the street had been left open. Young Alvens tried to stop them when they got to it, but Willi took him up by one arm and swung him away. They scrambled into the car and locked the doors, the windows darkening as bodies landed on top of it, hammering.

Grinding his gears, Willi drove blind for some yards until the two boys across the windshield saw the sense in dropping off it. Schmidt turned and glimpsed them rolling in the dust of the road. Others were still chasing.

"Don't stop, Willi."

"Fucking not going to," Willi said, swinging the car around a bend.

Eventually he pulled to a stop, turned off the engine, wiped the palms of his hands down his coat, reached into his pocket, brought out a tin of cigarettes, and offered one to Schmidt. "They're Manoli."

"Luxury." Schmidt took one and noticed that his hand was shaking.

"We'll have to close that place down, boss. Have a few of those boys up in court. Teach 'em a bit of respect."

Schmidt nodded vaguely. It wouldn't make any difference. What had animated those young men was a disease; you couldn't close down a disease. In any case, the only injury had been to his and Willi's pride, and he'd learned all he could.

He rolled down his window to let the smoke out. They were high up, on the edge of Viktoria Park. Down below he could see the network of railways leading to Anhalter, Potsdam, and Görlitzer stations.

It was quiet up here, and he heard a snatch of birdsong. He remembered that Mendelssohn was buried somewhere in this area of Kreuzberg.

Willi broke the silence. "Well, we got the names of some suspects, that's one thing."

"No we didn't. The surnames he gave me were mythological—gods and such."

"Was that it? I *thought* he gave in easy."

"When we get back, send some uniforms to bring in Röhm and Schwerte for questioning—at gunpoint if necessary." Wouldn't make any difference either, he thought; Röhm wasn't going to give anything away. But the man knew who the killer was; Schmidt had *seen* him know.

And he knows I'm going to find out if I have to sweat every fucking Brownshirt in Germany.

"Okay, boss," Willi said, and added, "Pity, really."

"What is?"

"Them kids. One of them was my neighbor's boy. Knew him right off. Bit of a sissy, I always thought, and look at him now. They teach 'em to be manly in that outfit, that's one thing."

Schmidt patted his sergeant kindly on his shoulder. "Reckoned they were manly, did you, Willi?"

"Didn't you?"

"You were better off with Yusupov." He flicked his cigarette butt out the window. "Drive on, my son."

BERLIN POSSESSED ONE network of information that was unavailable to both Inspector Schmidt and Prince Nick—its Jews.

Esther, leaving Bismarck Allee, turned north toward Moabit and walked through increasingly depressed and darkening streets until she reached a small wooden house next to a synagogue. All things considered, she would have preferred not to be out at night, but if she could help to find Natalya's killer, she was damn well going to, and time was pressing.

Rabbi Smoleskin chided her for infrequent attendance at the synagogue. "We haven't seen you in a while, Esther."

"There's been trouble, Rabbi."

"Troubles are what Jews are good at—troubles and chopped liver."

She was ushered into a passage where the only light came from the tallow taper in the rabbi's hand. The house smelled of chicken soup. In the thousand miles she and Rosa and the children had traveled from Siberia, passed along like parcels from settlement to Jewish settlement, sometimes in houses, often in huts, that smell had been the one constant, as if they had followed its trail by sniffing, like dogs. However poor their hosts, a hen had been killed in their honor because hospitality demanded it.

From the back of the house came voices and the clatter of crockery, but she was not paying a social call, and the rabbi took her into the cramped, cold room that served as his study, which was where troubles were dealt with. Books were what it consisted of, mainly; when her host had set his taper in the grip of a holder, its small, clear light showed them piled like bricks around the flaking plaster of the walls, as if holding up the room.

That had been another constant of her and Rosa's journey, Esther thought—always a book somewhere, even if the roof had holes in it big enough to see the stars, always a book.

When she'd told him everything, Rabbi Smoleskin pulled at his beard. "That was a sin you connived at, Esther. And seems two poor women died for it."

"And another girl is in danger. Help me put it right, Rabbi. It's a big hospital, the Elizabeth. There must be a Jew in it somewhere."

Knowing her demographic statistics, she had expected Jews in Germany to be few and far between—they were, after all, less than 1 percent of its population—and she had found it extraordinary when she'd finally arrived in Berlin to find that most of its citizens considered themselves swamped by them, an effect created by the Jews' visibility. They dominated large sections of business, the arts, the professions, owned many of the big department stores—out of all proportion to their numbers. Despite big class differences, despite quarrels between Orthodox and non-Orthodox, the Berlin synagogues were largely in touch, passing information across the great sprawl of the city. Moabit, which poor Jews left when they could, sent out its children, sometimes across the world, more often to better jobs in Berlin itself, and it knew where they were.

Frau Smoleskin was fetched in as a consultant. Hugging Esther, she asked, "How's Rosa?" Nobody forgot Rosa. She'd stayed in Moabit less than three months after the trek, her energy still unexhausted despite piloting her children, some of her neighbors, and a wounded, shell-shocked Esther through snow and summer, checkpoints, forest, and warring armies—to become a legend.

After the destruction of her village by the Cossacks, Rosa had seen that a Russia engulfed in civil war since the going of the czar was no place for her children. It never really had been; one gifted son had already left it and was studying in England. When the survivors had crept back out of the forest to see the dead and the ruined houses, Rosa had said, "We go." And they went. Rabbi Smoleskin had pronounced her *eshet hayil,* "a woman of valor." Which, in Esther's view, wasn't the half of it.

"She's left England now," she said. "I got a letter the other day. They've all gone to America. She's setting up a delicatessen business in the Bronx."

"Let us hope President Harding is prepared," the rabbi said, and turned to his wife. "Miriam, do we have somebody in the Elizabeth Hospital?"

Like a diplomatic posting, Esther thought.

But yes, there was. "Didn't the Schechter girl get a job in the almoner's office? Bright girl, that one." Yes, Elizabeth Schechter would help if she could. "But maybe they don't know she's a Jew among all those Catholics, so be tactful, Esther."

"Tactful," she said. "Bend with the wind, let well enough alone, consider the consequences, say 'sir,' don't make waves—when's it going to stop?"

"When Elizabeth Schechter don't lose her job for being a Jew," the rabbi told her sharply. "What's set you off, girl? Better tell Joachim to see her home, Miriam. In this mood she'll be attacking the Brownshirts."

But Esther refused to be accompanied. The Smoleskin boy, an adolescent with earlocks and the fuzz of a beard on his chin, was in greater danger from right-wing gangs than she was.

"I don't know what's happening," Miriam said on the doorstep, tucking the scarf more tightly around Esther's face. "This used to be a good city."

CONDUCTING INQUIRIES AROUND Prince Nick's club took time and was a frustrating business; Nick was reluctant to give a list of his membership to the police. "My members, they're big names, and they come here for relaxation." When threatened with arrest for hampering a murder investigation, he gave in. He was right about the names—they were very big: ministers of the Reich, half the German aristocracy, industrialists, theater people, film stars. Willi went through them with Nick's manager to pinpoint those of them who were also big in size, but, like the rest of the membership, these were people who traveled, often internationally, and not one of them was in Berlin on all the dates Schmidt was interested in. Often, when they attended the club, they brought guests, and as the manager pointed out, "Who can remember guests?" Certainly not the staff which, to a man and woman, swore they had not given any information to a big, military-looking man.

At the Pink Parasol, there was even more reluctance—the all-male membership wasn't listed under names at all, only numbers—but Willi, by this time losing his temper, had crashed open its door to find "a soirée" in progress and arrested every man in the place, taking a vanload of staff and very frightened big names, some of them in pretty dresses, to Alexanderplatz to be questioned.

After a useless bout of interviewing, Schmidt let them go without charge. As one of the more open interviewees told him, "Do I talk to big men? Darling, of *course* I do, and I never, *never* ask their names."

Damn it, he'd have to resort to tracking the killer along the befogged route of Anna Anderson's past.

At the Elizabeth Hospital, where she'd been taken after her immersion in the canal, he also had to throw his Polizei weight around, first to see the superintendent, who, like the hospital itself, appeared to be busy to the point of madness, then to persuade the man (a) to find Anna's medical notes and (b) to reveal what they contained.

"Our patients' histories are confidential, Inspector."

"Honorable, I'm sure, sir." Actually, it was; nobody could have been more indigent than the Anna Anderson dragged out of the Landwehr Canal, yet her privacy was being safeguarded like that of a paying patient. Schmidt shut the door that the superintendent had left open to a bawling corridor lined with patients needing attention while their relatives shouted for it. Was all Berlin sick? "But this is a case of murder."

"Been murdered, has she?"

"We're concerned that she might be."

The superintendent wasn't curious; if it didn't happen in his hospital, he didn't have to cope with it. "Wouldn't give her name, you say?"

"I understand you admitted her as Frau Unbekkant." Nice, he thought, that they'd given her the dignity of a married woman's title. Very German.

"Unbekkant, Unbekkant. Here we are. February 1920. What do you want to know?"

Schmidt was at a loss. "Whatever you can tell me."

The superintendent tsked with impatience. He ran his eyes over the report. "Admitted as suffering from shock and exhaustion. Weight 110 pounds. Lacerations to the upper body, not serious. Assigned to a 'quiet' ward. Refused to speak. Diagnosed as suffering from melancholia. Transferred to Dalldorf six weeks later." He looked up. "That's it. And now if I may be allowed to get on . . ."

Schmidt pondered while the man puffed and shifted. On the off chance, he said, "'Frau' Unbekkant. *Was* she married, do you know?"

"Oh, that was because she'd had a child." Tsking again, the superintendent went back to the notes. "Examination revealed she'd given birth at some time in the past."

"But . . . where's the baby? Did it turn up? Did she say anything about it?"

The superintendent closed the file. "Apparently not. And now . . ." He hustled Schmidt out of the room and disappeared into the corridor's hell.

Schmidt made his way outside to the hospital steps and lit a black-market cigarette. A child. That haunted little thing in Bismarck Allee had been a mother.

Once it would have been merely another factor in the case; today his own forthcoming parenthood made it infinitely pitiable. There was no child now. It had died or been taken away at some time in that unknown past. God Almighty, it could have gone into the canal with her, and Sergeant Hallman hadn't seen it. A jump of despair. A baby altered everything. If Anna was Polish, she was Roman Catholic; ergo, presuming her to be unmarried, she was a single mother and a sinner. She could have been hounded into the Landwehr by precepts that belonged in the Dark Ages. Schmidt, a shaky Lutheran, had no time for popery.

Or she could have been pushed into it by the child's father, a married man who wanted rid of her. Or anything.

He was, he realized, disappointed. The case had changed from black mystery to domestic tragedy—no less dark, but mundane in the wearying frequency with which it occurred. The killer whose reflection in Anna's terrified eyes had assumed ogreish proportions had dwindled into a figure just as lethal but a good deal more banal.

Schmidt threw the remains of his cigarette onto the step and put it out with a vicious twist of his foot. Then, like a good German, he bent down, picked it up, and looked around for a rubbish can.

He didn't see a rubbish can, but he saw a woman entering the gates. There were plenty of people about, but this one, dowdy as she was, he saw ringed, as if a pen had outlined her against the air.

He went toward her, put a hand under her elbow, and walked her back toward the gates. "What are you doing here, Fräulein?"

She's going to say she's ill, or visiting a patient, he thought. And legally I can't stop her, except that I'm damn well going to.

What she did say—and they were out of the gates by then—was, "I should have known you'd come here."

"You should," he said, and kept her walking, "leave it to the police; that's what we're for. I presume you came to do a bit of detection. Well, don't." He was angry. "What the hell did you think you were going to find out?"

"I don't know," she said. "What did *you*?"

They were nearing the Tiergarten, and he steered her toward it. There was a children's play area with swings and a bench. They sat down.

He said, "Did you know she'd had a baby?"

"Anna?"

"So they say. They examined her. At some point in the past, apparently. They don't know what happened to it."

"Anna," she said. "My poor Anna."

"It changes things."

Her head went up. "Why?"

"It means it's probably a domestic case."

She left the bench and walked to the swing opposite so that she could sit on it and look at him. The way she'd wrapped her scarves around it made her face armorial, like a shield battered on one side.

"I'm hearing you right, am I?" she said. "Natalya, Olga—their murders were *domestic*?"

She was an uncomfortable woman. He said, "Natalya was still murdered by mistake, but the killer probably has domestic reasons to kill Fräulein Anderson. He may be the father, he may have a position to uphold, and she could ruin it. For God's sake, I'm not saying that it excuses anything. I'm merely stating a case that would make it more understandable."

"Really?" He's just an ordinary male after all, Esther thought. Anna's related to the killer, so it's all right for him to murder her. "What else have you found out?"

She had no right to ask, and he had no compulsion to tell her, but there was a curious suspension to the moment; they might have been enclosed in a bubble that caused the surrounding snow and people and leafless trees to become indistinct.

"The killer's probably a member of the SA," he said, "one of Röhm's lot."

She dug the toes of her boots into the ground and swung slightly while she thought about it. "A Jew beater."

"An everybody-they-don't-like beater," he said.

"And *he's* concerned about his *reputation*?"

God, she was an uncomfortable woman. "He might be. For all I know, women ask him so many questions by day he goes around stabbing 'em by night." He added, "There's a lot to be said for it."

She had a snuffling laugh, like a faulty soda siphon.

He said, "You can't make rules for killers. As somebody once said, 'Everyone is dragged on by his own pleasures.'"

"Virgil," she said. "Virgil said it."

"He did." Schmidt got up, because if he didn't go now, he never would. "He also said, *'Latet anguis in herba,'* and I don't want it sinking its fangs into you, too, so leave the detecting to me, all right?"

She looked up at him. "It isn't domestic," she said. "It isn't. It's something else."

She scared him. He grabbed her by the elbow and hauled her to her feet. "Home," he said. "And stay there. Promise me."

"I can look after myself."

Deliberately, he looked at her cheek. "You've done a fine job of it so far. Promise me."

She pulled away. "Catch him," she said. And strode off.

He stood looking after her, wondering what gave her the right to dress in old clothes and still walk as if she owned the damn park. She thought she was steel; the heavier the beating, the stronger it became. In fact, he thought, you're as vulnerable as hell, and I don't know what to do about it.

ESTHER CIRCLED THE park, mourning for Anna and the lost baby. I'd have taken it, she thought. I'd have brought it up for you and been grateful to do it. Motherhood—the one estate I crave and won't ever have.

But at least she'd been spared the agony of losing a child, which Anna had not. No wonder she went mad, Esther thought. No wonder she went into that canal.

She tried inhabiting the cold space of Anna's past life and wondered at the strength it must have taken to emerge from it as intact as she had. *Tough as old boots,* Nick said, his voice rasping like the rooks' that were wheeling around the park's elms—and about as sympathetic. Natalya had thought the same.

Unfair, Esther protested, she's had too much to bear. But Nick's words had come unbidden and couldn't be unsaid. And they were true. Anna hadn't grieved for her lost baby; she'd grieved only for Anna.

Perhaps it's the same, Esther thought. How do we, the childless, know what is necessary to survive this worst thing?

She heard someone shouting at her and looked around to see a woman gesturing at a sign that said KEEP OFF THE GRASS. The lawn she'd been treading on was still covered in snow, but Germans liked their signs obeyed. She wandered back to the path, past other signs: KEEP DOGS ON LEASH. DO NOT PICK THE FLOWERS. TAKE YOUR RUBBISH HOME.

And yet . . . she began reliving life with Anna, trying to remember one word, one expression that had dwelled on the pain of a lost baby, a tear, an aching glance at children playing in the street. When Frau Schinkel's grandchildren visited, Anna had merely complained of the noise they made on the stairs—and not as someone who couldn't bear a reminder of young voices at play.

You don't like children, Esther thought. You like dogs.

That didn't mean Anna hadn't had a child, but it did suggest that she'd been prepared to abort it or have it adopted.

I'm being unkind, Esther told herself. But Anna-as-she-was persisted in asserting herself against the sentimental pictures from one of the mothers-for-Germany magazines.

It changes things, Schmidt had said.

Don't think about him, don't think about him. Damn him, he may be right in every possible way for a man to be right, but he's wrong about this.

If Anna had been compliant in the disposal of the child, why should its father go to such lengths—*such* lengths—to kill her?

Esther had been so preoccupied she had to look around to get her bearings and found she'd reached Dolls' Alley, the name Berliners gave to the avenue of statues with which Kaiser Wilhelm had insisted on enhancing the park. Up ahead was the sprouting column of *Victory* celebrating the former Prussian habit of winning wars. Berliners found it ridiculous and called it "Victory Asparagus."

Esther stared up at the kaiser. I don't think the baby comes into this, she told him. Schmidt's got it wrong.

Suddenly she was decided. "And so did you," she snapped at the kaiser before directing her steps back the way she'd come, to Lützowstrasse and the Elizabeth Hospital.

IT TOOK TIME to win Fräulein Schechter's trust and the secrets of the almoner's office, but at the end of the week, Esther Solomonova walked into Police HQ at Alexanderplatz and asked to see Inspector Schmidt.

"Not here, Fräulein," a duty officer told her.

"I have information for him. When will he be back?"

"Better leave a message."

He gave her paper and a pen. She wrote *"I know Anna's real name."* She signed it *"Solomonova."* She said, "You'll see he gets it, please. It's to do with the murder at Charlottenburg."

"Inspector Bolle's handling the case now."

She stared at him. "Is Inspector Schmidt ill?"

"His wife's been killed."

16

IT LOOKED LIKE an accident.

Accident, Schmidt thought mildly when he emerged out of the U-bahn on his way home and heard the ambulance go by with the bell on its roof ringing.

"Christ, an accident," as he turned the corner of his street and saw that the ambulance had stopped in the region of his building.

He began to run, dodging pedestrians coming the other way. One of them blocked him for a moment, and as he teetered, then dodged again, a voice addressing someone else said, "Your punishment, *mein Herr.*"

A crowd had gathered outside the front door.

A weeping Frau Busse tried to interpose her body between him and the open hallway. "No, Herr Schmidt, don't go in. Siegfried, don't. There's been an accident."

When he pushed her aside, the ambulance men attempted to stop him from seeing the body. "An accident," they said. "She fell downstairs. Wait for the doctor."

He pulled off the sheet they'd covered her with. There was no point in calling a doctor. The fall had flipped her beautiful hair to one side so that it spread itself almost neatly against the hallway's tiles. Her head was crooked at the angle made by a broken neck, like a dead bird's.

Around her, and strewn on the stairs leading up, were groceries—the two brown paper bags she'd been carrying them in had split and released their contents—tins, packets, bottles. Sugar was still trickling from its burst packet. A piece of raw rabbit stuck obscenely out of its newspaper wrapping.

She'd been to see Willi's wife again. Schmidt didn't think it then, but later he blamed and cursed himself over and over at having sent her to connive in the petty corruption that had helped to kill her. If both her hands had been free, she could have clutched at the banister.

His first reaction was rage that she'd always insisted on polishing and buffing the stairs. As he picked her body up and nursed it, he yelled at it, "I told you, how many times did I tell you? They were bloody lethal."

Weeping, Frau Busse persuaded him to put her down at last. "You did, you did. But she was such a good housewife, such a good housewife."

After the inquest—accidental death—he took her coffin by train back to Bavaria so that she could be buried in the church where they'd got married.

He was stone up to the interment, but the image of the little curled fetus in her womb that was going under the ground with her broke him, and he bawled until the mountains echoed back the noise he made.

Willi Ritte met him at the station when he returned, and offered to take him back home to Frau Ritte and the children. "You don't want to be alone for a bit," he said.

"Thanks, Willi, but I've got to face it sometime."

Willi was right, though. The apartment was intolerable. The unfinished baby jacket she'd been knitting from the wool of her sweater was on top of the needlework bag by her chair. Her cookbook was open at a recipe for "Rabbit in Morel Sauce" that she'd been going to make for him from her ill-gotten gains.

Frau Busse came in to ask him if he'd like to join her and the family for a meal. He thanked her but said he'd be going out and probably wouldn't be back for a few days.

He went to Ikey Wolff's parents' house in Wilmersdorf. They'd leaned on him when Ikey died; he leaned on them now.

Joe Wolff spent three days a week at his private dentist's practice; the rest of the time he provided free dentistry for the poor. Minna gave her services to a Jewish ex-servicemen's charity. She usually had trouble persuading Aryans that Jews had fought in the war. "I tell them Ikey got the Iron Cross. I tell them there was as many Jews fighting for Germany as goys," she said.

"Pro rata the population," Joe interrupted.

"You and your rata, but it's true, eh, Siegfried? Even in Herr Hitler's regiment there were Jews."

"Ikey was a regiment all by himself," Schmidt said.

They coped with grief for their son through hard work. "Not that it stops," Minna Wolff said.

"You learn to live with it," Joe said.

"You lock it up," said Minna. "Keep it in a room in your head."

"Comes out rampaging, of course, knocks you down," said Joe. "But yes, you learn to live with it."

Schmidt stayed with them for a week, but in the end he had to leave; they were talking about a different grief. His own was poisoned with guilt. Maybe at the moment Hannelore had been struggling up the stairs with her shopping, he had been thinking of Solomonova. The unease that had followed him on this case—not from any specific cause, just a heightened awareness of the quickness with which people could be erased—had been centered on a foreigner he hardly knew. He'd attributed vulnerability to the wrong woman.

All the times when he could have gone home to his wife but had stayed to work in his office returned to haunt him. He'd ripped Hannelore out of her natural environment, dumped her in a strange city, and then neglected her.

His defense that she'd seemed happy enough was overridden by stray words picked up from a stranger's conversation as he'd passed: *Your punishment,* mein Herr. Apt, they wrote themselves on every wall as at Belshazzar's Feast like a judgment. He hadn't loved her enough, and a ruthless Jehovah of the Old Testament had snatched her and the baby away from him. In the extreme moment, he had bumped into God coming the other way, speaking through His instrument: *Your punishment,* mein Herr.

Crumpling under the judgment, other times defying it, he found the Wolffs' stoical acceptance of an ultimate justice to be intolerable. He thanked them, assured them he loved them, and left.

He asked for and was granted one of the police flats near Alexanderplatz, then went back to his old apartment to arrange the move.

He arrived at the same time as the furniture van that was to take the Busses to their new home. Despite the inconvenience to her, Lotte Busse insisted on making him coffee and sat him down on a packing case to be entertained by her sister-in-law, catching up on Schmidt's news and imparting her own while she popped in and out of the room, directing the movers. The children were at school.

Maria Busse had her brother's obsessive stare and, in Schmidt's opinion, though not in that of Hannelore, who'd been fond of her, had always shown a simplistic and unhealthy devotion to religion. Her wide eyes regarded him out of the wimple of a novice nun at the Convent of the Holy Trinity down the road.

"Herr Schmidt, I have not had an opportunity of condoling with you. May the Lord and His mother help you through this time of trial."

He could tell from the look of her that she was building up a head of steam. He got up, but the nun's voice pursued him, telling him—*him*—of Hannelore's virtues.

". . . so strong in her faith, so gentle in her life. . . . You must take comfort. . . . She died certain in the love of God. . . . Even her last words were a blessing. . . . We grieve, but we must not be jealous that she has joined the holy saints in paradise. . . ."

If she mentions the baby, I'll knock her down.

Frau Busse came in with the coffee. Schmidt began saying he had to go, then stopped. "Her last words?"

"To the man who carried her shopping."

Schmidt looked from the wimpled face to Frau Busse's. "What man?"

"I didn't hear it, Siegfried," Frau Busse said. "Maria was visiting on another dispensation, weren't you, Maria? Sitting by the door to the hall, and she heard dear Hanne come in."

Sister Maria nodded. "And she said, 'God bless you, that would be so kind.' "

"Why? Who'd she say it to?"

"Well, it must have been to the man who carried her shopping, Siegfried," Frau Busse said. "Little Pieter was playing in the street, and he said she came back from shopping with a man who was carrying the bags for her."

"What man?"

"I don't know." Frau Busse was becoming frightened. "A big man, he said, but Pieter is so small he—"

"You didn't say this at the inquest."

"No, because he'd gone, Siegfried. He couldn't have seen . . . what happened."

Your punishment, mein Herr. Something was coming. He dragged in breath and fought for slowness. "Sit down," he said. "And you too," he told the nun. "Now then, a man, a big man, carried my wife's shopping down the street on the day she died."

"Well, Pieter said so, but—"

"And *you*"—he turned on Sister Maria—"heard her come into the hallway. What did she say exactly?"

" 'God bless you. That would be so kind.' I think so, but this door was between us."

"He must have handed her the shopping and gone," Frau Busse said. "When we heard . . . Oh, Siegfried, we heard her shriek and fall, like we told the inquest. We ran out into the hall. There was nobody there. He'd gone. The hallway was empty except for—"

"Had she closed the front door?"

"Oh, Siegfried." Frau Busse had her hands to her cheeks. "I can't remember, it was so terrible."

"No," Maria said. "The front door was open, but how could she close it with shopping in her hands?"

She'd have kicked it shut, he thought. It was a cold day, she'd have kicked it shut. But she didn't because he was carrying her shopping upstairs for her and would be going out again immediately. *Bless you, that would be so kind.*

Your punishment, mein Herr.

"He was carrying the shopping upstairs for her," Schmidt said. He thought, I'm not going to be able to take this. He was carrying her shopping upstairs. He pushed her.

"No, Siegfried." Frau Busse was kind but firm. "There was nobody with her. When I heard the noise—oh, dear, you know, when she fell—we went out into the hall, didn't we, Maria?"

He was standing on the landing upstairs, in the shadows, watching them.

"There was nobody there, only . . . And then we ran next door to the hardware store to phone for an ambulance."

Leaving the front door open for him to make his escape.

He left them both in tears without saying good-bye.

He went back to the Alexanderplatz and demanded an interview with Ringer. While he was waiting, he set the case before Willi—and did it badly. "She was murdered, Sergeant. The killer, the one who killed Tchichagova . . . this nun heard Hannelore thank him. *Not* just because he'd carried her shopping in the street. Because he was carrying it upstairs. She said, this nun says she said, 'God bless you. That would be so kind.' That *would be* so kind. Not 'Bless you, that *was* kind of you for having helped me,' but 'Bless you, how kind you are for helping me *now*.'"

"I see, boss," Willi said gently.

Oh, Christ, the semantics would defeat them. But he knew how she talked; they didn't. He *knew*. She was always polite and her grammar perfect.

"He told me, Willi. I came out of the U-bahn, and I was running down the street, and he . . . Oh, Jesus, he put himself in front of me. And he told me. I thought he was talking to somebody else. But he wasn't. He was telling me: *Your punishment,* mein Herr."

Willi walked with him to Ringer's office, holding his arm as if he were injured.

He said it all over again to the chief, just as badly, hearing his babble bounce back at him from a wall of incomprehension.

"I led him to her, do you see, sure as if I left a trail. Clever fellow, me, walking into their lair in Kreuzberg. I should have carried a sign: 'Come and get me.' I didn't need to. I threatened them, so I had to be hurt."

"I see," Ringer said, glancing at Willi. "Let me get this straight, Inspector. You believe your wife to have been murdered. . . . You received our condolences, I hope?"

"Yes." There'd been an official wreath as well as private ones from his fellow officers; he hadn't got around to thanking anybody yet.

"Your evidence—forgive me, Inspector—is a remark your wife made, heard through a closed door, and that of a child who saw someone carrying your wife's shopping for her."

"Yes." His fist on Ringer's desk made the silver inkwell jump. "For Jesus' sake, *listen* to me. They got her instead of me, to warn me off. They got her because I think small and people like them think big. It's their fucking universe; they can move around in it freely because . . . because they have no goodness. They're untrammeled. They don't have rules—"

He stopped, uselessness making him mute.

He started again. "Give me some men. Street interviews . . . somebody must have seen him. And Kreuzberg, I'll grill every one of those little bastards; somebody there'll know. Röhm contacted him, told him."

"Captain Röhm has already been to see me," Ringer said. "He has filed a complaint. He alleges there is a photograph missing."

And I bet he seemed your sort of man, Schmidt thought; ex-army, Old Germany, discipline *über alles*. But Ringer had rules, codes, procedures—he was circumscribed by them; Röhm had none.

He leaned forward. *"Did you give him my address?"*

"Of course not."

"Well, he fucking got it from somewhere."

Ringer's mustache twitched but his tolerance held for the discourtesy of grief. "Very well, Inspector, the matter will be investigated, of course. Not by you." He held up a finger to hold Schmidt back. "*Not* by you. Personal involvement conflicts with judgment in these matters. I'll put Inspector Bolle on it, a competent officer as you know."

Competence. He didn't want competence, he wanted action. He argued even as Ringer's face became more set, even as he knew that every word confirmed his lack of balance. It ended with Ringer suspending him for two more weeks on compassionate grounds.

He couldn't rest. He went up and down his street, questioning people, grabbing pedestrians, going into every shop. One or two said they might have seen a man carrying Hannelore's shopping, they couldn't be sure, and no, they couldn't remember the date. He went in to Alexanderplatz every day and pestered Bolle until the inspector banned him from the third floor altogether. Out of kindness, Willi met him most evenings for coffee. He said Bolle was doing all that could be done. At the Kreuzberg gym, Schmidt was remembered—not kindly—but there seemed general and genuine ignorance of his home address. Röhm, now back in Munich, had convinced the interviewing officer there that he knew nothing. Lotte Busse and her sister-in-law merely repeated their statements and could add no more.

"Could just have been an accident, boss," Willi said carefully.

"It fucking wasn't." He knew it wasn't.

Esther disliked Baron von Kleist on sight, but that was only fair—he'd disliked her as soon as he'd been given her name. Kept standing in the large hall, she heard the footman announce her and then the baron's loud "Solomonova? Now it's a damn Jewess! I suppose we'd better see her."

The footman who ushered her into the presence wore livery and a powdered wig—accoutrements she thought had died out with the waltz.

It was a large and beautiful room with wide windows looking over woods and a canal she couldn't quite place—the city could still confuse her.

"Fräulein Solomonova."

A man and a woman of late middle age were sitting in two easy chairs by a window, drinking coffee. Neither got up. The man crooked his finger. "Come here, young woman."

Esther moved closer. The woman put down her cup and raised a pair of lorgnettes on a gold chain around her neck with which to study Esther's scar.

"You are employed by Potrovskov?"

"Yes."

"Yes," Baron von Kleist said. He emphasized the word like someone who'd won a confession after intensive interrogation. "I believe you attended the grand duchess Anastasia for a while."

"Anna? Yes."

"The grand duchess, yes." They'd got that straight. "Well, look here, my girl, it must be made clear to him that Her Imperial Highness has moved on. She has been taken up by the circle to which she belongs, and any unfortunate alliances she may have made in the past are behind her. I want it understood that we cannot have unsuitable, I may even say coarse, women hammering on the door and shouting . . ."

Oh, boy, Esther thought with sudden happiness. Clara's been here.

"It upsets the servants, it upsets the grand duchess, it upsets *me*. We can't have every ragtag calling just when they like. We are doing everything to safeguard Her Imperial Highness."

"The Bolsheviks are out to murder her, you know," the baroness said.

"Filthy Reds. I've got no time for the Nazi Party, but the sooner this country's cleansed of all Bolsheviks and their Hebrew backers . . ."

It could be the Landwehr Canal, Esther thought, studying the view. She said, "I'd like to see Anna now, please."

The baron gave a disgusted "Tchah" and waved her off.

The baroness signaled to the footman waiting at the door. "Her Imperial Highness has agreed to receive you, but you can stay for only a minute or two," she said. "She is unwell, and we don't want her agitated. Hans, show Fräulein Solova to the grand duchess's room."

She was announced into Anna's room. It was nearly as magnificent as the one she'd just left, part sitting room, part bedroom. The curtains were carelessly drawn, allowing low winter sun to shine between openings and form shafts along the Aubusson carpet. Anna had done her best to untidy it but was presumably being thwarted by maids. Nevertheless, a breakfast tray had spilled on the bed, a towel trailed on the floor from an open bathroom door, clothes from a wardrobe.

If these were evidence of Anna's attempt to get up, she'd abandoned it and lay on the bed in a nightgown with her Pekingese clutched in her arms.

She looked at Esther without surprise. "This is Liu-bang, like the emperor. Who's his mommy's precious little baby, then?"

"Greetings, Liu-bang." Esther picked up a little gilt Empire chair and took it to the bedside to sit on.

"I do not like it here," Anna said.

"Why?"

"They bring people all the time. Always I tell them I want privacy, but no, they show me off to their friends. Madam Tolstoy comes and asks questions. Her, I do not mind—she knows I am Anastasia—but then they get Volkov."

"Alexis Volkov?"

Anna nodded. "Mama's groom of the chamber. They say he will report back to the dowager empress. He ask me questions, and when I answer, he cries and kissed my hand and said, 'Your Imperial Highness'—the baroness see it with her own eyes—but there is no word from Grandmama since he went back to Denmark to report."

And there won't be, Esther thought; the day the dowager czarina acknowledges Anna as her granddaughter will be The Day.

"You've got to stick it out for a while, Anna," she said. "You're safe here. I'm not keen on them either, but they believe in you and they'll protect you until the killer's caught. . . . Oh, lovie, don't."

Anna's small face had shrunk; she looked ill and old. Esther put out a hand to her. The dog growled. "Listen to me, Anna," she said. "It can't go on like this. You've got to help the police catch him. He can't hurt you then. He's not . . . fabulous—he's flesh and blood. They can get him for what he did to Natalya, finish him."

Anna's eyes wandered to the window. "These von Kleists, they tell everybody about me, show me like I am their pedigree cow, I am a display. It gives me a headache. My sight . . . everything is hazy."

"I know about the baby," Esther said. "The police know."

There was a long pause. Anna held up the Pekingese and pursed her lips toward its flat nose. "You protect me, Liu-bang. You protect your little mistress, yes you do, yes he does."

"Why didn't you tell me?"

"No baby."

"I went to the hospital. There's a woman in the almoner's office who remembers that while you were in there you signed adoption papers."

"No baby."

"Tell me."

Anna said calmly, "Sometime I wish I die then, so I would not remember now. At Ekaterinburg. In the Ipatiev House. For Special Purpose."

"You were raped?"

"You won't tell? You wait for me to die before you tell?"

"I won't tell."

"It was Bolshevik devils, many, many. I fight, but they hold me. Many hold me. The pain was not the worst. It was the *words,* the *terrible* words."

Yes, Esther thought, it's the words that stay with you. Wherever, whenever it had been done and whoever had done it, Anna had been raped; she was talking to someone who knew. Anna had transposed things that had happened to her with things she thought had happened to Anastasia. Like two different parasites, the experiences had twined themselves into her mind and fused; they could not be separated without tearing it apart.

"What happened to the baby?"

Anna shrugged. "Somebody adopt it. I don't think of it."

"You signed the papers with the name Franziska Schanskowska."

Anna shrugged again. "Any name."

"No, that was yours. You're Franziska. You're Polish. The man wants to kill Franziska Schanskowska from Poland. Why?" *Latet anguis in herba,* Schmidt had said. The snake hidden in the grass. "For God's sake, Anna, let's find him and scotch him."

"I am Imperial Highness the Grand Duchess Anastasia," Anna said. She looked ill.

"Don't. Don't do this. Not to me, not to yourself. You're condemning yourself to a lie. Your life will be artificial and . . . oh, static, not getting anywhere. You'll always be drifting around the edges with gullible posers. And for what? That throne has gone, thank God. It was built on bones. Every jewel, every bit of gold, every Fabergé egg—how could they look at them and not think of the misery each bloody thing had caused a people in their care? Beautiful ladies scattered coins as they drove by in their troikas, and starving children fought each other to pick them up. I saw them. Is that the inheritance you want? It's gone to the dust where it belonged. Leave it."

There was a tap on the door, and an anxious footman looked in. She realized she'd been shouting.

"Is all well, your Imperial Highness?"

"Yes," Esther said. "Get out."

He went, leaving the door ajar; the baron would be here in a minute. "Anna, *please,*" Esther begged.

"I am Anastasia."

Defeated, Esther looked around the stifling room. "I suppose it's better than Dalldorf," she said quietly.

"Yes," Anna said. "It is."

They looked at each other, and for a moment Esther saw something that, however misplaced, was nevertheless courage. Whoever this woman before her was, she had made a choice while she was still able to make one, and nothing would shift her from it.

"I'm so sorry, little one," Esther said. "I'm sorry."

She put out her hands to take Anna's, but the Pekingese snapped at her, making Anna smile. "You see, Esther. I have guard at last. Nobody will touch me again."

"Be safe, darling," Esther said.

"Who's his mummy's little Chinese dragon? Who breathes fire on nasty Cheka and burns them up? Yes he does, little treasure, yes he does."

Esther left her.

Ringer was calling him "my dear inspector" in the tone people used when they said "nice doggy."

"Under the circumstances, my dear inspector, you may wish to accept the appointment."

"What appointment?"

"Hanover." Sighing, Ringer began again. "The Hanover force has appealed to us for help in a particularly difficult case of unsolved multiple killings. And under the circumstances . . ."

"Hanover?" He was afflicted by a lassitude that made him almost deaf; the memory of Natalya's corpse lying in the snow was overlaid by that of another body, in a hallway, its fair hair spread out on the tiles.

Sometimes they fused together and became one image; sometimes he was worried by seeing only Natalya's, as if his mind wouldn't give credit to Hannelore's.

"My dear inspector, we would of course miss you, but the transfer seems preferable to losing you from the force altogether."

Force? Altogether? "Are you kicking me out?" he asked.

Ringer's mustache rose as he took a deep breath. "There is no question of that, but . . . if you do not wish to go to Hanover, then perhaps, in your present condition, another division here would be more suitable. Records, perhaps."

"Records?" Ringer'd got his attention now; the bastard wanted to put him in with paper filers and pencil fucking pushers. He sat up. "What's happening to the Tchichagova case?"

"It is being put on file as unsolved. Should more evidence come to light . . ." Ringer uplifted a finger. "But as far as you are concerned, it is closed, do you understand?"

Either he shut up about it or he became a filing clerk. Or he went to fucking Hanover. No, it was more basic than that. Either Hannelore and their baby rotted in the grave, unavenged, or he allowed himself to rot while still living on their behalf. Bolle had done his best; there was no proof that she'd been pushed downstairs, none that would stand up in court. Willi said there wasn't, and he believed Willi. He, Schmidt, could go on beating his head against that closed door for the rest of his life, losing his job and his sanity, or he could go to Hanover.

He said, "Suppose more evidence turns up?"

"My dear inspector, you will be told immediately. Of course."

He remained an active detective or he turned into one of the madmen to be seen shambling through the streets muttering their obsessions.

"I'll go to Hanover," he said. "But don't think the case is closed. One of these days, I'm coming back."

ESTHER TRIED TO contact Schmidt again but was transferred to Inspector Bolle, whose interest in her was little warmer than Baron von Kleist's—or in Franziska Schanskowska, for that matter. He was loyal to his colleague, but it was obvious that in Bolle's mind the connection made by Inspector Schmidt between the death of Natalya Tchichigova and the unstable Anna Anderson was so much hogwash. Natalya's killing was a straightforward case of murder by a person unknown, something to be expected when unwary women ventured into a lonely area late at night. When Esther asked after Schmidt, she was told that he had been transferred to another city.

Crossing Alexanderplatz, Esther cast a last look back at the great red building that was police headquarters. He'd gone from there, poor man. Retired into grief and another life in another city, fencing her out.

They'd been strange, those procedural and devastating minutes the two of them had shared, as if minds had met, as if, in the bare landscape of a killing field, they'd been aware of a secret tunnel to somewhere beautiful, they'd heard the flute of panpipes from the age-old forest.

Nitwit, she told herself, you were his suspect and then his witness, and that's all you were. The magic was on your side, only yours. He didn't even approve of you—you made sure of that.

But it had been magic to her, the first touch of warmth, the first moisture on the shard of ice that had kept her frozen for so long. Whether the thaw that was sending tears down her cheeks as she walked away from Alexanderplatz came from gratitude or chagrin that she'd ever met him, she wasn't sure.

Either way he'd awakened a part of her that had been dead, and if the recirculating blood hurt, it was at least a reminder that she had a life and must find a better way to live it.

PART TWO

17

Berlin, July 1932

A VISIT FROM Prince Nick was a rare event nowadays.

Esther offered him a cocktail and watched him prowl the apartment with the resentment of a man whose butler had bought the winning lottery ticket on his wages.

"Doing well," he said.

"Yes."

"You owe it all to me, you know."

"So you tell me."

"I gave you that damn camera."

"We are referring to the Leica I had to pawn when you left me and Anna and Natalya to starve, are we?"

"Got it back, didn't you?"

"No thanks to you." He'd cut her off without a pfennig when she'd told him she'd be neither sleeping with nor working for him again. He hadn't minded no longer having droit du seigneur, but the loss of a confidential secretary who spoke as many languages as Esther did had been a blow he'd made her suffer for.

Now, however, occasionally he turned up at 29c for advice, consolation, or praise—things that his succession of wives had run out of.

She wondered what it was this time.

She watched him studying a portrait of himself that she'd taken some years before, all sleek hair, hooded eyes, and cigarette holder.

"Good-looking fellow, that," he said. He still was, but the portrait, as with the man, was typical of an earlier time. To be fashionable now, he should have adopted tweeds and a pipe.

Like all speculators and black marketeers, he'd been hard hit when Germany had finally regained control of its economy and stabilized its currency. "Are they trying to ruin me?" he'd wailed at the time.

"Yes," Esther had told him, "that's exactly what they're trying to do."

He'd never got over it. The amusement tax had hit his nightclubs; so had a proliferation of casinos and cabarets that took away his trade to Berlin's newer West End. To compete, he'd lowered even his standards. It was said that there were clubs one admitted going to and others one didn't. The Green Hat, Esther was afraid, now fell mainly into the category of those one didn't.

She wondered why she was still fond of him.

"How's Anna?" he asked.

"She's not enjoying America as much as she thought she would."

"Damn good. That bitch has been a complete serpent's tooth to me."

Every mention of Anna in the newspapers—and hardly a week passed when she didn't pop up in the world's press somewhere—was gall and wormwood to him. "Not a word, not a fucking word. Not so much as a 'Thank you, dear Prince Nick, without you I'd still be in a fucking straitjacket.' Is that honor? I ask you, Esther, is that how Romanovs reward loyalty? No wonder the fucking peasants revolted."

The press had discovered Anna without him. Harriet von Rathlef, one of Anna's many supporters, had published a series of articles proclaiming her as the lost Anastasia. Peter Gilliard, the grand duchesses' former tutor, brought out a book declaring that she was a fake.

In 1928, with the death of the dowager empress, the czar's mother, things had heated up—an inheritance was at stake—and twelve of the surviving members of the imperial family had made a declaration that

Anna Anderson was not, definitely *not,* Anastasia Nikolaievna, daughter of the last czar of Russia.

On the other hand, the son and daughter of Dr. Botkin, the physician who had died with the Romanovs in the House of Special Purpose, were equally convinced that she was—and they had known Anastasia well as a child.

It seemed that half the world's population believed Anna to be the grand duchess and the other half didn't. What Esther found curious was that Anna was a celebrity in both camps; if possible, those who believed she was an impostor were as avid to know about her as those who proclaimed her to be the grand duchess. More books had been written about her—for and against. A film was in the offing. Dress shops sold frocks in "Anastasia blue." For a while there'd been a run on Anastasia-brand cigarettes.

Nick, ignoring the fact that Natalya's murder had panicked him into handing Anna over to the von Kleists, became a Rumpelstiltskin, stomping with rage at a woman spinning gold out of the straw with which he'd provided her. Esther tried pointing out that Anna wasn't making money; she was being kept in the style her patrons felt a grand duchess deserved, but she wasn't accumulating wealth, and if the supporters drifted away when the ballyhoo faded, she'd be as penniless as when Nick had found her.

"Let's hope for that," Nick said. "*I* sure as hell won't be picking her out of any more loony bins. And how come that assassin ain't taken a potshot at her? She's been public enough."

It was a question that had concerned Esther a lot; with Anna appearing in so many spotlights, it seemed impossible that the killer wouldn't seize his opportunity. But either he *hadn't* seen it or he'd passed it up; there had been no attempt on Anna's life. It had taken a long time for Esther to puzzle it out. After all, Anna was still the person she always had been and therefore presumably still the object of the killer's hatred.

"Do you know what I think?" she said. "She must know something from their mutual past, something that would harm the swine if it became public. Perhaps he murdered his wife, and only she knows where the body's buried."

"Or she abandoned the poor bastard after he'd given her everything."

"The point is," Esther said, "that if she tells the world what it is, she has to reveal that her past isn't Anastasia's. He knows now she won't do that; she's too famous; she can't give him away without giving herself away. He's safe."

"Or maybe he's just bored with chasing the bitch. Like I am. Or maybe he *was* Cheka, and they got bored too."

"Or maybe he's dead," Esther said. "Anyway, she doesn't seem as frightened as she was."

"How'd you know? I thought she'd dropped you, too. She become pro-Jewish all of a sudden?"

"Not exactly."

For a long time after their meeting in 1923, when Esther had challenged Anna with the name Franziska Schanskowska, the only intelligence she'd gained of her was through the newspapers. Until one day she'd answered a knock on the door of 29c to have Fräulein Anderson push past her and head in the direction of her old room. "I don't stay with stupid barons no longer."

Whether the von Kleists had got fed up with her or she with them, it was difficult to know. Anna said she was tired of being questioned about her history and presented with strangers she was asked to identify. "'Who this, Your Highness? Who that? Remember we meet at Winter Palace in 1908? Remember your mama visit me in the hospital in 1916?' Always on show, always questions. I don't do it anymore."

Anna scorned publicity. It was at least one trait she shared with the late czar and his family, who had fought to safeguard their privacy away from public occasions. She refused interviews and threw tantrums when they were forced on her or when enterprising reporters infiltrated wherever she was staying.

Esther thought it admirable. But those who'd taken Anna up in the hope that some of her fame would reflect on them found it a disappointment, which, allied with her erratic behavior, eventually caused a parting of the ways.

She left 29c a second time as abruptly as she'd come, this time at the behest of Duke George of Leuchtenberg, another believer, who'd installed her in his castle near Munich. That relationship, too, had petered out, and over the years Anna had been passed from hand to aristocratic hand like a baton as the previous recipient dropped exhausted. At which point Anna always returned to 29c Bismarck Allee.

Jewish or not, Esther realized she was about the only constant in Anna's life.

When, in 1928, America had beckoned and Anna set sail on the *Berengaria* for New York and the glare of popping flashbulbs, her hosts hadn't been the only ones to be relieved. Esther hoped, for Anna's sake, that she would make her home there.

Everybody else seemed to have forgotten Olga's and Natalya's murders. The police certainly had, and so had most of their friends. The flowers Esther put on their graves every year in the Russian cemetery were not joined by anybody else's.

Nick, she'd been sure, had forgotten, so he startled her now by suddenly asking, "Remember that police inspector? What was his name? Schmidt?"

"Yes." She remembered him.

"What did he say about Natalya's killer?"

"He said he thought he was a member of the SA."

"Sturmabteilung . . . Why do the Germans stretch words like that? Didn't he say anything else?"

"'One of Röhm's lot,' that's all he said." She could remember exactly. Every word.

"A queer, then." He raised his eyebrows at her surprise. "Esth-*er*. Everybody knows about Ernst Röhm. Ladies are completely *not* his cup of tea. He could get through bum-boys like . . . I tell you, just one of his visits to the Pink Parasol put up my profits for a week." Nick sighed. "He ain't been to Berlin lately. Not now the Nazis are gone respectable, I bet Herr Hitler's keeping poor old Ernst on a leash."

"Oh?" she said. "And when did the Nazis become respectable?"

"Don't you go Jewish on me. Some of my best customers are Nazis."

"What do you want, Nick?"

He held out his glass, and she refilled it from the shaker. "I dropped in for a chat, that's all. Old days, old friends."

"What do you *want*?"

He eyed her over the glass's wide rim. "That Schmidt . . . When he was talking about the killer, did he mention Munich?"

"No, he . . . Oh, God, Nick, is that where he comes from? Do you know anything?"

"Esther, Esther. If I had the goods on the bastard, wouldn't I take it to the police?"

"That'd be the day," she said. "Is it, Nick? Is Munich where he lives?"

"How would I know? We ain't sending each other postcards."

"Nick."

"It's just something Vassily said the other day—you remember Vassily? My sommelier? Well, he just brought the killer to mind, that's all. Esther, I swear on the saints."

"You don't believe in the saints. You believe in money."

And you're short of it, she thought. News of the imminent sale of the Green Hat had reached her. There were other signs: His hair was the uniform black that comes out of a self-inflicted bottle. One of the larger diamond rings was missing from his finger. His eyes were tired.

"Nick, if you were in trouble, you would tell me."

"Sure, sure. Who else? It's just a cash-flow problem, nothing. You know me, I got plans. I'm expecting to make a killing any day. Prince Nick will ride again."

He stayed a while longer, talking of other things, mainly his third wife, "a complete disappointment." His farewell, so like him, was a flurry, a glance at his watch, another appointment. "See you, kid."

Three days later she heard he was dead.

"WHAT THE HELL was he doing in Munich?" Schmidt wanted to know.

Since his return to Berlin, most of his sentences had begun with "What the hell . . . ?" What the hell happened to . . . ? Why the hell did they . . . ? It had become what-the-hell city: everything bigger, faster, more crowded. Trees had gone—which, to judge from the pulp required to print the city's enormous number of newspapers and magazines, wasn't surprising. New estates had arisen. Department stores were seven stories high and proudly declared Jewish names. Alexanderplatz had been refurbished but was no prettier. There was a new West End—ditto. A massive broadcasting center had sprung up; so had a radio tower that might have been spawned by Eiffel.

It was election time—it was always election time this summer—and every *litfass* in the streets carried posters that blamed the other parties for a sliding economy given its push by the Wall Street crash.

At first glance the Depression that Schmidt had seen turn industrial Düsseldorf into a ghost town was leaving Berlin unaffected. It appeared prosperous, but he knew that waiting behind the façade—in Moabit, Wedding, Kreuzberg, the docks—were the dreary lines of unemployed, the soup kitchens—and their faithful companions, Nazis and Communists.

When he got off the train, he'd been taken for a tourist and touted to ride on an open-topped bus to see the sights of "the biggest city in the world."

"I thought that was New York," he'd said.

"Biggest in population," he was told, "but Berlin's biggest in size. Do you know, sir, a sprightly pedestrian walking ten hours a day would take five days to circumambulate the two hundred thirty kilometers of Berlin's municipal boundary?"

"Poor bugger," Schmidt said.

His visits over the last nine years had been mostly confined to police headquarters, and much of the development had passed him by. Now that he was back for good, it seemed he'd have to learn Berlin all over again.

He'd met Willi in a bar across from police headquarters. It had once been the decently stolid Waffenrock and was now a star-spangled, overpriced lounge called "The U.S. of A."

"So?" He tapped the item in the newspaper. Willi had phoned him in Düsseldorf to tell him of it. He'd been about to take his leave of Düsseldorf anyway but at that had cut the farewells short and set out.

The *Berliner Morgenpost* he bought on the train showed a photograph of Nikolai Potrovskov below a headline: BERLIN NIGHTCLUB OWNER MURDERED.

"Throat cut. Found two days ago on the bank of the Isar under some trees," Willi said, repeating what he'd said over the phone. "No suspects so far, according to the Munich boys. Thought you'd be interested, boss."

He was, he was. "He seems to like beauty spots," he said.

"Who does?"

"Our killer."

"Now, boss." Willi pushed his chair an inch backward as from someone dangerously insane. "Don't start that again. Guy like Prince Nick, there's dozens of reasons for cutting his throat. They say gangland was lining up. Or it could've been one of his women. Coincidence, that's what it is. Wish now I hadn't told you."

They'd stayed in touch. Schmidt had twice returned to stand as godfather to extra Ritte children, now numbering seven in all. Willi's use of "boss" was a courtesy; he was an inspector himself—in Traffic, a busy division compared to the old days when it had consisted virtually of one man and a red flag.

"Coincidence, eh?" It could be, certainly it could be. Only it wasn't. Schmidt had been waiting for it to happen for nine years—not this particularly, but an occasion that Hannelore's killer could deal with only by killing again—and leaving some mark by which Schmidt would know it.

Here it was. Victim: someone who'd been connected to Natalya. Method: a cut throat, like Natalya's.

Location: Munich, which was where one of his initialed suspects in the Sturmabteilung had come from. R.G. of Munich.

"What the hell was Potrovskov doing in Munich?" he said again.

"Lot of people go to Munich," Willi said, still tender with the afflicted. "Winter sports, beer drinking, visiting their auntie. Very popular place, Munich."

"Yep. Been there myself." He patted Willi on the shoulder. "And in case you're worried, Inspector, I'm not going again. Not for a bit anyway. I presume nobody there saw who bumped off Potrovskov? No, he's good at that."

"What *are* you going to do?"

"I don't know. I got a letter from Ringer saying he wants to see me on my return. How is the old bastard?"

Willi sucked his teeth. "He's not happy."

"Somebody steal his mustache wax?"

More teeth sucking indicated that levity was not called for. "We got a new department, boss. Political."

"We've always had a Political Department."

"Not like this one. You ever heard of a man called Diels? Rudolf Diels?"

"No."

"You will. He's . . . I don't know what exactly. The Minister of the Interior's Special Representative to Police Headquarters or some fancy title, sort of government adviser on dealing with Commies and Nazis."

"About time somebody did, isn't it?" On the way into the Platz, he'd been passed by open riot trucks, klaxons blaring, carrying police stacked like milk bottles to a street battle near the zoo. "We're going back to the bad old days."

"We're back in the bad old days of unemployment as well, boss, but . . . Oh, well, you'll find out. Everything's got to go through Diels's crew. My boys attend a traffic accident, seems a report has to go to Diels. Ringer's not happy—he's being bypassed, like."

Schmidt didn't take much notice. Government ministers always tried to justify their existence by making changes in departments under their control; meddling was what they were good at.

The first real indication that this particular change went deep was Ringer's pleasure at seeing him. "Sit down, sit down, Inspector. A glass of sherry to welcome your return?"

Schmidt, seated in the comfortable chair provided for him, peered into the cabinet from which a decanter and glasses were being produced, in case it also contained a fatted calf.

"It seems we did rather well in Düsseldorf," Ringer said, toasting him.

"Did we?" Ringer hadn't been there. Over the years seventy-nine people had died at the hands of a man called Peter Kurten in ways Schmidt tried to forget. He didn't blame himself—he'd come late to the case—nor did he blame the Düsseldorf police. They'd all been flailing in the dark as, on his previous assignment, he and the Hanover police had flailed in the dark for the mass murderer Haarmann. But he didn't congratulate himself either.

"The trial's publicity reflected well on our involvement, I think," Ringer said. "We are being approached from several regions for advice on dealing with these"—the kaiser mustache waggled over a choice of words—"these killings in multiples with which the country seems afflicted. I have decided to set up a special unit to answer the call." He gave a congratulatory nod. "And you are the man to run it."

"Look." Schmidt sat forward. "It's a matter of luck, there isn't a method. You just have to wait until the swine makes a mistake. With Haarmann it was different, but Kurten didn't have a pattern—he'd kill anybody. In the end he more or less gave himself up."

"Luck, Inspector? It is my maxim that luck devolves on those who are prepared to grasp it when it is manifested. I envisage your job being public relations as much as anything—advice to forces, lectures on the subject. A new department for you to set up. I've given you a secretary."

"First I want some time off."

Ringer blinked.

"I'm owed," Schmidt told him. "I haven't taken leave in years."

"Of course, of course. As long as you like, within reason."

Ringer's face set suddenly, becoming a mask with a ridiculous mustache. Behind Schmidt someone had come into the room without knocking. He swiveled around and struggled for recognition of a familiar figure out of context.

"Ah, yes," it said. "I heard the inspector was here."

"You know Major Busse?" Ringer's was more an accusation than an introduction.

"Good God, Busse, how are you?" Schmidt rose. "What're you doing here?"

They shook hands. Franz Busse was in smart civvies, looking every inch the prosperous accountant. "Liaison, between Department 1A and . . . well, everybody else."

"Major?" Schmidt asked.

"Courtesy title." Busse shifted his spectacles on his nose. "Well, well, Schmidt, so you're to run our new multiple-murder department?" He was ignoring Ringer, Schmidt noticed; he might have been in the office of an inferior.

"*My* multiple-murder department," Ringer said.

"It has our full approval," Busse said, as if nobody had spoken. "And I am sure it could not have a better man in charge of it. Come along. I want you to meet Colonel Diels."

"Inspector Schmidt and I still have matters to discuss," Ringer said.

"Later, then," Busse said, clicking his heels. He went out, leaving Schmidt aware that there'd been a psychological chess game in progress in which he'd been a pawn.

The silence was painful. Ringer filled it by downing another glass of sherry.

"Very military," Schmidt said at last.

Ringer shrugged. "You are a friend of Busse's?"

"We were neighbors. I haven't seen him in years."

There was more silence. Ringer roused himself. "Well, I think that's all. Your office is ready for you when you're prepared to take up duty."

"Thank you, sir." He saluted and went to the door.

"Inspector."

"Yes, sir?"

"Keep me informed." It was a plea. Christ, Ringer was begging him.

"I shall, sir."

He'd been allocated his old office on the third floor, though the sign on its door was fresh. It still read GEHEIMPOLIZISTKOMMISSAR SCHMIDT, but the lettering was gold and had the added designation of his department: 7B. Inside, it had been newly painted, the filing cabinets were bigger and smarter, the telephone modern Bakelite, and the table desk was green metal with drawers and had a wastepaper basket to match.

There was a secretary. "Helena Pritt, Inspector." Another heel clicker. She wore tweeds and heavy shoes. Her graying hair was coiled in tight earphones, and her face, while it wouldn't have launched a thousand ships, would certainly have sunk them unmoved.

"They haven't changed the linoleum, I see," Schmidt said amiably.

"Do you wish me to order new?"

"No, no. Some of these cracks are old friends."

Frau Pritt didn't smile, probably couldn't. Schmidt opened his briefcase and brought out his film poster of *M*. "Let's start untidying. Got any pushpins?" The actor Peter Lorre had given him the poster and signed it *"To Inspector Schmidt, in gratitude and respect for his part in the arrest of the real M."*

He pinned it to the wall. "Fine film that," he said. "Did you see it?"

"No, Inspector."

"Based on the mass murderer Peter Kurten. Fitting for the new department, I think."

Frau Pritt's face suggested that she didn't.

Schmidt opened the filing cabinets. The drawers were empty except for a few official-looking forms. He said, "Would you go down to Records and bring up my personal files?" Old friends again, old arrests, his who-was-who among Berlin's criminal fraternity—out-of-date now, probably, but a starting point. Hell, he'd just feel more at home for having them around.

"I will need a signed C22 form, Inspector. For Department 1A."

"What?"

"Department 1A, Inspector. The transfer of files must go through the Political Department."

"Since when?"

"Since the order from Colonel Diels, Inspector."

"They're my files, Frau Pritt, collated while this Colonel Diels was still a corporal—if he ever was."

"They won't release them without a C22."

"All right, give me one." He signed the damned thing.

"Is there anything else you require while I'm downstairs, Inspector?"

"An ashtray and a cup of coffee. One other thing, Frau Pritt: you're working for me now, not the Political Department."

"Of course, Inspector."

"In which case I'd be obliged if you'd take that badge off."

Frau Pritt unpinned the little enamel swastika from her lapel and put it in her pocket.

When she'd gone, Schmidt tried out his new swivel chair. He took a pencil from a metal container on his desk and started drumming, staring at the telephone.

Eventually he lifted the receiver and gave her number to the switchboard operator. God knew how many times he'd thought of phoning her these last nine years, stretched out his hand to do it . . . and put the phone down again.

This time he let it ring. And ring. She wasn't in. She'd moved, emigrated.

Somebody lifted the receiver at the other end. *"What?"*

It was a man's voice. Why wouldn't it be? What else to expect?

"Can I speak to Fräulein Solomonova?"

"Out."

"When will she be back?"

"Oh, *God,* I don't know. Sixish, I expect."

"I'll come by at seven, if I may." He was about to ask whom he was talking to, but the man at the other end had put down the phone.

So.

Carefully, he put the pencil back in its holder. He saw he'd broken its point, crushed it. Well, Frau Pritt could sharpen it. With that face she wouldn't need a sharpener.

ESTHER DRAGGED HERSELF up the stairs to 29c and let herself in.

Marlene shouted from the bathroom. "Is that you, dear?"

"Better be," Esther said.

"How'd it go?"

"Awful." She took off her hat. "Boris was crying, everybody was."

"Do they know anything?"

"No." She'd found all Nick's staff gathered at the club, but the Green Hat wouldn't open tonight, partly out of respect for its late owner but mostly because, from Boris the manager down to the lowliest cigarette girl, the staff was too devastated by his death to function. Nick had underpaid them, shouted at them, slept with and then abandoned quite a few, but one and all wept for him as they got drunk on his vodka.

"To Prince Nick," Boris said, sobbing, throwing another glass into the Hat's huge and artificial fireplace. "No one fucking like him, Esther. Couldn't beat him. Remember how he palmed an ace at poker? Beautiful it was, beautiful. To Nick."

"To Nick." Her glass shattered. "What was he doing in Munich, Boris?"

"'Zactly. What was he doing there?" He tottered toward her, steadying himself on her shoulder. "'I'm off to make a killing, Boris,' he said. 'We're going to have good days from a bad man.' That's what he said, 'good days from a bad man.' I told him, I said, 'Nick,' I said, 'Little Father, don't you have anything to do with bad men.' He just laughed, you know the way he did. 'Boris,' he said, 'Boris, my trusted friend, any fish is good if it's on a hook. That's what my father, Prince Wladislaw, told me.' Bless him." Boris wiped his eyes on Esther's sleeve. "He never knew his father. Lying to the last, he was, may he join the holy martyrs."

"Why on earth would anyone kill him?"

"They got husbands in Munich, Esther, lots of husbands, thousands, thousands Bavarian bastards. Martyred by a fucking husband, bless him."

"Is Vassily here?"

"Vassily? No, Vassily found a boyfriend and happiness and fucked off to America. Why?"

"He told Nick something. I think that's why Nick went to Munich."

She'd gone upstairs to the office. His diary told her nothing except that by flying to Munich, Nick had missed a dentist's appointment, a Grand Lodge meeting, a summons to his bank, and a tryst with someone called Wanda (*"Send orchids"*).

She gave up the search among his papers; he'd always kept details of his more nefarious activities in his head. There was no correspondence with anyone in Munich.

You went after him, didn't you? You found something out, somebody said something. A bit of blackmail, Nick? Oh, Jesus, why does it hurt so badly? You stupid, stupid, second-rate crook, why have you taken so much of me with you?

The silence became unbearable, and she'd gone downstairs to smash more glasses to his memory before she left.

Marlene was calling again from the bathroom.

"What?"

"A man phoned for you."

"Who was it?"

"Didn't say, dear. The bastard woke me up. Nice voice. Says he's coming around at seven."

Oh, God, no. She was too tired for visitors.

All at once she was on her feet. Nine years. She'd been expecting him for nine years. She looked at her watch. Half past six.

"Marlene."

"What, dear?"

She had to make him pay for those nine years, but she had to look her best to do it. "Get out of that goddamn bathroom."

She opened the door and looked at him without surprise, as if she'd been expecting him. There was no greeting. She just said, "Do you think it was Natalya's killer?"

"Yes."

"So do I. Come in."

She'd changed quite a bit. She'd had something done about the scar—it was still there, but not so prominent, less a badly mended wound, more a plain scar. Her bouncy hair had been beautifully cut. Her ears were studded with plain gold disks, matching the buttons of her dress. She looked groomed, svelte—he supposed, fashionable.

She led him into the living room. Like her, it had become very modern, very smart. The furniture was streamlined, and instead of being gathered around a stove—there was no stove, just white radiators—it stood back to permit a centerpiece of an enormous round rug in geometric patterns of cream and red on which stood a similarly round glass table with some art books stacked on its top.

The walls were hung with huge and arresting photographs; one of them—a portrait of Potrovskov—was lit by a globular lamp placed below it. At the other end of the room, she'd installed French doors where the window over the courtyard had been, and they were open onto a small balcony, letting in the last of the July light and the mixed smells of summer and city.

Snatches of song in a contented baritone, such as a man emits when he's dressing, came from the room he remembered as Natalya's. She didn't comment on it.

He felt rabid contempt. No need to offer consolation on Potrovskov's death, then; the poor bastard had already been swapped for somebody else. Not that he'd been about to sympathize; he'd disliked condolences from people who hadn't cared about Hannelore—and he sure as hell hadn't cared about Potrovskov.

"Cocktail?"

"Beer if you've got it. You never moved, then?"

"No, I stayed to annoy Frau Schinkel. The place suits me." No need to tell him that one of the reasons she'd stayed was so that he would find her again.

He was given a beer and a chair. She perched on the table as if their interview were to be short.

"I won't stay long," he said. "I came to see if Potrovskov told you why he was going to Munich. Did he say who he was going to meet there?"

"No."

"Oh."

So that's that, Esther thought. See you in another nine years. Why else would he have come? Death was his business.

He'd changed; the gentleness she remembered had gone, presumably with the loss of his wife. She'd seen his name in connection with the murders in Düsseldorf when they'd been headline news—*"Inspector Schmidt of the Berlin police, who is in charge of the case"*—and had wondered at the time what that involvement would do to somebody. It wasn't that he'd aged, she thought, more that he'd set in concrete, thinner but somehow heavier, like a man who'd built an inward bulwark against intruders. He'd come trailing ghosts: Natalya, his wife, the dead of Düsseldorf. And angry, so *angry.*

Well, if he was nothing else, he was a policeman, and there was a killer to be caught. She said, "About Nick. He mentioned the Sturmabteilung and Munich in the same breath."

He watched her as she related the conversation she'd had with Potrovskov, then the one with the Green Hat's manager. She was being brisk about it, efficient. Couldn't wait to get rid of him before her man emerged from the bedroom.

She said, "He used the same phrase to both Boris and me. He was going to 'make a killing.'" She sneered, and he saw how badly hurt she was. "There's irony for you."

"Blackmail?"

"I imagine so. When I told him you'd thought the man was SA, it seemed to confirm something for him. He knows a lot of Nazis." Her fist clenched. "I should have kept on asking. I . . ."

A bee had come into the room and was blundering. She urged it toward the balcony, closing the French doors behind it. She hung on to the door for a moment, her back to him. "Stupid," she said. "Stupid. He was so stupid."

From the other room came a spirited burst of "What Is This Thing Called Love" in English.

He saw the shake of her head. She turned around, came back, and stood in front of him. "All right," she said. "What are the police doing about it?"

"Not much. No clues. In Munich they think it's a random killing."

"But you don't."

"No." He gave her his reasons; he supposed she had the right to know.

"All right," she said again. "What are *you* going to do about it?"

"Officially? Nothing. I've been transferred to a new department."

"And unofficially?"

He said, "He was always going to kill again if anybody got too close. That's why I didn't want you meddling in the case."

"Oh, how nice," she said brightly. "You've been worrying about me for nine years. You should have said."

He nearly shouted, I was keeping you safe, woman. Hannelore died because I was getting too close, because she was there, something to be smashed because I valued it. He'd ensured Solomonova's safety by staying away from her.

"This funny thing called love," sang the singer.

He said, "They won't let me touch the case. I reacted badly when he killed my wife." He wanted to punish her with it.

"*He* killed her? He *killed* her?"

"I'd tracked him to the SA. I was on his trail. He pushed her down the stairs. A warning." He spoke in staccato to get it over with. "And it worked. I was taken off the case. They kept me busy with other murders. There was no proof anyway. But it was him. She was pregnant."

Her shoulders slumped. "I didn't know." After a while she got up and fetched him another beer. She pushed a cigarette box toward him, and a table lighter. "Do you want something to eat? An omelette? I'm good at omelettes."

"No, thank you." Solicitude to the bereaved. Why the hell had he told her?

She went into the kitchen and made him one anyway; she had to do something for him.

He sipped his beer, looking at the portrait of Potrovskov, wondering what her new man was like, all at once too tired to care.

She came back with the omelette and set the tray on his lap. "Eat." Very Jewish. She watched every mouthful and saw some energy come back. "You're going after him on your own, I imagine," she said.

"Yep." He told her about R.G. of Munich. He wanted more information from her, and the only way to get it was to give it.

"So all we've got to do is go through the Munich telephone directory for men with the initials R.G.," she said.

"That's it."

"Well, I've got a contribution." She told him about Franziska Schanskowska. "I'm pretty sure that's Anna's real name. When she signed the adoption papers at the Elizabeth Hospital, she had to sign them in the name under which she'd given birth—and she'd had the baby in Poland. The name wasn't in the hospital records as such; I was lucky to find someone in the almoner's office who'd made a mental note of it. I told Inspector Bolle at the time, but he didn't seem to think it was relevant."

Parroting her, he said, "So all I've got to do is search through old Polish telephone directories and see if a Franziska Schanskowska was ever listed."

"We," she said. "*We've* got to search."

"No."

Her head came up. "I'm involved in this. He's killed two people I care about, three when you count Olga. He's picking us off. He's got to be finished. He's Argus—he's got eyes everywhere. How do I know he's not out there now, watching us?" She got up and went to the windows, opening them wider. "I can't go on like this. He's got to be gotten rid of. He's invisible, but I can smell him; he stinks of death. Sometimes I think I've never known anything else."

His anger was almost uncontrollable. "He's not Argus. He's not superhuman, for Christ's sake. He's just another fucking killer. He kills when he's frightened. He stinks because he stinks. And I can get him."

They heard the man in the bedroom call, "Anything up, sweetie?"

"Nothing, lovie," Esther called back. She gathered herself together. To Schmidt she said, "I'm going to make some coffee."

She went into the kitchen. Does he think it's my fault? I'm alive and his wife's dead? I'm sorry, I'm sorry. But I can't take that on; I gave up feeling guilty just for surviving a long time ago.

He'd done one thing, though: he'd diminished the killer for her. Nick's death had sent the shadow looming over her head again, and she'd cowered under it, helpless. Schmidt had cut it down to size. The killer wasn't some arbitrary force of nature; he had initials, weaknesses, he was afraid. He was *gettable.*

When she came back with the coffee, Schmidt said more quietly, "He's not out there. He's in Munich and what he's got is a damn good spy network—*two* spy networks. He's a homosexual—at least I think he is, because he's under Röhm's protection—and he's a Nazi."

"Which makes him almost universal."

"No," Schmidt said, "it doesn't. It gives him access to two societies who'll go to considerable lengths to protect their own. Röhm knows that our man killed Natalya because I told him, and he doesn't care—it was Röhm who set him onto me. He's not all-powerful, he's just very well-informed. He's like a rat—when he's threatened, he kills. So far he's gotten away with it, but sooner or later he'll make a mistake."

"But why? Why does he kill? This isn't one of your random murderers. This man's selective."

"Ask your Anna Anderson," he said. "She knows. She was his first victim. He chucked her in the canal, and when that failed, he came after her again. She knows whatever it is he wants to keep quiet; she's got something on him that even the Nazis wouldn't tolerate. Maybe he once spoke slightingly of Hitler's mustache. *If* she's Franziska Schanskowska, whatever-it-was happened when she *was* Franziska Schanskowska. And *if* she's Franziska Schanskowska, she can't expose our friend without admitting that she's not Anastasia." He realized he was pounding on the table, and stopped.

"Yes," she said quietly, "I'd worked that out."

"They're locked together," he said. "He knows that by now. He won't try for her again, only for anyone getting too close." He added, "Or their wives."

"Don't blame Anna," she said quickly. "She doesn't calculate like that. In her mind she *is* Anastasia; her fear of him is . . . well, a sort of residue from her past, a reasonless terror that she doesn't analyze. It's not her fault."

Of course it's her fucking fault, he thought. The woman's a carrier infecting anyone she comes in contact with. She's Typhoid Mary.

Instead he said, "Anyway, she's been safe enough these last nine years—so have you, and you'll oblige me by keeping it like that and staying out of it. Just get on with whatever you're doing."

He was making her as furious as he was. "If you don't want my help, why the hell are you here?"

"I told you. To find out if you knew why Potrovskov went to Munich."

"Well, I don't."

He shrugged. "In which case I'll drink my coffee and be on my way."

"By all means."

"You do something to me." Natalya's door was thrown open, and a man came out. Six foot two in high heels with the build of a coal heaver, scarlet lips, platinum hair, and a smart, short-skirted two-piece dress in pink velvet. "Oh," he said, then fluttered his lashes. "Ooh-*er*."

"Inspector, this is Marlene Leicester," Esther said. "Marlene, this is Inspector Schmidt of the Berlin police."

"So this is the famous Schmidt, is it?" Marlene said. He put out a manicured hand. "How do you *do,* darling. And little me off to work, what a shame. *Well* . . . " He looked from Esther to Schmidt and back again. "I sense *atmosphere,* so I'll leave you two alone. But *you,* my dear inspector, can inspect me anytime." He pranced off, taking most of the ghosts with him.

Esther said tenderly, "She's not always like that. She just tends to show off when she meets new people."

Schmidt felt anger seeping away like bad weather, leaving a laundered blue sky under which he could have slept for a week. A homosexual transvestite, bless her. That's all right, then. He tried to show interest. "How did you acquire her?"

"She does an act at the Pink Parasol—it was one of Nick's clubs in the old days. Her landlord turned her out. I was glad of her company and her rent. Funnily enough, Frau Schinkel adores Marlene. It's me she can't stand. Give her a transvestite Aryan over a heterosexual Jew any day. And Marlene's aristocratic, an English milord's son, German mother. Went to Eton, everything. She was just born into the wrong body. Berlin's been heaven for her." She squinted at him. "She manages to shock most people."

"Not me," he said sleepily.

"I know. Why not?"

He roused himself. "Oh, Hanover and Düsseldorf. Murderers who were freaks of nature, mental mutants. When you've been wading through atrocity for nine years, you're grateful for every human quirk that doesn't involve killing somebody." He yawned. "Anyway, in the Haarmann case kids died because their parents didn't like to admit that their son was homosexual."

He thought, Marlene's all right by me. I love her. "I'd better be going," he said.

And if he hadn't looked so damn tired, she'd have let him. She was still angry; he'd got what clues she could give him—it was all he'd come for. But apparently the meal had done him in; with his legs stretched out and his head resting against the back of her most comfortable chair, his eyes kept narrowing and then opening as he tried to remain awake.

She lunged to take the coffee cup from his hand before it dropped.

"I'm sorry," he said.

"Where are you staying?"

"I don't know. I only got in from Düsseldorf today."

She clicked her tongue at the inefficiency. "There's Marlene's room. She won't be back until the morning." She told herself she'd have done as much for a dog.

She pointed him in the right direction and went off to find a pair of Nick's pajamas that were still in a drawer somewhere, but by the time she got back with them, he'd fallen onto Marlene's bed and was asleep.

Strange, strange man, she thought. One minute I was something the cat threw up, and the next I wasn't.

Nine years, she thought. She stood looking down at him for a moment, replaying their conversation in her head. Good God, she thought, that's why.

You stayed away for nine years in case what happened to your wife happened to me.

She turned off his light and went to bed but not to sleep, listening to the rattle of the late-night trams in Bismarckstrasse.

In Schmidt's dream Solomonova fell downstairs, her limbs flailing and breaking while Peter Kurten stood in the shadows on the landing above.

The door opened. "Are you all right?"

"Shit," he said. "Yes. I'm sorry, I get these nightmares."

She said, "There isn't much time, is there?"

"Time for what?"

"For us."

She came to him, and it turned out he wasn't as tired as he'd thought he was.

SHE WATCHED HIM wake up. It was a pleasure. He looked better. And so he should, she thought. It had been an invigorating night.

"Good morning."

"Good morning."

She said, "In view of the circumstances, calling you 'Inspector' seems somewhat formal. What's your first name?"

"Siegfried," he said. "My parents believed in joy through victory. Boy, did they get that wrong."

His eyes took in Marlene's befrilled bedroom. Pink was not just the motif, it was the only color: walls, curtains, ruched valance, cupboards, bedclothes, bed, the tasseled tester above it—all ranging the pink spectrum from light blush to damn nearly mauve. "Good God," he said.

"Marlene likes pink," she said.

"I thought I was waking up in someone's entrails."

To get it out of the way, she said, "I never loved Nick; you ought to know that. I was fond of him, and he was kind to me. I owed him a lot. In a way he was my best friend."

"I didn't love my wife enough," he said. "She deserved better."

"We never love anyone enough."

He reached for her. "We're going to change that."

She would have stayed in bed forever, but he was worried that Marlene would return and find them in it. "How very bourgeois of you," she said, reluctantly clambering out.

"Where I come from it's called respectable."

He helped her strip the bed and put on clean sheets, and then she made him breakfast—another omelette.

It was luxury to see him in her surroundings. She sat at the table in the kitchen, her chin in her hands, watching him eat and look around at its modernity, its only color the green-and-yellow chinaware. He pointed at a potbellied machine rumbling away in a corner. "What's that?"

"A washer-dryer," she said. "It's doing your shirt and pants so you can go to work. Pink's not your color." He was wearing one of Marlene's negligees. Actually, she thought he looked wonderful in it.

"My old mother had to make do with a boiler and a mangle."

"Good for your old mother," she said.

"Seems funny to ask," he said, "but what do you do?"

"Well, I'm not a kept woman, haven't been for nine years—not that I ever was, really. All this is the fruit of my own labors. So's the flat—I bought it."

She conducted him into the living room. "My showcase," she said. She'd framed some of her best studies in metal, putting a full-length shot of Marlene the transvestite against one of Marlene the film star. Apart from Potrovskov there were black-hatted men emerging from the Moabit synagogue, a landscape, a shot of the futuristic Karstadt department store in Neukölln.

"You're a photographer."

"Your powers of detection amaze me, Inspector," she said. "Have you heard of Cicatrice?"

"No."

"It's me. French for 'scar.' It's my professional name. I'm highly thought of in artistic circles."

He shook his head in wonder. "What started you on that?"

"Nick. He gave me my first camera. A Leica, thirty-five-millimeter." It had been Parsifal finding the Holy Grail, Wellington meeting Blucher. "I left his employment and his bed when Natalya died and began earning my own living. I didn't want to be involved after that."

"Was it hard going?" That had been 1923. All Germany had nearly died in 1923.

"Hard." She'd started with happy-snaps, shivering in the Tiergarten while she took photographs of tourists and developed them by night in a primitive darkroom she set up in Anna's old bedroom.

Then, merely because it made a terrific picture, she'd photographed some street children using packets of currency to build a playhouse. She'd taken it to an American news agency in Fischerstrasse, which had sent it to *Collier's* magazine in New York, which had paid her for it.

"After that I just recorded Berlin life—wheelbarrows filled with banknotes, the breadlines, Wandervogel kids without shoes, prostitutes, Einstein—"

"Einstein?"

"Through the synagogue. He'd just had his breakdown and was taking things easy on the lake at Caputh. It made my name."

"I didn't know he'd had a breakdown."

"Lovely man," she said. "I like people who have breakdowns."

She amazed him. While he dressed, he kept coming into the living room to watch her tidy the place up. Cicatrice, he thought. It was typical of her to make a virtue of her scars. In the night he'd found that her upper body was pitted with old wounds. "Who the hell did this to you?" he'd asked.

"Pogrom," she said. "Not worth talking about. Don't let them put you off."

They hadn't.

"Tut, tut," she'd said. "There's a name for men who are excited by disfigured women."

"It's 'lover,'" he'd told her, and it was true. For him the flaws highlighted the beauty and mystery of the rest of her; she made other women look dull.

He wasn't going to be much use at work today; when they hadn't been making love, they'd been talking.

"Was it awful?" she'd asked. "Haarmann and then Kurten? I read about them."

"If you want an authority on how flesh gets torn apart and how to tell the mothers it's been torn and wait to find the next one and tell that mother, send in a request. I'm setting up a department in it." He had memories that were beyond discussion.

She said gently, "But you caught them in the end."

"They caught themselves. And you know what? They were glad. I saw the relief in their eyes; they were tired of it."

Heaven would have consisted in neither of them having to go to work, but through the euphoria came the drum of duty.

As she buttoned him into his shirt, he said, "Did you ever get Anna to say where she came from?"

"No."

"Franziska Schanskowska," he said, musing. "Christ, there's got to be some record of where she was born. I've got to go back to her beginnings."

"We," she said. "*We've* got to go back to her beginnings."

"No." He was suddenly furious with her. "He killed my wife because I was meddling. I'm not having it happen to you. Jesus *Christ,* don't be stupid. In fact, I want you to move out of here."

"I'll do no such thing," she said. "He's forgotten about me. He can't possibly know that we've been to bed together—you said yourself, he's not superhuman." She said more gently, "I've got my darkroom here. This is my business address. I'm damned if he drives me out."

He supposed he didn't have the right after just one night to insist, but she frightened him. "We'll see," he said.

After a while she said, "Nick couldn't find out, but I was thinking. . . ."

"Thinking what?"

"The agency that dealt with the adoption of Anna's baby. They might know—if you could use your clout to discover which one it was. Might have been German, might have been Polish."

"I'll find it." He kissed her, picked up his coat, and moved toward the door. "Just don't talk to any strange men."

"I've got two of them living here," she said. "At least . . . I suppose there will be two." She gave a marked cough. "I'm a busy career woman. I just need to know—are you coming back?"

"I am. Get something nice for dinner." He half closed the door and opened it again. "Not omelettes." And went out.

"Oh, thank you," she said.

18

GOING ALONG the third-floor corridor toward his office, Schmidt was waylaid by Eisenmenger. Literally waylaid; Eisenmenger had been waiting for him. "I expect you want to buy me a drink on my retirement," he said.

He took Schmidt by the arm, and they went on, not downstairs to the hall but toward the door leading to the fire escape that in turn led to the police parking lot.

That a man of Eisenmenger's dignity and bulk should lurk, let alone use a fire escape, indicated that something was up.

A hut was up, for one thing—new since Schmidt's day—at the entrance to the parking lot. Men were working on it and a barrier. "Note that," Eisenmenger muttered as they walked around it.

"What we want is a beer cellar of dubious reputation. Noisy if possible," Eisenmenger said. It was like accompanying a cartoon conspirator who had a bomb peeping from his cloak.

There were plenty of old-fashioned dives near the Platz. Schmidt chose the Wrestlers on the grounds that, even though he'd arrested its owner several times for fencing stolen goods, they'd maintained mutual respect.

Apparently they still did. "Nice to see you back, Inspector."

"Nice to *be* back, Boxer."

It was too early for the quartet and crooner that usually covered the denizens' conversations, but the place was dark enough. They ordered beers—Eisenmenger added a schnapps chaser to his—and took them to a corner table.

"To your retirement," Schmidt said. "Bit young, aren't you?" Eisenmenger was of the ilk to have looked fifty when he was eighteen and would continue to look fifty when he was eighty.

"Dear boy," Eisenmenger said, and Schmidt suspected he was drunk, "I am fifty-six, and I intend to become older, a happiness that may be denied me if I stay."

"Nonsense. You're the doyen of the political department. Nobody knows where more bodies are buried than you do."

"Indeed. However, since I fear that the body count will rise to a level which not even I can countenance, I am going." His enunciation was as perfect as ever, but he was definitely drunk. "I am taking myself and my wife to Tübingen, where I intend to grow orchids, reflect on the works of Marcus Aurelius, and thank God that we had no children."

"Christ, Carl, what's . . . Is it this fellow Diels?"

"Ah, yes, Colonel Purely-a-Courtesy-Title Diels." Eisenmenger looked long into his beer, then drank it. "Did you see the new addition to the parking lot?"

"The hut? Yes."

"A guardhouse. Have you used the phone since your return?"

"Once."

"Note the double click as the operator connects you to your number. Not only is your call—and the person to whom it is made—being registered, but somebody is listening to every word you say."

"For goodness' sake."

Eisenmenger looked up and raised an eyebrow. "You think I fantasize?"

"Frankly, yes."

"What a remarkably fine establishment this is." Eisenmenger screwed his monocle into his eye socket to look around at the fly-ridden sausages hanging from the beams and the cauliflower ears and tattoos of the clientele. "The beer is excellent. You may get me another."

Schmidt fetched the drinks. "I'm glad we met. I was going to ask you about Röhm's SA in Munich—"

Eisenmenger waved a hand. "Already an anachronism, dear boy. Röhm has become too powerful and therefore, like all threats to Herr Hitler, will be dealt with. He's a homosexual anyway, and our Adolf loathes queers. The SA will be used as auxiliary police. No, if we are trading initials, I suggest you consider the new force, Hitler's own, the SS, the Schutzstaffel, for which happy band our own Department 1A and Major Diels serve as an instrument."

Schmidt's mouth, open for follow-up questions, closed.

"We are being infiltrated," Eisenmenger said. "I consider it my duty to warn such honest men as still remain. Has your new department been allocated staff?"

"I've got a secretary who clicks her heels."

"Party member," Eisenmenger said. "She will report back on your every move to Diels with a salutation of 'Heil Hitler.'"

"Report what, for God's sake? I'm just doing my job."

"So is Diels. His task is to prepare a new police force for a new Reich. A secret state police, the Geheime Staatspolizei, or, to use its acronym, the Gestapo."

Schmidt looked into eyes that were suddenly as sober as his own. "Is Hitler that close to getting the chancellorship?"

"Depending on the next election, or certainly on the one after that, an Austrian housepainter will be declared chancellor of Germany. Nearly all the center parties are caving in to him; the nationalists think that if he is allowed the respectability of power, they can control him."

For the first time, the acidity of Eisenmenger's speech left it and he sounded merely humanly troubled. "They don't believe him, you see. They don't believe *in* him—none of us really do. We think him merely mad. We refuse to recognize a phenomenon the world has never seen before." He took a deep breath, and the old tone was back. "Oh, yes, my boy, there is nothing to stop him. Diels, a farmer's son, or someone of equal breeding, will be made minister of the interior. Almost immediately a new bill will be passed, the Enabling Act." Eisenmenger's hand gripped Schmidt's. "I tell you, I've seen the draft. If you are acquainted with a trade unionist, liberal, Communist, beggar, homosexual, alcoholic, Jew, Jehovah's Witness, Gypsy, anybody mentally afflicted, or any bastard just too clever, I suggest you say good-bye to them now."

Schmidt grinned. "That's half the population. I can't see—"

"They're setting up camps," said Eisenmenger. "SS camps, SA camps, correctional camps, camps where those who stray from the Nazi path can be . . . corrected. Also killing grounds. That's where they take the worst strayers. The ultimate correction."

Schmidt was silenced.

"Jews especially," Eisenmenger said. "I hope you are not on friendly terms with any of God's Chosen?"

"As a matter of fact, I hope to marry one."

"Unwise," Eisenmenger said.

Schmidt was suddenly sick of the man, his snobbery, his monocle, the measured sentences, the smell of fear that emanated from him like a contagion; sick of being frightened by warnings in the moderate newspapers so poundingly repetitious that, merely to continue to work, he'd dulled himself to them; sick of living through crises; sick of political broken reeds; sick that he hadn't even voted in the last election because his chosen Social Democrats had proved themselves unfit to be voted for.

"There'd be civil war," he said, and drank the last of his beer.

Eisenmenger's fingers still gripped his hand. "And who is to provide the other side in this conflict?"

"Well, the workers, the Communists." Fine thing, he thought, when you started looking to the Reds for a safeguard to democracy.

"The clenched fist. Of course. The hammer and sickle. The fact that they are attached to a limp wrist does not concern us." Eisenmenger leaned forward until his sweating face was close to Schmidt's. "They're terrified, man. They have come up against a force even more brutal than their own. Watch the Nazis in action, see the stomping jackboots, listen to the abuse. We are witnessing something new: terror as a political ploy."

"Well . . ." Schmidt said, fetching money from his pocket.

"There's a killing ground, you know," Eisenmenger said. "They take them there and shoot them."

"Shoot who?"

"The disappearers. Awkward buggers, troublemakers. Debris to be cleared away so that our Führer's got a nice clean space to move into. One place where SS and SA meet in unanimity, the burial ground."

He wagged a finger. "Under the greenwood tree—lovely phrase, that. *That's* where the bodies are buried, my son."

"I've got to go," Schmidt said.

Eisenmenger didn't move. "Get out of the country, Inspector. There'll be no place for honest men in the new Reich. And take your Jewess with you."

As Schmidt paid for the beer, Eisenmenger lumbered beside him to the bar and demanded to be introduced. "Herr Boxer? Allow me to shake the hand of an honest crook."

The last Schmidt saw of him, he was embracing the barman and advising him to get out of the country.

Schmidt went back to the Alex in a temper unimproved by the clusters of men gathered around every *litfass* apparently mesmerized by screaming red posters with a black swastika. Hadn't they anything better to do?

Probably, he thought, they hadn't. Six million unemployed.

Fuck 'em; they were poisoning a morning that had begun in Arcadia. He'd been going to phone her every hour, like a moony adolescent, just to hear the sound of her voice. Now he wanted to phone her every hour to make sure she was safe, not from Natalya's killer but from Jew haters. *Now,* thanks to fucking Eisenmenger, he didn't dare phone her at all—at least not from the Alex.

He was brusque with Frau Pritt. "I want the telephone number of every adoption agency in Berlin. Start with the Roman Catholics. If necessary, we'll move on to the Polish agencies."

She was emptying his ashtray, one of her activities to show her disapproval of his smoking. She flapped the air a lot with her handkerchief. Schmidt had been tempted to give up cigarettes lately but had decided that to stop annoying Frau Pritt was too big a price to pay.

"It would help if I were acquainted with the circumstances, Inspector," Frau Pritt said.

"I'm thinking of having you adopted. Now, get on and do it." He congratulated himself on not saying "please" and then thought, Christ, I'm getting as bad as they are.

Give the woman her due; she was efficient. By noon he had a list as long as his arm. He retired with it to the Wrestlers, commandeered its phone, and began dialing.

Esther spent the morning in her first-floor studio in Cicerostrasse, photographing a film director who wanted a decent portrait for the publicity for his next movie, *The Last Testament of Dr. Mabuse*. He said it would be his final film in Germany; he was getting out.

"I'm on Hitler's List," he told her.

She lunched with her agent, Morry Linderer. He said he was on the List and would probably be heading for Palestine. "You ought to get out, Esther. You'd make a fortune in the States."

"I'm not fashionable enough to be on the List."

"A Jew's all you gotta be," he said.

Her afternoon was passed at the Kronprinzenpalais, talking over an exhibition of her photographs to be held in its small upper gallery in January. Dr. Justi, its director, was depressed. A new collection of modern art in the main gallery had been attacked by the Nazis' art critic, Alfred Rosenberg, as "intellectual syphilis."

"They've probably put Kandinksy and Picasso on the List," she said, which turned out not to be funny, because Dr. Justi thought they had.

Going home, she was passed by truckloads of stormtroopers on their way to cause trouble somewhere. They were singing one of their anthems: "'*Blut muss fliessen! Blut muss fliessen!* Blood must flow. Let's smash it up, let's smash it up, this goddamn Jewish republic!'"

They would not depress her, could not; today she was undepressable—she'd been waiting for somebody to notice the gap between her feet and the ground. The shadow of forthcoming death that had been gathering over her had folded itself up like an umbrella, leaving her with only one concern: what to get a policeman for dinner.

She was not a good cook. Anna had never noticed the fact; Natalya, onetime recipient of meals by the sous-chef at Czarskoe Seloe, had borne it; Marlene ate out. But a German liked his food.

After careful thought she purchased some veal, potatoes—he'd be a potato man—green beans, and a lemon.

She opened the door to him with a rolling pin in her hand.

"Bit early in our relationship for that, isn't it?" he said.

"I'm trying to get the bloody schnitzels flat."

"I was thinking of getting you flat first," he said.

"Marlene's still here, but we could go to my bedroom; she's broad-minded."

He wasn't. "I'm bourgeois enough to be inhibited. Besides, you're a screamer."

"I am *not* a screamer."

"Damn well are."

"Damn well not."

The meal was prepared with banter and eaten with exchanges of their day's news. "*Is* there a List?" she asked.

"I don't know. Eisenmenger would say there was, and he's nearer to events than I am. Christ, he was chilling. Drunk, but chilling."

"Lang said Einstein was on it. I don't believe it. I can't. I mean, what would be the point of getting rid of a brain like that? I don't understand the theory of relativity, but I know it's important; even Hitler must know that—it's ridiculous. It's just Nazi bluster. Germany needs its Jews."

He'd kept his good news until last. "I'm going away tomorrow," he said casually.

"And I thought we were getting on so well."

"I'm going to Poland."

She put her hands together and waggled them, like a petitioner with an answered prayer. "You found out where Anna comes from."

"Franziska Schanskowska. Born eighteenth May, 1901, Bagna Duse, near Pinsk. Poland."

She ran for maps.

Marlene, ready to go to work, emerged from his bedroom while they were studying them and peered over their shoulders, smelling of shaving soap and scent. "'Polesie,'" he read. "How sweet. Minsk, Pinsk—kitty-cat names. It looks about as far as you can go without hitting Russia."

"It *was* Russia," Esther said, absently. "We occupied it."

"Everybody seems to have occupied it." Schmidt had got hold of a Baedeker. "It was Belarus, then Lithuania, then Poland, Russian again, briefly Polish again when Napoleon went through, Russian again—'now democratic Poland having defeated the Red Army.'"

"No wonder the Poles are so gloomy," Marlene said. "Bewildered, poor darlings." He'd been combing his wig and put it on over his balding head, adjusting it and moueing at his reflection in the mirror. "Well, I'm off, little ones—a cabaret girl's work is never done."

"Before you go . . ." Schmidt said. He produced the photograph that had once hung on the wall of the Kreuzberg SA headquarters. Always with him, it was getting worn; he showed it to everybody. A line of men standing behind a line of boys kneeling on one knee; if he'd met any of them in the street, he could have recognized them by the shape of the head, the very earlobes. "Have you ever seen any of these faces before?"

"The men or boys?"

"The men." Although the boys would be men by now.

"I'd like to have, sweetie. *Very* butch. But no," Marlene handed it back. "Friends of yours?"

"Actually . . ." Schmidt found this awkward. "I wondered, if I got copies made, whether you'd show them around. And be careful. The man I want is a killer, and I think he's more likely to be found among people you may come into contact with. He's a friend of Ernst Röhm's."

"Ha-*ha*." Marlene took the photograph again. "We're in the Realm of Faerie, are we? Faggots? Poofs? Queens? Buggers? Queers? Or, as my Cockney friends in England used to say, Brighton piers?"

"Nazis as well," Schmidt said.

"Even butcher." Marlene fluttered his mascara. "Those jackboots, my dear, *so* masterful. Well, if Esther makes some copies, I'll do my best. Does this mean little Marlene will be helping the police with their inquiries?"

"Yes."

"*That'd* make a change." He blew a kiss and left, swinging his handbag.

Esther was still studying the map. "It's not on here. We need something larger-scale. Still, if we go to Pinsk and inquire . . ."

"We?"

She looked up. "I'm coming, too."

"No." He'd have liked to take her, but Eisenmenger's talk had made her hideously vulnerable. Political terror had enhanced personal fear, mingling the two together. The killer's authority had gained that of his party; their private enemy had joined his individual malevolence to that of the army bearing down on them—both of them centered on Solomonova.

Tonight he'd done a ridiculous thing and doubled back before reaching Bismarck Allee, using his streetcraft to ensure he wasn't being followed to her flat, knowing even as he did it that he was crediting the killer with sorcery. "We don't know what I'm likely to stir up in Poland," he said.

"He's hardly likely to be in Poland, is he?" she said. "You said yourself he wasn't ubiquitous."

He evaded the issue for something more pressing. "Alone at last," he said, and dragged her off to her bedroom.

Later she said, "Are you going to Poland officially? I mean, will the Polish police be helping you?"

"Good God, no. It would entail to-ing and fro-ing between the Alex and Warsaw. And as far as Berlin is concerned, the Anastasia file is closed. I'm just taking time off, that's all, and wandering around Poland in it."

"You speak Polish, of course," she said.

"Ah."

"And Russian? Because the villages where you're going speak a dialect that's a combination of both. And Yiddish? You speak Yiddish?"

"No."

"Lot of Jews in Polesie. Lots. It was part of the Pale of Settlement." She glared at him. "You don't even know what the Pale of Settlement was, do you?"

"No."

"There you are, then."

Actually, the journey was a swine once they got to Poland; the trains lacked the comfort of German compartments, any comfort at all sometimes, and they had to keep changing because of the country's three different railway systems. An incipient anti-Semitism showed itself every time Esther had to produce her passport, which was often, and resulted in obstruction.

At Warsaw Station, Schmidt argued with railway officials who said their papers hadn't been stamped properly at the frontier.

"Just give them money," Esther said.

"It's nothing to do with that. The bastards are being racist."

"Here." She shoved some zlotys into his hand and held his hand out to the official. "It's politer for a man to do it."

"It's bloody corruption, that's what it is," Schmidt said. The official was now signing papers with a flourish.

"Haven't traveled much in the East, have you?" she asked.

"First and last damn time," Schmidt said.

The Poles had celebrated their emergence from occupation under Germany, Austria, and Russia by making familiar place names unaccountably Polish. The onetime Brest Litovsk, which he'd heard of, was now Brześć nad Bugiem, which he hadn't, and couldn't have pronounced if he had. Station-name signs ran the length of the platform and were strangers to vowels. Distances were immense. How Napoleon's army had crossed them on foot and then gone on to Moscow, he couldn't think. Or why.

And she loved it: the delays, the discomfort, the waterless washbasins, the dirty lavatories without paper—she'd brought her own supply—the beautiful flourish with which they were directed to the wrong platforms, even the breath-strangling smoking compartments she went into for his sake so that he could have a cigarette.

"Stop smiling," he said.

"I can't help it. I'm catching happiness on the wing."

"You're catching attention; it's like traveling with a three-ring circus." Heads turned to watch her, but not because of the scar; she radiated joy. He couldn't take his eyes off her.

Waiting for yet another train under another station sign with more consonants than was good for it, he asked her to marry him.

She said no.

"Why the hell not?"

"Lots of reasons. I can't have children, for one thing."

"Who says?"

"Oh, doctors," she said vaguely.

"We can adopt. Is it because of the Jewish-faith business? I don't mind being up to my knees in little Yids."

She smiled. "I know you don't. It's just not a good time for marrying Yids. Or bringing them up, for that matter."

He persisted, but she stopped him. "Let's enjoy what we have while we've got it."

Which made it worse. He wanted permanence. She believed that happiness was rain in the desert; you collected what you could and stored it for a long, long drought.

Disappointment made him surly. He was impatient with the train that eventually chugged into the station, as well as with the people who crowded onto it on their way to market, all of them straight out of a Brueghel painting—complete with livestock.

"We're well into the Pale of Settlement now," Esther said, looking out the window.

"We're into the bloody Middle Ages. Does that pig have to be in here?"

"It's a pleasanter traveling companion than some," she said.

He had to do better. He reached for a cigarette, saw her look, and put it away; the pig was probably sensitive. "All right," he said. "What *was* the Pale of Settlement?"

"It's where Jews were allowed to live under Old Russia," she said. "Part of it was here in Poland under Russian rule, part of it in Russia itself. Got very crowded." She looked out the window again. "Made it easier to carry out pogroms, I suppose, having them all together."

"Did you live in the Pale?"

She shook her head. "We were rich. If you're rich, you can live anywhere."

"Where did you live?"

Her eyes stayed fixed on the window. "Lots of places," she said.

Forbidden territory, he thought. But if we're traveling so deep into Anna/Franziska's past, why the hell can't we venture into yours?

It was dark before they drew into Pinsk, and they had to check in to the nearest hotel, where the elderly woman behind the reception desk responded to the halting, room-renting Polish he'd picked up on the way with what sounded like abuse.

"Is she haggling?" The hotel foyer was lit by one bulb, and the number of keys hanging on the board behind the woman suggested that she had empty rooms to spare. A gruesome crucifix had been plastered into the wall above them.

Esther was snuffling her soda-siphon laugh into his shoulder. "I don't have a wedding ring. It's a Roman Catholic hotel, and she doesn't approve of us. She says *all* naughty Germans and their secretaries sign in as 'Herr and Frau Schmidt.'"

"You see?" he said furiously. "We've got to get married."

She took over, speaking with a rapid command that produced submission and a key.

"What did you say?" he asked as they went upstairs.

"I said you were the German representative of an American travel company, and that if she wanted tourist dollars, she was going to have to wake her ideas up. They're very moral here, but they're also very poor, and I'm afraid they're used to being bullied."

The next morning Esther walked out into Pinsk alone, leaving her lover asleep. He was looking better every day, but the fatigue imposed by Hanover and Düsseldorf had gone deep, she thought. He needed all the rest he could get.

It was going to be hot; the sun was already striking strong and yellow on the stepped fronts of the churches. A typical, old-fashioned, Russianized, provincial Polish town; she'd never been here before but knew it well.

The dread she'd felt at venturing back into her past had been ameliorated by the man she'd brought with her, and it hardly hurt at all to look on the unpaved side streets, take in the smell of horse manure and garlic and an air filled with strummed music, see the men in business suits drinking tea in the cafés with men in tall astrakhan caps while women did the work.

Automatically, she turned toward the Jewish quarter. Quarter? In Polesie, Jews were 70 percent of the population, yet 150 years of Russian occupation had left Poles and Jews distinct and uncombined. Same unpaved streets, same wooden buildings, but a different smell, this time caraway and fish. Other, sadder melodies from the cafés where men in business suits sat drinking tea with hirsute rabbis and women still did the work.

She'd dressed dowdily. In boots, a long skirt, a loose blouse, her head bound in scarves, she more or less blended in. He wouldn't, of course; he looked like what he was, a German, or even a damned Englishman, sure that if he addressed foreigners loudly and slowly enough, they would understand him. Perhaps the most honest man she'd ever met; last night, at the reception desk, he'd been put out as much by her lie as by the proprietor's rudeness. It was what made him a rare and excellent policeman, she supposed. She was not going to be responsible for ruining a career that went deep into the bone.

But if she wouldn't marry him, she could at least save him embarrassment. She turned into a tiny jeweler's shop to look at wedding rings. She took time making her selection, asking the jeweler about the marshes—there'd be as many Jewish villages in them as Aryan. "My husband and I are thinking of visiting Bagna Duze," she said casually.

And saw his face change.

As she returned to the hotel, Schmidt was coming from the opposite direction. He'd been looking for her. She waggled the newly ringed finger of her left hand at him. "We've got to go by boat," she said. "And I can tell you this much—something terrible happened in Bagna Duze when Anna Franziska was a girl."

SHE'D MANAGED TO hire what appeared to be the only motorized transport on the great river Pripyat. It was a low-gunwaled, narrow boat, like all the others in which Pinsk's fishermen plied their trade, but this one had an outboard engine. True, it made a noise like a lawn mower and had been manufactured in Milwaukee much earlier in the century, but Jan, their boatman, was proud of it, and Esther said they were lucky to get both it and him. "We're going into marshland, and the roads are unreliable for ordinary cars. This is quicker," she said. "Unless you want to go on horseback."

He didn't want to go on horseback. He didn't particularly want to go by water either, but water was what there was in thousands of square kilometers that had more or less filled in since the Ice Age—more where it had formed peaty islands, less where it was still lakes and sinuous little rivers that snaked through tunnels of alder out of which they emerged onto yet other stretches of water with masses of birds lifting up at their approach like a lid being sucked off a boiling saucepan.

Schmidt stopped trying to brush bird shit off his shoulders and let it dry. "How are we going to get back?"

"Jan'll come and fetch us," she said comfortably, and added, "In a day or two, I expect."

He said, "Does he have to keep singing?"

"We're paying him well. I think he feels he's got to do extra for his money. Very Venetian of him, if you ask me. Very honeymoon."

The prune-skinned, gap-toothed old Polesian at the tiller wasn't Schmidt's idea of a gondolier. His singing wasn't exactly bel canto either, but since this looked like the only honeymoon Schmidt was going to get . . . "Does he know what happened at Bagna Duze?"

She shook her head. "Whatever it was, it was bad. The Jews I talked to wouldn't say anything, just warned me not to go. So I put on my Gentile hat, like I told you, and tried the Polesians along the river, but they weren't any more forthcoming. Whatever it was, I think it happened during the Great War, yet I get the impression it wasn't anything to do with the war."

The point was, did it have anything to do with Anna? A confirmed city man, he found wilderness disconcerting, and the pleasure of playing Adam and Eve in it was tinged with a professional's guilt that he'd miscalculated in thinking that by coming here he'd learn anything more than geography.

He looked about him; they were going through another tunnel of alder. An otter slithered up the bank and disappeared in a shake of glittering water drops. "Even the war'd get lost around here."

"I know. I keep trying to fit Anna into these surroundings. She just doesn't."

He couldn't picture that strange little soul in this morass either. But he could imagine her wanting to leave it.

His woman, on the other hand, was reveling in the journey, taking picture after picture with her camera. "Oh, look," she kept saying. "Oh, look," at a heron frowning at them from a tree, another bird-covered lake, another set of reed-thatched huts, some watermen scouring weed from a dike.

She'll run out of film, he thought as she licked a roll closed and tore open yet another.

His own knapsack included two bottles of Scotch whisky for the purpose of loosening tongues.

Such natives as they saw seemed friendly, if web-footed. They waved and exchanged shouted consonants with Jan. Compared with most peasants, he supposed, these were well-off; the water and air were full of food if you could catch it, and the boat was beginning to pass meadows fat with cattle. No Depression here; they were back in a primitive but contented eighteenth century.

"Jan says Bagna Duze is quite a big village," Esther said. "Got a church, school, everything. It serves a hunting lodge belonging to"—she talked to Jan again—"the Count and Countess Zorawski. We can stay there if we have to."

He didn't question it. In this neck of the woods, barging up to some aristocrat's house and asking to stay was probably normal behavior.

It was what they did. Bagna Duze might have been the metropolis of the marshes, but if its population topped five hundred, Schmidt would have been surprised—nearly all of it crammed into tweedy little cottages that were also part barn. The only stone buildings were an overlarge church and, in the far distance, among beeches, a house, more like a French château than a hunting lodge.

THE SOUP WAS hribnoy sup (mushroom and barley), the next course hrybi v smtane (mushrooms with sour cream), the entrée kotleta pokrestyansk (pork cutlet in mushroom sauce).

"Danuta went mushrooming today," the countess said unnecessarily, "but tomorrow you shall have lampreys. Lampreys tomorrow, Danuta."

Sagging, Danuta tottered off. So far, to Schmidt's knowledge, she'd picked dinner, cooked it, served it, and prepared the guest room. Apart from a retainer in a powdered wig, even older than herself if that were possible, she appeared to be the only servant in the place.

"A king of England died of a surfeit of lampreys. Did you know that, my dear?" The count leaned as far as he could from his place at the top of the table to lay a liver-spotted, lecherous hand on Esther's.

"We mustn't let that happen to you," the countess said, signaling impatience at her husband with her fan. "We are *so* pleased to have you. A book, you said, Frau Schmidt?"

It was the first time she'd shown curiosity. You had to say that for aristocratic Polish hospitality, Schmidt thought: it didn't ask questions. He and Esther had been welcomed without a second's hesitation, and not just because they were an inrush of freshness into a moldering house; they were travelers and therefore entitled to courtesy.

The count and countess had been more eager to show who *they* were than find out about the couple who'd landed on their doorstep. They spoke German well. The Almanack de Gotha—a book to which Schmidt had been introduced within half an hour—declared their rightful position among the *Szlachta*, Poland's nobility.

The scarlet-and-white flag of Poland flew from a turret roof. Tattered standards from various battles for Polish freedom hung from the high, cobwebbed ceiling of the great hall in which the four of them were now dining. The motto *"Nic o naz bez nas"* (Nothing concerning us can be settled without us) was on each piece of beautiful, tarnished silverware on the table.

Decay was everywhere, in the mildewed portraits of Zorawski ancestors lining the walls of the enormous staircase, in the bulwark of planks that held up the door of a disused wing, on the rusted faces of clocks that had stopped as if too dispirited to tick on.

Like their house, the Zorawskis were museum pieces. The countess's dress echoed that of the empress Maria Theresa, and her dentures made disconcerting attempts to escape. The count was half the size of his wife, a wizened, embroidered-waistcoated manikin, animated by the energy that had seized him on seeing Esther, as if a ferret had sat up at the sight of a rabbit.

The couple talked of other residences, a castle near Warsaw—"our son keeps it now"—a schloss in Austria—"but we are becoming too old to keep moving from place to place as we used to, so we summer here. For the shooting, you know."

And it's cheaper, Schmidt thought.

He wondered when Esther would get to the point. Now she did. She took her hand from under the count's and rested her arms on the table, the picture of a woman at ease. "Yes, we're writing a travel book about Polesie," she said. "At least my husband's writing it—I'm taking the pictures. Of course, we *had* to visit the wetlands, and we heard about Bagna Duze in Berlin from a friend who used to know someone that lived here—Franziska Schanskowska."

There was a pause, but only one attributable to an elderly couple searching failing memories. "Goodness gracious," the countess said, "little Franziska. I haven't heard that name in years. You remember her, Casimir, Józef Schanskowska's daughter?" To Esther she said, "He was the village wheelwright. Dead now."

The count strummed the table, squinting to remember. "Wasn't she the girl involved in all that nasty business? I thought she got drowned."

"She did," the countess said. She turned to Esther. "More honey truffles, my dear?"

19

Esther stared at her hostess as at a gorgon, then pulled herself together. "I beg your pardon, Countess. No, that was excellent."

"Herr Schmidt?"

Fuck it, fuck it. "What? No thank you."

"I'm sorry," the countess said. "Did your friend believe Franziska to be alive? I'm afraid she died years ago . . . 1919."

"*Annus horribilis* for Bagna Duze," said the count.

"For all Poland," said the countess.

"They threw everything at us that year, but, oho, we beat them all in the end." The count's little face was a triumphant demon's. "Russians, werewolves, floods, Gypsies, Jews—we beat them all."

"Casimir." The countess snapped it out, then smiled apologetically at her guests. "Such a nuisance, werewolves. A peasant superstition, of course. But indeed there were an inordinate number of deaths in the village that year, and I'm afraid young Franziska's was one of them."

"Never found her body, of course," the count said.

"Yes they *did,* Casimir," said the countess with a patience frayed by long-standing irritation. "Her father identified it. It *wasn't* the

Gypsy girl's. Józef was quite happy on that point, if you remember." She turned back to Esther. "The floods, you see. So many were swept away that recovery was rather gruesome and *not*"—this was to the count—"a subject for the dinner table."

"We survived, we survived it all," the count exulted.

"Actually, we were in Warsaw at the time," the countess interjected.

"And then 1920, *annus mirabilis*. We fought the Red Army and won, oh, yes, we won. Poland defeated them, and Bagna Duze did its bit." Another stroke of Esther's hand. "If the dead ever rise from these marshes, my dear, there'll be sorry ghosts among them."

The countess employed her fan, as if the hall were too warm, though walls a meter thick kept it cool. She pushed back her chair. "Frau Schmidt? Shall we leave the gentlemen to their port and cigars?"

Glancing helplessly at Schmidt, Esther followed her.

A traditionalist, the count told dirty stories over the excellent port and equally excellent cigars, refusing to be diverted from the subject of sex and women except for tales of his prowess against the might of the Red Army. "Thought they'd export communism to the Western world, did they?" he said. "Oho, they didn't reckon on Poland and Casimir Zorawski."

In the countess's cluttered drawing room, which smelled of lavender and cats' pee, Esther focused her hostess's attention on the subject of Franziska Schanskowska.

"Such a strange child," the countess said. "Of course, I blame her father. He sent her away to school at the convent in Pinsk—education is *such* a mistake for peasant girls, don't you think? It isolated her from the other village maidens, of course, and made her discontented on her return."

"And the Gypsy girl?" Esther asked.

"Now, that *was* an odd thing. A band of Gypsies came wandering through the marshes—from Russia, as far as anyone could tell, getting away from the civil war, one supposes. In 1919, this was. Was it? Or was it earlier? Well, of course, they weren't welcome—the *thieving*. People's geese went missing, washing off the line. A totally dishonest people, you know, despite all that rubbish that's talked about how romantic they are. *Anyway,* there was this girl with them—she didn't seem to belong to them, and . . . I've forgotten how it was that Józef took her in. On Franziska's insistence, I think. She had some weird fixation that the girl was a changeling, either stolen from a royal nursery or . . . I don't know, something highly improbable. They were inseparable, the two of them. And, poor things, they were swept away together when the floods came."

"And they didn't find the Gypsy girl's body?" Esther asked. But the countess's head had lolled in the same instant; she was asleep.

Reunited with Schmidt to stroll on the terrace before going to bed, Esther said, "I don't see how they identified Franziska. The floods were dreadful; this area was inundated, whole villages swept away. They were recovering bodies for months, and the only thing recognizable on Franziska's when they found it was the cross on the chain around her neck. But every girl in Poland wears a cross, except the Jews, of course. And some of the bodies were carried away into the Pripyat and never found. Her father said the cross was hers, but for one thing they're mass-produced and, for another, I expect that after all that time he was desperate to put an end to uncertainty and lay his daughter to rest."

"So it could have been the Gypsy girl?"

"Could have been anybody that was female."

"So what you're saying is that they buried someone else while Franziska, who's been swept away by floodwater, manages to drag herself onto a riverbank, thinks 'Bye-bye, Bagna Duze,' and squelches off." His mind was turning to bed.

There was a reluctant snuffle in the darkness. "I'm saying there's a strong possibility that Anna is Franziska. Similar character."

"Or she could be the Gypsy who was really the grand duchess Anastasia in disguise, having been picked up by this band of kindly nomads on their way through Ekaterinburg."

"All right, then, smarty-pants. What did you learn from the count?"

"Apart from the fact that he fought off the Bolshies single-handed, very little."

"He was in Warsaw at the time, hardly heard a shot fired, according to the countess," Esther said. "It was their son. He was with Pilsudski in the counterattack that drove the Red Army back. My God, the Poles were brave. And stop doing that. They'll see us."

Schmidt withdrew the hand he'd placed companionably down the front of Esther's blouse. "We haven't done very well, have we?"

"I don't know. We came to investigate Franziska's past, and we find it to be odd. And I'll tell you another thing: They're hiding something. Everybody is. Why didn't my jeweler in Pinsk want to tell me what it was, if it was just floods? Nobody can help floods. I tell you, something awful happened here in 1919."

"I should think it did. 'Russians, werewolves, floods, Gypsies, Jews.' Only need the Four Horsemen of the Apocalypse and you've got the set."

"The Russians were later," she said.

They'd ventured into the garden. Neglected lavender bushes threw off a scent as they brushed past them. The faces of statues made white patches in black, entangling ivy.

"All I'm trying to point out," she said, "is that Anna is quite possibly Franziska Schanskowska and is definitely *not* Anastasia."

"You're not making a very good case for it," he said. He caught her up and kissed her. "But you might as well go on with it now that we're here. Try to get the count on his own tomorrow."

"He's been trying to get me alone all evening," she said. "He's a droit du seigneur man if ever I saw one."

"Small price to pay for information."

Her laugh had an echo, perhaps from the lake or from the forest that began at the back of the house. Inside, the count had sat himself down at the piano, and the despairingly sweet notes of a Chopin nocturne cascaded onto the terrace.

"*'Et in Arcadia ego,'*" she said.

He wished she hadn't said it. His schoolmaster had claimed that the phrase was wrongly attributed to the world of nymphs and shepherds. "It was inscribed on a tomb," old Müller had said. "It's a statement by Death: 'I am even in Arcadia.'"

I don't want this, he thought. I don't want Arcadia. I want slippers and quarrels and possibly a dog, I want everydayness. I want her to get old and have an ear trumpet. I want her ordinary and safe.

After a while she said, "And what will you be doing while I'm surrendering my honor?"

"I'm interested in the werewolf reference. Werewolf equals murders. Murder is my business." Death again, he thought. He said, "There was a mass being held in the church when we passed it. I'm going to ply the priest with liquor and talk to him."

"Can you?"

"It was a Latin mass," he said. "We should manage all right. Only thing I was good at in school, Latin. Lousy at everything else, but . . . I remember having to translate the Gallic Wars and thinking, This is Caesar. He's on some blasted heath surrounded by his centurions, there are blue-painted barbarians howling in the distance, and he's telling me about it."

"It's a long time since I heard any Latin."

" 'Ite domum saturae, venit Hesperus, ite capellae.' "

She puzzled over it. "She-goats?"

" 'Go on home, you have fed full, the evening star is coming, go on, my she-goats.' It's the only bit of Virgil I can remember."

They went in and said their good nights. The canopied bed in their room could have accommodated both them and a platoon of Napoleon's army. Tonight, with moonlight and the smell of water and forest coming through the window, it was their world.

"Of course, there's an early reference to werewolves in Pliny the Elder," Father Teofil said, rising to run his finger along one of his bookshelves. "And—I think I'm right—he got it from the Greeks. Euanthes, I believe."

"You say that people around here still believe in them?" It had taken an hour to get the priest this far. Several pages of Schmidt's police notebook were already full of geological and social information. Father Teofil had been overjoyed to meet another Latin speaker, if one somewhat rusty, and was flattered at featuring in a book, eager to display his learning, which was considerable.

"You did not expect to find a classical scholar in the marshes, I imagine, Herr Schmidt, yet the wilderness and the solitary places shall be glad of him, to paraphrase Isaiah."

Schmidt was sure they were, though the dusky flush of Father Teofil's skin, his extreme thinness, and a collection of empty vodka bottles in a reed basket, to which one of Scotch had just been added, suggested other reasons for the priest's lack of advancement.

He repeated his question. The man's Latin was classical, and if he spoke slowly, Schmidt was able to keep up with him.

"I fear so, I fear so. Trying to eliminate paganism from their souls is the work of Sisyphus. Oh, here it is." Father Teofil took down a book and collapsed into his battered wicker chair. "Yes, Pliny tells us, a man of the Antaeus family . . . mmm . . . hung his clothing on an ash tree by a lake in Arcadia and swam across, thus being transformed into a wolf."

"The count was saying there was an incidence of werewolves around here some while ago."

"Just as I thought, it was from Euanthes."

Schmidt unscrewed the top off his second bottle but kept his hand on it. "The count," he persisted. "Werewolves. Around here." He wasn't sure whether the subject was worth pursuing, but he was damn well going to pursue it. He'd traveled into Anna/Franziska's past to find what it was that linked her to a murderer. Franziska might or might not be dead, but werewolves had been mentioned in virtually the same breath as her name. There was a connection in people's minds between murderers and werewolves—both Kurten and Haarmann, his multiple murderers, had been designated werewolves at one time or another. Ergo . . .

"It happened around here, didn't it?" he said, tapping the bottle.

"There were killings, but you don't want to put that in your book."

"Certainly not." Schmidt put away his notebook, reached for the priest's glass, and held it, like a biscuit in front of a puppy. "When was this?"

"Oh, years ago. About 1918, I think, or was it '19? A little boy from the village disappeared. He'd been mushrooming in the forest with his mother. She was found murdered there—particularly brutally, I'm afraid—but no sign of the child. Her wedding ring, the only thing of value she had, was gone from her finger. The police were informed, yet little was done. It was wartime, and officialdom was in chaos. People became afraid for their children." He shrugged sadly. "What would you, the werewolf legend was resurrected. . . ."

He was under way now. Schmidt poured the man's whisky and handed it to him.

"Then, some weeks later, a little skeleton was found in a dike not far from here. There was . . . trouble. The villagers now assumed they knew who had killed both mother and child." Father Teofil looked at Schmidt over his glass. "It was Easter, you see, and it was assumed these were ritual killings."

Schmidt was being told something, but he didn't know what. "Go on," he said.

The priest looked relieved. "It was thought the killer or killers had been found, action had been taken, the matter was over."

"Yes?"

Father Teofil looked down at the floor, as if searching for something he'd dropped. Schmidt poured more whisky into the glass, but for a while Father Teofil's eyes desperately scanned the dirty reed mat at his feet.

"Go on," Schmidt said again. There was no place for pity at this point in an interrogation; time for that when you'd got the truth.

"Then the child's father came forward. . . ."

"I wondered if it was the father," Schmidt said. "Most murder victims are killed by their nearest, if not their dearest."

"Oh, no, Herr Schmidt, no, no. It wasn't him. I doubt if poor Tadeusz ever killed anything bigger than a fish. A most gentle person, almost effete for a villager, a mother's boy. Indeed . . ." The priest's eyes swiveled toward Schmidt and away again. "I had been greatly relieved when he married, if you understand me. You come from a metropolis; perhaps you are conversant with these matters."

Schmidt nodded gently.

"He came forward in church," Father Teofil said, "I have never witnessed such a scene and hope never to do so again. Ravaged, raving—we had thought it to be grief, you see. It was guilt. He pointed . . ."

His own arm swung out in accusation toward a worm-eaten grandmother clock in the corner. "He pointed at a young man who had been his friend. There . . ." The priest's hand stabbed again toward the clock. "Sitting in the congregation, a young man we all knew; indeed, I had baptized him, taken his confirmation. Mary, Mother of God, have mercy on us sinners, Almighty God, who seest we have no help in ourselves."

"And this friend had killed his wife and child."

Father Teofil looked up and nodded. "They had been lovers, it seemed," he said simply. "Ryszard had wanted them to go away together, for Tadeusz to leave his family. . . . Ryszard, oh, a strange, afflicted boy. In the confessional he would burden me with recitals of such sins, as if he took pleasure in it." Father Teofil's voice, which had begun to slur, suddenly sharpened. "And I only tell you that now because he must be dead."

"What happened then?" Schmidt poured more whisky into the old man's glass, a hunter dripping the blood of a goat to attract the tiger. The killer's near, he thought. He's coming toward me.

"In my own church," Father Teofil said. "A scene from the *Oresteia,* accusation of slain innocence, the audience my own horror-struck congregation." He lapsed into Greek, where Schmidt couldn't follow him, holding out his glass. Schmidt filled it.

"Tadeusz, my poor boy, my poor, poor boy, he made his accusation, then ran from the aisle to the door, pursued by the Furies." Tears gathered in the hollow of the priest's eyes and tipped over to slide down the planes of his cheeks. "He drowned himself. They found him in the dike afterward. He'd put his mother's flatiron in one pocket and his wife's in the other to weight him down."

"And Ryszard?"

The old man's hands lifted and fell in helplessness. "We could not believe it. What would you? These people do not belong in the world of Aeschylus. This is a simple village. They are born, they worship, they marry, they give birth, they die. Such things are as far away from them as the stars. A young mother slaughtered? Her child butchered? Because one man wished ownership of another? They did not move. They could not believe it of one of their own."

"No," Schmidt said. "I can see that. He got away."

"He went that night. Even then we could not believe. . . . But there came the testimony of his cousin, a girl. Their two families shared a smallholding. She had always suspected Ryszard, she said, had been in terror of his violent nature all her life. She took us to his room. There was the young mother's wedding ring, other things . . . an ax."

"Was the cousin's name Franziska Schanskowska?"

"Franziska, yes."

Schmidt had become merely a chorus, the prompt that moved on the protagonists of the tragedy being reenacted in the room by the old man's memory. "And Ryszard? Do you know what happened to him?"

The priest shook his head. "He escaped human justice." He looked up. "But it may be that he was subject to God's, because soon after that the floods came, the Lord's punishment on wickedness, a deluge visited on the innocent and guilty alike. Poor little Franziska was swept away with so many others. Her Gypsy friend, too. How the ripples of evil spread out and out, on and on, to this very day."

"Oh, yes," Schmidt said. "What was he like, Ryszard?"

"Oh, a big boy, tall, the Galczynskis were all tall. Very big, very clever. I think often that the village was too small for him and that had he been allowed . . . But his father was a harsh man, a brutal man. I baptized him, taught him his catechism. That he should have . . . So terrible. I look at his picture sometimes, pray for his soul . . . pray for his victims."

"A picture? You've got a picture?"

It was a matter of bullying now. Schmidt scrabbled through a dresser drawer, holding up photograph after photograph of Sunday-school picnics, church processions, a cart bearing a statue of the Virgin Mary with white-clad, palm-carrying little girls walking beside it, a confirmation class. "Is that him? Is that him?"

He went on searching. "Is *that* him?"

"Ah."

It was of a boys' church choir. He took it over to the old man. "Which one?"

"Lord have mercy on his soul, and . . . and there's Tadeusz. . . ." The priest's finger glissaded across the photograph from a tall figure to a slighter one. "My boys, my boys."

"I'm sorry," Schmidt said. He took the glass out of the priest's hand, where it had begun to tip, lifted the thin, cassocked body more comfortably into its chair, and stood looking down at it until its breathing became regular. "I'm very sorry." He put the photograph into his pocket and went to find a neighbor who would sit with the old man and make sure he didn't vomit in his sleep.

Walking back up the street toward the hunting lodge, he attracted bright Polish greetings that he neither heard nor returned.

R.G. of Munich. Ryszard Galczynski of Bagna Duze.

That was it, then. Now he knew the face Hannelore had seen. The heavy features of the boy in the photograph in his pocket were those of the man third from the left in the picture of the Sturmabteilung's sports conference, at the moment in his pack up at the hunting lodge. He had the motive, the name, and a photograph. Two photographs.

R.G. of Munich. The man had changed his name and probably his nationality. He'd taken German citizenship; no Pole could have possessed the influence that had protected the identity of this one—but he'd kept his initials. And his nature.

What was needed now was proof. There'd be no trouble connecting R.G. with the murders he'd committed here in the marshes; the crimes would be on file somewhere and the Polish police probably delighted to extradite him so that he could be charged.

But I want you to pay in Germany, for Natalya, for Hannelore, and for the others you've dispensed with on your way. I want you in *my* dock in front of *my* judges, so the nation can see what sort of animal the fucking SA nurtures in its bosom.

And that would be more difficult. An examining magistrate was unlikely to make the imaginative leaps that Schmidt had in order to connect a storm trooper with the shadow in Charlottenburg. There'd been no proof at all that the man had killed Hannelore and, it seemed, very little for the murder of Potrovskov or of Olga. The witnesses who'd seen him in the streets near Charlottenburg would be unreliable nine years later—even supposing they hadn't died in the meantime.

The only link was Anna or Franziska or the Gypsy girl or whoever the hell she was, the only one who could point the finger.

"Hello," said a voice.

She was sitting on a bench in the Zorawskis' garden—he hadn't realized he'd reached it.

"I've got him," he said. "He was here. He killed a mother and her baby because he was having an affair with her husband."

"I know."

"How do you know?"

"The count told me." She seemed strangely unexcited. "I want you to come for a walk with me."

"All right." He fell into step beside her and began to reconstruct the sequence. "He got away. It was wartime . . . chaos . . . and he escaped. But we know where he went, don't we? He went to Germany, changed his name. Christ, I don't know how he walks on two legs; he kills like a stoat. Something stands in his way and it's dead. He chopped down that woman and child to get them out of the way, didn't think twice."

He looked at Esther. "They were fair-haired, you know. I saw their picture. Even Röhm couldn't countenance that; Hitler certainly wouldn't. Jew killers are one thing, Aryan killers another—and the man's a homosexual, another species Hitler's got no time for. No wonder he wants to keep the past quiet. He's risen through the Nazi ranks. Be a shame if his career's spoiled by a dead woman and child in Poland. Power's important to him; it satisfies his bloodlust—it *is* a sort of bloodlust. And he's clever. He's directed it. The Sturmabteilung's a spiritual home for him. God, what a whale of a time he must've had—breaking limbs with impunity. He's the Nazis' sort of man, a monster who doesn't care."

They were in forest now, autumn leaves soft under their feet, but Schmidt was back in Berlin in wintertime, near the Landwehr Canal. "That's where they met again, him and Anna, the girl from his home village, I damn well know they did. Him up from Munich for a day out smashing Communists. Her . . . I don't know what she was doing, but she's walking along the Landwehr and comes face-to-face with a nightmare. There, right in front of her, the man who's always terrified her. She sees him, he sees her. It blasts them both, him as well as her. She'll tell, take away his power . . . she knows. He's got to kill her or— *Where the hell are we going?*"

"There was a village somewhere along this track. A Jewish village."

"Have you been listening to what I said?"

"Yes," she said. "I know. I'm glad." She tucked herself under his arm and put her own around his waist. "He comes from here, he's a killer, you've got him."

"Well, more or less," Schmidt said. "Could you stop a minute?"

"I love you so much," she said. She was crying.

He put a hand under her elbow and guided her to a fallen tree. "Sit down." He sat down beside her and fished in the pocket of her jacket for the toilet tissue she always carried on foreign journeys. "Blow," he said.

She wiped her eyes. "But that wasn't everything," she said.

"What else?"

"It was Easter, you see," she said. "Before Ryszard was declared the murderer, this was. They found the little boy's body in the dike at Easter. Passover. They thought it was a ritual killing."

An old, dark phrase out of history; he'd felt a brief unease when the priest had used it, but hadn't stopped to run it down.

"Ritual killing," she said. "It was always the same if an Aryan child was found dead. It happened in Russia . . . oh, how many times. Someone to blame and be killed in turn. The same excuse to murder Jews—they were killing Christian children or poisoning the wells, one or the other. Always. And then would come the pogrom."

It was a warm day. The mist hiding the waterways at dawn had risen, momentarily scarlet, and dispersed into an enamel-blue sky.

She said, "They found the body, and . . . It was night, but immediately most of the men here set out to the village where the local Jews lived. Zorawski told me. He wasn't here at the time—he and the countess were in Warsaw—but I don't think he'd have stopped it anyway."

They were sitting so still that a quail came bustling out of the trees, then turned and went back into them. The rattle of a woodpecker came from farther in the forest.

She took a deep breath. "He said . . . Zorawski said, 'It was a ghastly business, but one good thing came out of it—we got rid of the Jews.' "

"What did they do to them?"

"I don't know; even the count doesn't know. He'd have told me, believe me, he'd have told me." She turned her head to look at him. "I don't want to go back to that house, Schmidt."

"No."

She stood up. "I'm going to the Jewish village. Blociska, it's called. There's something I want to do."

It was a long walk and very beautiful, following the ruts in the track through shafts of sunlight, into shadow and out again, birdsong. He thought how blithely nature had ignored killers who passed through it—a youth dragging the dead body of a child, men with torches.

The trees thinned. "This is it, I think," she said. "Zorawski said the priest stopped them from burning it down."

It was eerie. Blociska had been a village almost indistinguishable from Bagna Duze, but now it was dead. There were still signs above the doors of the shops in the wide, muddy main street, but the roof of one of them had fallen in. Rusted chains hung over a well. Sparrows pecked in empty hen runs. No sound apart from the singing of birds. Where the track widened out into what had been the village street, there was a huge, round, black scar made by fire.

"No need to imagine things," he said. "That's recent."

She nodded and walked on, turned a corner—and there was the building that made Blociska different from Bagna Duze.

"Good God," Schmidt said.

He'd seen synagogues in Berlin—two years ago he'd attended the funeral service for Minna Wolff in one—but not like this. "Chinese" was his first thought, but its successive diminishing roofs topped by a little pyramid were pitched straight, not with the curls of a pagoda. Yet it was Eastern, huge, alien, strange, exotic, and constructed entirely from wood.

It was wooden magic. It was rotting. It had a blurred look. Some of the roof shingles had slid to the ground; the Star of David held in one of the cloisterlike arches adorning the ground-floor walls was falling sideways.

"There was one like this in Rosa's village," she said, "not so big, though."

"Rosa?"

"Rosa was the one who mended me."

She unwound one of the scarves from her head and then put it on again so that it draped. "There's something I've got to do. I'm not sure how to do it, and Rosa would say I shouldn't be doing it at all according to the Law. Women don't play much part in the synagogue—there should be more of you, for instance, to make a minyan. But I'm going to do it anyway, for whoever died here, for his victims. You don't need to come in. I won't be long."

"I think I will."

"Well, you go in that way. I go up here. Separate entrances for men and women." Gingerly, she began mounting the outside staircase.

"Be careful," he called. She'd slipped as one of the steps gave way.

"Don't worry."

He pushed open the main door and left it open so that light could get in. The few windows were allowing only dusty shafts of sun to come through. It was even more astonishing inside than out. They hadn't been able to afford gilding; they'd had only wood, and they'd carved it, fretted it, ornamented it, turned it, polished it, so that once it had gleamed like gold and even now leaped out, like glorious bramble bushes, to catch the soul of the beholder. The walls formed bays, and in the center of the hall stood the pulpit—no, Joe Wolff had called it the bima—an octagonal plinth with a lacelike balustrade around it.

He could smell damp and, he thought, the oil that had once burned in the hanging lamps. Some bats dangled from the cupolaed ceiling.

He heard a door scrape open in a gallery above his head, and she began praying for the dead in Russian. In a low, clear monotone, the complex, mighty syllables echoed into an empty synagogue for the souls of men, women, and children, Aryan, Jewish, for a people that were gone and, perhaps, for the bereft and ignorant parents who had driven them away, for Natalya, for Hannelore, Potrovskov, Olga. On and on it went, until he wondered at the power of words, mere exhalations of breath, useless against cudgels and racial hatred but still so compelling that he found himself adding his own Our Father in a plea to a God he didn't believe in, because in this place, at this time, it was appropriate.

Then there was silence, and he could hear the birds again.

When they met outside, she was brisk. "There."

They set off toward the forest. She was still full of words, as if the prayers had loosened them. She said, "In the pogrom I lost everybody, *everybody*. They killed my mother, my father, my siblings, friends, my dog. To this day I don't know how I got out alive—or why. I was too injured to remember. There's a space in time I still can't cope with. I just woke up in Rosa's village. I get flashes of it, I hear the shots, see the bayonets slicing down, my head explodes. I think I hear my little brother whimper."

She paused for a moment and went on, still brisk. "Rosa took me in and nursed me. She was the wife of the village rabbi, an ordinary woman, you'd think, rough. She had too many dead of her own to be sentimental about mine, and soon she had more because, while I was still recovering, Cossacks came riding into the village. They were being chased by a contingent of Bolsheviks. You wouldn't think they'd stop to kill and burn, but they did." She smiled. "Rosa said it was force of habit."

He handed her over a fallen tree, and she resumed the long, rhythmic stride that helped to keep the words pumping. "She hid me along with as many as she could. When they'd gone, when we came out, there was nothing left. Her elder son had already emigrated to England; Russia was in civil war, so why stay?" Her hands spread out in a very Jewish query, as Rosa's must have done. "So she took us survivors out of Russia, through Poland, into Germany. I decided to remain in Berlin. I didn't want to go to England. When I got the job with Nick, I persuaded him to get me papers for her and the others. They were forged, of course, but they got Rosa and the rest to England. We still keep in touch. She's in New York now, doing well."

He caught her arm to slow her down. She looked up at him. "So that's it. My past. Two pogroms. Unlucky, really."

"And you're still standing," he said.

"There was Rosa."

He delved into her pocket and produced another set of toilet tissue. "Blow." He sat her down on a log and knelt beside her.

"Oh, I don't know, Schmidt," she said, weeping. "It's strange when you ought to be dead and aren't, when you want to be. My life was somebody's carelessness. A sort of oversight. For a long time, I didn't know how to fill it. God was irrelevant. Rosa said that was narcissism—well, she didn't use the word, but that's what she meant."

"Is it?"

"Yes. You have to have worked that out long before it happens to you, because it's been happening always. God has to be fitted into a past of massacre. To believe in God when you're exempt and then stop believing in Him when you aren't is not only presumptuous, it's bad history."

"Or a nonexistent God in the first place."

She waggled her hands, as he'd seen Minna Wolff do a hundred times. "Maybe. But even if you don't believe in Him, if you're a Darwinist, it's the same thing. Think of the millions of years of your species struggling to give you this amazing accident of life, and how sinful, how bloody ungrateful, it is to throw it away. It's our duty to the dead not to waste the million-year gift they can't have by being guilty because they can't have it. We have to forgive ourselves for being alive."

He applied more tissue, and she took it out of his hands and scrubbed her face with it.

"Or perhaps in my case God just overdid it. He took everything that had mattered and everything that didn't. It was too massive to take in. I was reborn at sixteen, naked, raped, with a face somebody'd slashed open. Rosa didn't know who I was—for a long time I didn't either. Didn't matter to her. I was hurt and needed mending. Rosa doesn't fit into Darwin's theory, Schmidt. It didn't help her survival or her children's to waste time and food and care on me. For part of that awful journey, I slowed her down."

"So Rosa is God."

"A facet of Him," she said. "Or Her. God's what stops you from slitting your wrists."

He helped her up, and they walked on.

He wanted to tell her about Ikey Wolff, but it wasn't the time. One day, though, he'd talk about Ikey, another aberration of Darwin's theory, and how Ikey had got him through the war, not by heroism but because the man had been proof that decency was still a human attribute.

The forest was thinning now, and they could see the Zorawskis' house in the distance.

She stopped for a moment. "And there's you," she said.

20

In the train out of Pinsk, he gave her the two photographs. She saw the killer's face immediately; *now* she remembered it. It was coming up the staircase of the Green Hat toward her.

She forced herself to study it for a long time, knowing it was ridiculous to feel that those flat, dull, vaguely Slavic eyes were watching her. "It's the same face," she said. "He didn't change at all; he just got older. Stolid, secret. You wonder what sort of childhood produced that look."

"Lousy, I expect. They generally are. And I don't bloody care." He handed her another filched photograph. "These are the ones he butchered—see that young woman there, with the baby in her arms, the one smiling?"

She handed the pictures back.

At Warsaw Station the only German paper he could get was *Berliner Morgenpost*. When he settled back with it in the compartment, another face he knew stared back at him from an inside page. "Good God Almighty."

Under a picture of Anna, the caption read *"Mystery woman*

claims a share of the Romanov inheritance." Below was a brief story. He read it to her.

"'*Anna Anderson, the woman claiming to be the Grand Duchess Anastasia*' blah, blah, blah . . . '*has hired lawyers to begin a fight in the German courts for recognition of her title as heiress to the murdered czar of Russia. . . . Mrs. Anderson is at present in the United States.*' Shit. That means she'll be coming back at some point. Did you know about this?"

"No." Esther rubbed her forehead.

"Well," he said, "Ryszard must know by now that she's not going to give him away. Tell the world who he is and she tells the world who *she* is. She should, but she won't. She's been secure for nine years by proclaiming she's Anastasia. The killer knows that while she's Anastasia she can't be Franziska and a witness against him. He's safe from her. She's safe from him."

"Are you sure?"

"Yes. It's in our man's interest. If she's Anastasia and alive, nobody's going to inquire into the whereabouts of Ryszard Galczynski from Bagna Duze."

"You blame her, don't you?" Esther said. "For not pointing the finger at him. She can't. I've told you, she believes she is Anastasia."

Whoever she is, she's a pain in the ass, Schmidt thought. The woman was a complication he didn't want to deal with. "What's she been doing in the States anyway?"

"Some American millionairess called Jennings was planning to finance an army to invade Russia and put her back on the throne."

"Are you kidding?"

"No." She shook her head at him. "Schmidt, you don't realize how . . . she gets taken up by really extraordinary people. Rachmaninoff—I mean *Rachmaninoff*—was fighting her cause at one point."

"And they drop her again," Schmidt said.

"Well, she's difficult," Esther said. "She can't help it. God, I wish she wasn't coming back. I'd hoped the States would suit her, but now I come to think about it, she was beginning to complain at the publicity the American papers were giving her, she didn't like her hosts, she thought she was being exploited, she'd stepped on her parrot—"

"Stepped on a parrot?"

"Some sort of accident when she was having hysterics. I should have known she wasn't happy from the fact that she phoned at all. It's only in between patrons that she turns to me."

"You'll take her in, I suppose? If she comes back?"

"If she wants me to. She's my responsibility."

"She's not."

"Yes she *is*." Her eyes got bluer when she was stern.

Anna Anderson, Schmidt thought. Female. Known to be trailing gunpowder. Four dead so far. Many wounded, including one parrot.

THEIR TRAIN SLOWED entering Berlin. Esther watched a setting sun slant across the posters lining the railway tracks. Election time again. So far 1932 had consisted of little else. The wrangling of parties without a majority in the Reichstag was reflected by fighting in the streets.

Sooty terraced windows displayed Communist posters; an enclave of houses with nice gardens was placarded with swastikas. Nearly every party was portraying the German people as a half-naked giant. The Nazi giant towering above a bank, destroying it with a swastika-decorated compressor. The People's Party giant was in a loincloth sweeping aside soberly dressed politicians. A Social Democrat giant threw tiny Nazis and Communists out of the Reichstag. More swastikas, hammers and sickles, raised fists.

She thought how violent and masculine it all was. They've forgotten women. The Nazis even made a virtue of their refusal to put forward women candidates: "Politics is too unclean for women to participate."

Hoardings again. Pictures of President Hindenburg, Chancellor von Papen, Hitler, Hitler, Hitler.

"What exactly does von Papen stand for?" she asked.

"Von Papen," he drawled deliberately, screwing a metaphorical monocle in his eye, "stands for the Good Old Days. Army, Authority, Aristocracy. No nasty democracy. You remember the Good Old Days? When anybody who applied for social benefits wasn't allowed to vote?"

"He doesn't want Hitler in, though, does he?"

"No, but rather Hitler than the Reds. And the Nazis are now the second-largest party."

"I don't understand politics," she said. "We didn't have any in Old Russia."

"Better learn," he said.

The train was hissing quietly to itself, having stopped before entering the station. Opposite the window was another Nazi poster on which an anemic-looking angel, depicting the Social Democrats, was walking hand in hand with the usual caricatured Jew—squat, fur-coated, cigar-smoking, hook-nosed. Somebody with a paint pot had enforced the message: KILL THE JEWS!

Their cab had to take a circuitous route to get to Bismarck Allee; the police had set up a barrier to block Potsdamer Platz and surrounding roads.

"Kozis and Nazis been fighting down there all day," the driver said. "Bloody Reds."

"Why not bloody Nazis?" Schmidt asked.

"That's different. Wasn't for them, we'd have bloody Bolshies in power."

It was dark by the time they got home. Marlene had left a note with the day's date in slashing green ink on the kitchen table: *"Tell the inspector that little Marlene of Scotland Yard solved his case yesterday! All shall be revealed! What DID you get up to in Poland?"*

At three o'clock in the morning, the phone rang. She handed it to him. "For you."

It was Willi. "You left this telephone number, boss."

"What is it?"

"Just thought you might be interested, knowing you and Prince Nick and Munich. Probably nothing to do with it but . . ."

"What?"

"One of his old clubs, boss, the one for queers. There's a riot. Call's just come in from one of my lads."

Jesus. "The Pink Parasol?"

"That's the one."

"Send a car. I'm at 29 Bismarck Allee."

She was sitting up in bed. "What is it? The Pink Parasol. Is it Marlene?"

"No, just a disturbance. Homo club, there's always some sort of trouble." He dragged on his trousers.

"Oh, God," she said. "It's Marlene."

When he got there, the Parasol's bouncer was being put into an ambulance. He'd slammed the street door on the truckload of storm troopers that had pulled up outside and given fight when they broke it down. As the stretcher was carried past him, Schmidt glimpsed a cauliflower ear sticking out from what was otherwise a bloody mess.

Willi had turned up in a traffic car. Tudjmann of Vice, under whose aegis this was, stood on the pavement among a ring of uniformed police, watching his men collect wooden clubs and truncheons from stormtroopers as they came down the stairs and hurried off into the night.

"Aren't you going to take their goddamn names?" Schmidt demanded of him.

Tudjmann shrugged. "What for?"

"Well, I am." He made for the stair, yelling, "Police!" with Willi behind him herding descending Nazis back up. One or two pushed past him, but the rest retired in front of him to the first landing where a door read JUSTUS MARCKS. THEATRICAL AGENT. The Pink Parasol was another floor up.

The storm troopers gathered on the landing were uniformly young and sated. They stared at Schmidt with curiosity, almost affront. He demanded, "Who ordered this?"

"What do you care?" one of them asked, and another said, "We're doing your job for you. Cleaning Germany of vermin."

"Take their names, Willi," Schmidt said. "Check every identity card."

He went up the next flight of stairs.

The Pink Parasol was like hundreds of clubs in Berlin described as "intimate," meaning small—a room with discreet lighting that kept its clientele in near darkness and focused pink spotlights on the small stage at the far end, where some storm troopers were still doggedly smashing up the band's instruments and music stands. Splintered chairs and tables littered the floor among broken glass.

Some men in business suits were gathered together in one corner of the room, fearful but, as far as Schmidt could see, unharmed. The assault had been on the staff and entertainers. A black man lay facedown on the floor with blood coming out of his head, a dented saxophone thrown on top of him. A young man hung by his tied hands from a light fixture. His glittering leotard had been ripped down to his ankles, and his back was scored like a slashed painting. Two more were unconscious on the floor, others were staggering on their feet, one was retching and trying to catch his teeth as the effort sent them out of his mouth.

Schmidt gestured to the businessmen in the corner and then to the hanging figure. "Get him down." He walked up to the stage where the storm troopers were still too busy to notice him. "Police," he said, clearly, without shouting.

One by one they lowered weapons and turned to face him. A couple were smirking. Not one of them was older than twenty.

"Who put you up to this?" Schmidt asked conversationally.

The smirk on one face grew wider. "Decency."

Schmidt looked at the wooden club in the boy's hands and knew he could take it from him and smash his face with it and knew, too, that if he did, he wouldn't stop.

He heard Willi's voice behind him giving orders. "Send these men to the Alex. And get the medics up here."

He looked around. The Parasol boys were either too shocked or too injured to be coherent. He went up to their customers. "Was the one they call Marlene here tonight?" he asked.

A short, fat man stepped forward, settling his jacket. He sported a mustache and a wing collar; he looked like everybody's bank manager. "I should make it clear, Inspector, that my friend and I had no idea what sort of club this was. We merely stopped in for a drink."

Schmidt smiled, took him by his lapels, and raised him to tiptoe. "And I should make it clear"—he rocked the man back and forth—"that I do not care a fuck about you and your friend. I want to know if Marlene was here."

A younger man stepped forward. "They took her. Him, I mean."

"Where? Who did?"

"Two of them. They took her through there." He pointed to a curtain by the side of the stage. "She was just starting her act."

"Thank you," Schmidt said. "Willi, here."

They barged through the curtain into a small corridor, yelling, "Police!"

Some bolts were drawn back and a door opened, a man peeped out. "Who are you?" Willi demanded.

"Have they gone? I heard the rumpus."

"Where's Marlene?" Schmidt shouted at him.

"I don't know. I heard the rumpus and—"

Schmidt pushed past him, opening doors. A dressing room, smelling of cheap scent with bulbs around a huge mirror. A less fragrant lavatory. A broom closet. And, at the end, a door leading onto a fire escape that descended into a yard made dark by the loom of surrounding buildings. "Get a flashlight, Willi."

Light showed an open gate and overflowing trash cans. One was overturned, and there was blood dripped on its scattered contents. "She was struggling."

A tiny, rubbish-filled alley raised Schmidt's hopes. They'd leave her here. Above the rattle of the nearby S-Bahn, he yelled, "You go that way, I'll go up here!"

He stumbled to the end of the alley.

He met Willi coming back. "They took her out the other end, boss. A waiter having a smoke saw a big woman being forced into a Mercedes, a Silver Arrow, he said it was."

"Get a description out, Willi."

"Who *is* this Marlene?" Willi asked. "Important, is she?"

"Yes. I want that car stopped."

"Can't be too many of them about," Willi said. "Rich man's auto, that is."

"*Now,* Willi." But he knew there wasn't any rush; the transvestite was probably already dead.

He didn't say so to Esther when he phoned to tell her. "We'll find her, darling."

There was silence at the other end of the line.

"We'll find her," he said again. Because she still didn't say anything, he put the phone down so that he could get on with his job. This was no time to indulge in guilt; she'd flagellate herself enough for the two of them. If it was anybody's fault, it was his—that's what came of using unofficial channels. Had he given the photograph to the uniform boys to flash about . . .

He should have known. Giving Marlene the picture had been lethal. The killer had come for her, and he'd gotten her. The poor old queen had shown the sports-club photograph to somebody who'd recognized the face on it. Recently. Very recently. *"Tell the inspector that little Marlene of Scotland Yard solved his case yesterday!"* Just now his anger was too great for self-blame; he could feel it licking out of him, lighting up the figure caught in it, scorching it until it shriveled.

You're in Berlin now. I'm getting close, you bastard, and you know it.

IN 29C BISMARCK Allee, Esther continued to hold the phone to her ear long after the connection had been broken. Crazily, the only words in her head paraphrased a line from an English play that had once made her laugh. *"To lose one flatmate, Mr. Worthing, may be regarded as a misfortune; to lose two looks like carelessness."*

After a while she put the receiver back—very slowly. I'm a web, she thought. Everyone dies that gets caught up in me.

She'd heard the fury in Schmidt's voice and envied it; anger was not an option for her. The massacre of her family would have blasted her apart if she'd given way to it; the crime had been too vast for anger, too impersonal, a political act. She'd disciplined herself to seeing the killing in context, as a legacy of impersonal hatred, czar on Jew, Bolshevik on czar, Red on White, White on Black. And now that it was personal, now that a malformed mind had slithered out of the Polish marshes and was defending its disguise by striking at other people she loved, it was too late for her to resurrect anger; she could feel only shame that she'd helped to lead it to them. And grief that they were dead.

It was a warm night for October, but Esther sat at her window watching it turn into day, wrapped in a blanket because she was so cold.

STRETCHING INTERDEPARTMENTAL COOPERATION to the limit, Willi managed to stay on the case with him. "Finding that car is Traffic business," he said.

"Anastasia case," he said when Schmidt had explained the circumstance. "Like old times. Um, Bismarck Allee . . . you living there now, boss?"

"Any objection?"

"I ain't, no. But I was thinking . . . in view of the lady's, um . . ."

"She's a Jew, Willi. You can say it."

"I'm not saying anything. It's just that . . . our Major Diels . . ." He jerked his thumb in the direction of Department 1A. "Might be wiser to give a different address, for every day, like. They reckon he's got every Yi— Jew in the city on file."

"Major Diels can go fuck himself."

The Silver Arrow had been seen heading west. It had passed along Bismarckstrasse, Kaiser Damm, and onto Heerstrasse, where a police car had pursued it because it was going too fast but had lost the chase to the Mercedes's superior speed. The police driver thought it might have turned left into Grünewald Forest; he'd taken its number, though. A Reichstag deputy had reported it stolen.

Just after dawn a foot patrolman on the banks of Havel reported having seen a silver car going over the bridge leading to Schwanenwerder; he'd been too far off to tell the make or license plate, but he'd noticed it because it had driven only a little way onto the island before turning around and speeding off again.

Almost immediately there came another report: the car had been found abandoned near Tempelhof Airport.

"Airport, boss?" Willi asked as they set out.

"No," Schmidt said, "Schwanenwerder. That's where he's dumped the body."

"How do you reckon that?"

"I'm getting to know him." And he's getting to know me.

Autumn was extending itself in the latest and longest Indian summer Berlin had known for years. Tapestry-colored leaves still clung to the trees of villas that became bigger and more widely spaced as Willi drove westward.

"Schwanenwerder," he said. "Yid country, ain't it? Oh, sorry."

"It's all right. It is Yid country," Schmidt said. "Exclusively and exclusive." Once inhabited only by rabbits and landscape painters, it was now home to some of Berlin's wealthiest Jews, who'd built mansions on it. "It's our man's little joke."

"*Their* joke, boss. There was two of them took the homo out of that club."

"He's getting help. And he's getting careless." Literally without care, he thought. The more power the Nazis got, the more R.G. gained confidence that he was untouchable.

The radio crackled the car's call sign. "To Inspector Ritte. Body found on Schwanenwerder."

Willi clucked with admiration and stepped harder on the pedal. "On our way."

They had to slow down through Grünewald behind horses and riders out for a morning canter and parties of young men and women with picnic hampers going out to the lake for a swim while the weather lasted.

"Had my first girl here," Willi said lovingly. "Bivouacking with the Wandervogel, I was. Getting back to nature, the leader called it. And a camp of female Wandervogel not far away. Lotte, she was called. Never forgotten her. We got back to nature under the trees, all right, her and me." He sighed.

Schmidt nodded, trying to tell himself that there was still health in the world. He thought of the forest vibrating with Berlin slums' randy adolescents under the Grünewald trees, the only beauty and greenery available to them. Probably still was, except he couldn't imagine Fascist youth having beautiful moments.

He'd had a girl here himself, though she wasn't his first. Trudi Menzel, bless her. He'd borrowed a bicycle so he could bring her here, and she'd sat on the handlebars all the way, his chin resting on her plump shoulder while he pedaled, getting hotter and hotter and more and more lustful. He remembered the effect of sun coming through the leaves onto Trudi's skin. Like Willi said, beautiful.

They were running past Havel now, its water dotted with little sailboats. Willi wrenched the steering wheel to the right, and they were over the bridge onto the island.

Somebody'd hung up a piece of canvas, a sail from the look of it, between two trees at the lake's edge, and a policeman in a skiff had stationed himself on the water itself to keep boat-owning onlookers away from what lay in between.

Some uniforms were having a smoke nearby and tossed the butts away as the car drew up. One of them saluted and came forward.

"Was it you found him?" Schmidt asked.

"Yes, sir. It was me saw the car, sir, and so I come over to have a look. Seems like they tried to chuck the body in the water, but I reckon it got caught on a tree root as it rolled down the bank."

"What's your name?"

"Baum, sir."

"Well done, Baum. Is Dr. Pieck here?"

Baum wiped his hand across his mouth. "Just arrived, sir. Examining now. We caught him before he left home." The police surgeon lived nearby in Wannsee.

"Is that your vomit?" Schmidt pointed to a small heap by one of the trees.

Baum nodded. "Sorry, sir. Thought I'd seen everything, sir, but this . . ."

"Does you credit," Schmidt said. He walked around the canvas. Kneeling by the body, the police surgeon nodded to him and sat back so that he could see better. His assistant stood by, looking over the lake.

They'd left Marlene clothed, which he hadn't expected, but had ripped the long, slinky, pink satin gown she'd worn for her act from neckline down to the mess at her crotch, exposing the large, flesh-colored falsies with which she'd padded its bust, a shaved chest, and a hairy belly, all now crusted with blood from her cut throat, where flesh gaped open on the left side. Presumably agony and then rigor mortis had kept her teeth clamped on the genitalia that had been stuffed into her mouth, so that, unwillingly, irresistibly, Schmidt was reminded of a dog carrying some smaller animal's entrails to its master.

Her right hand lay stretched out where the tree root had interrupted her body's roll, and water was gently lapping against long, red fingernails.

A coot came bobbing out of the reeds and set off farther down the lake. A slight southerly breeze brought the shrieks of the bathers from the Wannsee beaches.

"What's that across the head?" Schmidt asked.

"Yes, I had difficulty with that," Dr. Pieck said. He stood up, brushing his knees. "Done with the same knife that severed the carotid artery, and he'd have been struggling at the time, of course, but you can just make out letters." He addressed the corpse: "Somebody carved the word 'filth' into your poor, bald head, didn't they?"

"Struggling?"

"Oh, yes. All the injuries were inflicted before death, except of course the one to the neck that caused it. Water, Plancke, if you please."

His assistant had a kidney basin and soap ready. Pieck washed his hands and dried them on a small white towel. The basin was emptied, more water poured in from a jug, and Pieck washed his hands again and, again, dried them. "A transvestite, one presumes. Dear, dear, how these sorts of fellows hanker to become women. Prepared to go to Cairo for the operation, I'm told." He looked benevolently down at the thing at his feet. "Didn't want it done this way, though, did you, old chap?"

"Sir." The policeman in the boat had retrieved something from the water that hung from the oar like a dishrag. It was a wig.

"Send it with the body when they take it in," Schmidt told him. Whoever came to do the official identification should see Marlene as she'd wanted to be seen. Oh, Christ, he thought. It'll probably be Esther.

Raised voices were coming from behind the canvas. When Schmidt appeared around it, Willi said in the monotone he reserved for the unwelcome, "This is Herr Fuchs, sir. He's a banker. He lives in that house over there"—Willi pointed to a richly chimneyed house among distant trees—"and he wants us to go away."

"I didn't exactly say that." Apart from being short, Herr Fuchs was not the Nazi depiction of a Jewish banker. He was slim. His speech was cultured and without lisp. He was dressed for tennis. "I do appreciate that you have your work to do, Inspector, but if you could speed this up."

A jackass, Schmidt thought. "It's a murder case, sir," he said stolidly.

"Exactly. My wife and daughters want to come down here and take our boat out." He pointed a few yards along the lake to where a gleaming launch was moored to a small pier. "I just wondered how long you're going to be."

"As long as it takes, sir."

"Mmm." Herr Fuchs lingered. "I just wish these gangs would keep to the streets and not intrude their . . . machinations into our little haven."

"Yes, sir." Schmidt had lost interest. Why here? he was thinking, looking around. Why dump her here? Long way to drive. Risky. There was something else. "What's that, sir? That thing there, near the bridge?"

"Ah, a little bit of our German history."

They strolled together to look at it, a single Corinthian column of stone to which a broken piece of architrave was still attached.

"A fragment from the Paris Tuileries," Fuchs said. "It was brought back by our soldiers after the Franco-Prussian War. Rather amusing, don't you think? Read it."

Schmidt peered at the brass inscription. THIS STONE FROM THE BANKS OF THE SEINE, PLANTED HERE IN GERMAN SOIL, WARNS YOU, PASSERBY, HOW QUICKLY LUCK CAN CHANGE.

So there it was.

"Pity that poor fellow over there didn't take the warning," said Fuchs.

"It's a warning to all of us," Schmidt said. To me, he thought. That's why he brought Marlene here. So that I'd read it.

Fuchs raised his eyebrows. "Very well, Inspector, I'll leave you to hurry things up. I'll send one of the servants down with a drink for your men, lemonade or something."

Schmidt watched him go, so agile and smug in his shining whites, so sure he was divorced from the horror that lay at the bottom of his garden. What do you read? The financial pages? Try *Mein Kampf,* where Hitler says you're a disease. Do you think this silk cocoon of yours will protect you from storm troopers?

He went back to the lake's edge.

IN THE POLICE morgue in the basement of the Alex, Esther looked down at Marlene's bewigged head where it lay outlined against the sheet. "Yes," she said obediently, for the record. "That is William Edward Leicester."

Schmidt would have spared her, but there wasn't anybody else. Marlene's friends had been frightened off, and the upper-class family in England, when contacted, had refused to come. He led her away.

"I don't know what to do," she said.

"I'm sorry. My love, I'm so sorry. My fucking fault. I shouldn't have involved her."

She looked up at him. "Why do we blame everybody but him? He's the disease. But, Schmidt, she was so joyful, I couldn't understand how her family could cast her off and not miss her company." She began to weep, and he put his arms around her. "It's like being aboard some hideous Noah's Ark," she said. "We send out a raven and a dove to find something for us, and they don't come back because the something has torn them to bits."

"Come on, Mrs. Noah, I'll buy you a coffee."

In the café she asked, as he had known she would, "How bad was it?"

He wouldn't lie to her. "It wasn't good."

She rubbed her forehead with the heel of her hand. "We're not going to get him, are we? If the Nazis take power, he's just going to blend in; he'll be lost in the bigger evil. They won't care who he's killed."

"They're not in yet," he said. "And until they are—*if* they are—he's as big a menace to them as to anybody else, if they only knew it. Once he's exposed, he's hardly going to be a vote getter."

"Once he's exposed," she said.

He took her hand. "I'm getting close. Just one piece of luck, that's all I need. One lucky break."

At Schwanenwerder, as they'd followed the police van taking the body to the forensic lab, he'd made Willi stop while he walked back to the column from the Tuileries. "'. . . how quickly luck can change,'" he read again.

"And so can yours, you bastard," he'd said. He'd felt a bit ridiculous as he'd said it, but it needed saying.

"I'll see to the funeral," she said. "I'll talk to the undertaker. I don't want her buried without makeup."

"Esther."

"Yes?"

"Time you moved out of Bismarck Allee." He expected protests—he was going to override them—but he wasn't prepared for fury.

"NO." She attracted the attention of the entire café.

"For God's sake, be sensible," he said. "Why not?"

"Because he'll have won. Because I'm a Jew. Because Jews are always having to run away, get shifted, move on, leave your home and possessions and get the hell out. They're not shifting me—not now, not ever."

"Not 'them,'" he said. "Him."

But for her the killer's shadow was being subsumed in the greater storm cloud; he was among the truckloads that went past singing death to the Jews, in Hitler's voice on the radio, in the raids on synagogues, the very fear that she found when she visited the Smoleskins in Moabit and that she felt herself—and would not give in to. Here is where I stand. Here, and no further.

"All right," he said.

She became quieter. "I'd be diminished if I ran away."

He watched her go back to her work, disappearing into an Alexanderplatz in which election posters on every lamppost shouted for her vote. A Communist had set up a soapbox and lectern and was doing a good imitation of Lenin at his loudest but was being drowned out by a group of men with swastika armbands blowing whistles.

He tried thinking logically, and logically there was little danger to her. It was doubtful if the killer had even known Marlene's home address but rather had been alerted by one of his homosexual friends who'd encountered Marlene at the club when he was showing the photograph around.

But the image of Hannelore spread-eagled on the hallway floor was a persistent terror to him. And Schmidt was no longer the investigating officer on the case. He'd been taken off it. Ringer had insisted that the investigation of Marlene's killing be handed over to his old enemy, Bolle.

"This sort of killing is not your business, Inspector," Ringer had said. "Your job is to set up the Multiple Murder Department."

"This *is* multiple murder, for Christ's sake. How many more deaths are you going to let the bastard get away with?"

But the fact that Natalya and Marlene had both lived at 29c and that Potrovskov had been its frequent visitor was regarded as an unfortunate nine-years-apart coincidence. In Ringer's opinion, Natalya, a stripper, Marlene, a transvestite, and Potrovskov, a dealer in everything shady, were the sort of people who, through their very nature, turned up on police mortuary slabs.

Schmidt, Ringer's manner had indicated, was showing a regrettable tendency to return to the obsession that had gripped him at the death of his wife.

"Fräulein Solomonova seems merely unfortunate in her acquaintances," he said. "A personage to be avoided, in my opinion."

Which told Schmidt that Ringer knew he'd taken up residence at 29c.

The evidence he'd collected in Poland, if anything, made matters worse.

"You went unofficially, without any reference to the Polish police." Ringer lectured him, "What did you think you were doing?"

"Finding out he killed a woman and a child there, then came to Germany, where he's now committed at least five more murders, let alone the original attempt on the life of Anna Anderson—that's what I was doing. What are we supposed to do? Let him roam the country slaughtering anybody he fancies? How many multiple murders do you want? I thought that was *my* bloody department."

The kaiser mustache whiffled, but the old man kept his temper. Which—Schmidt reined himself in—was more than *he* was doing.

"I shall, of course, speak to my opposite number in Warsaw," Ringer said, "and I shall attempt to present matters in such a way that we receive Polish cooperation. In the meantime I suggest you contact the Immigration Department."

Schmidt already had. "Immigration hasn't got an entry for a Ryszard Galczynski. Not under that name. He came in illegally."

It wouldn't have been difficult; the country had become awash with illegal immigrants from the east—a fact that was causing dissatisfaction and swelling the ranks of the Nazi Party. Buying the requisite papers wasn't difficult either, if you had the money; Potrovskov hadn't been the only one who supplied forged identities.

"Indeed?" Ringer handed him back the Anastasia file that Schmidt had resurrected from Records. "You will pass this over to Inspector Bolle. By all means bring it up to date with your Polish findings if you think it necessary. Discuss it with him, but it is his responsibility now, not yours. Confine yourself to setting up the new department."

The one concession Schmidt had been able to extract from the chief had been a uniformed officer detailed to patrol Bismarck Allee and keep a watchful eye out for any unauthorized person approaching number 29.

In his office Schmidt attached the case notes on Marlene's murder to the file and added the statement by Father Teofil he'd made the priest sign before he left Bagna Duze, along with another from the count. He put the resultant bulging folder on Frau Pritt's desk. "I want everything in here duplicated," he told her. "Everything."

He went down to the Alex's new photo lab. "Can you make copies of these, Hugo?" He handed over the two pictures of the killer as a boy and the killer as a storm trooper.

"You'll need to sign a form for Department 1A."

He signed it. When he had duplicates of notes, statements, photographs, lab reports, then—and only then—did he take the original down to Bolle's office and give it to him.

Bolle was a pipe smoker and one of those men who refuses to show surprise. Having to explain all over again to that smoke-wreathed, stolid face the motive for Marlene's murder and the probable identity of the killer reinvoked a nine-year-old anger in Schmidt. This stupid, slow sod wouldn't see the links, hadn't believed him over Hannelore's death, wouldn't believe him now.

"So that's the case," he said, finishing. "Or is this another accident, and the poor bastard cut off his own balls while shaving?"

"No need for that," Bolle said, removing the pipe from his mouth. "I'm not saying you're right. I think this was a queer killing pure and simple. But it was nasty, and if you've got a line on the fuckers who did it, we'll go after them."

"Really?" Schmidt hadn't put Bolle down as a champion of the transvestite community. He said so.

"I'm not," Bolle said. "Unnatural bunch of shits in my opinion, but there's too many SA gangs barging into places and hauling people off. It's getting out of hand. At least this pansy's body turned up; some never do."

"Really?" Schmidt hadn't put Bolle down as anti–storm trooper either.

"Old fellow lived down my way," Bolle said, "trade-union man, a docker at the Westhafen. He'd been calling for the ban to be put back on the SA. Three weeks ago they broke into his house and took him away. Told his wife he was Communist scum. Not been seen since. I got my boys on it, but so far we haven't been able to make an arrest. They scared the wife so she couldn't identify her own mother." He wagged his pipe at Schmidt. "Opinionated old codger, Jan was, and I'm not saying we didn't have our arguments, but he wasn't a Red—he was a Roman Catholic *and* he fought for his country in the war, which is more than these young bastard Brownshirts ever did."

Schmidt left Bolle's office with an apology owing and an unspoken *nunc dimittis* on his lips. It was the election, he thought. The stridency of hatred made you forget some people still believed in law.

Bolle even allowed him to sit in on the interrogation of the men who'd invaded the Pink Parasol—on the understanding that questioning was left to Bolle.

All of them were young and came from outside Berlin. Not one professed to know the name of the man who'd turned up in plainclothes at one of their meetings and said something along the lines of "Let's go, boys, and strike a blow for the Fatherland by destroying a nest of queers."

"You obey any civilian who turns up?" Bolle asked.

"He wasn't a civilian. He was Intelligence; he had authority from Munich."

"And you didn't ask his name?"

"Not necessary. We obey orders."

Shown the photograph of the 1923 sports conference, they recognized Ryszard's face but confessed to not having seen him before the incident.

"He spoke with a bit of a foreign accent," one of them admitted.

"Not a German, then."

"Neither is our Führer." The youth gave a Hitler salute. "We are still proud to serve him."

"By beating up nancy boys," Bolle said. "Who was with him? Who helped him kidnap the one dressed as a woman?"

"They were all stinking women," the youth said, and spit.

"The victim was killed, you know that? Tortured to death. You were accomplice to a murder."

"Trash like that deserve it."

"Where did they get the car they used to take him away?"

"What car? We came to Berlin in a truck."

The boy had a lovely complexion, cream tinged with russet; he should have been herding cows on the farm his father owned outside Potsdam.

Bolle asked, not unkindly, "What the fuck are you doing here, son?"

Red flooded the boy's skin, and he hammered on the table. "Because it is necessary. Germany is in the hands of degenerates. My father's gone bankrupt; the stinking Yids own our farm now. *It is necessary.*"

When they got outside the interrogation room, Bolle said, "I'm going to have to let them out on bail. Their lawyer's screaming about decent boys like that being in jail while perverts pollute the streets."

"Decent? Let me take the little shit down to the morgue and show him the body and ask him if *that's* decency. What about the kid whose back was ripped to shreds?" But he knew and Bolle knew that the youths' likeliest sentence was a fine. Their lawyer would emphasize the Pink Parasol's wickedness. They'd be dressed in suits, the flower of German youth carried away in a campaign against indecency. The farm boy would return to his village and be greeted as a hero.

In a disintegrating situation, where beatings, battles, woundings, and killings were reaching record levels, Nazi propaganda was presenting the storm troopers as a form of auxiliary police—indeed, in some areas they had more or less become such—the only force capable of standing between good Germans and the powers of darkness as represented by sin, inferior races, and, above all, Bolshevism.

Bolshevism. The death of millions of Russian *kulaks* from starvation owing to Stalin's collectivization was a terror stalking a Germany that still regarded itself as an agricultural nation. The Nazi Party was enforcing the message with energy—going door-to-door, holding rallies, meetings, leafletting. Hitler had taken to the sky and was flying from city to city, wooing massive crowds in the machine-gun voice that never gave out.

And I've got to go back to Bismarck Allee and tell Mrs. Noah that her dove's killer is still free.

Nevertheless, it hadn't been a fruitless exercise. He was throwing aside the branches hiding the killer crouching in cover; he was getting glimpses of the thing that had followed Natalya into Charlottenburg Park, that had carried Hannelore's shopping for her. Every time it sprang out to kill, it was more difficult for it to reconceal itself.

In fact, he didn't have to tell Esther anything, because she wasn't home when he got in. A note on the kitchen table read *"Couldn't get you on the phone. Anna returning tomorrow on the* Deutschland. *A friend's flying me to Hamburg to meet her. Love."*

He went back downstairs to find the patrolman whose job it was to keep an eye on number 29.

"Left in a car with a man." The patrolman checked with his watch. "About half an hour ago."

"A big man?"

"Biggish. On the fat side. They were laughing together."

It wasn't the killer; Ryszard could never have made anyone laugh. Going back upstairs, Schmidt told himself he had to stop being frightened for her; she'd lived nine years without him keeping an eye on her. And if she wanted to go off with jovial fat men, why should anyone stop her?

Searching in a badly stocked refrigerator for something to eat, he found himself answering his own question.

I should. I can't do without her.

21

THE CONTACT IN the New York Port Authority who'd cabled Howie Meyer with the tip-off that Anna Anderson was on the *Deutschland*'s passenger list had neglected to say whether she was traveling first, second, or third class.

He also appeared to have tipped off half the German press, to judge from the crowd of reporters and cameramen also waiting in the rain on the dockside, a fact that annoyed Howie. "I wanted an exclusive."

"I don't know why you're bothering," Esther told him, "or them either. She won't talk to you. She hates the press."

"But she'll talk to you, kid," Howie said. "Why d'you think I brought you along? Where the hell is she? They're letting steerage off now."

It was extraordinary, Esther thought. There'd been halfhearted flurries of activity by the press corps as a minor film star and an auto-racing playboy had descended the gangplank, but the person for whom the cameras and notebooks were patiently poised on this wet Hamburg morning was an ill-tempered, untidy, nervy little woman who didn't want anything to do with them.

To Howie she was even important enough for him to have hired a private plane to fly them up to Hamburg in time to meet her.

A nice man, Howie Meyer, one of the slangy, cultured Americans. Esther had taken a liking to him—and he to her—when she'd provided the pictures for one of his features for *Collier's* magazine. Even so, she wouldn't have told him of her connection with Anna; Frau Schinkel had done that while chatting to him in the hall of number 29 one morning, boasting of the famous grand duchess who'd once lived upstairs.

He'd badgered her ever since. "Is she Anastasia or isn't she? You can tell me, kid, I'm a reporter."

"No comment, Howie."

"Where the hell is she?" he said now.

"Hiding on board, I expect," Esther said.

"The hell with it. I'll find her." Howie shoved his umbrella into Esther's hand. "Keep a lookout." He put up his coat collar and went off.

Esther found herself looking carefully at the backs of big men in the crowd, edging around to see their faces just in case this one or that should belong to the man who had climbed the staircase of the Green Hat all those years ago.

It was the reason Esther had agreed to come when Howie'd asked her along, to make sure the killer wasn't waiting for Anna.

For God's sake, she'd told herself, you're getting paranoid again.

She'd gone along anyway. It was one thing to theorize that Anna was safe from the killer, that the two of them balanced each other's hidden identity. But for her, Anna and danger had been synonymous from the beginning. Olga had been the first who'd died for her, then Natalya, Schmidt's wife, Nick. And now Marlene. It had reinforced the fear. And the grief. Sheltering under Howie's umbrella, the rain fenced Esther around with tears for unnecessary, ubiquitous death.

"You've got to stop being afraid," Schmidt had said. "He's not a superman."

Maybe not, but he was everywhere. Maybe here, among the rain-soaked welcomers, blank-faced and lethal, waiting.

She wondered if Anna was even now peering out from behind one of those portholes, as she'd peered from number 29c's kitchen window all those years ago.

The last of the steerage passengers were coming off. She wasn't on board. It was a mistake. She wasn't coming. Thank you, God.

Somebody put a hand under her elbow, making her jump. "She's gone," Howie said.

"Gone? Where?"

"Sshh." Howie steered her away. "Let's have some coffee."

They found a table in the arrivals hall's large and dreary café. "I crossed one of the stewards' palms with dollar bills," Howie said. "The ship docked in the early hours, and she was taken off right away."

"Who took her?"

"Hush, will you?" Howie looked around. "I don't want anybody else to get this. Seems she was shanghaied over in New York. Who was it putting her up in the States—somebody called Jennings?"

"Miss Burr Jennings."

"Annie Burr Jennings?" Howie whistled. "Daughter of the American Revolution and Standard Oil, one very rich old bird. She can sure pick 'em, your Anna."

"More that they pick her. What happened?"

"Seems she outstayed her welcome."

"Yes, she does that."

"Boy, did she outstay it. The Jennings clan had her smuggled on board in charge of a Finnish nurse—a lady with muscles, my guy said. She was locked in her cabin the whole passage over, never allowed out. Five o'clock this A.M. she was smuggled off again, still in the charge of the muscle-bound Finn, and taken away to"—Howie consulted the back of his hand—"the Ilten Sanatorium, near Hanover. The Finn was heard to say her patient was crazy and the Jennings family'd had enough and was committing her to a German asylum where she belonged."

"Can they do that?"

"They done it, kid." Howie grinned. "Unusual way to get rid of a difficult guest, but effective—slam her in the nuthouse."

"It's not funny," Esther said. She was thinking. "Hanover . . . I have a friend who knows Hanover pretty well, and he's got authority. Find me a phone."

Howie and the American dollar could find anything. Esther, settled in an office of the Hamburg-American Line, phoned Schmidt. "Yes, it looks as if she's been committed, practically kidnapped. Somewhere called the Ilten Sanatorium. Can you find out what's happening and call me back? Oh, shut up."

She put down the phone. "He thinks it's funny, too."

"Who is he?"

"A police inspector. Name of Schmidt. He was in Hanover on the Haarmann case, and then Düsseldorf—he specializes in mass killers."

"Siegfried? Siegfried Schmidt? Whaddaya know? An old pal of mine. We watched the guillotine take Peter Kurten's head off together."

"For God's sake."

"He had to be there officially," Howie protested, "and I had to be there because, hell, it's big news when the biggest mass murderer in the world goes to his end hoping he'll hear the sound of his own blood gushing from his neck. He murdered more people than anybody, and I said that was a record, and Siegfried said no, the record was held by Gilles de Rais five hundred years ago, and I said it was nice to meet an educated cop, and he said it was nice to meet an educated hack, and we exchanged hats. Good man."

"Yes, he is," Esther said, and paused. "I'm living with him."

"Aw, shit, Esther."

She smiled at him. She wouldn't hurt him for the world, but Howie fell in love the way a speculator gambled on the stock exchange: if one company failed, there were always others.

They went to the bar, and she bought him a drink to cheer him up while they waited for Schmidt to phone back.

HAARMANN, "WEREWOLF OF Hanover," had not only killed his victims by biting through their windpipe in a sexual frenzy but had subsequently sold their flesh to the town's meat peddlers. At his trial it had become apparent that several of Hanover's citizens had probably eaten their own children—an aftermath that had caused its mental homes to be particularly busy and brought Schmidt into contact with most of them.

He remembered the superintendent of the Ilten Sanatorium as a man devoted to the welfare of his patients. He still was. The voice coming down the telephone line expressed outrage that one of them had been virtually kidnapped in the United States and sent across the Atlantic to arrive at his establishment like a parcel.

"It is so irregular, these Americans. It is immoral. The poor woman . . . She has no medical records with her. I have no idea of her history, who has treated her and how—if indeed she has been treated at all."

"What does the Finnish nurse say?" Schmidt asked.

"She has gone, just dumped her patient on us and disappeared. I have never—"

"What are you going to do with her—Fräulein Anderson?"

"We have admitted her, of course, what else? She is in a state of collapse. We have not had time to observe her, but I hope that time and rest—"

"I'd be obliged if you'd keep her arrival quiet, Doctor. I don't want the press or anybody else getting in to see her."

"Neither do I, Inspector. She will need calm, regularity, time."

And lots of it, Schmidt hoped, putting down the phone. The longer Typhoid Anna was hors de combat, the better. He refrained from saying so when he rang Esther back. "She's in good hands, and she's going to stay there. There's nothing more you can do. Come home."

Bolle peered around the office door. "I'm off to SA Headquarters and have a search through their records for this Intelligence fella that young Nazi told us about. You reckon your man's stationed in Munich, do you?"

"I think he travels back and forth. Liaison, maybe."

"Want to come along?"

Schmidt reached for his coat, then thought better of it. "The SA guys aren't exactly fans of mine. You'll do better without me. But take some strong-arm boys with you. The last time Willi and I ventured into an SA nest, we had to make a run for it."

"I'm not standing for any of their nonsense," Bolle said stolidly. "Mine's a lawful police inquiry."

"So was ours."

If he'd thought that Bolle was going to get any answers, he would have gone with him, but he didn't—he'd made a few inquiries of his own. Captain Schwerte, Röhm's friend and the same bastard who'd been in charge of the Kreuzberg SA nine years before, had risen to the rank of colonel and was now a power to be reckoned with in the national storm-trooper hierarchy. The man hadn't cooperated with the police in 1923, and, the SA being even more rampant than it had been then, he wasn't going to cooperate now. Bolle wouldn't get anywhere.

So Schmidt reckoned, as he followed other lines of inquiry. What he hadn't foreseen was that Bolle would be taken off the case altogether.

"They *haven't*."

"They have. I got in to see this Colonel Schwerte," Bolle said. "Told him I wanted a look at his list of military personnel. He laughed at me."

"*Did* he, now?"

Bolle lit his pipe, blank-faced as ever, but the match in his hand shook as he applied it. "'I am an officer of the law, sir,' I told him. 'You are required to answer my questions.' And he laughed. He picked up the phone and asked to be put through to Department 1A. 'I have an officer here wanting to look at military records. Some case he says involves one of my men.'"

Bolle pursed his lips, and a drift of Old Lüneburg wafted into the air to join Schmidt's cigarette smoke. "Next thing I know, the bastard's grinning again and handing me the fucking phone, and it's Diels on the other end, and what the hell am I doing, and return at once and report, Inspector. And I did." Another waft of Old Lüneburg. "And I'm off the case."

"Who's on it, for Christ's sake?"

Bolle shrugged. "Department 1A, I suppose. Set a Nazi to catch a Nazi."

"Shit." Schmidt stubbed out his cigarette. "Does Ringer know?"

"Doesn't matter, does it? Ringer's not running this division anymore. Department 1A is."

Frau Pritt put her head around the door. "Major Busse wants you in his office, Inspector."

"Which inspector?"

"Inspector Schmidt."

Schmidt's eyes met Bolle's. He left him puffing his pipe and ignoring a tutting Frau Pritt as she tried to flap its smoke toward the window with her handkerchief.

He went into Busse's office on the attack. "I hope I've been dragged in to hear that your department's going to demand the personnel list from the SA."

Busse frowned. "What? What are you talking about?"

"That." Schmidt stabbed a forefinger at the Anastasia file lying open in front of Busse where he sat at his desk. "A multiple-murder case. Accordingly, it comes under my department, Busse, and I want some bloody cooperation on it. If your people are the only ones who can get a list of military personnel out of the SA, then get it."

"Ah, yes," Busse said, turning over a few pages and marking a place with his finger. "The killing of the sodomite. Your mysterious R.G. of Munich."

"Can you get the list or not?"

"From the Sturmabteilung?" Schmidt's nostrils twitched with the same distaste they'd displayed at the word "sodomite." "Shall we say that there are . . . internecine difficulties? Captain Röhm guards his . . . fiefdom somewhat jealously."

"Even from you people?" Schmidt sat down, interested despite himself. Fiefdom, eh? The Nazi powers were quarreling among themselves.

"For the moment, yes. However . . ." Busse settled his glasses more carefully on the bridge of his nose; he had a trick of extending his little fingers as he did it. His dark hair had a middle part as straight as a flare path. Damned old woman, Schmidt thought.

"At present I am not concerned with your R.G. of Munich."

"I am," Schmidt said. "He killed my wife."

"Yes, I see you have made a statement to that effect." Busse tapped the file. "Frau Busse told me at the time you seemed overwrought on the subject. She assures me it was an accident."

"It wasn't."

"I had a high regard for Frau Schmidt," Busse said. "The finest example of German womanhood, I always thought her. Her loss would unhinge anybody, but it is to be hoped that you will eventually marry again, to someone of equal racial purity."

So Busse, too, knew where he was living. What the hell did they care who he went to bed with? "I wasn't unhinged, and I don't want marital advice. I want help catching a killer."

"Yes, yes." Busse was impervious to rebuke. "However, at the moment I am interested in the matter of the woman Anna Anderson. She has since attracted international attention. America, for instance, appears to have welcomed her as the grand duchess Anastasia."

"What's that got to do with anything?"

"But you," Busse said, ignoring him, "seem to have gone to some lengths to throw doubt on her authenticity by suggesting that she may be some Polish peasant. Can you prove that?"

"Look," Schmidt said, "I don't care who she is. For all I know, she's the Queen of frigging Sheba. It's only that this whole case began with somebody trying to kill her."

"For instance . . ." Busse wet his thumb and forefinger to leaf through the folder's pages. "Dear, dear, where is it now?" He was the sort of man who said "dear, dear."

What he wasn't, Schmidt thought, was the sort of man whose soul—if he had one—could be snatched by romance, not the sort of man who'd read bedside fairy tales of lost princesses to his children. Balance sheets, yes; fairy tales, no. This very office spoke of utilitarianism: tidy to the point of rigidity, its only decoration a portrait of President Hindenburg. Schmidt couldn't work out whether the man wanted Anna to be Anastasia or whether he didn't.

"Here we are, yes, a reference to some woman at the Elizabeth Hospital who asserts that Anderson once signed adoption papers under the name of Franziska Schanskowska. Have you a statement from her?"

"No. She's emigrated since. To Palestine."

"One of those." Busse's nostrils were afflicted again. "Her evidence would have been suspect in any case, then." He uncapped a fountain pen and made a note on the file.

"Look," Schmidt said, "I'm interested in linking Anderson to the killer so I can put handcuffs on the bastard. Whether she's Anastasia is immaterial."

"You must learn to leave political matters to us, Schmidt. Now, then . . . ah, yes, the matter of the supposed Gypsy girl who also went missing from—where is it?—from Bagna Duze. It says here she arrived at the village from Russia."

Schmidt was curious. "Since when did all this grand-duchess stuff become political?"

"The Gypsy girl," Busse said. "She came from Russia?"

"Apparently. Why? You thinking she escaped from Ekaterinburg?"

"I wish to know the weight of such evidence as you have provided on Fräulein Anderson's identity. Now, then . . ."

And he continued to do it, asking questions, making notes in the margin of the file, then making them again on a pad of paper, testing the link between Ryszard Galczynski and R.G. of Munich only so far as it also provided a link between Anna and Franziska. And doing a good job of breaking it, Schmidt thought.

"So." Busse sat back, settling his spectacles. "In fact, there is no actual proof to connect Fräulein Anderson with your Polish peasant."

Schmidt shrugged. In effect, it didn't matter; he'd gone to Bagna Duze to find R.G. of Munich, not Anastasia. "I wouldn't advise you to buy shares in Anna Anderson as the grand duchess, Busse. I don't think her lawyers would like that file produced in court when they ask for the Romanov inheritance."

"No," Busse said slowly. "No, they wouldn't. It is not a tidy story." He tweaked his glasses again. "You have a duplicate copy of it, I believe."

Frau Pritt, the bitch. "Of course. It's a multiple-murder case. My baby."

"We'll have it back for the time being, if you don't mind."

"I do mind. What the hell is this? *You* aren't showing any interest in catching the bastard."

"Our interest is political," Busse said. "And I should like that copy. I may have to . . . insist." Not so much the accountant now. His sibilants had the sound of a bayonet coming out of its sheath.

"Then you can insist to the chief of police. My new department has been approved at Reichstag level."

"So has ours."

"Not as recently as mine."

They were playing "so there." Two boys in a playground arguing over whose football it was. An appeal to the headmaster would probably end up with Department 1A winning, Schmidt thought—the bastards had been given unheard-of authority—but he could also count on it taking a long time.

"We shall see." Busse recapped his fountain pen. "In the meantime we must not quarrel. We are both on the side of order."

"*Law* and order."

Busse nodded, smiled, and got up. "You must tell me about the Kurten case, I am most interested. Did you bring a record of it back with you?"

"A summary."

"Good. Perhaps you would let me see it. I am making a study of the diseased mind." He accompanied Schmidt back along the corridor, chatting.

While Schmidt pulled out the drawer of the filing cabinet, Busse looked around the office as if making a mental note of the untidiness. When Schmidt handed him the Kurten papers, he was regarding the poster of *M,* the haunted, toadlike eyes of Peter Lorre as the murderer staring back at him, so unmistakably Jewish that, the year before, the Nazi publicity machine had used the poster to suggest that all killers were Jews and all Jews were killers.

" 'To Inspector Schmidt, in gratitude and respect for his part in the arrest of the real M,' " Busse read. "You liked the film?"

"It was excellent."

"It showed sympathy for a degenerate."

"I helped catch Kurten. I'd have gone down to hell to catch him. I felt relief when they cut his head off, if that's what you're asking. The film showed a man in the grip of an obsession he couldn't control. Maybe we should all be grateful we're not born like that. I can't even give up smoking."

"Lorre is a Jew, of course," Busse said.

"So I believe. Well, there you are. Have fun with your diseased mind."

"Thank you."

Schmidt held the door open for him and watched him go until he was out of sight. Then he closed the door and locked it. He got out the copied Anastasia file, put it in his briefcase, picked up his hat and coat, and went out.

"EISENMENGER?"

"Who's that?"

"Schmidt."

"Where are you calling from?"

"The Wrestlers."

There was a heavy sigh. "Dear boy, I am in the middle of moving. At this moment louts are loading an eighteenth-century escritoire onto their van with somewhat careless sangfroid. Give me the number, and I'll ring you back."

Schmidt gave him the number.

Boxer said wearily, "Don't they got a phone in the Alex? There's other people want to use that one now and then."

"This one's helping the police with their inquiries." He ordered a beer and waited.

Even entering the Wrestlers, he'd taken the precaution of ensuring that he wasn't followed. And I'm a damn policeman, he thought, serving the state's interest in trying to catch a killer; it shouldn't be like this.

But he heard two clicks on his telephone every time he used it, he was concerned with a case that "they"—whoever "they" were—didn't want him to pursue, he had a secretary who was an informant, and the fact that he was living with a Jew had been noted. The tentacles of cancer creeping through the body of Germany were enwrapping him. And he'd begun to be afraid. That's what they feed on, he thought. Surveillance, brutality, disappearances—those aren't merely to get rid of the unwanted; they're a strategy to break down our resistance.

The telephone rang.

"I had hoped to make it clear that I was gambling on a long and happy retirement," Eisenmenger said. "You, young man, are shortening the odds against it. What do you want?"

Schmidt was curious. "Where are *you* phoning from?"

"My neighbor's house. I am alone in his study, and I've shut the door."

"What *is* Department 1A?"

"I hope you have not fallen foul of it."

"It's taken over a case I'm interested in."

"Department 1A"—Eisenmenger's voice became that of a schoolmaster—"is the embryo of what will, should Herr Hitler be made chancellor, become the Secret State Police, the Geheime Staatspolizei, the Gestapo. It is designed to rid the state of its enemies. It is the baby of Hermann Göring, and, believe me, you don't want to stay around and watch it grow bigger."

"Why would Hitler, or Göring, be interested in Anna Anderson?"

"The Anastasia female?"

"Yes."

"She'd be a useful tool, always supposing she were the grand duchess. Take up her cause and Hitler would get White Russian support, show the capitalist world his determination to fight Bolshevism. Have her by his side when he drives in triumph into Moscow."

"Hell of a risk for him, though. Suppose she's a fraud? He'd look a fool."

"Hitler has intuition. He prides himself on it. He cannot be made to look a fool—if he says white's black, his minions ensure that white turns a very dusky color. They call it 'working toward the Führer.'"

"So if he decides Anderson *is* Anastasia, his minions would be keen to wipe out any suggestion that she wasn't?"

"Indeed so. Is that all, dear boy? I have to get on."

"What are the internal politics? I mean, this Gestapo doesn't seem particularly friendly with Röhm and his SA gang."

"No. It is devoted to Hitler. Röhm is somewhat unwisely setting himself up as a rival power to Hitler. I leave you to draw the conclusion."

"Röhm will be dispensed with, will he? So . . . oh, fuck it, I can't talk generalities. Look, the man I'm after is a killer; he's murdering anyone who can give him away. He's an SA man, and what I want to know is, would Department 1A or the Gestapo or whatever it is bring him to trial if they caught him?"

"Depends whom he's killing. If it's Jews, they'll probably promote him."

"Aryans. Would they bring him to trial?"

"No. He would simply disappear."

"Yes," Schmidt said slowly. "Yes, I was afraid of that."

"Continue to be afraid," Eisenmenger said. "And don't ring me again."

"SO THEY DON'T bring him to trial," Esther said. "So they kill him themselves. Well, I don't care, just as long as he's dead."

They were at dinner in the flat.

Schmidt was appalled. "You can't do that," he said. "There's something called law. Perhaps you Russians didn't hear about it, but it's . . . it's a living thing. It's what separates us from apes. It's taken a thousand years to grow. People died for it. No law, then no republic—just barbarians with axes. He's *got* to go on trial. For Christ's sake, woman, people have to see what he did. Unless it is *shown* and proved that he killed Natalya, Hannelore, and the rest, you don't redress the balance, don't you see?"

"No," she said, "I don't. I just want him dead."

"Quietly shoved in a hole somewhere. I'm told they have a nice little killing ground."

"Yes."

"Then you might as well shove all his victims in with him. They'll be as faceless as he is. They might have had revenge. They haven't had justice."

"But you'll be safe," she said.

He looked up, realizing. "Is that what's worrying you, Mrs. Noah?"

"All the time."

He got up and went around the table to kiss her. "None of us would be safe," he said.

The next morning, on his way to work, he made a diversion to the home of Joe Wolff, stopping off to pack up his Anastasia file and put on the requisite stamps.

"Look after this, Joe. If anything happens to me, I want you to send it to the editor of the *Berliner Tageblatte.*" It was a newspaper he'd always trusted.

"Why should anything happen to you, Siegfried?"

"You never know. And, Joe, do it anonymously." If trouble came to his old friend, Ikey's shade would never forgive him. He'd never forgive himself.

Continue to be afraid, Eisenmenger had said.

He was.

The next night, returning late from dinner at a restaurant, he and Esther found the door to 29c hanging open. For a second, Schmidt thought a grenade had been thrown inside. The big table in the living room had been smashed, books scattered from the shelves, cushions ripped open and thrown on the floor. . . .

"I'll kill 'em." Schmidt stomped over broken glass to the phone and then stopped. "What's the fucking use? At least they didn't get what they came for."

He looked around. Esther was still standing in the doorway, her eyes large and remote. "He's been here," she said.

For a moment he didn't understand; then he did. "My love, it's not him. Did you think it was him? He's not a burglar. Darling, I know who did this. They won't do it again." He kept talking as he righted a chair, fetched her to it, and held her.

She drew in a deep breath to stop herself from shaking. "Who was it, then?"

"Oh, just some little friends from Department 1A. They were looking for a file I won't let them have—the wreckage is their way of showing they were miffed because they couldn't find it."

She took in another breath. "And that's all right, is it?"

"It's better than the bastards getting it," he said. "I'll have a couple of my boys around in the morning, help clear up. And I'll get you nice new furniture, some chintzy material, how'd that be? Red and black. Nazi colors."

He was sorry for the damage, he was angry, but the thought that he'd thwarted Busse buoyed him up.

"Look at it as an interdepartmental dispute," he said.

Marlene, it turned out, had not only been the scion of an English Roman Catholic family but on most Sundays had tottered on high heels to mass at the tiny church near the Charlottenburg Rathaus, where, Schmidt thought, her confessions must have enlivened the day for the priest now conducting her burial service.

Schmidt had attended reluctantly and more as a policeman than a mourner, feeling that the best he could do for Marlene was to find her killer—and find him before the gentlemen of Department 1A did.

He'd never had much time for the Roman Church, even less since most of its bishops had begun hailing Hitler as a new messiah who'd sweep the German Temple of its Jewish money changers. But Esther had asked him to come.

Marlene's friends were there, in droves. The nave of the church was almost full, and sunlight coming through stained glass cast daubs of color here and there on lavish widows' weeds and veils, some of them concealing the faces of real women while others emitted deep, masculine sobs. The Pink Parasol boys were there, most of them in sober, well-cut lounge suits, recognizable by the bandages, sticking plaster, and arm slings they wore like campaign medals.

The priest, a wizened little man, was unexpected. He referred to Marlene as a sinner, "but a loving sinner, killed by the fiends of a godless organization," a declaration that led Schmidt to shake him by the hand after the committal.

Esther had arranged transport for the journey back to her apartment and the wake, an unnecessary expense, Schmidt had thought, since the distance between the church and Bismarck Allee was short.

But she'd been rightly cautious; the queens especially became outrageous on exposure to the public, waving and shrieking abuse from the cab windows as they passed a couple of storm troopers sticking up bills on a hoarding.

"Behave yourself," he had to tell one of them, dragging her back in.

"They've got to be stood up to, darling."

"But not antagonized." Bad as the bloody Reds, he thought; couldn't resist confrontation and lost public support by doing it.

The flat had been restored as well as possible in the time available. The front door had been mended and provided with new locks. Chairs and the table had gone to the dump, and guests would have to sit on hastily bought cushions, but the place looked tidy. Busse's men had wreaked no havoc on the bedrooms, bathroom, or kitchen, merely searched them. The message had been the damage to the living room. Frau Schinkel had heard nothing—she slept like the dead—and the flat below was empty.

Esther had covered a table borrowed from Frau Schinkel with canapés and cocktails and hung her walls with photographic portraits she'd taken of Marlene, some in Dietrich mode—with top hat, tails, and fishnet stockings, seated provocatively on a stool—others in pensive mood. The queens wept.

A blond young man touched Schmidt on the shoulder. "Inspector?"

"Yes."

"Can we talk?" Walking stiffly, he led the way out onto the balcony that Esther'd had built outside the French windows, adding a fire escape that led down to the garden into which she'd transformed Frau Schinkel's former backyard.

The last time Schmidt had seen him, the youth had been hanging from the light fixture at the Pink Parasol. "How's your back?" he asked him.

"All right," the boy said. The bad match of sallow skin and brilliantined, peroxided hair—almost pink in a November sunset—aged him.

He had the hopeless eyes that Schmidt had seen in the faces of long-term prisoners, and he turned them away, putting his hands on the balustrade to look down at the garden.

Ottmar Keysterling, Schmidt remembered. Age nineteen. YMCA, Sophienstrasse. Four convictions for soliciting. Waiter and part-time dancer at the Pink Parasol. Statement taken by Sergeant Hoffner while the boy was still in the hospital having his back stitched together. Said he didn't know any of the storm troopers who'd attacked him, wouldn't recognize any of them again.

"I liked Marlene," Ottmar said.

Schmidt prompted him: "Did she happen to show you a photograph?"

"No. I knew she was flashing one around, but I didn't see it."

Schmidt rested his arms companionably on the balustrade and joined the boy in looking down. Esther had planted the little garden so that there would be color even in winter, and the bare boughs of a small willow showed russet against a whitewashed wall. He waited.

The boy sighed. "But . . . I think once upon a time . . . I think I met the man who took Marlene away."

"Which one? There were two of them."

"Yeah. I didn't know the other one. This was the big one."

Thank you, God.

"He didn't notice me," Ottmar said. "They all came rushing in, yelling. It was some others roughed me up—one of them had a whip. But the one I'm telling you about, the big one, him and another one went straight for Marlene. He had a scarf around his face. . . ." He squinted sideways, either to see if Schmidt believed him or to make sure he understood.

Schmidt nodded.

"It was jumbled," the boy said. "They were yelling and hurting me, and I couldn't remember anything, like I told the other policeman, but now it keeps coming back." He lifted his hand, opening and closing it to indicate illumination and darkness. "Must have been just a glimpse, but I keep seeing this face, his face, among all the others. I guess the scarf slipped off, or Marlene pulled it off him." For the first time, Ottmar smiled. "She was a big girl. She put up a fight."

Schmidt nodded again. Keep going, keep going.

"And I knew him," Ottmar said simply.

"His name?"

"No. Well, it was at a party. In Munich. I was in Munich then—must be a year or more ago—and there was this party. Me and a friend . . . and some other friends, we were the entertainment, if you know what I mean. We'd been asked along by a man called Stratz. Wilhelm Stratz. Know him?"

Schmidt shook his head. Munich, he thought. R.G.

"Big shot, Stratz is," the boy said in American. "Very big shot around Munich. Friend of Röhm's." He glanced at Schmidt as if trying to enlighten a yokel. "You must've heard of Röhm. Head of the SA?"

Yes, Schmidt said, he'd heard of Ernst Röhm.

"Yes, well, him and Stratz are like that." The boy crossed his third finger over his forefinger. "Lives in a fucking huge schloss, Stratz does. Anyway, we all went. There was this big limo that came to get us. And he was there, a guest, like."

"The big man? The one who took Marlene?"

"Yeah, him." Ottmar's voice had lost its energy, and he looked down at the garden again. "He's not a nice person."

"And you can't remember a name?"

"They don't have fucking introductions at that sort of party," the boy said, "just fucking." He frowned. "I think they called him Reinhardt. Yeah, that was it. Reinhardt. Any good to you?"

Reinhardt: Ryszard. Yes. Ryszard Galczynski of Bagna Duze had become Reinhardt G-something of Munich.

"Was he in uniform?"

"Wasn't that sort of party. He wasn't in anything."

"And you'll swear to this? I'm going to get him, Ottmar. Not just for Marlene. He's killed before, and I'm going to bring him in, and when I do, I want you to identify him."

"He's a Nazi, a big one, you could tell. They were all Nazis at that do."

"I'm still going to get him."

The boy sneered. "You and whose army?"

"Just me."

The boy shrugged. "Won't do any good. You don't know 'em."

"Yes I do, and yes it will."

"Didn't do Marlene any good."

"Which is why he's got to be stopped. You see him again, you come and tell me. *Run* and tell me."

"Suppose so," Ottmar said drearily. "All right."

Schmidt put out a hand to clap him on the back, remembered just in time, and put it over the boy's for a moment. "You won't be sorry."

"That'll be a fucking change," Ottmar said.

WASHING UP the glasses when they'd all gone, Esther said, "Don't get him killed, too."

"Who?"

"That boy you were talking to on the balcony. Ottmar."

"Reinhardt. He says the bastard's first name is Reinhardt. He's Reinhardt G. Of course, he may not be in Munich anymore. He could be anywhere—in Berlin, in bloody Bremen, anywhere. How many SA are there now? Hundreds of thousands. How many with the initials R.G.? Oh, God, don't let Department 1A find him before I do."

There were ways, he thought. Find someone to infiltrate the SA, maybe. Or get one of the burglars from Wrestlers to break into headquarters and steal its army list. Or blackmail someone on the staff.

He's not hearing me, Esther thought; he's looking beyond me. The only face he wants to see is the one in the photograph. Everyone's expendable. He'd tether himself like a goat if he thought it would attract the tiger.

She was angry enough with him to bring up another complaint. "And what are you going to do about Anna?"

"Nothing," he said. "She's tucked up nice and safe where she belongs."

"It should happen to you," she said. "She can't stay in an asylum forever. You'll have to get her out."

"It has nothing to do with me."

"You're so keen on the law," she said. "But you'll let a woman be caged up like an animal. There must be somewhere else she can go."

"I thought you wanted her safe," he said.

"I didn't want her in Bedlam."

It was their first quarrel, and he won it. "It's up to the doctors now. She'll be all right. You said yourself she's as tough as old boots."

"I'm afraid for her."

"Well, stop it. I've told you and told you. He hasn't gone after her in nine years, and he's not going to now—he knows she's no threat to him."

You know it, she thought. I just hope he does. But in one way he was right: the killer was part of a greater darkness. Cower from it and it would overwhelm them all.

The November election results suggested they didn't need to cower. The economic situation was improving, and the Nazis had lost seats—aggressive, grandiose electioneering had begun to fail in impact.

Berlin had never given the Nazis a majority anyway, and when, desperate to bring down the government, they had allied themselves with the Communists in a transport strike, they had scared off the middle-class voter. A low turnout and a national vote of 11.7 million compared to 13.7 million the previous July reduced the party's representation in the Reichstag to 196 seats. It was still the largest group by far, but the combined seats of the other parties well outweighed them.

Schmidt took Esther out dancing to celebrate at a party given by some of her arty friends, where champagne corks popped like rifle fire against deafening salvos of jazz.

Howie Meyer joined them at their table. Esther was asked to dance, and the two men watched her—she was a good dancer.

"I love her! I love that woman," Howie shouted above the noise. "But she won't leave you." He was slightly drunk.

So was Schmidt. "Best man won," he shouted back. He liked Meyer, the only journalist that had attended the Peter Kurten trial whose reporting of it he'd been able to stomach.

"You want to take her away, pal," Howie said. "Get her out of the country. Before Hitler gets her."

"Howie, old friend, we're celebrating the fact that he won't. Hindenburg's said no. Won't make him chancellor now." Schmidt had no regard for his president, but the latest storm-trooper atrocity had awakened even that old fart to the Nazi threat.

Meyer shook his finger under Schmidt's nose. "Want to bet? Little Adolf'll be chancellor within the year, maybe quicker."

"No. Hindenburg's found backbone from somewhere."

"Sure, Hindenburg's said boo to his goose," Meyer said. "Only Hitler ain't no goose, and boo ain't going to stop him. You analyzed the election results?"

"No."

"I have. I'm Nazi watcher for my American readers, who, I may say, can't get enough of it. Want another Scotch?"

"Sounds as if I'd better." He was sobering.

Meyer lumbered back with the drinks, dodging the dancers. "See, it may have escaped your notice in the euphoria, but the Communists in the Reichstag are vetoing anything that'll get this fucking country back on track. Reds? Reds don't give a shit about stabilizing the situation. What they're good at is yelling Marxist and Trotskyite slogans at the Nazis across the floor. You come to the public gallery sometime—just you come; it ain't a parliament, it's a zoo. Scares the hell out of me and scares the hell out of the voting public. And when people are scared, they want a leader."

"Not Hitler, for Christ's sake."

"Why not?" Meyer suddenly stood up and put his forefinger across his upper lip. "'We will silence the Bolsheviks. We will not rest until every German has a job. Jews who control the banks will threaten our farmers no longer. We will protect German family life; mothers will stay at home to bring up the country's children without fear of crime or pornography. Foreigners will be denied citizenship.' And that's word for word, folks." He bowed to the laughing, booing crowd on the dance floor who'd paused to listen to him. "Vesuvius is going up, my friends," he shouted at them. "You're dancing in Pompeii. Get out, get out. The lava's coming."

He sat down. "He'll be chancellor, pal. Depend on it."

"Fuck," Schmidt said.

"My sentiments exactly," Meyer said, and he tossed back his drink.

Schmidt waited until the stares attracted by Meyer's performance had gone. "Do something for me, Howie, will you?" He outlined the case against his killer. "I think he's in Berlin now, I think he's an officer in the SA, and I think his initials are R.G. Reinhardt Something-beginning-with-G. This is his photograph." He handed over copies Esther had made for him, the face of the killer circled on both of them.

"Gloomy-looking bird," Meyer said. "Want I should show this around my Nazi pals?"

"Jesus, no." Schmidt paused. "Have you got any?"

"I use a long spoon," Meyer assured him.

"Well, don't. Last person who did that got his throat slit and his balls cut off."

Meyer handed the photos back. "Did I mention I'm attached to my balls and all Nazis look alike to me?"

"What I wondered was . . . You know people at your embassy. They must keep a list of Nazi activists. What I need to know is—"

"If American intelligence has come across the fucker?"

"I want to bring him to trial, Howie. I don't want the Nazis finding him first and getting rid of him because he'd give them bad press. I want justice, and I want it seen to be done."

"You sweet, old-fashioned thing, you," Howie said, taking the photographs. "Did I tell you I'm in love with your woman?"

"Yep. And I'm taking her home."

Esther, busy in her darkroom at 29c, heard a knock on the downstairs door and knew that Frau Schinkel, who'd gone out shopping, couldn't answer it. She stood for some minutes, adjusting the wet prints hanging on the line. It was too early for Schmidt to come back from work, and she was expecting nobody else to call.

Damn it, she thought. I've got to stop this. I will *not* be afraid. He won't make me afraid. She went downstairs and nearly called out, "Who's there?" through the door, and then didn't.

She jerked the door open. "Yes?"

A small face glared out at her above one of the loveliest mink coats she'd ever seen. "You take a long time," the person said crossly. "They let me out. I tell them I am not mad, and now they believe, but there's reporters and reporters all the time, so I got to stay with you. Nowhere else to go."

Esther started to laugh, and Anna Anderson pushed past her. "Left my suitcase in the cab," she said. "You have to fetch it—too heavy for me."

22

"DOES SHE HAVE to stay here?" Schmidt wanted to know.

"Yes," Esther said.

"Well, does she have to be so untidy?" He wasn't a tidy man himself, but Anna took disarray to championship levels. It wasn't that the woman intruded; she spent most of her time in her room and was virtually monosyllabic—to Schmidt at any rate—when she didn't. And usually she'd been fed by the time he got back, so that he and Esther could eat alone. She was just there. Or had been there—he'd arrive home to find Esther clearing up the mess Anna had left behind like a Hansel and Gretel trail of bread crumbs leading into the chaotic forest she was creating out of Marlene's room.

"She really *must* be royalty," he said.

"That's what Natalya used to say. Natalya tried putting peas under her mattress to see if they made her uncomfortable, like the Hans Christian Andersen princess."

"And did they?"

"She didn't notice them."

He was, he realized, taking up the position Natalya had occupied when the three women shared the flat, and with much the same resentment; it irritated him to see Esther, who was busy, waiting on someone who was not.

He looked toward the door of the silent bedroom. "What does she do in there?"

"Nothing much."

It was a nothingness that intruded as if the woman inside were pounding a drum kit.

"Look," Esther said, "she's got nowhere else to go, and the press doesn't know she's here, so nobody can bother her. I don't mind, and I don't see why you should."

Apart from the fact that he was paying half the bills, he didn't see why he should either, but he did.

"And she's company when you're away," Esther said.

He was away a lot now. His new multiple-murder section—now generally known as Department MM—entailed his traveling around the country, giving lectures, setting up training courses, advising. Whether there were more multiple killers on the loose than there ever had been or whether he was being alerted by the various police forces dealing with them, he wasn't sure. The former, he thought—political violence was unleashing individual savagery.

A national rage made them almost coincidental. He would be taken to police morgues to look on the slashed, often dismembered, victim of a murderer and find that lying on a neighboring cart was a body riddled with bullet holes sustained in a riot. A killer in custody slavered the same loathing for mankind that he heard over the radio in the voice of a politician. In the Reichstag, deputies fought like rats in a cage.

Only at 29c did the air remain unpoisoned. Perhaps, he thought, it was why he minded the presence of Anna, as if her breath took away some of the freshness he found in it.

Esther had abandoned the Latin poets for Goethe. "'Know you the land where the lemon-trees bloom?/In the dark foliage the golden oranges glow;/a soft wind hovers from the sky, the myrtle is still/and the laurel stands tall—do you know it well?/There, there, I would go, O my beloved, with thee!'"

"Would you?" he asked.

She snapped the book shut. "No. It'd give me hay fever."

Howie Meyer kept urging him to take her out of the country. "Don't wait till Hitler's ax falls—and, believe me, it's poised over the head of every Jew in the country. Take her now."

"She won't go."

"She won't go without you, you mean."

"Keep an eye on her while I'm out of town, Howie, if you can."

"I do," Howie said. "And you might have the goddam grace to be jealous."

This was the rub. If he went, she'd go with him, but there were some things you couldn't live with, and, for him, leaving the killer uncaught was one of them.

The only solution was to find Reinhardt G. of Munich—and quick.

So far he wasn't making any progress in doing it. No record of an SA officer with the first name of Reinhardt had come to the attention of the Intelligence Department at the U.S. embassy. Nor had Howie Meyer, who, like most American correspondents, was being courted by the Nazis, seen him at any of their functions to which he was invited.

The burglar sent into SA headquarters to steal its list of personnel not only had come away empty-handed but considered himself lucky to have come away at all. "They got trip wires, they got alarms, they got guards with fucking guns. I didn't get close. What they got in there? Give me a nice quiet bank any night."

"Thanks for trying, Mo-mo."

Esther twitted him for upholding the law by illegal means, so he didn't tell her that, through Ottmar, he had made contact with a young corporal in the SA.

"Friend of Marlene's, he was," Ottmar had said.

"How can he have been a friend of Marlene's *and* a storm trooper?"

Ottmar's world-weary eyes looked on him as on a child; obviously the one did not exclude the other. "I'm not saying he'll do it, but he's a Berliner, see, not like the fucking clodhoppers that tore into the Parasol. And he cried when I told him about Marlene."

A meeting was set up at the Wrestlers. The young man's name was Wolf; he was large and surly looking, and his Brownshirt uniform caused the same flutter of unease among the bar's clientele as would the sight of a fox in a turkey shed.

"All I want you to do is keep a lookout for an officer with the first name of Reinhardt, fair-haired, big, in Intelligence," Schmidt told him. "If you see him or hear of anyone with that description, come and tell me. Nothing more." He handed over an envelope of bills.

Wolf took it. "He the one cut up Marlene?"

"Yes, so be careful."

After the boy had gone, Boxer came over. "Can't say I like that class of customer, Inspector." When storm troopers ran out of Jews and homosexuals and Communists, they'd been known to rampage into the smaller police stations and attack those confined in the cells.

"Who?" asked Schmidt innocently.

"Ah." Relieved, Boxer tapped the side of his nose. If the meeting had been illicit, that was all right, then.

What the hell am I doing? Schmidt wondered. And then answered himself: he was doing his job, and doing it in the only way left to him. The thought that the faceless agents of Department 1A might have secretly done it for him, that his killer was already dead from a bullet in the back of the neck—*and he would never know it*—kept him awake at night.

With Esther asleep beside him, he wove fantastic ideas into more fantastic plans; using Nick Potrovskov's forger to devise papers that would get him into SA headquarters in some capacity or another—letters from Röhm, perhaps, demanding a list of officers. Or setting himself up as a target that would tempt the killer into the open. An entry in the personal columns along the lines of *"Reinhardt, I know who you are. Come and get me."*

But I *don't* know who he is. And the bastard knows I don't.

In the meantime he could only cast his bread upon the waters, get on with his official job, and hope that the men of Department 1A were kept busy with theirs—whatever that was.

AT CHRISTMAS HE took Esther and a wreath to the Jewish cemetery in Weissensee. "It isn't the anniversary of his death or anything," he said. "I just come at Christmas. He used to enjoy Christmas, Ikey did."

She read the inscription on the gravestone as he propped the wreath against it. "So he got the Iron Cross," she said.

"Yes, his father's very proud of that."

She read the inscription: "'He died for Kaiser and Fatherland.'"

"His father's proud of that, too."

FOR MOST OF January Esther was occupied at her studio in Cicerostrasse preparing for her exhibition at the Kronprinzenpalais. It was also a particularly busy month for Schmidt, and the only way he was going to be able to attend her opening party was by flying into Tempelhof in the evening and catching an overnight train back to Bremen later.

Since Esther could not, Howie Meyer met him at the airport with a car. Howie was wearing a dinner jacket, making Schmidt conscious that he wasn't. "It's an Event, pal," Howie said reprovingly. "The Kronprinzenpalais doesn't give up one of its rooms to any old happy snapper. Don't you read the art pages?"

Schmidt usually flicked through them as he turned to the sports section. "I don't know much about her work," he said. "I'm ashamed."

"You should be. She's a first-class camerawoman. *Collier's* takes anything she sends, you know that? *Cicatrice*—jeepers, that's style. My little secretary was going to paint a scar on her face the other day so's she'd look like Esther. Save it, kid, I told her, you need mystery and cheekbones. That's the thing about Esther—there's all these lousy Russians claiming Peter the Great's their great-granddaddy, but don't none of 'em have what that woman of yours has got."

Schmidt's focus was suddenly on Meyer, fat, funny, with the gloss that all educated Americans had. He told himself he wasn't jealous; at least, this wasn't the jealousy he'd felt for Potrovskov and the shameful shot of relief he'd experienced in the first moment when reading of the Russian's death. This was envy. Meyer could offer her what he couldn't—security, prosperity, a new life in the Land of the Free.

The brightly lit room at the Kronprinzenpalais was crowded. Smartly dressed men and women that Schmidt felt he ought to recognize were studying the pictures, wineglass in hand. Peter Lorre and the man who'd directed *M,* Fritz Lang, were the only two he could put a name to, and they were engaged in discussion with other people.

Howie grabbed a drink and disappeared into the crowd. Schmidt grabbed another, looked for Esther, couldn't see her, and started studying the photographs.

He didn't like them too much—he wasn't meant to; Esther's photography hurt. Here was Berlin's underbelly, the toppling cards of the Weimar's paper republic. No landscapes, no studies of film stars. Instead a barefoot toddler in a roadway raised its arm in a Hitler salute to storm troopers' marching boots. An old woman dragged herself through the puddles of a Moabit alley, Communist flags strung like washing above her head. A long, magnificent shot over massed steel helmets and, at the far end of the ranks, outlined against swastikas, a tiny, screaming, gesticulating figure.

Somebody next to Schmidt addressed somebody else. "She's putting the branding iron to our eyeballs again. Isn't she marvelous?"

Peter Lorre came up and insinuated Schmidt to a quieter corner. "May I ask you something, Inspector?" The froglike little face looked shiftily worried, but it always did. "Dr. Goebbels has let me know I'm on his list. He is saying I should get out of Germany. Can he do that?"

A few months ago, Schmidt would have said no. Now he found himself saying, "Christ, I hope not."

"Lang thinks he will go," the soft, breathy voice went on, almost to itself. "Maybe I should."

What can I say to him? Schmidt wondered. Stay, the country needs you? They couldn't mean it; get rid of Jews and the gap would be ruinous. It had to be merely an election ploy, an appeal to anti-Semitic panic. You couldn't exile people because you didn't like them; it was against the law.

The law. The great governess, upholding, upheld. For the first time, it came home to him, *really* came, like a shrieking succubus sinking its claws into his entrails, how frail she was; he saw her in the dust, her gray head kicked in by jackboots. It could happen. Was happening.

He stared down at Lorre, dumb.

The actor nodded, shook Schmidt's hand, and turned away, bumping into Esther. "Wonderful shots, my dear. You should be in cinema. You have the eye."

"Thank you," Esther said. She faced Schmidt. "What do you think?"

He wanted to kiss her in front of them all. No, he wanted to pick her up and walk off with her, growling his ownership like a Neanderthal.

She snuffled and fluttered her eyelashes; they hadn't been to bed together for three days. "I know," she said.

He smiled back at her. "You don't go in for sunsets, do you?"

"It *is* a sunset," she said. "I'm merely recording it." Her gaze went past him to a group just coming into the gallery, a tall fat man, a tall thin one, and a small thin one. "Good God," she said.

"Who's that with Göring?" Schmidt wanted to know. Whoever he was, he was a worried man.

"That's Dr. Justi, he's the director here. The little one's Alfred Rosenberg; he's the one who thinks modern art is intellectual syphilis."

From his face, it was obvious that Rosenberg was applying the same judgment to modern photography and looked at it as if he might catch something. But Göring liked it. He lumbered along the walls, pointing with his dog whip, saying, "Yes, yes, yes, this is why they vote for us."

He had wonderful blond hair, heavy and sculptured, like his face. He stopped at the picture of the saluting urchin and gave a rich, catarrhal laugh. "Now, here is the future. We should give this one to Goebbels for his propaganda, eh, Doctor? Introduce me to this Cicatrice. I will congratulate him."

Dr. Justi wiped the sweat from his forehead. "Frau Cicatrice, may I introduce Herr Göring?"

Göring lifted Esther's hand to his lips. "Madam, I can pay you no higher compliment than to mistake your camera for that of a man's. I should like to see you do a study of our Führer."

"I'd love to," she said. She would, too, Schmidt thought; a gleam had come into her eye he'd seen in that of newspapermen and vultures.

"Justi here has been giving me a private view of the Impressionists downstairs," Göring said. "Also some very fine Klees and Chagalls."

There was a mutter from his small companion. "Jew-inspired daubs."

"Rosenberg here thinks modern art is not founded sufficiently on race," Göring said smoothly. "His preference is for paintings of warriors and big women, but there is some of the new I find most . . . collectible." He grinned at the director and slapped him on the back.

Dr. Justi sagged.

There was an interruption from a dark Russian. "Hermann, my friend, please to come, the grand duchess Anastasia has expressed a wish to meet you."

They watched Göring stride off to a small figure in a corner of the room, ringed by people apparently hanging on its every word, one of them Howie Meyer. A little hand was regally extended. Göring bent to kiss it.

"You brought *her*?" Schmidt asked.

"The press viewing's not till tomorrow. She wanted to come. She's beginning to feel more secure."

And was as big a celebrity as anyone in the room, Schmidt realized; everybody was watching the encounter.

He took Esther to the window. "I have to go. Get Howie to take you home, but don't invite him in—he lusts after you."

"I know he does, bless him."

"Does America beckon?"

"It will if you don't get back from Bremen pretty quick. I'm sex-starved."

He went to get his coat and bumped into Göring and his entourage getting theirs.

Hell, why not? It might smoke the bastard out.

"I'm glad we met, Herr Göring," he said. "Do you happen to know an officer in the SA? Christian name Reinhardt. Big fellow, fair-haired? Midthirties, I'd guess; speaks with a Polish accent?"

It was a massive face. It turned on him slowly, like a buffalo attracted by a gnat. "And you are?"

"Inspector Schmidt. Berlin police. Department MM."

"Your interest in this person?"

"He's a murderer."

"I shall make inquiries, Inspector."

"Thank you."

. . .

From the window Esther watched her lover emerge into Unter den Linden and hail a cab. Watched it drive away.

Behind her the room's conversation hissed with sibilants. The List, the List. Not just Jews, the avant-garde itself was on it. Art had become a risk. Risk, risk. What theater would put on a Brecht play if They took over? What concert hall would include Schoenberg in its program? Or Berg? Would Klemperer be allowed to conduct? Who'd dare hang a Kirchner on their walls? The Nazi-controlled town council of Dessau had already closed down its Bauhaus. Storm troopers in Spandau had thrown Remarque's book *All Quiet on the Western Front* onto a street bonfire; cinemas showing the film version were having their seats slashed. Truth was unpatriotic. The barbarian was at the gates.

She knew that the artistic community had turned up partly out of loyalty to her, but mostly for the chance to huddle together, like travellers who'd heard the howl of wolves getting close.

And you ask if America beckons, she thought. One word from you and I'd follow you, like Eurydice led out of the underworld by Orpheus. Because this *is* the underworld. Göring, that monster with taste, wants to show my depiction of a child perverted by savagery as propaganda for that same savagery.

Yes, America beckons. And you'd be lost in it.

How would that man of hers, that so-German best of Germans, endure the life of a refugee, always a transplant, always aware—as those who lived in it were always aware—that the earth you drew sustenance from was not your own? That you were tolerated in another person's house like an inconvenient aunt who'd lost her money? She knew the life of a refugee, none better. It was not for him.

In any case, he wouldn't go until he'd caught R.G. of Munich.

So I'll stay in hell with you—and gladly, because you can't live anywhere else.

But, by God, if she could photograph Hitler, she'd show them. She knew just the angle, the right light to emphasize those eyes, like a shark's at the moment it rolled over and opened its teeth. She'd show them truth; she'd sell it to *Collier's* for America to see. Get her name on the List of Honor before they wiped it out.

And her.

"I LIKE HERR Göring, Esther," Anna Anderson said over her shoulder from the front passenger seat as Meyer drove them home.

"I was afraid you would."

"Why you say that? He had proper respect. He will help me, I think. He has great hopes for me."

"He said that, Esther," Howie said. "I heard him. He actually said that."

Anna ignored him. Her sojourn in the United States, where not all the huge publicity she'd received had been good publicity, had added Americans to a list they now shared with pressmen. Meyer's being both, she rarely addressed him, and when she did, she was rude.

She said, "He liked your pictures. He told me." She paused graciously. "I didn't tell him you were a Jewess."

And I didn't tell him you were an impostor, Esther thought. It had been a long day.

"Here we are, ladies." Howie switched off the engine. It was late—the guests had been reluctant to leave one another's company. Bismarck Allee was nearly deserted.

"Stay there," Esther said to Anna. And to Howie, "It's cold. Let me open the front door before she gets out."

Perhaps it was the light snow that had begun to fall, perhaps it was because she was tired, but she was prey to old terrors tonight. She looked up and down the street. The doorway across the road gaped at her.

"Okay." She hustled them both indoors. "Coming up?" she asked Howie, reluctant to face the empty flat. She wished now she hadn't had a fire escape fitted, but the temptation to have access to the yard and make a garden out of it had been too great.

"Sure."

Anna went straight into her room without saying good night. Esther made her a hot chocolate and set coffee to brew for herself and Howie. She took Anna her drink.

"Was a nice party," Anna said. "I tell them all how I meet Cole Porter in America but I do not like the jazz. Herr Göring said Herr Hitler doesn't like the jazz either. He said the Führer likes Wagner. I said I like Wagner, too; we are soul mates."

"Good."

Esther went back into the living room and poured Meyer a brandy to go with his coffee. "Come on, Esther," he said, "tell Uncle Howie. Is she or isn't she?"

"So that's what you've come for," she said. "Not my company, not the coffee—the lowdown on the grand duchess. I've told you and told you, Howie, it's not my business. No comment."

"She's news. Once she goes to court to claim the inheritance, it'll be *big* news, and I want a feature ready for my great American public."

"You won't get it from me," she said. "I want nothing to do with it. Lawyers will just bleed her dry."

"It's what lawyers are good at." He leaned forward. "I'll tell you this, kid, the Nazis are backing her."

She stared dismally at him. "Schmidt said something like that. . . . Oh, it's too fantastic. I thought Göring was just being polite."

"Polite? *Göring?* No, they've been talking a lot about her at their feeding troughs. Looks like Hitler's got a grand design for our grand duchess."

"What?"

"They say his intuition's telling him she's the real Anastasia, and we all know the Führer's intuition is infallible, don't we? See it from his point of view: he wants to reassure the aristocracy; also, he needs the landholding vote, the farmers. Look at me, boys, I'm the only guy in Germany who can save you from Commie revolution. Words, words, words. But how about a symbol? How about picking up the remnant of the flag the nasty Bolsheviks trampled in the dust and giving it a wave? Who but our grand duchess?"

"Oh, God," she said, rubbing her forehead. "I'm so tired of all this. Why can't he have a grand design for Grand Uncle Ernest or Grand

Auntie Olga or Grand Cousin Dmitri or any of the other grand panjandrums? They're Romanovs."

"Because Anastasia is the czar's child and they aren't. Because she's a world figure now and they aren't. Because even Hitler believes in fairy tales. And she's prettier than Stalin."

"Oh, God. Howie. Oh, God."

"I'm just warning you, kid. I could be wrong." He saw that he was worrying her too much. "Come on, she'll be dandy. I can't see a court turning down her claim if she's got little Adolf's backing. It's you who ought to get away."

It was his constant theme. He took hold of her hand. "Listen to me, Esther. Tomorrow, maybe the day after, maybe the day after that, Hindenburg and the rest of 'em'll give in to Hitler's demand for the chancellorship. The army's backing him. So's the conservatives; they figure that by inviting him in, they'll control him." He ran his hand through his thinning hair. "It'd make a cat laugh. Sheep opening the gate to a wolf: 'Come on in and be nice.'" Gently, he kneaded her fingers. "I don't want to scare you, kid, but it's time to go. What'll happen won't be pretty. You don't want to be around. See, I might have to go, and then what'll you do?"

"You'd leave?"

"Not if I can help it, but I might get the bum's rush. Goebbels wasn't too pleased with me the other day, can't think why."

She tried to smile. "Couldn't be because your last piece called Hitler a jumped-up, Jew-baiting little jackanapes whose politics would cause raised eyebrows in the camp of Attila the Hun?"

"Nah. Good line, though, huh?"

"Good line."

He said, "Well, it was time I stuck my colors to the mast. The point is, I just wouldn't feel right leaving . . . friends behind."

"I love him, Howie," she said.

"Yep, that's what I was afraid of." He let go of her hand.

She walked him to the door and kissed him. "Please take care."

"You, too."

To watch him drive away was bleak. If he left the country, she realized, the last shred of normality would go with him.

However, there was something more urgent than that to consider. She closed the door, bolting it, and went upstairs. In the living room, she began walking its length, up and down, up and down.

Schmidt had said he suspected something of the sort, and she'd ignored the possibility as too fantastic. But tonight Göring and then Howie had solidified the terrible possibility. Hitler and Anna. Anna and Hitler.

What to do? What the hell to do? Get her away?

She wouldn't go.

All right, get her to admit publicly that she's a fake.

She wouldn't do that either.

But something had to be done, *had* to be done.

She's news.

Suppose Hitler were to take up this newsworthy grand duchess, using his infallible intuition. And what if that intuition were shown to be fallible, if someone followed the trail to Bagna Duze, to a Polish peasant, a mysterious Gypsy, and irrefutable proof that Anna was one or the other. He'd look like a fool—and Esther didn't think Adolf Hitler would enjoy looking like a fool.

What was it Schmidt said that the Nazis did to their embarrassments? A bullet in the back of the neck?

Esther sat down and poured herself a brandy.

The thing is, she thought, she's not really a fake at all. Anna was possessed in the medieval sense, had opened her mind to the spirit of a dead grand duchess and allowed it in. Her own persona had become intolerable to her, so she'd adopted one more pleasing. A mere playactor would be more regal, more gracious, instead of remaining an obdurate pain in the ass that eventually wore down everybody's patience. Hiring lawyers to pursue Anastasia's inheritance through the courts was not cupidity; as grand duchess, Anna thought it to be hers by right.

Esther thought, I cannot desert this neurotic, Jew-despising little bugger; there's something about her—vulnerability, courage, a refusal to conform to what people expect of her, an endurance.

She drank her brandy and poured another, deciding that tomorrow she would go to the bank and draw out most of her money, in case she could persuade Anna to use it in making a getaway.

But if Anna wouldn't go, if this new Caesar should adopt her, it was a Caesar that must not be mocked.

Very well, then. Let us make sure that he is not.

She got up. Fatigue and brandy and the thought of what she had to do made her stagger slightly. She opened the door to Anna's room, which was dark. "Anna."

"I am asleep."

"Well, wake the hell up. Hitler, Anna . . ." She shut the door behind her, felt her way to a chair, tipped its contents off it, and sat down in the total blackness. "Hitler," she said.

"What about Herr Hitler?"

"This is important. I want you to listen very, very carefully. If he takes you up . . . if he calls you in . . ." She was burbling, so she coughed and started again. "Anna?"

"Yes, Esther."

"If Hitler should take up the cause of the grand duchess Anastasia . . . Are you listening? This is what you must do. . . ."

She spoke for a long time into the darkness.

THE NEXT DAY—IT was January 30—Adolf Hitler was made chancellor of Germany.

23

SCHMIDT HEARD the news at a working lunch in Ernst-Reuter-Platz, where, having that morning returned from Bremen, he was discussing with other inspectors and local authority officials the training of police officers.

A page brought in a note to Herr Stirner of the mayor's office. Stirner read it and stared at his plate for a minute before standing up. "Gentlemen, we must postpone this gathering. I have just been informed that President Hindenburg has invited Herr Hitler to become chancellor of Germany."

There was silence.

An inspector from the Spandau department said, "Well, can't we go on with the meeting? Nothing's changed, and this is important stuff we're discussing."

"Everything has changed," Stirner said. "For one thing, I am no longer in office. Good day to you, gentlemen."

On his way back to the Alex, Schmidt heard wildly happy cheering outside the Kaiserhof, where Hitler had returned from his appointment with President Hindenburg.

Sparse snow was melting as it hit the pavements. In the

shopping arcades, groups of people were gathered outside the radio shops listening to the news. More groups blocked the way in places, some people shaking others' hands in congratulation, some shaking their heads. A woman dashed up to a storm trooper and kissed him on both cheeks before rushing off again.

What was marvelous to Schmidt was how little else had changed. People were still going about their business. The hot-chestnut seller was in his usual place, a street cleaner brushed frozen rubbish from the gutters and put it in his barrow. A woman coming out of the hairdresser's tied a scarf around her head and then put up an umbrella as if everything were normal.

That was until he reached Alexanderplatz.

"SO," HOWIE SAID to Esther, "the loonies have finally taken over the asylum."

He'd come to say good-bye; he was catching the night plane. The previous night, getting out of his car to enter his hotel, he'd been roughed up in the street by a couple of storm troopers. *Collier's,* frightened for one of its best correspondents, was recalling him.

"I wouldn't be leaving now," he said, licking his cut lip, "only the good Dr. Goebbels has canceled my visa. Schmidt still in Bremen?"

"He's back—he was going straight into the office. He'll be home tonight."

They were sitting in the kitchen over a cup of coffee, listening to the radio. Anna was wandering the living room, waiting for Meyer to go.

"Only three Nazis in the cabinet, can that be so bad?" Esther switched off the radio. "Howie, can it?"

"They got the posts that matter, kid."

The phone rang, and they heard Anna pick it up.

Howie jerked a thumb in her direction. "Now then, sweetie," he said, "before I go. Is Sleeping Beauty the real princess? Aw, come on."

"Maybe one day, Howie, not now."

Anna was in the doorway. "That was Herr Hitler," she said, carefully casual. "Well, was his equerry. I am to go see him. He sends his car for me." She smiled at them. "You see?"

. . .

A crowd of more than fifty uniformed policemen stood outside the Alex, shouting. Passersby had stopped to watch them, and more were gathering.

Schmidt pushed through and tapped one of them on the shoulder. "What's happened, Bollo?"

They'd worked together, but he didn't think Bollo recognized him; the man's face was idiotic. "We been sacked," he said. "They sacked us."

Schmidt said, "Nonsense."

"They won't even let us in to report," Bollo said. "Look."

Schmidt looked. Storm troopers stood outside the entrance to the Alex with rifles trained on the policemen.

"Let me through." He walked forward until he was opposite the guns. "What the hell are you doing?"

One of the storm troopers passed his rifle to a colleague and took a list out of his pocket. "Name?"

"I am Inspector Schmidt, I work here. Now, what the hell are you doing?"

"Your warrant card."

"What?"

"Show me your warrant card."

Schmidt showed it.

"Very well. You may go in."

He went straight to Ringer's office, but Ringer's secretary, white-faced, told him that the chief had been summoned to Department 1A.

Schmidt went down to the canteen and found it virtually deserted. The cooks were putting chairs on tables and wiping down the empty counters. In one corner, Tudjmann of Vice was finishing a cup of coffee.

"What the hell's happening to those men out there?" Schmidt asked him.

Tudjmann shrugged. "It looks as if we're being cleansed of dross at last."

"What?"

"They're all troublemakers," Tudjmann said. "I've seen the list."

"Guns were being trained on policemen, Tudjmann. Policemen."

Tudjmann stood up. "Did you think the country could drift in the Weimar's imbecilic way forever? We have a leader at last. *Now* we will see."

On the stairs Schmidt bumped into Willi Ritte hurrying down them.

"Come to my office."

"I'm in a hell of a rush, boss. There's to be a parade."

"My office, Willi."

Willi refused a chair when they got there; he was agitated. "There's to be a fucking great victory parade tonight; they're pulling out all the stops. Block the streets, line the route."

"What's happening to those men outside?"

Then Willi sat down. "Bad business. They been sacked—most of 'em pushed before they could jump. Ohliger was spokesman for the federation, so I suppose they wouldn't want him around. And Todt's brother's a Red. Schott's married to a Jewess. Things like that. Fifty-two of them. They were all on a list."

Lists, Schmidt thought. They're good at lists.

"And right away fifty-two SS came in to take their place," Willi said.

"On whose orders?"

"Department 1A. Seems they've got authority from the new Prussian minister of the interior."

"And who's that?"

"Hermann Göring."

"Christ." When he'd left Bismarck Allee this morning, the minister of the interior had been Wilhelm Groener. Three hours, he thought. They'd been planning for this so that it was all ready to slip into place. The efficiency daunted him. In three hours the world had shifted on its axis; he could feel the vibration from it through his shoes, making his legs tremble.

"About the list, boss." Willi's big feet scuffed the linoleum. "They say it's not just the uniform boys."

"I see." So it wasn't merely haste to organize a victory parade that was making Willi Ritte nervous in his office. "I'm on it, am I?"

More feet scuffing, and then Willi looked up, pleading, "Boss, I got seven children and a wife."

"I know you have." He felt a deep sadness. He got up and went around his desk to pat his old friend on the shoulder. "Give them my love."

"Fuck it, fuck all of it." Willi's hand came up for a moment to clutch at Schmidt's. He got up and saluted. "Good-bye, sir."

"Good-bye, Sergeant."

"Today?" Esther asked. "Hitler's sent for you *today*?"

"Why not? He has power to see me now."

"When?"

"Now. He sends his car."

Esther turned for help to Howie. "Today."

"He knew this was coming," Meyer said. "He's had time to make his plans—apparently Her Imperial Anna's on them."

"Not a word, Howie. Promise me, not until I see what it means for her. If you love me, not a word."

"Okay," Howie said. "But take your camera."

"I will."

"You do not come, Esther," Anna said. "I do not take a Jew to see Herr Hitler. I am the grand duchess."

"I don't care. I'm coming."

"Listen, Your Highness," Howie said, "grand duchesses don't turn up alone, they take ladies-in-waiting along. Looks kinda poor, a Russian princess going by herself."

"What you know? You're a newspaperman."

"Listen, kid, I've interviewed Hitler more times than you've put on panties. I've interviewed royalty, for Chrissake. I know things about England's Prince of Wales and a certain American divorcée that'd curl your hair, and I tell you no blueblood goes visiting without an attendant. Take it from Uncle Howie. In fact, how'd you like to take Uncle Howie along?"

Anna sat down. "You come, I don't go."

"Okay, okay. He wouldn't be pleased to see me anyhow."

Esther tried phoning Schmidt at the Alex, eventually slamming down the phone. "An idiot on the switchboard keeps saying that he doesn't work there."

Anna allowed them to dress her. Esther did her hair while Howie polished her best pair of shoes and displayed unexpected knowledge of ladies' couture. "No, not the dress, the suit. She doesn't want to look cute, she wants to look businesslike. No, no, kid, not that hat. Try this one. And she'll need gloves—she got any gloves?" Anna's nails were bitten to the quick. "Here, these'll match."

"I wear my mink. The Duke of Leuchtenberg gave it me."

"Yep, it'll impress Adolf."

Esther, brushing the coat down, had a searing moment of doubt. "I shouldn't be letting her do this."

They both turned on her.

"I go," Anna said.

And Howie said, "You kidding me? You don't turn down the chancellor of Germany on his first day. Sweetheart, this is a *story.*"

It was. And, with luck, a picture; her nose was twitching for it. She gave in to the inevitable and resumed brushing.

The car, a shining, swastika-pennanted Daimler, was at the door while Esther was attempting once more to phone Schmidt at the Alex. Eventually she gave up. "That idiot's still saying he doesn't work there. Should I take the plate camera? For a portrait?"

"No," Howie said, "look too much like a setup. You're hot stuff with the Leica. Take that."

She was still stuffing film into her pockets as a black-uniformed corporal of the Schutzstaffel, Hitler's personal bodyguard, opened the Daimler's door for them. While he went around to the driver's seat, Anna muttered, "I do not introduce you. I just say my lady-in-waiting."

"Anything, anything." Shutter speeds, depth, exposure—oh, hell, should have brought flashbulbs, no, must be natural light. I'll get him on a balcony or something with her, he's always on a bloody balcony. Shaking hands with her? Kissing her hand? Yes, please, *please.* And then a portrait, a close-up, the eyes.

Howie, standing on the pavement, saw them off with an elaborate bow.

"Where are we going?" Anna asked the driver.

"Kaiserhof." The SS obviously didn't believe in courtesy, but then neither did Berlin cabdrivers.

"The Kaiserhof." Anna settled back comfortably; she loved good hotels.

"All officers to report to the canteen," Frau Pritt said. The swastika brooch was back on her lapel.

The canteen was comfortless; its kitchens were closed and empty, its counters bare. Men gathered in groups, speculating, spreading rumor, drifting like wraiths.

After an hour somebody said, "The hell with this," and a posse broke into the kitchen cupboards and made black coffee for the rest. There was no milk.

One or two tried to return to their offices and start work but were sent back again. "Good day for crime," somebody said, and raised a nervous laugh.

Ringer came in, and there was a move toward him. "Any news, sir? What's happening?"

Ringer didn't answer. He went and sat at a table, staring into space. He was given a cup of coffee, and after that nobody went near him.

At four o'clock a storm trooper came in with a list and pinned it on the notice board: *"The following personnel are hereby dismissed from the service and are required to leave the building by 1730 hours. By order of Hermann Göring, Prussian Minister of the Interior."* Ringer's name was at the top of the list, Schmidt's about halfway down.

The Kaiserhof had been Hitler's Berlin campaign headquarters for some time now—ruining, as far as the avant-garde was concerned, a congenial watering hole. It was still a hotel, and other, less discriminating clients were gathering for tea in the lounge, its plush furniture and even the smartly dressed women being made to look fussy by the sharp, black lines of SS officers scattered around the room. Cheers and laughter came from the American Bar where more SS were celebrating, and champagne corks popped in staccato salvos.

Anna and Esther were shown upstairs to where the Nazi entourage had taken over an entire floor. Esther heard ticker tape clicking in one room, typewriters going in another marked PROPAGANDA. Female clerks scurried quietly in and out of doors; uniformed men stalked the carpeted corridors. The air smelled cleanly of paper, good cigars, and suppressed excitement.

The *money,* Esther thought. She compared it to the Moabit Communist Party HQ, where a disused factory contained the phones, typewriters, ticker-tape machines, fierce argument, and cigarette smoke thick enough to choke you, all on one open floor and where nobody could afford more uniform than an armband.

And the *discipline.* Their Führer was in office at last—the day they had worked and waited for had dawned after years of planning—but that same planning now moved them forward as if on ball bearings. That's the terrifying thing, she thought. They know where they're going. They're programmed.

She and Anna were put into an anteroom to wait, sustained with a tray of tea and the assurance by a butler that the Führer was sorry, he was naturally very busy and would attend to Her Imperial Highness as soon as he could.

There were men in the room, wing-collared, bemedaled, some with sashes, one or two in uniform with ceremonial swords getting in the way of their thighs, few of them talking, inhibited by the presence of the butler standing at the door. Every five minutes the door would open and let an ambassador out before the butler ushered another one in. "His Excellency the Italian ambassador . . ." "His Excellency this." "His Excellency that."

All going in to congratulate Hitler on behalf of their country, she supposed. And all being given exactly five minutes. Could she get her picture in five minutes? Should she start clicking the moment she went in? Would he let her?

Half an hour went by, and the door kept on opening for another dignitary to be announced, then closing as he went, opening again. . . .

Esther worried about the light and kept wandering to the window as if that would encourage it to stay in the sky. If the grand duchess were this bloody important to him, she shouldn't be kept cooling her heels. On the other hand, all these representatives were kept waiting—it was probably deliberate.

Anna enjoyed it, sipping her tea and glancing through the Fascist *Der Stürmer,* absolutely at ease.

Waiting on Hitler, Esther thought. Everybody's waiting on Hitler.

"The Führer will see you now."

Esther and Anna got up.

THEY LINED the hall to say good-bye to Ringer, those who'd been sacked and some of those who hadn't. But the old man didn't look at anybody, just walked past them and out onto the steps. They saw him dither for a moment, accustomed to having the police limousine waiting for him, then square his shoulders, signal to one of the taxis in the stand opposite the Platz, and step out toward it.

There it goes, Schmidt thought, Old Germany with its waxed mustaches, marching steadfastly into oblivion.

He felt a deep pang of grief, the first time since the list had gone up that he'd felt anything. Shock and anger—though they would unseat everything else in a minute—were being overridden by numbness. No, disbelief. Not just at the sacking of some of Berlin's best policemen, himself included, but at the brutality of it. Nobody, not Hermann Göring in whose name it was being done, not Diels, no official of the new order, had put in an appearance. Just storm troopers with lists. And guns. The maximum of humiliation with the minimum of effort.

He lingered at the doors for a moment before going upstairs to fetch his coat and hat. Snow fell clearly in the shrill, flashing light sent out by signs for Pilsner, Opel cars, for the latest American movie, *42nd Street.* A pretty young woman in a beret was wearily taking off the cardboard sign that had hung around her neck saying HELLO, I'M LOOKING FOR WORK, I CAN DO SHORTHAND, TYPING, AND I CAN SPEAK FRENCH AND ENGLISH. Sparks flew out from underneath the trams as they crossed connecting lines. Soon people would be going home.

Gunpoint, Schmidt thought. Didn't they see policemen being threatened with guns?

Across the Platz, outside a bookshop, he could see a storm trooper watching the sullen owner remove a display of books from its window.

Schmidt had been meaning to buy Alfred Döblin's *Berlin Alexanderplatz* for some time—probably couldn't now; Döblin was a Jew.

He waited for anger, but all he could summon up was awe.

THEY WERE SHOWN into a large and beautiful room with an enormous table desk against the big window at its far end. The single occupant was out of proportion to it, too small, the sleeves of his brown uniform just slightly overlong, giving him the look of a child in hand-me-downs.

"Yes," it said, "the woman I most want to see."

Hitler crossed the floor swiftly and clasped Anna's hands in both of his own, staring intently into her eyes as if reading her soul.

Rasputin's trick, Esther thought.

She was introduced—"My lady-in-waiting"—and he repeated the maneuver, though not for as long, and this time merely shaking her hand.

"I hope my people have looked after Your Imperial Highness. You have had refreshment? I would not have kept you waiting." He clapped his little hands together. "But this is a special day; business must come before pleasure."

He'd learned it all, the graciousness of a tyrant. Where had this common, unsophisticated little man got his impenetrable self-belief? And the ability to impose it? Genius, Esther thought. Criminal genius. It was the confidence trick of all time.

"Yes, this is a great day, a great day—not for me but for Germany. And for you, too, madam. For Russia. Let me tell you . . ."

They were signaled to sit down. He remained on his feet, pacing, giving Anna the benefit of his worldview.

Esther tried to concentrate; Howie would want her to remember every word, but at the same time she must assess angles, the pearly natural light from the windows, the planes of the face, the eyes, blue as Anna's and her own, the silly mustache, the hand-me-down sleeves.

Anyway, the voice that enraptured masses didn't work with an audience of two, not for her; it was machinery. Occasionally it rattled out something so staggering it caught her attention: "Russia must be cleansed of Jewish Bolshevism, that racial tuberculosis threatening the globe. . . . The Bolshevik commissars are Jewish. . . . England will change her attitude when she sees that such is my aim and will join us in the enterprise. . . . Old Russia must learn Nationalist Socialist principles. . . ."

At last he said, "The throne shall be returned to the last of the true Romanovs." He bowed to Anna, who inclined her head, smiling.

He has no perception of her, Esther thought; he doesn't see people except in relationship to himself. He looks, but he doesn't see. She's what he wants her to be—perhaps she is.

Ten minutes gone. She's being given more time than the others.

"But I should tell Your Highness, Germany's need for living space is predominant; much of western Russia is ethnically German and must be returned to the Fatherland."

This was what he meant by *Lebensraum,* then. Russia. He actually *is* insane.

Anna nodded graciously. He could have Russia's ethnic-German bits.

"Russia must look eastward for her own expansion."

Oh, all right, Anna's nod said, she'd look east.

Children, that's what they are; not just her, the two of them. I've seen children play like this. You be Russia, I'll be Germany.

"I have Your Imperial Highness's blessing, do I not?"

"Of course, my Führer."

Where did she learn to do that? Extend her hand like a queen?

Hitler shook it in both of his. He was pleased.

"Allow me to present you with a copy of *Mein Kampf.*" He and Anna moved toward the desk, and Esther, recovering, said, "Sir, Her Imperial Highness would very much like a photograph of you and her together."

Hitler wagged his finger at Anna. "A snapshot for your personal album? Very well, then. Soon you and I shall have our official portrait taken."

I'll give him damn snapshots. She maneuvered them into position by the desk, metered the light, and started clicking. "A handshake, thank you. Now a little farther apart. . . . Sir, if you'd move to your right as you sign, just there, wonderful." She changed lenses. The light wasn't bad. "If you'd just rest on the desk, that's very nice, and perhaps put your chin in your hand. Oh, that is so . . ." Anna was out of the shot now, and he knew he was her sole subject, but he liked it.

She went on shooting, grateful for every second. He continued posing. She even changed film, and it could have gone on, but there was a tap on the door and the butler put his head around it. "I am sorry, my Führer, but Major Günsche is back from Munich and says it's urgent."

Hitler raised his hands in mock dismay. "Forgive me, my dear Anastasia. But we shall meet again. Soon, soon."

Esther, still standing by the desk at the window end of the room, took another shot of their farewell. A couple more of them moving together toward the door. And another one as Anna stopped.

Hitler, who'd taken two steps forward, had to pause and turn around to her. "What is it?"

It was a man who'd taken the butler's place in the doorway. He was big and dressed in the uniform of an officer and carried a folder of papers under one arm. He'd taken off his cap, ready to salute his Führer, displaying fair hair and the Slavic slant of his cheekbones.

It was as if the Medusa stood between him and Anna, invisible to all but the two of them. They had become stone.

Somehow—and for what remained of her life, Esther was proud of possessing the wit to do it—she lifted her camera to her eye, focused, and took a picture of Hitler, Anna, and, clear in their background, the man who'd killed Natalya.

"WHAT ABOUT MY pension?" Bolle asked. "Twenty-four years, I'm entitled." He slammed his hand on the table. "I'm entitled to respect. Not . . ." He pointed to the list still on the noticeboard.

They'd gone back to the canteen and made themselves coffee, because Bolle couldn't yet bear to go home and tell his wife he'd been sacked.

Schmidt nodded and sipped his coffee, some sense beginning to return. *Lists,* he thought. Christ, they'll have access to all my files.

Bolle buried his head in his hands. "They can't do this."

"They've done it," Schmidt said. "They've changed the world. And all in one day." He still marveled at it.

"Never mind a fucking day," Bolle said, "I've been a policeman twenty-four years. Quarter of a century of duty. Shit, I even voted for 'em. What've I done, that's what I want to know? How do I tell the wife? How'll we manage if they don't give me a pension?"

His voice mingled with the distant screech of S-bahn trains entering and leaving Alexanderplatz Station, a lament for a city that, outside, insisted on going about its business as if nothing had happened.

Schmidt was able to think now. He'd gone from shock to anger—his hands were still shaking from both—and eventually into coherence. His detective mind began fitting things together, his own personal abasement—a mere dot—sprouting lines that went out and out, curling, entangling, into a bigger picture that formed the mouth of the abyss. Eisenmenger had been right, Meyer had been right, even he himself had been right—merely hadn't applied it, hadn't believed.

In a minute he would go upstairs and phone Esther. We're going, he would tell her. Draw out any money you've got, I'll withdraw mine, and we'll go; it doesn't matter where. They're taking over the police; law has broken down. He wouldn't say there was no safety anymore, especially for her. She'd know that.

He imagined her saying, "You can't leave Germany. You love Germany."

He would say, "I don't love it more than I love you. Besides, it isn't Germany anymore, it's another country."

At the table Bolle maintained a savage keening, reluctant to face his wife and the outside world. "Why me?" he kept asking. "Why me?"

Yes, *why* him? Most of the others whose names had been on the list were Social Democrat voters, like Schmidt himself. They certainly had reason for firing Inspector Siegfried Schmidt, known liberal, consorter with Jews, a man who in Ringer's words was "a good detective but a bad policeman," unreliable when it came to obeying orders.

Bolle, however, *was* a good policeman, not an imaginative one but stolid, dutiful, typical of a middle class that, with its memory scarred by 1923, had voted National Socialist in a time of trouble.

Would Bolle have obeyed their orders if they'd kept him on? Probably. Asked to arrest radicals, Jews, queers, and Bolshies without charge, he would have drawn no parallel with the arrest of his unionist friend by the storm troopers. It would have seemed to him merely a way of establishing stability—until it dawned on him that his stability was a tyranny that could arrest any protester—his own son, even.

So why Bolle? Why Bolle *and* him?

The Anastasia case. It was the only common denominator. Bolle had worked on the Marlene murder, had the description of a killer the Nazis wanted left undescribed, had read the Anastasia file.

Christ, they're efficient, Schmidt thought. Take no chances, take no prisoners. "Time we went," he said gently. But Bolle shook his head.

There was no comfort to be given; Schmidt rested his hand on Bolle's shoulder for a moment and left him sitting alone in the corner of a huge and empty canteen.

A storm trooper standing at the bottom of the stairs stopped him.

"I'm going up to my office to fetch my hat and coat," Schmidt said.

"Wait." The man got out his list to consult it.

"Oh, fuck off." Schmidt pushed past him and went up the stairs. He'd had enough of lists.

Nobody shot him.

It was getting dark, and he had to switch on his office light.

He picked up the phone, surprised it was still connected, and phoned Esther's number, hearing it ring and ring. She wasn't in.

Outside, in the parking lot, an armored car, known accurately but without affection at the Alex as "The Kettle," was grinding past the barrier, on its way to break up some demonstration or another.

God, he thought, let there be demonstrations somewhere, riots, protest. Let somebody fight back—they're snatching the law. The Law. They've stolen it, like a goddamn necklace. Who *is* protesting? The minister of justice? The Reichstag? Where are they? Criminals are taking over the country. It's a fucking putsch, and they're getting away with it; they're stealing Germany. Cassandra must have felt like this, seeing that the Greeks were coming and not a single fucker listening to her. Well, they're in now. The Alex is their Trojan horse.

And what are *you* doing about it?

He felt under his desk for the metal wastepaper can, took it out, then went over to the filing cabinet and the drawer that contained his personal files, records of old arrests, old contacts, informants. He scooped them out and carried them over to the can, stuffing them into it.

Thieves, queers, prostitutes, con men—not the new chancellor's favorite people, but, compared to him, clean and upright men and women. Schmidt would be damned if he left their addresses for the SS. He took out one of the sheets at random and saw that it was the record of Rudi the Flasher, Rudi who'd been stalking the streets around Charlottenburg on the night Natalya Tchichagova had been killed, Rudi now an impotent old man.

He got out his lighter, lit a cigarette, and then applied the flame to poor old Rudi and dropped him, burning, into the can.

Frau Pritt was in the doorway. "Stop it. What are you doing? Stop it."

He began shaking paper out of the other folders and stuffing them into the fire in the can.

"Stop it," Pritt screamed. "You are destroying government property. It is against orders. Stop it." She lunged at the can, trying to lift it off the desk, but an eruption of flame drove her back.

He heard her running down the corridor shouting.

Not much of a protest, this. Not much to weigh down his end of the unbalanced scales, but, Christ, he had to do something to put a spoke in their wheel and prove he was a man and not a dog they'd kicked out of its home.

It was quiet on this floor. Virtually all the officers and men who hadn't been sacked were being briefed in the lecture hall on their duties for the forthcoming victory parade.

Victory parade.

He kept grabbing more folders, amazed at the number of people he'd persuaded, bribed, or blackmailed into giving him information over the years: small-time crooks, mainly, *Winkelbankiers,* illegal backstreet currency dealers, pickpockets, Gypsies, smugglers, counterfeiters, unlicensed hawkers—Jews, mainly—racketeers, bigamists.

Innocents, all of them, their combined sins a mere peccadillo compared to the political crime about to overwhelm them.

The smell was making him cough, so he raised the window just a fraction to cause a draft. Smoke from the can poured toward the wintry outside air as if along a chimney. Pinched faces were transferred out of his memory and onto paper, where the heat curled and flared them into ash; he might have been burning them alive.

"Stop that, please," Busse said. He was in the doorway, wearing an SS uniform. Light glinted off his spectacles, and he had a Luger pistol in his hand.

Entering the flat, and finding that Schmidt wasn't in it, Esther went straight for the phone to call him at the Alex. All the way back in the car, she'd been desperate to tell him: I've seen him. I know his name. *I've got his picture.*

The same idiot on the switchboard, obviously a trainee, insisted that Inspector Schmidt did not work for the police, so for now she slammed the receiver down and set about the other thing she'd been dying to do. She went into her darkroom with her camera. Then she popped her head around the door. "Anna, I'm developing. Do not, repeat *not,* come in." It was a prohibition Anna had twice broken, to the ruin of some spectacular film.

The shock to Anna of seeing the man who'd pursued her for most of her life had been very great, and when they'd got to the lobby in the Kaiserhof, she'd had to sit down. But once she'd seen that he was not coming after her, she'd rallied surprisingly well, as if her fear had been automatic. Perhaps she'd realized there was no danger, that he and she would keep each other's secret. "I am under the Führer's protection now, am I not?" she'd said.

At home she'd kicked off her shoes and collapsed expansively onto the sofa, humming to herself, smiling a grand-duchess smile.

Esther shut the door, turned on the safelight, and got to work. Even while the film was still in the developer, she could see that the work was *good.* The shot of Anna, Hitler, and the killer would need some toning, but, by God, she'd caught it—Hitler off balance because the other two had switched attention from him, the rigidity of Anna's neck, and the eyes of the killer alive, appalled, in that lumpen face.

Genius. And genius to have inquired of the butler as they were being shown out. *"The officer, ma'am? That's Major Günsche. SA Intelligence. He liaises between the Führer and Colonel Röhm when the Führer's in Berlin. Yes, I believe his first name is Reinhardt."*

It was one hell of a photograph in its own right, shrieking with tension.

As a document to damn with, it was clear as clear. Got him. Got him. I've got him, Natalya. Nick, Marlene, I've got him.

The darkroom had seemed loud with exultation; now it died away, and in the quiet came the first squeak of fear. She was doing what those three had done; she had gone out and met a killer. Literally, she was exposing him.

She washed the negatives, not rushing, but wanting to. Hung them up to dry. Stepped out into the empty living room. It was quiet there, too.

"Anna!"

Anna's voice came from her room. "Why you shouting?"

"It's all right. I didn't know where you were."

She walked to the phone, lifted the receiver, and dialed. This time she didn't confuse the idiot by asking for Schmidt by name. "Multiple Murder Department, please." And sagged with relief as she heard the call being put through.

Schmidt raised his arm. "Heil . . ." Then he batted his forehead. "Don't tell me. . . . On the tip of my tongue. I'll get it in a minute."

Busse didn't waver; neither did the pistol. "You are destroying Reich property."

Schmidt grabbed more files.

Busse walked up to the desk, putting the Luger against Schmidt's back. "Stop or I will put you under arrest."

Schmidt doubled up the last of the files, stuffed them in, and watched them take. He moved away from the Luger, went around the desk, and sat in his chair, opening a drawer; there was a notebook in here that might be useful to them. He took it and dropped it into the can. Finally he looked up. "Yes? What do you want?"

The uniform suited Busse. Clean black lines, lightning flashes on the collar tabs, the death's-head on the cap band. It gave him dash, authority, menace, as if the accountant in spectacles had merely been a chrysalis that had burst into something more beautiful and more terrible. Still with spectacles.

"I hope the Anastasia file isn't among those ashes," he said, "No. Of course it isn't. Where is it? We didn't find it in the Jewess's flat."

The gloves were off—if, Schmidt thought, they'd ever been on. "You've got it," he said.

"We have one copy, you have another. And we would like it, please."

"Why? Adolf going to take up the White Russian cause, is he? Kiss the sleeping grand duchess and wake her up? Put her on the back of his horse and charge off to Moscow?"

"Please don't try to rile me, Schmidt. The Führer is waiting on our findings, but we have not yet finished our investigation."

"I see," Schmidt said. "You haven't shown him the file yet."

"Evidence as to the lady's authenticity is still inconclusive." Busse allowed himself a quirk of the lips. "As you have found out, we have been rather busy."

"I'll give you that," Schmidt said. Even pretty uniforms designed down to the bloody buttons and waiting in their closets.

He noticed an instruction lying on top of papers in his In tray: *"From today all staff will use the Heil Hitler greeting and farewell. By order of Hermann Göring, Prussian Minister of the Interior."* The good Frau Pritt, no doubt, preparing for his successor. He crumpled it and tossed it in the still-smoldering can. "Well, Busse, arrest or no arrest, I'm hanging on to that file for a bit. You never know. Adolf might get voted out next time, and the police will start catching killers again."

"Tell me where it is, Schmidt, and then you can go home." Busse was being quite reasonable about it. They'd been neighbors, old friends. A reasonable old neighborhood Nazi—with a gun.

"No."

Busse glanced at his watch—the Luger didn't move. His wrists were knobbly and very white, hairless. "I am due to take part in the victory parade," he said, "but I think there is just time to bring your Jewess here. I am certain she knows where the file is and can be persuaded to tell me and one of my storm troopers downstairs—under pressure."

The last trail of smoke from the can drifted back into the room with some snowflakes—a breeze had sprung up, swinging a slice of cold air into the fug like an ax, ruffling the *M* poster and distorting Lorre's face.

He's a family man, Schmidt thought; there's a nice Frau Busse and a lot of little Busses. Nazis get married, they have children; they've sat by a sick child's bed, seen a parent die. They know the budding and the falling like the rest of us. What withers them? This thing in front of me is a stalk.

The phone rang, and without thinking he picked it up; this was his office. "Inspector Schmidt."

Esther's voice came over the line, high and clear with excitement. "I've got him, Schmidt. We went to the Kaiserhof, Anna and me. Hitler sent for her. He's thrilled with her. We were just leaving, and, Schmidt, oh, *Schmidt,* he came in. It was him. It was R.G. And I've got him. I took a photograph of him and Hitler and Anna. He's Major Reinhardt Günsche. SA Intelligence. Schmidt, Schmidt, we've got him."

Everything narrowed down. Busse evaporated into irrelevance. The constriction against Schmidt's throat became a different fear. He saw Hannelore's killer climbing the stairs with her shopping and waiting for her at the top.

"Schmidt. Are you there, darling? I've got him."

Gently, he said, "Esther . . ."

"Yes?"

"Get out of the flat. Take Anna and get out. Don't stop to pick anything up. Do you hear me?"

"Yes. But the film."

"Do it." He was shouting and didn't hear the rap on the door of 29c, but he heard Esther call, "No, Anna, don't open it. Anna!" and a distant scream and then a long, slow knocking as from a telephone receiver swinging against a table leg where it had been let fall.

"Esther!"

Over the line he heard the far-off clatter of boots and shoes going down the stairs.

24

"WHERE'S HE TAKING them?" Schmidt asked conversationally, walking around the desk.

"What?" Busse was staring at the phone.

Schmidt gave him a push in the chest. "R.G. of Munich. He's just raided my flat. His name's Günsche. He's SA. He's going to kill my girl. Where's he going to do it?" He gave Busse another push.

"I don't know. The SA are a law to themselves. Why should I know?"

"Because you do. There's a killing ground. They've got a place where they torture people and kill them. He took Marlene there before he dumped her at Schwanenwerder. Where is it?" He pushed Busse again.

"Marlene?" Busse wasn't keeping up.

"This man," Schmidt said, still speaking pleasantly, "has taken Solomonova and Anderson out of their flat. I just heard him do it. They'd been to the Kaiserhof to meet your Führer. They bumped into R.G. of Munich. Recognized him. He's got to kill them." All the time he was pushing Busse in the chest, and Busse was letting him. "Don't tell me you haven't been keeping an eye on the SA. Tell me where they've gone."

The last push sent Busse staggering so that the Luger hit against the wall. "He's going to kill her, Busse, you bastard. He's going to kill your Führer's grand duchess, because he's going to kill my woman and he daren't get rid of one without the other."

"Stop that. *Stop*." Busse brought up the gun. "I don't know."

"The Anastasia file is with a friend and will be published if anything happens to me or Solomonova. I'm quite clear on that point, am I? Anna Anderson has just been to tea with Hitler; he's thrilled with her. The czar's daughter, his Russian puppet. He hasn't read the file, has he? You haven't shown it to him yet. He doesn't know she's more likely a Polish peasant, or even a Gypsy. Who had an illegitimate baby at one time. But *you* know, Busse, you've read the statement from the hospital. Let me think. . . . Are Gypsies on Adolf's list? I believe they are. A newspaper's going to print all that, Busse, and when your Führer reads it, he's not going to be pleased, because he'll look like a fool."

He was using dirty ammunition, but if he didn't, Esther would die.

"These are dramatics," Busse said. "Why will this man take them anywhere?"

"He likes to kill in the open. Tell you what I'll do," Schmidt went on. "I'll give you the file. I'll give you the file and my word that Fräulein Solomonova and I will say nothing. Ever. Just get me there in time."

He watched Busse assess the balance sheet. It was a matter of whether the Führer would persist in his choice against the evidence, whether he preferred his fairy tales untrammeled by facts, whether—God help us all—he'd carry an oriflamme that had pitiable humanity's stain on it.

There was throbbing in his temples: she's dying, R.G.'s going to kill her, she's dying, he'll kill her. But Schmidt was a hunter, always had been, and he was holding out fresh meat for Busse to snap at.

"No good trying to make black white this time, Busse," he said. "Everybody'll see what color it is."

"Yes," Busse said, not listening. He sat himself in Schmidt's chair to consider. "But at least the Führer has made no public declaration so far."

Schmidt stood and watched Busse reject the meat and knew he hadn't been offering bait, he'd been digging a trap. And had fallen into it.

Busse had been dubious about Anna, it was why he'd wanted all copies of the file under his control. Now he had to jump one way or the other—and was jumping out of reach. Hitler would be persuaded to reject Anna as an impostor; the Führer would be stopped from making a fool of himself before the public got wind of the fact that he had.

Busse stretched a hand to the phone . . . then brought it back. Diels, like almost everybody else in the building, had gone to the parade. He looked up at Schmidt, settling back. "It is regrettable, but there is nothing to be done."

Esther was dead, then. The world didn't hold her anymore. The particular, irreplaceable thing that she was to him was going and taking all that mattered with her.

Busse was bothering him, suddenly standing beside him, asking questions. "You say Günsche? Is that Major Günsche? SA Intelligence?"

"Yes." Schmidt looked up. There'd been a change.

"Röhm's bum-boy. Well, well," Busse said. "There *is* a place. Unauthorized, of course—those SA get above themselves—but I've heard about it."

"Take me there." He grabbed his coat.

They were out in the corridor, its dreary Bakelite shades directing pools of light down onto the linoleum in patches that left areas of darkness in between. He'd never seen it so empty. Or so quiet.

Busse paused, and Schmidt was impatient with him. "What now?"

"I might need reinforcements."

"For God's sake, he's on his own—he's always on his own. You've got your damn gun."

Busse didn't move; he was considering. When he looked up, he said, "Yes, I have."

They went down the fire escape that led to the parking lot.

"Where is this place?"

"Grünewald."

"Shit." Far west. And Alexanderplatz as far east of the old city as you could get.

The cold was reviving; freezing air dulled the throbbing in his head.

No good to Esther if he didn't think. His mind narrowed down to a wicked point of light that made some things gleam with clarity and left everything else in blackness.

The snow was thin but beginning to settle. Behind him Busse gave a "Tcha" as he slipped on the steps. All the police cars were out, even the antiriot Kettles. The only vehicle in the lot was a four-seater Mercedes tourer, an SS pennant on one side of its hood, a swastika flag on the other.

The parade, Schmidt thought. They've sent everybody to the parade. Good night for killers.

A storm trooper on guard at the back entrance met them at the bottom of the steps, revolver at the ready before he recognized Busse. "Heil Hitler."

"Heil Hitler." Busse pushed Schmidt past him.

The storm trooper trotted anxiously behind them. "Sir, sir."

"What?" Busse was already unclipping the weather cover off the tourer. "You drive," he told Schmidt.

"I can't." There'd never been a need; he'd had police drivers or public transport.

Busse looked at him, surprised. "Oh, very well." He got into the driver's seat, putting the Luger on his left side where Schmidt couldn't reach it. Schmidt got into the passenger's seat.

The storm trooper was still bothered. "Sir, this man, sir. He's on the list."

Busse said, "I'm arresting him, Corporal. Go away."

"Heil Hitler."

At the gate the guard, not to be caught napping, had the barrier already raised for them and Heiled them through, his arm popping up and out like celery on springs.

Into the alley, turn, into Alexanderplatz, across the lines of a tram coming toward them, and they were speeding down Liebknecht toward the Linden. Hell of a lot of traffic about. One thing about the Nazi pennant—people got out of the way.

They were being halted at the Brandenburg Gate by a barrier and a policeman with a lantern. "Sorry, sir. Heil Hitler. You'll have to go around. We're closing it off for the victory parade."

"Move that thing out of the way," Busse said. "Führer's orders."

They were through. Schmidt settled deeper into the leather seat. "What does this thing do?"

"Hundred and twenty."

Good. With luck, R.G. wouldn't have anything as fast as this.

Through the Tiergarten, making good time.

"Left," he said. "What the fuck are you doing? Turn *left*."

"No, Bismarck Allee first. He might still have them there."

"He won't. He'll take them to Grünewald. Go south, go fucking south!"

"Be quiet."

"He likes to kill in the open," Schmidt said. "Oh, God, you're wasting *time*!" He heard his voice break.

"We'll see."

It's what his bunch would do, Schmidt thought. Kill them in the apartment and explain afterward. But R.G. doesn't dare explain; he's got to make them disappear.

Bismarckstrasse. They were turning into Bismarck Allee, very nearly knocking down an old man crossing the avenue. There was a kerfuffle outside number 29 that made him catch his breath, but it was an agitated Frau Schinkel surrounded by neighbors. The policeman who was supposed to have kept an eye on the house was with them. The front door stood open.

Busse pulled up. "What happened?"

Frau Schinkel's face was framed in Busse's window. She saw Schmidt. "A man in uniform took them away, Herr Schmidt. In a car. I told him, 'Fräulein Anderson is not a Jewess.' I said, 'Why do you take her?' but he took them. He took them without their coats."

"What sort of car?"

The patrolman's voice said, "It was an Audi. He sat in the back. He made the Jewess drive. He was an officer; I couldn't do anything."

"How long ago?"

"What does it matter how long ago?" Schmidt yelled at him, "Get on." Without their coats they'd die of cold before the bastard could cut their throats.

The image of her body, thin, scarred, infinitely beautiful, came into his mind so strongly that his fingertips felt her skin. "Get *on*."

They were driving again. Past the entrance to Charlottenburg Palace, and *now* they were turning left toward the Grünewald.

He could have taken them north toward Tegel or Reinickendorf, plenty of woodland there. And lakes. They could have gone north. They could have gone east, west. . . .

"You say you haven't been to this place before?" He had to shout. The force of their speed was making the hood flap loudly where one of the studs hadn't been done up properly.

"No. It's SA territory."

Shit, *shit*.

No streetlights now and houses becoming infrequent. Less traffic. Busse was driving well—the car's speedometer needle was trembling on the 90; the flap of the hood turned into drumming.

Good, that's good, go faster.

Without taking his eyes off the road, Busse reached out for the knob on the neat little radio in the dashboard. Turned it.

"*. . . the crowd is immense, threatening to overwhelm the cordons, and the police are trying to push it back, ready for the marchers.*"

You had to hand it to them. One day in power and Goebbels had commandeered State Radio to make an outside broadcast of the Nazis' celebration of victory.

And Busse was going to kill him. Schmidt had no doubt about it; he just didn't know what for. It hadn't come in a revelation; the knowledge had accreted like the freezing slush gathering along the edge of the windshield. Something had happened back there in the Alex; Busse had stopped to consider. He'd thought of taking reinforcements, of turning up at the killing ground in force, and then he hadn't. Instead of putting Schmidt under arrest and leaving him behind, he'd taken Schmidt along with him.

Which was illogical.

But Busse was a logical man. The eyes looking out from the glasses were those of Death playing chess. There was nothing left of the father and husband who'd lived downstairs, the knobbly-kneed, lederhosen-wearing, hiking accountant. Unlikable but understandable, that man had gone, and the creed of the Nazis that anything—*anything*—could be achieved if you were ruthless enough, had infused the thing that had taken his place.

When Busse had looked at him back there in the Alex corridor, Schmidt had seen himself reflected in those glasses—expendable.

Busse was going to kill him.

"Already we can hear the first blare of the trumpets from beyond the Brandenburg Gate. . . ."

The lights of oncoming vehicles appeared and were gone in the same second.

"You're missing the parade," Schmidt said. "Shame."

Suburbs. Houses, petering out to become more and more infrequent.

"And here they come!" shouted the radio announcer. *"Magnificent . . ."*

Think, think. You're a detective. Detect.

If Willi Ritte had been sitting on the hood of the Mercedes looking inward, he would have seen Schmidt's face go blank and his jaw slacken. And Willi would have read the signs.

I am Busse. I have read the Anastasia file and it worries me; Anderson may be an impostor, but my impulsive, intuitive, little Führer has adopted her cause, though, thank God, he has not yet declared for her in public.

"For a moment we return you to the studio for the announcement of the new chancellor's cabinet, which met at five o'clock this afternoon. . . ."

So if R.G. of Munich kills her, no harm done. Sorry, my Führer, she's dead as mutton. Just as well under the circumstances.

But if Major Günsche of SA Intelligence kills her . . .

Schmidt's eyes opened. That's when it had changed. That's when Busse had sat up and taken notice—when he'd realized who it was had taken the women.

Trees flashing past, white phantoms in the lights of the car, a glimpse of a lake, and then it was gone, air cold on the ears and smelling of pine and water. They were near Grünewald.

Think. Eisenmenger told you. He told you twice: *Röhm has become too powerful, and therefore, like all threats to Herr Hitler, must be dealt with. He's a queer anyway, and our Adolf loathes queers.*

Röhm's bum-boy, Busse had said of Major Günsche of the SA. And if Schmidt had heard loathing, he'd heard it then.

The Gestapo hadn't been able to dispose quietly of R.G. of Munich because Röhm had been protecting him; Röhm, the too-powerful, Röhm, the homosexual whom Hitler was finding to be a threat to his own position.

But we can dispose of him now, *mein Führer.* And Röhm with him. I, Busse, of your Secret State Police, am in a position to rid you of them both, because Röhm's bum-boy has killed your pet, the grand duchess. Günsche is a homicidal maniac, out of control; he has a long record of killing, and Röhm has countenanced it.

The radio droned with the announcer's voice: "*. . . Vice Chancellor, Herr Franz von Papen; Reichs Minister of the Interior, Herr Wilhelm Frick; Reichs Minister of Agriculture, Herr Alfred Hugenberg; Reichs Minister for Public Enlightenment and Propaganda, Herr Joseph Goebbels . . .*"

Yes, thought Schmidt, the death of Anastasia by one of Röhm's henchmen would be news all over the world. It would infuriate Hitler. It would certainly provide the excuse to topple Röhm.

But for that, Anna needed to be the real Anastasia. Adolf wouldn't care too much about the death of an impostor—which publication of Schmidt's file could prove that she was.

That's why he's brought me along, Schmidt thought. It's why he hasn't got men with him and why he's hurrying. He'll let Günsche kill Anna. But if Esther's still alive, Busse can threaten to kill her as well, unless I give him the file. And when I have, he's going to kill both of us, the two living creatures who can validate the truth of it.

"*. . . in charge of military production, Herr Einwen Braun . . .*"

"Aaah" A long-drawn-out expulsion of breath from Busse made Schmidt look at him. "Excellent, excellent." The man was smiling and tapping the wheel. "My brother-in-law," he said. "The Führer has just appointed him."

"He married the nun?" Schmidt was momentarily diverted by the incongruous.

"My other sister," Busse said.

"A high-placed brother-in-law," Schmidt said. "Useful."

"We get on well," Busse said. "The Führer approves of happy families."

"That's nice."

Busse was slowing down, reaching out to turn off the radio. On their right was the cold, black water of the Havel. "It's somewhere along here. Put the top down. There's a flashlight in the glove compartment."

Schmidt struggled with the hood's snaps. His detective memory clicked away, frantically sorting through old records.

"There's a turn along here," Busse said. "On the left. And a name, I can't remember, like a Wandervogel name, but it is not for Wandervogel."

"I bet it fucking isn't," Schmidt said.

Several wooden fingerposts indicated footpaths, hiking tracks, bridleways meandering into the trees and darkness; one or two pointed to where various Wandervogel groups had built a cabin. Schmidt stood up in the car, holding on to the windshield with one hand, playing the flashlight beam on them as they crawled past. "'Berlin Falcons' Camp.' That one?"

"No, it was another name . . . something. Keep a lookout for the Audi."

"Here's another one, slow up. 'Graf von Wartenburg's Young Wolves'?"

"No."

"Snotty little bastards, they were. We used to fight 'em." Why am I saying things like this? Because I can't bear whatever's coming. "Slow down. 'Black Riders'?"

"That's it." They'd almost gone past. Busse swung the wheel, and they bumped over the verge and onto a track that stretched ahead, gray in the headlights before Busse switched them off. He got out of the car, carefully transferring the Luger into its holster.

Without lights and the noise of the engine, the darkness and silence of the forest fell on them; the only thing to be heard was emptiness stretching hopelessly far, beyond exploration. Nobody had been in it, nobody would ever be in it.

"Go ahead—and be quiet." Busse's voice was tense.

Schmidt began walking, shining the light toward the ground, trying to protect the beam with his other hand so that it didn't show too far ahead of them.

"What's that?" Busse was beside him, bending down, examining the ground like a good little Wandervogel looking for tracks.

Schmidt didn't join him. He was being sapped by a sense of unreality, the sheer fatuity of what they were doing. He was in a forest, and she was somewhere else, being hurt. The heavy shadow of an owl swept overhead, emitting on his behalf the shriek lodged in his throat. They're dead. The sort of luck we need doesn't happen. She's dead. He was lost in the nothingness she would leave behind. His head pounded with the memory of voices that had told him to take her away from Germany.

"A vehicle has been along here," Busse said. "Recently. Look." And there was a tire print in the snow, its serrations only just beginning to blur from flakes coming through the canopy of branches overhead.

God, if you let me get her back . . . Let me get her back. Help me, Lord, to use what knowledge I have to get her back. Compared to her, Germany was dust that he'd shake from his heels, and happy for the chance to do it.

Busse was grabbing the flashlight out of his hand. "Hurry." He went ahead at a jog, aiming the beam just before him so that light off the snow on the track reflected back on his lower legs, and Schmidt followed a gleaming pair of jackboots.

A mile. Maybe more, maybe less. He was getting tired. They should have brought the car. Busse kept up an unwavering pace. Fitful snow touched his face in icy dabs. She didn't have a coat.

After a while Schmidt ceased thinking. Fatigue and pounding jackboots became routine. When the jackboots stopped, he was cross. *"What?"*

Busse had extinguished the light. Cloud came and went, letting the moon switch the scene in front of them on and off, like a flip-page peep show. The track had widened and spawned another one leading from it to the left. A wooden barrier intended to bar the way stood open, decorated with boards that continued along a barbed-wire fence stretching into the woods on either side. FORBIDDEN ENTRY, KEEP OUT, DANGER, ELECTRIC FENCE—posters with skulls and crossbones hung at regular intervals. More effective were the small corpses scattered untidily along its length—birds, a deer calf, a fox in midsnarl.

Busse's head went up. "Do you hear it?"

Schmidt could hear only the pounding in his ears. He listened harder—there was the silence of the forest. And then, frail as the snow, a far-off tapping like a woodpecker, somewhere behind and to their left.

"Woodpecker?"

Busse of the Wandervogel shook his head. "Digging," he said. He began following the track to the left, past the open barrier, having to stop every now and then when the moon went in and put them in an avenue of blackness.

The smell of pine was becoming laced with something sourer. They bring them down here, Schmidt thought. The dead and the soon-to-be-dead are brought down here.

The regular hit of a pick crunching into hard earth was recognizable now, the familiar sound of war when men dug trenches. And graves.

Somebody began playing the flute. Frail and sweet, it weaved in and out of the pick's metronome like Pan playing to the dryads.

Light ahead.

The noise of the pick stopped. He'd heard them.

But the fluting went on, unencumbered now. Not a flute, a voice.

They moved forward until they were behind trees on the edge of a large clearing of packed earth. There was a hut on the far side. The Audi was parked ten yards off, facing away from them, engine running quietly, its headlights on full beam, illuminating a scene like a stage set. Four people stood on it, not one of them moving.

A stormtrooper, waist-deep in a small trench, had shouldered his pick and was staring up at Esther and Anna, who stood above him, on the edge. At the other side of the trench, facing the two women across it, stood a big man in an SA officer's uniform, pointing a revolver at them.

Esther had her arms crossed on her breast, clutching her shoulders in an effort to keep warm, a pose that, curiously, gave her the appearance of someone who'd just stepped out into a chilly dawn to hear the birdsong.

Anna was out of sight on the other side of Esther, but the voice was hers. The other three were listening to her.

In a surge of gratitude, Schmidt thought, That's what delayed him; he had to pick up one of his boys for a gravedigger.

A peace descended on him and with it thankfulness that he'd been allowed to live for this—to have Hannelore's murderer in his sights and at his mercy. The man hadn't heard them; he stood like a statue, expressionless, the barrel of the revolver in his large hand pointing at the two women. Tall but not exceptionally tall, not fat, it was more an effect of mass, of concentrated muscle beneath the gray uniform.

For Schmidt it was as if the two of them had been carrying on a correspondence, and here the anonymous letter writer stood, everything Schmidt had dreamed: big, blank-faced—and vulnerable.

He nudged Busse beside him, whispering, "Shoot him in the leg." He could still get the bastard back for trial.

Busse nudged him in turn—with the Luger. "Move," he said.

With the gun in Schmidt's back, they walked forward, past the Audi and onto the stage set of its lights.

"Major Günsche?" asked Busse pleasantly. As the man turned, he shot him.

Günsche dropped.

Schmidt stumbled forward. Oh, Christ, not so quick, not so easy, not after all these years. Not at somebody else's hand, my job.

It was like a grief. The Minotaur lay on the edge of the pit, its eyes open and uncaring, not even knowing it was dead.

Busse had come up behind him. "Join your friends, please," he said. To the stormtrooper he said, "Keep digging. There are more to go in."

The stormtrooper was young. His cap hung down the back of his neck from its chin strap; his close-cropped, fair hair was shiny with sweat. He looked up at Busse with his mouth open, then at Günsche's body, up again.

"Dig," Busse said. "I order you to dig."

The boy was used to orders—he raised the pick from his shoulder and brought it down, and the metronome started up again. Günsche's revolver lay on the edge of the trench where it had fallen from his hand.

"No," Busse said.

Schmidt stopped looking at it. Busse picked it up. "Join your friends, please."

Schmidt walked around the trench to the women, unbuttoning his coat and then his jacket. Esther smiled at him, closing her eyes, as if she'd been expecting him.

"In a line," Busse said.

Schmidt positioned himself between the two women. He put his coat around Esther. "I'm sorry, sweetheart."

She took his hand.

Anna was addressing Busse across the grave. "Have you come to kill me, too?"

The stormtrooper stopped digging, looking at her. They all looked at her.

"But I am explaining to that man there that I do not die," Anna said, almost querulously, pointing to the body as if it had committed a breach of etiquette. "Not before, not in the House of Special Purpose, not all these years. Always they try to kill me, always I do not die."

Busse stared at her. Schmidt, with his jacket ready to put around her shoulders, couldn't move.

She was resuming a story she'd been telling. "Mama said it. She said, 'You will not die, little one.' But I did not believe her then. Only now, when I know. Then I was afraid the new men who come will kill us. . . . Some of them are Magyars, but all have been sent by the Cheka. We hate them worse than the other guards. Their leader, Yurovsky, he is Russian Jew, cold, cold man. My father says he is sinister but do not worry because friends smuggle news in to us that the Bolsheviks are weak from civil war. An American and British force has landed at Murmansk. We will be rescued."

Ekaterinburg. She was talking about Ekaterinburg.

"It is a warm night when they come for us, I remember. . . . July. . . . Yurovsky tell us to get dressed. You are being transferred. Get dressed. And I do not want to put on my bodice. No, Mama, it is so uncomfortable where Demidova has sewn the jewels in it, but Mama says, 'Never mind, little one, you must.' "

It was a pretty voice. Schmidt had mainly heard it using monosyllables, and none too graciously. In prolonged speech it was like a syrinx, fresh and tripping. His arm was touching hers, and he felt it shivering, but her eyes were directed calmly at Busse opposite, holding him as spellbound as the rest. She wasn't seeing him; she was watching some other drama being played out in front of her. And making everyone else watch it with her.

"So we go downstairs. Papa first, with his military cap on. He is carrying Alexei, who has not walked since the last attack. Alexei is sleepy and has his arms tight around Papa's neck. We all follow. I have Jemmy in my arms. . . ." She blinked for a moment. "Do I tell you Jemmy is my spaniel?"

The stormtrooper, still standing in the grave with the pick on his shoulder, nodded; yes, she'd told him. Busse gave a slow, wondering shake of his head.

"Demidova is carrying the pillows, one for Mama's back, the other has more jewels sewn in it. We are taken to a room, a bit like a cellar but not a cellar. It is smelly. Wait, they say. Transport is coming. Papa says they must bring us chairs: 'The czarina should not have to stand while she waits.' So they bring chairs, and Mama sits down. Papa lays little Alexei across two of the chairs and sits to hold him."

Anna unclasped her hands, to tap her mouth thoughtfully. "I get this right. I tell no one before. And you will see why I survive, why I survive always, no matter what you do. I, yes, I stand behind Mama's chair, and Olga, Tatiana . . . yes, that's right, all four of us girls in a line behind Mama. And Dr. Botkin and Trupp, they are to our left, I think. Kharitonov and Demidova stand together."

Anna smiled. "Demidova is clutching the pillow with the jewels, tight, so tight I think, Oh, no, they will suspect."

She stopped smiling, her eyes widening.

"Yurovsky is coming back. Behind him come men with guns, all the guards, all with guns. Even then I think they are the guards for our journey. But Yurovsky says, 'Your relatives have try to save you. Now we must shoot you.' And he shoots Papa as he try to stand up, straight in the head. And then all is shooting, shooting and noisy."

Slowly, Anna's hands went to her ears to cover them.

"Mama falls forward . . . plop, like that. I do not see what happen to Olga and Tatiana and Marie. The bullets hit my chest, and I fall back—oh, such pain; even still my breasts are marked with scars where the jewels push into my skin. But is Demidova I see, she is running around and screaming, and the bullets going puff into the pillow and feathers coming out, and they are chasing after, poking her with bayonets. And

Jemmy is barking, and he stops, and it is quiet, but I think I hear Alexei moan once before it is quiet again."

It was quiet in the forest, too, except for the hum of the Audi's engine.

Anna took her hands from her ears; she held them out as if she were displaying stigmata. "So they kill me," she said. "But I do not die. I do not die in the House of Special Purpose. What happened, I do not know. Maybe one of the guards still is loyal to us. Maybe he sees me alive and pushes me off the cart that takes my family away. When I am better, I am with Gypsies. They find the jewels, perhaps. They do not kill me either."

She smiled across the grave at Busse. "I do not die now if you shoot me. Always you try to kill me, always I do not die. I am the grand duchess Anastasia."

Busse was staring at her, mesmerized. "Yes," he said. Then he said, "Yes, Your Imperial Highness."

Anna closed her eyes. "That is good," she said, and fell against Schmidt. He held her up. Froth was coming out of her mouth.

"What is it?" Busse demanded.

"She's fainted," Schmidt said, trying to put his jacket around Anna's shoulders as she flopped against him.

"She *is* Anastasia," Busse said in awe. "You heard her."

"Yes," Schmidt said, He picked Anna up in his arms and edged Esther back so that he stood in front of her on the lip of the grave.

Busse still pointed the gun at them, but he was flustered. He shifted his spectacles.

In the pit the storm trooper stared across at Anna, bewildered, then back up at Busse. His young face was streaked with dirt across his cheek where he'd wiped off perspiration.

Busse made up his mind. When the stormtrooper looked up again, he shot him through the forehead. The boy fell back against the side of the pit, eyes open, his head resting against Günsche's dangling hand.

Schmidt felt Esther flinch.

"About the Anastasia file," Schmidt said. His voice intruded on the air, breaking an echo left by the pistol fire.

"Carry Her Highness to the car," Busse said. "Carefully. Then come back. The Jewess stays where she is."

Schmidt shook his head, as much to clear it as anything. He'd underestimated Busse—or overestimated him, he didn't know which. Even Busse, clinical, Nazi Busse, wasn't proof against fairy tales. He'd made up his mind to be Anastasia's knight, her savior. Anna, laid at Hitler's feet. Here is the true, proven grand duchess, my Führer, rescued from death at the hands of one of Röhm's killers.

It would still work.

"About the file . . ."

"Quiet about the file," Busse said. He gestured toward the car. He had Günsche's gun in his hand—they were going to be shot with Günsche's bullets. "I do not need it. It is irrelevant now. Inconvenient, perhaps, because of the baby, but we shall deny that. It was mere Communist propaganda to blacken her name."

He was thinking on his feet, Schmidt saw, planning. Nothing was going to mar the image of the unsullied Sleeping Beauty awakened by a Nazi kiss—certainly not the two witnesses, Schmidt and Esther, who could attest to the inconveniences the file contained. They would disappear.

"She is the grand duchess without a doubt," Busse said. "Only one person could know what she knew. We shall put her on the radio, and everyone will hear her. That was the truth we heard."

"Yes," Schmidt said, "it was. But you should have read the file more closely."

"I'm taking her back to the Führer," Busse said. "Get her into the car."

Schmidt hoisted Anna so that her head was against his shoulder; he was finding her heavy now, but Busse couldn't shoot him without hitting his Anastasia, and both their bodies were protecting Esther behind him.

"There's a list in that file," Schmidt said. "Men who were interviewed about Yusupov on the night of Natalya Tchichagova's murder. You remember? In 1923? Prince Yusupov? Günsche put Yusupov's name on the note that took Natalya to her death."

"What? *What?*" Busse was becoming angry. "Put Her Highness in the car. I order you."

"These men had been with Yusupov at a nightclub called the Pink Parasol. You wouldn't know it—it's a homosexual club."

Busse began to move, walking along the edge of the grave, coming around it to get behind Schmidt, to shoot Esther.

"They were brought in for questioning, and they gave Yusupov an alibi," Schmidt said, watching him. "One of them was called Braun. Common enough name. On the list, he's down as Braun, E. Just the initial. But I interviewed him—he was still in his ball gown."

Busse stopped still.

"And I remember his Christian name," Schmidt said. "I have a memory for detail, and anyway it was unusual. It was Einwen. Einwen Braun, same name as the fellow Hitler has just promoted to some office or another."

He watched Busse's Adam's apple move in his throat.

"I remember the address, too," he said. "It's in the file. I'm surprised you didn't notice it, but the list's a long one, so perhaps you overlooked it. E. Braun lived in Mariendorf. Your brother-in-law ever live in Mariendorf, Busse?"

There was silence.

"Still does?" Schmidt asked gently. "Well, you know what these newspapermen are like; when they get the file—and they will—they might notice the name of an E. Braun living in Mariendorf and wonder if it's got any connection with *the* Einwen Braun and look him up. He's got a record, Busse. I remember that too. Just one offense—soliciting in a men's lavatory."

He waited. Busse didn't say anything.

"The offer still holds," Schmidt said. "You get the only remaining copy of the file. Fräulein Solomonova and I go free."

We're going to stand here forever, he thought. We're in some obscene enchantment.

Busse lowered the Luger. He twitched his spectacles. "We'd better go," he said. "Someone may have heard the shots."

And I will believe in You and all Your works forever.

"After you," Schmidt told him. Carrying Anna, he followed Busse and Esther to the Audi.

As he passed the grave, he looked down to where Günsche lay, his hand hanging down against the head of the dead stormtrooper.

Nazi justice. No trial for him, no public acknowledgment of the monster he'd been. Hannelore's death, Natalya's, all of his victims'—mere cases moldering in the unsolved section of the Records Department. Obliterating dirt would be shoveled on top of where he lay. Long live the law of the Luger.

Busse had got himself in hand. "Put Her Highness in the back," he said, opening the Audi's rear door for them. "Carefully."

Schmidt lowered Anna onto the seat. Her eyes were closed, and she was moaning. He wiped her mouth gently with his shirtsleeve.

"You." Busse pointed the gun at Esther. "Reverse and go up the track. Turn right at the top. You"—this was to Schmidt—"in the front with her." He got in beside Anna.

They drove to where they'd left the Mercedes. "Same order as before," Busse said. "The Jewess drives."

"Her name is Fräulein Solomonova," Schmidt said. "Use it."

They changed cars, leaving Günsche's Audi on the edge of the forest.

Esther started the Mercedes, put it smoothly into gear, reversed, and they were on the road. Her hands were white on the wheel. Schmidt touched them. "All over now," he lied.

She nodded.

"How is this to be worked?" Busse asked from the rear seat.

"I'm thinking," Schmidt told him.

The Luger touched the back of his neck. "Think well."

"Bismarck Allee," Schmidt told Esther.

"The file's not there," Busse said.

"Bismarck Allee," Schmidt said again.

After that nobody spoke. Esther drove well, going at a medium pace. Schmidt tried to get her to look at him, but she might have been a wooden statue with its eyes fixed on the road. They could hear Anna muttering in the back and Busse trying to comfort her.

As soon as they were passing streetlights, Schmidt looked at his watch. It said eight-fifteen. "What's the time?" he asked Busse. "My watch has stopped."

Busse pulled back the edge of his left-hand glove. "Twenty hours fifteen."

Just an hour and a half since he'd been in the Alex, burning files. Ninety minutes. It had felt like a lifetime. For two men back there, it had been.

"Still got time to join the parade," he said.

Busse said nothing.

The sky had cleared, and a hard-edged moon showed busy streets on which the main trend seemed to be eastward, toward the West End.

They pulled up in front of number 29. Schmidt and Busse supported Anna while Esther opened the door and helped her upstairs. She was beginning to come around. They steered her to the sofa, and she lay down, closing her eyes.

The flat was warm and tidy, and Esther stood in the middle of it as if seeing it for the first time. The phone still dangled from its wire.

Schmidt said, "Hot drinks all around, I think," and moved to the kitchen.

Busse stopped him. "Where is the file?"

"With a friend, I told you."

Busse said, "Come here, Fräulein." The gun pointed at Esther. He took her by the arm and walked her to the phone table and the hard-backed chair beside it. "Sit." He picked up the receiver and held it out to Schmidt. "Tell your friend to bring it here." The gun was against Esther's cheek.

"I want your word that when you've got it, she and I can go free," Schmidt said. "There's a flight from Tempelhof we need to catch."

"Of course."

God, how that man did need that file. It would be in flames seconds after he got it. Whether he'd known about his brother-in-law or hadn't, it *really* wasn't information he wanted to reach Hitler's ears.

It would be handy to have it suppressed in any case. Hitler could have his pristine grand duchess. Busse, her rescuer, could have his reward. Nobody need know anything else, and the dance could go on.

Schmidt said, "You won't mind if I make sure of that." He went to the other side of the table and turned the phone around so that its dial was out of Busse's view. He dialed. Let him be in, God. Don't let him be out.

Joe Wolff's voice, which always reminded him of richly squashing fruit, said, "Hello?"

"It's Siegfried."

"Siegfried, my son. How are you? You only just caught me. I was thinking I'd go watch the parade."

"You can. But I'm in trouble, and I need a favor."

"Trouble?" A thousand years of anxiety came over the line.

"That folder I gave you. Have you still got it?"

"Yes, yes, it's on top of Minna's wardrobe. Still wrapped up. You want I should get it?"

"Yes. I need you to take it to the West End—hold on a minute." He covered the mouthpiece with his hand and looked toward Busse. "Pick a hotel, any hotel."

"Tell him to bring it here," Busse said. He had hold of Esther's hair, pulling her head back so that her throat was exposed to the gun barrel.

"It's packed up and addressed to my favorite newspaper. You want me to tell him to mail it? Pick a bloody hotel."

"The Kaiserhof."

"Oh, yes, I'm sure my friend's going to walk into a nest of Nazis. Pick another one."

"The Esplanade."

Nice and central. He said, "Take the folder to the Esplanade. You know it?"

"Of course I know. Bit pricey, but Minna and I brought Ikey to tea there in the palm court on his twelfth birthday. He was very taken by the éclairs, I remember."

Schmidt was wrenched by a vision of the little suburban family that spent its annual holiday in a bed-and-breakfast at Baden-Baden staring around them at the plush and chandeliers.

"Quick as you can, then," he said. "When you get there, phone me at this number." He gave Esther's number. "If I don't answer or you see anybody who looks as if they're searching for you, put the folder in the mailbox. Can you do that?"

"Sure, I can do it. But is it bad, Siegfried? Can I help?"

"You are helping." He put down the phone.

Busse said, not unadmiringly, "You *have* been thinking, Inspector."

"It's what I'm good at. You all right, Mrs. Noah?"

Esther nodded. She pushed the gun away from her neck and got up. Busse let her. "Coffee, everyone?" she asked.

God, he was proud of her. He leaned over the table and put his hand to her cheek. "That's my girl."

He looked at his watch. For Joe, the journey by S-bahn would take less than ten minutes, give him time to get the folder and his coat, walk to the station, walk to the Esplanade at the other end. "Half an hour," he said. "And I'll get the coffee. Esther, you pack us a suitcase—nothing heavy. If they can squeeze us onto the night plane, they won't let us take a lot of weight. Just the essentials. Passports. Oh, and a thick scarf; it's going to be cold. Put in an extra coat."

He went into the kitchen, Busse with him, following his every move with the gun.

Good, very good. So far.

"As a matter of interest," he said, "what explanation will you give Hitler as to why Günsche wanted to kill Anna Anderson in the first place?" If Busse was cutting the connection between Anna and Bagna Duze, Günsche's action would seem not only arbitrary but reasonless, even to Adolf.

"It is obvious," Busse said. "Major Günsche was secretly a Communist assassin. The Bolsheviks infiltrated him into Röhm's organization years ago, under cover, to eliminate White Russians."

God Almighty. It was beautiful. A Red ogre to be added to the fairy tale for Hitler's delight and the disparagement of Röhm, who had nurtured it. Olga, Natalya, Potrovskov had all been White Russians. The murders of Hannelore and Marlene, if they came up at all, would be explained away as extraneous—attempts by a Bolshevik assassin to cover his tracks.

"You've been doing some thinking yourself," Schmidt said.

In the living room, he held the cup out to Anna. Her blue eyes stared at him. "I do not die," she said.

"Immortal, Your Imperial Highness."

From the darkroom doorway, Esther said, "She'll need someone to look after her when we go."

"We are in charge of Her Imperial Highness now," Busse said. "I shall phone and order my people to come and look after her."

"No," Schmidt said. "On our way out, we'll ask Frau Schinkel to see to her." He looked at his watch. Ten minutes gone.

"At least let me ring my wife," Busse said, moving to the phone.

"No."

"She is expecting me. She will be worried that I am late."

Schmidt said, "Touch that phone and I won't answer it when my friend calls." Whoever Busse called, it wouldn't be an anxious wife. Frau Busse wasn't waiting up for a husband she knew to be taking part in the victory parade.

"This is foolishness," Busse said, but he sat down.

"You can listen to the wireless, if you'd like," Schmidt said kindly. "Hear what you're missing." He got up and turned on Esther's radio set.

"Magical splendor." Off the scale with excitement, a commentator's voice shrilled into the living room. *"Exhilarating. A million torches are issuing in a new dawn."* Behind it came the noise of bands and cheers and marching boots.

Not a commentary, Schmidt thought, it's propaganda—a word picture of a hundred thousand marching Nazis was being transmitted into millions of German homes.

"In the torchlight the banners flame with color as they pass us."

And most of Berlin's police lining the route letting them do it.

Esther came out of the bedroom carrying a suitcase. She'd put on a light suede coat, and a smart cloche hat was pulled down over her hair to shade her cheek. A scarf was tucked inside the fox collar. Good girl.

"Now I pass the microphone to the Prussian minister of the interior," screamed the commentator. *"A new dawn, Herr Göring."*

Göring, sonorous: *"We bring national rebirth to the Fatherland. This is the Day of Awakening."*

The phone rang. Schmidt got up. The Luger, which had been wavering in march time, pointed immediately at Esther.

"Yes?"

"Is that you, Siegfried? Such a time I have had. The crowds."

"Where are you?"

"At the reception desk. Sweating like a pig, but here. The place has got bigger, Siegfried, and so modern. All these rich young people, where do they come from?"

Schmidt thought of Joe in his off-the-peg suit among Berlin's smart set. Oh, Christ, I've made him noticeable.

"Good man. Unwrap the parcel, just enough to show the receptionist the folder inside, and then put him on the phone."

He passed the receiver to Busse. "Check it," he said.

Busse took over the phone. "This is Major Busse of the Schutzstaffel. Are you the receptionist at the Esplanade? I shall make sure. Give me the number. I will ring you back."

Doesn't trust me any more than I trust him, thought Schmidt. "I'll dial the number, thank you," he said. Busse gave him the number; he dialed and passed the receiver over.

Busse spoke to the receptionist: "You have a folder? What does it say on its first page?"

He listened, nodded, and handed the phone back to Schmidt.

"Put me back to the gentleman with the parcel, will you? Is that you, my friend? I want you to wrap it up again. Then go and get yourself a drink. Take it *and* the parcel to a window looking out onto Bellevuestrasse. In a little while, a car's going to drive up and park on the other side of the street. There'll be three people in it: me, a lady, and an SS officer. If the officer gets out on his own, finish your drink, leave the parcel on the table, and go. But if it looks like one or both of us is being forced to come in with him, I want you to pick the parcel up very quickly, get out by a side entrance, and shove it in the nearest mailbox. In the name of God, don't let the Nazi see you. Got that?"

"What is it, Siegfried? What is this trouble?"

"A misunderstanding, that's all. We're clearing it up. Have you got that?"

He was aware of sounding abrupt. He wanted to call Joe by his first name, say good-bye, thank him for past kindnesses, mention Ikey, but he didn't dare. Busse was listening to every word, and there must not be the slightest trace that would lead the bastard to that good old man.

"I got it. It's exciting, Siegfried. Like I am a spy."

"I love you, old friend. Do one more thing for me. Very important."

"Anything, Siegfried, you know that."

"Get out of the country."

He put the phone down. "Satisfied?"

"There is no need for this elaborate nonsense," Busse said. "I have given my word."

"Indulge me. Shall we go?"

On the way out, Esther stooped down to kiss Anna, who'd taken herself to sit by the wireless. "Good-bye, darling. Take care of yourself."

"Good-bye," Anna said.

Busse waited, his gun on Schmidt, while Esther called in on Frau Schinkel and asked her to keep an eye on Anna.

They got into the car. Busse switched on its radio before Esther drove off. *"And there is Herr Hitler himself, taking the salute."* The commentator might have glimpsed God. *"Listen to the acclamation as the columns pass him."* The roar wasn't just from the radio; it came through the hood of the car, a tidal wave of sound washing through the Tiergarten from Linden and the Brandenburg Gate.

Half the West End was blocked by detour signs, and they had to take a long way around to Bellevuestrasse. "Here," Schmidt said. "Park here."

The street was busy with people, families, all moving toward the parade, most of them carrying little paper flags with swastikas on them.

As ever, the Esplanade was crowded with the haute monde getting themselves ready for the nightclubs, its great windows showing groups of glittering people standing in groups, talking and laughing. Schmidt looked for Joe Wolff's face but didn't see it. He'll be there, though, always trustworthy—like father, like son. But this is the tricky bit.

Busse was lingering in the car, staring toward the hotel; Schmidt could almost see his mind measuring times and distances. *If I take them with me under arrest, can I get into the bar before the folder disappears?*

No, you can't, you bastard. And you can stop looking about for a policeman—they're lining the procession route. Never one around when you want one.

"How do I know this isn't a trick?" Busse asked. "Have you a code, you and your friend?"

"We'll stay in the car until we see you wave from the window," Schmidt said. He tried to sound casual and hoped like hell Busse didn't see the sweat on his face. "I've kept my word, you keep yours. How about driving us to Tempelhof afterward? See us off the premises, as it were. Getting a cab tonight will be impossible, and the lady's tired."

"Very well." Busse took the keys out of the ignition. He started to cross the road, looked back, and then went on.

Schmidt leaned forward and put his face against Esther's. "Got the passports?"

"In my handbag."

He began struggling with the suitcase in the restricted space of the backseat. "Did you bring another coat?"

"It's in there."

"Yeah, here it is. Put it over your arm. Leave the rest. I'm not carrying this bloody case to the station—too damn heavy."

Esther's voice was deliberately calm. "Do I gather we are not going to Tempelhof?"

"No, we're not. They'll be waiting for us. At this moment Busse is making the necessary phone call. He doesn't intend to leave us alive."

"Oh, God." He heard the fear in her voice. So did she. She said, trying for control, "What are we going to do?"

"We're going to watch the procession like everybody else. Ready?"

"Yes."

"Let's go."

As they left the car, he tore the swastika pennant off its hood. He caught sight of Busse's face in one of the Esplanade windows, saw it slide out of view as the man made for the exit.

"Run." He caught her arm, and they ran toward Pariser Platz, dodging around families heading in the same direction. Crowd and noise loomed up like a turbulent sea, and they dived into it, squirming and pushing. Schmidt's hand was pulled out of Esther's, and for one minute he panicked; if he lost her now, it would be forever. Then he saw her struggling and had to fight to go back for her. He grabbed hold of her and dragged her along like an angry father with a recalcitrant child.

If Busse was following them, they couldn't spot him—wouldn't, even if he were only a few paces away; they were hemmed in toward the rear of massed chattering, cheering people, most of them staring upward at the tips of banners and eagle standards being carried by men they couldn't see.

"Take your coat off," Schmidt said.

"What?" The noise of the bands and the crowd was deafening.

"Take your coat off. Put the other one on."

She nodded and slipped one arm out of her light-colored coat, then the other, letting it fall to the ground. The people on either side didn't notice, wouldn't have noticed if she'd stripped naked. In the crush it was difficult to put on the new coat—it was black, Schmidt was glad to note, very different from the one Busse had seen. A man who was pressed against her complained, "Stop shoving!" without looking to see what she was doing. She took her hat off. For the first time, he noticed that she had her camera on a strap around her neck.

"Scarf," he said.

"What?"

"Put your scarf around your face."

They started to move in the direction of the Brandenburg Gate; it was impossible to keep in the center of the press, and in wriggling through they found themselves near the front and for a minute glimpsed the columns passing by—and were transfixed, like everybody else. The marchers came on and on, sweeping through the pillars of the great gate surmounted by *Victory* in her chariot, one phalanx, then another, another, as they had been all night, as they would continue, units Schmidt didn't recognize, bands, more columns, more swastikas, as if monstrous, human-size ants were invading the city, glorious and terrible.

More terrible was the crowd watching them. "Look, Hans," a man shouted to the child on his shoulders. "You are seeing history." People cried, "Heil, Heil," and stomped in time to the marchers. A divided, suffering, and humiliated city was being healed by spectacle, its pride raised high on poles, its people ready to be led by a tiny figure waving at a window.

Schmidt didn't know it anymore.

He spotted a gap that would let them double back, but it meant going along the front of the crowd. He handed Busse's swastika pennant to Esther. "Wave that."

"No."

So he waved it instead, pulling Esther behind him, running, stooped, along the space between the crowd and the police lining the route, making for the gap. He thought he glimpsed Willi Ritte and that Willi glimpsed him, but it could have been someone else.

They were nearly back where they'd started. They took a side road, aiming for Königrätzstrasse. Above them a great penumbra of light rising from the procession was diffused against the night sky, as if reflecting a burning pine forest on the march.

Esther was limping, and he put his arm around her shoulder to help her along, waving his swastika in time to the beat of "Watch on the Rhine" coming over the rooftops, hoping like hell they looked like a happy couple on their way home after a good Nazi night out.

Up ahead was Berlin's biggest hotel, the Excelsior, opposite the Anhalter, Berlin's biggest railway station. Kings and foreign dignitaries had used both in their time, but Schmidt was aiming for a remembered greasy café in a side alley used by track workers, a place that once had served Stettin beer and possibly the best pork knuckles and sauerkraut in Berlin.

A wireless on the counter was relaying the commentary on the parade. Some men playing cards looked up as they came in, then went back to their game. The only other customer was either asleep or unconscious.

Schmidt helped Esther to a corner table and sat down opposite her. "Made my first arrest here," he told her. "Fellow who'd beaten up his aunt for her pension."

She tried to nod. Her eyes were closed.

He said, "You can go to pieces now. We've got time to spare."

She shook her head. "Too tired." She said, "You know what was the worst thing? He didn't say anything. Günsche. He never spoke a word from the time he came into the flat, not on the journey to the forest, no word. I knew he was going to kill us, but the silence . . . It was like being in the jaws of an animal. As if he were . . . just death."

Schmidt had very nearly asked, "Who?" Günsche was the past; they were in the jaws of a bigger animal now.

"I'd thought of him as a sort of beast," she said, "waiting in the shadows and killing us one by one, and now he'll always be that. . . . Inexplicable. Not human."

"Yes he was," Schmidt said. "He was a pox-ridden, nine-pfennig whore bastard."

Her eyes went wide with surprise and relief, and she began to laugh. "I do love you, Schmidt."

A voice from the other side of the room said, "You ordering or not? No waiter service here, you know."

"Merely charm," Schmidt said. He got up and crossed to the counter. Either the man he remembered behind it hadn't aged or this was his son—same anchor tattoos on his forearms, same dirty apron, same bad temper. Schmidt had a giddying sense of déjà vu that might have been sheer, blind fatigue. He ordered beer for them both, knuckles with sauerkraut and potatoes for himself, herring and sauerkraut and potatoes for Esther. It was a long time since they'd last eaten; it would be a long time until they ate again.

The food-bespattered wireless on the counter blared out "Hail to Thee, Crowned in Victory."

The men at the table were arguing over their cards. The drunk hadn't moved. The café owner was relaying the order through a hatch.

Schmidt reached over and turned the wireless's volume down low, adjusting the wavelength to a fraction above the AM band. *". . . a brown coat,"* a dispatcher's voice was saying. *"The woman has a distinctive scar on her cheek and is wearing a light suede coat with a fur collar and a tight-fitting black hat. Arrest on sight. Use force if necessary."*

The café owner turned around. Schmidt flicked the knob back to the state radio band.

"Policemen," the café owner said, and spit. "Smell 'em even when they're off duty."

Schmidt went back to Esther and sat down.

She'd been watching. She said, "Are they broadcasting our description?" She had a hand to her cheek.

"It's all right," he said. "The scarf hides it. And you've changed your coat."

She said dully, "We're not going to get away, are we?"

"Yes we are. When we've eaten, we're going to walk into Anhalter and I'm going to buy us a pair of tickets for the Munich express. Nice place, Munich, Hitler country, but he won't be expecting us. Where do you want to go? Switzerland? America? England?"

"They'll stop us at the frontier," she said.

"No they won't. When we get to Munich, we're going to buy ourselves— Have you got money with you, incidentally?"

She nodded and patted her handbag. "I'd drawn out nearly everything in my account in case Anna should want it. I've left her some, but tonight, when I was packing, I decided we'd need a larger amount than she would."

"Good. Well, we're going to buy some nice warm clothes and walking boots, and we're going to take a nice long bus ride into the mountains, and we're going to cross over into Austria by a track I know."

He and Hannelore had walked it once, from the last inn in Germany over the border to the first inn in Austria, not a frontier guard in sight.

But that had been in summer, he thought.

"With every policeman in the country looking for a man accompanied by a woman with a scar on her cheek," she said. "I'm not going to do it to you, Schmidt. We'll go separately."

"We go together," he said.

She was looking toward the café window, its glass almost obliterated by advertising stickers, and he knew she was seeing beyond it to the ticket inspectors, the railway police, the wanted posters—HAVE YOU SEEN THIS COUPLE?—the hundred identity checkpoints of a new Germany.

Two steins of beer were slammed on the table, two steaming, aromatic plates shoved in front of them. She didn't notice.

No point, he wanted to tell her. No point to life without you. He said, "Esther." He tapped her hand to get her attention. "Mrs. Noah."

"What?" She picked up her knife and fork.

"And still they come." The commentator's voice was hoarse. *"The flower of Germany, marching into a glorious future."*

"About Anna." Now that he'd got to it, he wasn't sure what to say. "In the forest, when she was . . . About the executions . . . the House of Special Purpose."

Esther cut into a herring. "She was amazing, wasn't she?"

"Yes," he said. "Yes, she was. How did she know?"

"Know what? This is nice herring. I didn't realize how hungry I was."

"Know about the House of Special Purpose. Busse was right; we were hearing what happened. She couldn't have made that up."

Esther sighed. "I suppose not."

"So either she is Anastasia or somebody else got out of that cellar and told her."

"I suppose so," she said; her voice was very tired.

"About the bullets hitting the jewels in her bodice and making scars—*has* she got scars on her body like that?"

"No."

"But you have."

"Yes."

"*You* told her."

"Yes." She put down her fork as if her hands needed to be free for this.

He'd known. Part of his mind not occupied with other things had known ever since the forest; it had been waiting for him. What would he feel? Now he didn't know what he felt. Yes he did—he was angry. Not much, he was too fucking tired, but . . . angry.

"And you wouldn't tell me," he said.

"I had to do it," she said dully. "Hitler was taking her up. I didn't want her trying to fool Hitler. She had to be the real thing. I thought I might be saving her life. As it turned out, she saved mine." She put out a hand to lay it on one of his. "And then you came along and saved both of us. How did you know where we were?"

He ignored it. "Which one are you? There were six women in that cellar. You're too young to be the maid or the czarina—or Olga. So which of them are you? Marie? Tatiana? Anastasia?"

"Anastasia," she said.

The men were putting away the cards and calling for the bill. The drunk at the other table raised his head, said, "More beer," and collapsed again.

After a while Schmidt asked, "Were you ever going to tell me?"

"I don't know." She looked at him square in the face. "Maybe, one day. But Anastasia's dead. She died in that cellar."

All at once she was baring her teeth like a dog. "You want to know? All right, if you want to know, Anastasia saw her mother try to make the sign of the cross as they opened fire and then drop. Just drop. She didn't see her sisters die, any of the others, she only saw Demidova scuttling—she was *scuttling,* bullets everywhere and feathers and men going after her with bayonets. Then I was in a corner, my hands like this." She put her hands over her eyes. He saw her nails digging into her forehead. "The noise . . . Jemmy was barking. Demidova screaming. My chest was on fire. . . ."

She dropped her hands; her mouth was ugly with pain. "And then it was quiet. Except I heard Alexei whimper . . . and then a crack from a rifle butt, and it was quiet again. Oh, God." She was knuckling her forehead. "Oh, God."

He gripped her hands while she fought it.

Her scarf had fallen back, and the scar was livid against whiter skin. The men at the other table were looking in their direction. She didn't see them. She said, "Anastasia died in that cellar. What survived, how it survived . . ." She tried to smile. "Your guess is as good as mine."

He wasn't angry anymore. "What survived was one hell of a woman," he said. He leaned over and rearranged the scarf, not to hide her face but so that he could touch it.

"A different woman anyway," she said. "Christ, I'm so tired."

Schmidt snapped his fingers toward the counter. "Brandy," he said.

"Brandy?" Now everybody was looking at them, the owner, the men. Even the drunk had opened his eyes.

"Schnapps, then." God, he thought, we should have taken out an advertisement and a brass band. He made her drink.

"Telling Anna . . ." she said. "It near killed me. I'd learned not to relive it. Matter of survival."

Yes, he thought, resurrecting that memory to give to someone else—one of the great acts of generosity.

"We are seeing the triumph of the will of one man, our leader, Adolf Hitler!" screamed the commentator.

"And the Gypsies?" he asked.

"We had to say Gypsies; it fitted in with Anna's Franziska past. She believes it anyway. But there weren't any Gypsies. There wasn't anything, nothing I remember, except hurting. Until Rosa."

"So that was true."

"Rosa is true," Esther said. "Except she's unbelievable. This injured thing rolled off a cart at her feet one day, another bit of detritus from the civil war. I'd been raped, there was the great gash in my face. Sometimes I think she suspected who I was, but if she did, it made no difference to her. We'd persecuted her people, refused them education. We sent soldiers against them, encouraged pogroms. . . ."

We, he thought.

"But Rosa had seen so much death she just liked things to be alive. When the Cossacks came, she hid me as if I'd been her own. I became a Jew because of Rosa. All those adopted children we'll have, they're going to be Jews. For Rosa. If the Nazis catch me, I'll shout in their faces, 'I'm a Jew and proud of it.' For Rosa." She attempted another smile. "We of the House of Romanov owe her that."

Gently, he put the fork back in her hand. "Eat," he said.

She looked at her fork, then at her plate, and began eating again. With her mouth full, she said, "Does it make a difference?"

"Does what make a difference?"

"Ekaterinburg. Me."

"No, no," he said. "I just like to know who I'm on the run with, that's all."

The color was back in her face now. "I expect I'd have told you eventually," she said.

"Good, that's good."

"I don't think about it," she said, "nor the life before that. We walked in a dream, we girls, folded in love. So loved, we were, so loving. So happy, so untroubled, apart from Alexei's illness." Her voice was matter-of-fact now, but her fist clenched on her fork. "That's why we can't have children, you and I. It's carried by the female line, a legacy from Great-Grandmama."

Hemophilia. He'd once heard it said that if it hadn't been for the czarevitch's hemophilia, the czarina wouldn't have turned to Rasputin, who could ease some of her son's pain. No Rasputin, no revolution. A dynasty ended by the illness of a little boy.

"I'm sorry," he said. "Sweetheart, I'm so damned sorry."

"What for?" She opened her eyes. "Finding us? For saving our lives? Being magnificent?"

Great-Grandmama, he was thinking. Queen Victoria. "Takes some getting used to," he said.

"Don't think about it," she said. "I'm the woman who loves you."

The workmen had picked up their knapsacks and were leaving, saying, Good night. As he passed, one of them said, "You all right, missus?"

She smiled at him. "Very well, thank you. And you?"

The café owner went to the door, struggling with the drunk to throw him out. He came back, dusting his hands. "You two going to be much longer?"

"Probably," Schmidt said. "We'll have two more glasses of schnapps."

"And coffee," Esther said.

"I looked up 'pogrom' in the dictionary once," Schmidt said. " 'An organized massacre in Russia for the annihilation of any body or class: especially one directed against Jews.' Pogroms don't have to be against Jews."

"Two pogroms," she said. "The House of Special Purpose. Then one against Rosa's people. Oh, don't look at me like that. What has changed?"

"Nothing. It just . . . takes some getting used to. I'll get over it. I still want to get you into bed."

"Good," she said briskly. "And if you don't mind, I'd rather we didn't settle in England. Admirable country, I'm sure, but Uncle George could have offered us asylum and didn't—too afraid of a revolution on his own account."

Uncle George, he thought. King George V of England.

He said, "Suppose Anna wins her case, gets the inheritance?"

"She can have it. But she won't win; the family will never let her. I doubt if they'd have let even me have it if I'd declared myself—I haven't seen most of them since I was a little girl. They quarreled with Mama." She gritted her teeth, ugly again. "They left her isolated, suffering for Alexei, with only Rasputin to turn to."

She's seen history, he thought. Legend happened to her.

"It was a terrible thing I did," she said, "letting Anna happen. But at the time . . . Nick would have dropped her like hot coals if he'd known she was a fake, and it seemed a way of getting her out of that awful asylum. I would have taken her away, but I couldn't support her." Esther shook her head. "And she *was* Anastasia—more like something that had come out of the House of Special Purpose than I was—she *wanted* to be Anastasia."

"At least you speak Russian," he said.

She was watching his face. "Don't," she begged. "Don't even think of it. I don't want it, I don't *want* it. It was a fraud—we ruled one-sixth of the world's land by a confidence trick. We conned one hundred and thirty million people into giving us allegiance. I remember riding in Aunt Xenia's troika and scattering coins to the poor as we passed and thinking how kind we were being. They took off their caps and bowed to us. They should have had us arrested." She shrugged. "In the end they did."

He toasted her in schnapps. She toasted him back and drank her coffee. The radio commentator, temporarily exhausted, was allowing his microphone to pick up the passing strains of another "Deutschland über Alles."

"Will she be all right?" she asked. "Sins escalate. Oh, God, how they escalate. Mine did. Suppose Hitler does use her?"

"I doubt he will in the end," Schmidt said. "Anyway, Mrs. Noah, if there's one thing I'm sure about in this whole fucking business, it's that little Anna Anderson will survive Adolf Hitler."

She grinned at him, astonished and astonishing. "She will, won't she? I do love you, Schmidt. Who do you love?"

"Esther Solomonova," he said.

"That's right." She cleared her plate. "I feel better. I'm going to miss German herring."

"Think you can make it now?"

The grand duchess Anastasia put on her coat, tied her scarf more tightly around her head, and picked up her handbag. She leaned over and kissed him. "We'll make it," she said.

AUTHOR'S NOTE

IN TURNING the story of the woman, Anna Anderson, who called herself Grand Duchess Anastasia, daughter of the last czar of Russia, into a thriller, I have taken great liberties with her life. But then, so did she.

I think she was a fraud; the DNA tests after her death showed that she was. As one of my characters says of the slaughter of the eleven people, the czar's family and his retainers, at Ekaterinburg in 1918: "Nobody got out of that cellar." It's fairly certain that Anna was, in fact, a Pole called Franziska Schanskowska.

Nevertheless, she was a mystery. Her knowledge of the Romanovs was minute and the impassioned, ongoing belief of her supporters that she was in truth the grand duchess is understandable—photographs show a marked likeness between the two. Also, rumors that there were at least two survivors from the massacre began very early—Romanov impostors were beginning to present themselves in the 1920s. Even after investigation of the mine the corpses were thrown into, only nine bodies were discovered.

Prince Nick, Esther, Natalya, and Schmidt, et al., are fictional, of course. As far as one can tell, the only person who groomed Anna to play the part of Anastasia was Anna herself. There were no murders in her life apart from the fact that she lived through the years of one of the greatest serial killers of all time, Adolf Hitler. And from what is known of the real Franziska, she came from Pomerania and not Polesie, which is the birthplace I've given her.

However, what I *don't* think I have distorted too much is Anderson's character. Despite severe illnesses, mental and physical, she was amazingly tough and lived until she was eighty-two years old, fraying the nerves and fortunes of nearly everyone who helped her as well as the man she eventually married. She was an anti-Semite and even if she *didn't* meet Hitler—and as far as I can make out we have only her word that she did—she certainly approved of him.

It is not an anachronism to present the SS as more or less taking over the Prussian police in January 1933, despite the fact that their official formation wasn't until April. That particular section of the SS had been infiltrating the police force for some time, even if it did not use the name "Gestapo."

I owe three people for help on this book. Sarah Molloy, enduring friend. Emma Norman, for her intuitive and exhaustive research. And Helen Heller of Heller Agency, who provided the basic plot and who, being the Isambard Kingdom Brunel of thrillers that she is, so brilliantly and patiently engineered me through it. Thank you.